OTHER BOOKS BY THIS AUTHOR

THE SEQUEL TO BACKWARDS TO OREGON

A HISTORICAL ROMANCE

JAE

TABLE OF CONTENTS

ACKNOWLEDGMENTS

Once again, I want to say thank you to my "creative staff." Without these women, this novel wouldn't be the same.

First of all, I want to thank my wonderful critique partners, RJ Nolan and Alison Grey. I appreciate your honesty and your support.

I also want to thank my beta readers, Pam and Erin, who spent countless hours helping me improve this novel.

Thanks to Margot for helping me with the Dutch names and for recording the correct pronunciation. An "honorable mention" to her mother, who happens to have a nice name and a nice daughter—or rather two of both.

Thanks also to the people who took the time to test read the first edition of this novel (in alphabetical order): Aim, Andi, Caren, Corinna, DK Hawk, Gail Robinson, Henriette, Jackson Leigh, Jean Alston, Jeanine Hoffman, Judy Currier, Kathi Isserman, Koda Graystone, Laurie Salzler, Levine Sommers, Marie Logan, Mary Buchanan, Nancy Pierce, Nicki, Nikki Grimes, Sabina, Speed, Tarsilla Moura, and Vicki Lolich.

Thank you to Glendon from Streetlight Graphics for creating another beautiful cover.

A big thank-you goes to Fletcher DeLancey. She went above and beyond her duties as my copy editor and did a fantastic job line-editing my manuscript.

DEDICATION

For my grandmother, who taught me that love is thicker than blood.

And for the hundreds of readers who sent feedback e-mails and asked for a sequel to *Backwards to Oregon*.

"We tell lies when we are afraid," said Morgenes. "Afraid of what we don't know, afraid of what others will think, afraid of what will be found out about us. But every time we tell a lie, the thing that we fear grows stronger. It is, in fact, a kind of magic—perhaps the strongest of all. Study that, if you wish to understand power, young Simon. Don't fill your head with nattering about spells and incantations. Understand how lies shape us, shape kingdoms."

"But that's not magic," Simon protested. "That doesn't do anything. Real magic lets you... I don't know. Fly. Make bags of gold out of a pile of turnips. Like in the stories."

"But the stories themselves are often lies, Simon. The bad ones are. Good stories will tell you that facing the lie is the worst terror of all."

Dr. Morgenes in *To Green Angel Tower* by Tad Williams.
Quoted with permission of the author.

MACAULEY COTTON MILL
BOSTON, MASSACHUSETTS
MARCH 5, 1868

"R UN!" RIKA'S CRY STARTLED TWO crows into taking flight. "They'll close the gates!" She gripped Jo's thin arm and dragged her over cobblestones slick with snow. Dawn hadn't yet broken through the clouds, but Rika knew they didn't have much time.

Jo gasped, her breath condensing in the chilly air. "I can't." A coughing spell shook her slight frame and bent her in half. When she straightened, a streetlamp's yellow gaslight revealed angry blotches on Jo's otherwise pale cheeks. She gave Rika a smile. "Go on without me. I'll be there in a minute. Just need to catch my breath."

What she needs is to find new work, Rika thought.

The stuffy, lint-filled weave room made even the healthiest women cough. But, like Rika, Jo didn't have much choice. With no husband and no family to take care of her, the cotton mill was her only means of support.

"No," Rika said. The first horsecar of the day clattered up the hill, and Rika raised her voice so Jo would hear her over the stamping of hooves. "I won't leave you here alone."

Another cough prevented Jo from answering.

Rika's throat constricted. She handed Jo a handkerchief and wished she could do more. But what? Maybe if she gave her this week's pay, Jo would agree to see a doctor.

"Come on." Rika took hold of Jo's arm. "If we're late..."

Just yesterday, an Irish girl had stumbled from Mr. Macauley's office, crying and pressing a ripped sleeve against her bleeding lip.

"That's for letting my looms sit idle after the five o'clock bell," William Macauley had shouted after her.

No one had said a word. No one dared to.

One arm still around Jo, Rika hurried them along rows of elms that bent beneath the harsh wind. They struggled across a small bridge. Rika sucked in a breath as the wind's icy fingertips drove a spray of water through her worn skirt. "Careful," she said. "Don't slip."

Finally, the flickering streetlamps revealed the mill's four-story brick building. The tall chimney already leaked sooty smoke into the dark sky, blotting out the stars.

The shrill ringing of a bell shattered the silence.

"Run!" Rika shouted.

A girl, no older than thirteen, pushed past them and hurried up the steps, probably on her way to the spinning room on the first floor.

The bell rang a second time as they raced through the doors of the cotton mill. Beneath the soles of Rika's worn boots, the floor vibrated. Even the walls, though made of brick, seemed to quiver.

Darn. Rika dug her nails into her palm.

The overseer had already pulled a cord, setting the gigantic waterwheel in motion.

She slipped into the weave room, hoping to get her looms going before the foreman climbed onto his high stool and found her missing. *What's this?* She squinted through the lint-filled air.

Jo's looms were already moving, the shuttles hissing back and forth. One of the women winked at Jo.

Lord bless them. They covered for us. Rika squeezed Jo's hand and hurried to her own workplace. Her steps faltered and her smile waned when she saw her looms—three unmoving objects in a sea of bustling activity. No one had set her looms in motion. No one had even noticed her missing.

No one but William Macauley. He towered over her looms, a golden pocket watch in his hand, and tapped the faceplate with a chubby finger. Thick lips blew cigar smoke into her face. "You are late, Miss..."

Rika struggled not to cough. "Aaldenberg," she said, knowing he never remembered the names of his employees. "I'm so sorry, Mr. Macauley. It won't happen again."

"Damn right, it won't." He snapped his watch shut. "I don't need lazy gals running my looms."

Rika trembled. Was he about to fire her? *Think! Say something!* She pressed her palms together as if praying. "I swear I left the boarding house on time, but um...I had...um... female problems and had to visit the outhouse." It wasn't a lie, just a creative interpretation of what had happened. After all, a female had made her late.

Mr. Macauley's plump cheeks flushed, and he bit down on his cigar.

Rika held her breath. The lump in her stomach rose to her throat.

He stabbed his finger at the rows of looms rattling and whirring around them. "Then how come all the other womenfolk started work on time?"

Because they didn't care enough to stop and help Jo. But saying that would get Jo fired. Once, a girl had fainted in the weave room's humid heat. The overseer had told her, "We've got no place for a sickly girl," before putting her out on the streets.

Rika bowed her head. "It won't happen again, Mr. Macauley. I promise."

His cheeks still flushed, the old goat grunted but seemed to accept the apology.

Ha! Rika clamped her teeth onto her lower lip to hide a triumphant smile. She knew he wouldn't be eager to discuss the particulars of "female problems."

"I'll take the delay you caused out of your wages." Mr. Macauley puffed on his cigar and blew smoke into her face. "I'm sure you agree one week without pay is fair."

One week? Rika coughed and bit the inside of her cheek. She would have to dig into her savings to pay for her room and board. How would she ever save enough to make it out of the mill if things continued like this? Worse, she wouldn't be able to give Jo money so she could finally see a doctor. She clenched her fist behind her back. For a moment, she thought about arguing, trying to offer him one day's wages, but she knew any protest would anger him even more. "Of course," she mumbled, gaze lowered to the floor.

Mr. Macauley brushed lint off his cravat. "I'm warning you, girl. I'll have the overseer keep an eye on you. If you're late again," he stabbed his hand forward, making cigar ash rain down on her, "you'll be out of a job." He pocketed his gold watch and strode into the whirl and hiss of the looms.

Rika pressed a hand to her stomach. Fear snuffed out her momentary relief. She'd avoided disaster this time, but how much longer would she be able to care for Jo and keep her job?

Hours later, Rika's ears were ringing. All around her, water-powered wheels and leather belts whirred. Two hundred looms clattered as the harnesses lifted and lowered the warp threads. Her gaze flew left and right, following the paths of the shuttles. After each pass of the shuttle, a comblike bar hammered the woven threads into the cloth's web.

Darn! A broken thread.

Rika sprang into action. She hit the lever, bringing the loom to a shuddering halt. She reached into the machine, fished out the broken ends, and, without looking, tied a weaver's knot. It had taken her a long time to master the skill, and the Macauleys weren't generous enough to let the women learn the technique during work hours. Rika had practiced under Jo's tutelage by candlelight in their room, tying knots until her fingers bled.

She shook off the memory and jammed the lever back into place. The loom roared to life again. Rika glanced at her other two looms. Sweat ran down her face, and she dabbed at her forehead with her apron. Her damp bodice clung to her chest no matter how often she tugged it away from her overheated skin. Despite the cold outside, steam wafted through the weave room. It kept the cotton threads from drying out and ripping, so she didn't dare open a window.

Rika took a deep breath and then coughed when she inhaled a lungful of floating lint. Dust and the lingering odor of sweat and oil burned her nose.

Finally, the bell rang, announcing the end of their workday.

Thank the Lord. Rika signaled for the cloth boy to gather the woven cloth and walked toward Jo, who still hurried from loom to loom. "Jo," she shouted.

Her friend kept on working. After three years in the mill, Jo's hearing had been affected by the noise of the machines. Rika vowed to make it out before the same happened to her.

"Johanna Bruggeman!"

"Oh!" Finally, Jo seemed to notice the other women filing out of the room. A tired smile flitted over her face when she turned to Rika. "Let's get out of here. My feet are hurting something awful." Damp strands of normally white-blond hair, now darkened to the color of wheat, stuck to her thin face.

When Rika opened the mill's heavy door, darkness had fallen. Cold air hit her like a punch, and she shivered as the wind cut into her sweat-dampened cheeks. After the weave room's humidity, the dry winter air burned her lungs.

She tugged Jo against her side, hoping to protect her friend's thin body from the wind, and they set off for home. *If you can call it that.* Rika slowed her steps to adjust to Jo's shuffle. Like most mill girls, they were renting a room in the crowded part of town east of Tremont Street.

"What did Mr. Macauley say to you this morning?" Jo asked when they paused to let a beer wagon rumble past. "He didn't catch you being late, did he?"

Rika lifted her skirt and stepped over a half-frozen puddle. "Don't fret. He just gave me an earful, that's all."

Candles flickering in the boarding house's narrow windows beckoned, promising rest, warmth, and food, at least for a few hours. But when they crossed the street, half a dozen young women sat on the stairs or perched on the banister, bundled up in their coats.

"What are you doing outside?" Rika asked. "Don't tell me there's vermin again?" Her scalp itched at the memory of last summer's lice, and the thought of again finding tiny teeth marks on her brown bread made her stomach roil.

"No," one of the women answered, shivering. "Too cold even for vermin. Betsy is inside, talking to her gentleman friend. She's giving each of us a penny so that they can have the parlor to themselves for an hour, and we don't want to be cooped up in our rooms."

While Rika longed for some fresh air too, she worried about Jo catching a cold, so she led her inside and up the creaking stairs.

Mary-Ann's voice came from within their third-story room. "It's my turn."

"But I got to it first," Erma answered.

Not again. Rika was sick and tired of the old argument. She opened the door. "Stop squabbling. Let Jo have the washbowl first."

"That's all right." Jo sank onto the bed she shared with Rika. The small room lacked other places to sit. "I think it's your turn anyway."

Huffing, Erma retreated from the washbasin. "I'm going down to write a letter home."

Rika folded her coat and apron and set them on the trunk next to their bed. Without looking at Jo or Mary-Ann, she slipped out of her bodice, skirt, and petticoat. Goose bumps pebbled her flesh in the chill air. She stepped toward the washstand and ran a wet cloth over her pale skin.

After slipping into her only clean skirt, she shoved her feet back into the worn shoes. They no longer seemed too large, as they had this morning. When she had first started working in the mill, Jo had taken her under her wing, happy to befriend another girl from a Dutch family. She taught her to buy shoes one size too big so they'd still fit her swollen feet in the evening.

The ringing of the supper bell made Rika jerk. "Hurry, Jo!" She passed her friend the washcloth and laid out a clean skirt and bodice for her.

"You go on." Jo didn't move from the bed. "I'm not hungry."

Not hungry? Rika eyed her slight friend. Jo had lost weight during the last few weeks, and she couldn't afford to miss meals. "Jo," she said. "Come on. Just a few bites."

"No. Go on." Jo shooed her away. "I'll stay and read my letters."

The sound of feet dashing down the stairs made Rika look up. If she didn't hurry, her place at the table and most of the food would be gone. "I'll try to bring you some bread and cheese. Are you sure you'll be fine? I can stay and keep you company."

"No, go."

"Promise you'll go see a doctor. They got lady doctors at the hospital now."

"What would they tell me? To rest? To quit working in the mill?" Jo shook her head. Her voice was calm, as if she had long ago accepted her situation. "I can't afford either."

Rika drilled torn fingernails into her palm. "But maybe there's a tonic or syrup that can help."

"I can't waste money on that. I need every dime when I go west. Now go, or the others will eat your supper."

"But—"

Jo opened her mouth to interrupt, but coughs cut off her words. Her face flushed, and she waved Rika away.

With one last glance, Rika hurried to the dining room.

Tin plates clattered, and chairs scraped over the floor. Girls and women shouted up and down the three long tables, adding to the roaring in Rika's ears. She squeezed in between two girls and snatched the last potato. The first few forkfuls of beans landed in her stomach without her taking the time to chew thoroughly or enjoy the taste.

At breakfast and lunch, the factory bell hurried them along, and Rika gobbled down her food to satisfy her growling stomach. Now she found it hard to eat slowly. Minutes later, she mopped up the bacon grease on her plate with a piece of brown bread and became aware of the other women's conversation.

"Did you hear about poor Phoebe?" Mary-Ann asked.

The women shook their heads and stared at Mary-Ann.

Rika listened but said nothing, using their distraction to slip a slice of bread into her pocket.

"What happened?" Erma asked.

"She got her hair caught between a belt and one of the shafts," Mary-Ann said. "Scalped her from forehead to the back of her neck."

The girl next to Rika gasped.

Rika touched her own hair. Factory rules demanded that the women wear their hair up and tucked under a scarf, but accidents still happened. Last week, a weaver had lost a finger in the machinery, and the month before, an unsecured shuttle put out a girl's eye.

"I'm taking up a collection for the hospital fees," Mary-Ann said. "So if you can spare a few pennies..." She looked at the other women.

Rika reached into her apron and rubbed her thumb over a coin in her pouch. Five cents that could help fulfill her dream: getting out of the cotton mill and finding a place to call her own, maybe running a seamstress's shop or a small boarding house. Five cents that could help Jo, buying better food or a syrup for her cough. She clamped her hand around the coin until it dug into her skin.

"Hendrika?" Mary-Ann tilted her head. She held out her hand, fingers cupped around the coins the other women had given for Phoebe.

Sighing, Rika handed over the nickel.

When Rika returned to their room, Jo was sitting up in bed, slumped against the pillow. Her eyes were closed, and an unhealthy flush painted her normally pale cheeks.

"Jo?" Rika whispered, then remembered that Jo wouldn't hear her. She raised her voice and repeated, "Johanna?"

Jo opened her eyes. "How was supper?"

"Good." No use telling Jo about Phoebe's accident. It would upset her and cause another coughing spell. Rika reached into her apron pocket. "Here. I brought you some bread." The bread's aroma evoked childhood memories of being forced to leave the warmth of her father's bakery and walking Boston's frozen streets, peddling her father's wares until her feet blistered. Back then, she'd dreamed of a better life, of a place where she belonged and was loved for who she was, not just how much bread she sold. She shoved the thought away. Love was a childish dream. All she wanted was to own a home, no matter how small, that no one could take away from her.

Jo took the slice of bread and held it in her hand without eating. "Thank you."

Rika's gaze fell on Jo's feet hanging over the side of the bed as if she hadn't possessed the strength to take off her boots. She sat on the bed and grasped one foot. Cotton dust colored the worn boots a mousy gray, and Rika tried to give them a good polish with the edge of her apron.

Groaning, Jo lifted her head. "Don't bother. You won't get these old things to shine."

Rika gave up, unlaced the boots, and took them off to make Jo more comfortable. "Want me to help you wash up some?"

"I'll do it in a little while, when I get up to use the necessary." Jo pulled herself higher up in bed. "For now, I just want to rest a bit and read my letters."

"Read?" Rika looked at the creased pages and the battered envelopes on Jo's lap. "You mean recite by heart. Don't you get tired of reading them over and over again?"

"Tired?" Jo pressed a handkerchief to her lips. "Never. Listen to this: 'The land here is lush and green, and the air smells of pine, spring grass, and apple blossoms. I do believe that you will find it a real healthy climate when you come to live with me.' Doesn't that sound heavenly? How could I get tired of it?" She sighed. "Just one more week until I catch the train west."

"Then why are you sighing?" Rika asked. It had sounded like a sigh of resignation, not one of longing. "I thought you were looking forward to marrying your Philip."

"Hendrika Aaldenberg! You know quite well that his name is Phineas." A smile curled the edges of Jo's lips. It was a game they had often played in the past few months, meant to lift Jo's spirits and ease Rika's gnawing worries about Jo's health. "Of course I'm looking forward to going west and becoming his wife. I just wish you would change your mind and come with me."

The conversation was as old as Rika's pretending not to remember the name of Jo's future husband, wrapping around them like a worn coat that comforted with its warmth and familiarity. "Go west and marry a man I don't even know?" Rika shook her head. An image of Willem flickered through her. She shivered as she again felt his bloodshot eyes staring at her as if she were a stranger while she helped him to bed. "He could turn out to be a drunkard or—"

"Or…" Jo coughed. "Or he could turn out to be the man of your dreams."

"I haven't dreamed of any man." Rika placed Jo's boots next to the bed. "But I hope you become real happy with Paul."

Jo held her ribs, this time from laughter, not coughing. "Phineas."

Rika rolled around and pulled the thin quilt over her ears. Nights in the boarding house were as noisy as days in the weave room. Jo coughed and wheezed next to her, and in the other bed, Erma snored more loudly than Rika's brother and half siblings had ever managed.

With a grunt, Rika turned to face the wall. The lumpy straw ticking beneath her rustled.

The snoring stopped for a second, then resumed twice as loudly.

She wanted to yell. How would she make it through a fourteen-hour workday without a wink of sleep? She threw her boot across the room. It thumped against the wall above Erma's head.

At last, the snoring ended.

The popping and chirping in her ears never stopped, though. Sometimes at night, when everything was quiet, she still heard the incessant clattering of the looms. If she wasn't careful, she'd end up as hard of hearing as Jo.

Finally, long after midnight, Jo's coughing ceased, and Rika fell into an exhausted sleep.

<hr />

"Hey, Hendrika!"

A hand on her shoulder pulled Rika from sleep. She blinked open sleep-crusted eyes and stared into the semi-darkness of the room.

Erma stood next to her. The glow of the kerosene lamp created a halo around her head. "I think this," Erma set one dusty boot on top of Rika's chest, "belongs to you. And 'cause you were so busy throwing boots tonight, you and Johanna slept right through the bell. You'd better hurry if you want to make it to the mill on time."

"Darn!" Rika threw back the quilt. The boot dropped to the floor, and she scrambled after it. "Jo, get up. We can't be late again." Her tired arms and legs protested as she struggled into her petticoat and pulled up her skirt.

Jo was still bundled up under the covers. One arm stuck out beneath the extra blanket she had heaved on top of herself.

"Jo!" Rika gave her a shove.

Jo didn't move.

The slice of bread lay untouched on the trunk next to the bed. In the low light of the kerosene lamp, Rika caught a glimpse of a crumpled handkerchief, dotted with brownish spots and tinged with the gray lint that had accumulated in Jo's lungs. Hastily, she closed the buttons on her bodice and bent to shake Jo awake.

Her hand gripped a cold shoulder.

The coldness raced up her arm and through the rest of her body. An icy lump formed in her stomach. "Jo?" she whispered. "Jo, please!"

No answer.

With trembling fingers, Rika rolled Jo over and stared into the face that had lost its feverish color. "Oh, no. No, no, no." She pressed both hands to her mouth. "One more week. Just one more week. Then you get out of here."

Tears burned her eyes. She stroked the stiff fingers. They were still clamped around one of Phineas's letters.

"Hendrika, Jo, come on," Erma called, already halfway out the door. "If you're late again, you're gonna be fired."

Rika didn't move from the bed. She slid the creased paper from Jo's hand, folded the letter, and returned it to its envelope.

TRAIN STATION
BOSTON, MASSACHUSETTS
MARCH 7, 1868

"NO, MA'AM." THE MAN BEHIND the counter shook his head. "I can't give you a refund on this ticket."

"But you don't understand." Rika held out the ticket. A plume of dark gray coal smoke rose from the locomotive huffing and puffing its way out of the railroad station. Soot tickled her throat, and she coughed. "The ticket is valid, and I need the money."

"No refund," he shouted over a whistle blast and pointed at a small mark stamped on the ticket. "See? You have to either use the ticket by boarding the train next Friday or let it go to waste."

Rika stared at the square piece of paper in her hand. So Jo's beau hadn't trusted her not to turn the ticket in for cash. *And why should he? He doesn't know her from Eve.* Only a fool trusted strangers.

She shoved the ticket into the pocket of her thin wool coat, nodded a thank-you, and walked away.

What now? How else could she pay for Jo's funeral? Her savings and Jo's would cover it, but then how would she continue to pay rent now that she'd lost her job?

As she stepped off the curb, a horse let out a startled whinny and veered to the left, almost colliding with a cart.

"For heaven's sake, pay attention, Miss," the driver of the brougham yelled.

"Sorry," Rika mumbled and hurried away. She stumbled along streets and alleys.

Where to? Erma and Mary-Ann couldn't help. They'd already given half their wages to Phoebe, the scalped girl. Even if they had money, Rika doubted they would help. They'd been Jo's friends, not hers, and now that Jo was dead, they wanted to save their money for the living. Everyone had liked smiling

Jo, but Rika knew her own gap-toothed grin didn't warm any hearts.

Certainly not Mrs. Gillespie's. When Rika reached the boarding house, her landlady dragged a carpetbag through the front door and set down a slender box next to it.

Rika trudged up the steps. She stared at the box with its familiar purple and green stains. *Mama's box of paints!* She glared at Mrs. Gillespie. "What are you doing? These are my things."

Mrs. Gillespie dropped Rika's old pair of shoes onto the box. "The mill is sending over half a dozen Irish girls, and I need the space."

Trembling, Rika clutched her fingers together. "You can't just put me out on the street."

"I can't afford to keep you on if you're no longer paying rent," Mrs. Gillespie said.

Bile crept up Rika's throat. She swallowed. "I'll pay. Really, I have enough to pay for a month."

"And then what?" Mrs. Gillespie crossed her arms and peered at Rika from her position on the top stair. "How will you pay the month after that, now that you lost your place in the mill?"

So she had heard already. Rika's shoulders slouched.

"Good luck, Miss Aaldenberg." The landlady turned and stepped into the boarding house.

"No, no, no, you can't just—"

The door swung closed between them.

The sound sent a thousand panicked thoughts ricocheting through Rika's mind, leaving behind a hollow feeling in the pit of her stomach. Her knees gave out. She sank onto the cold stairs, between the carpetbag and the paint box, and cradled her head in her hands.

"Amen." The pastor closed his Bible, nodded at Rika and the gravediggers waiting nearby, and walked away.

Rika stared into the open grave. *Oh, Jo. Why is life so unfair sometimes?*

When one of the gravediggers cleared his throat behind her, she gave herself a mental kick. No use lamenting over things she couldn't change. She said her final good-bye to Jo and left the cemetery.

She wandered Boston's streets, keeping on the lookout for offers of work or an inexpensive place to stay but finding neither. Her steps led her to the colorful stands and carts of the market, where she clutched the carpetbag to her chest and squeezed past two men haggling over a fish. The smell of bread and smoked meat made her stomach growl. She hadn't eaten since yesterday, and market day with its smells and sights made her head spin. In search of food she could afford, she stepped around the yardstick of a vendor measuring cloth.

"Crunch bread," a deep voice called across the street, trying to be heard over the other peddlers. "Boston buns! Apple bread fresh from the oven."

That voice! She knew it. A shiver raced through her. She ducked behind a stand piled high with vegetables and peered at the man.

The white apron covered his barrel chest, and the hands resting on the pushcart were as large as she remembered. Rika's heart stuttered, then calmed. It couldn't be him. Her father was in his fiftieth winter, and the man selling breads and pastries seemed younger than Rika.

"Nicolaas," Rika whispered. It had to be him. When she'd left home six years before, he'd been just a boy, not yet twelve years old. Now her little brother was all grown up. She craned her neck and let her gaze slide over the crowd, making sure her father wasn't with Nic.

When she realized he was alone, she blew out a long breath and hurried across the street.

Nic grinned a welcome. The twinkle in his brown eyes still reminded her of their mother. "Want a loaf of apple bread? For you, just two pennies."

"No, thanks, I—"

"Seed bread, then?"

"I don't want any bread. I'm—"

His grin turned into their father's angry grimace. "Then get out of my way. I don't hand out charities." He kicked her as if she were a stray dog.

Rika cried out at the sharp pain in her shin. She clutched her skirt and stared up at Nic. The brown eyes that had once looked at her with adoration now held only cruel indifference.

"Want more of that?" he asked when she still didn't run.

So her brother had become a man who kicked people when they couldn't afford his bread. Rika's chest burned. "If Mother could see you now, she would be ashamed."

"How dare—" He lifted his fist, then stopped and blinked. "Rika? Hendrika? Is that you?"

Rika nodded but kept her distance. She no longer knew him or what he was capable of. Six years under their father's tutelage had changed him from a shy boy into a hard man. To their father, being kind was a sign of weakness.

"Lord, you have changed!"

"So have you," she mumbled.

"What are you doing here? Are you returning home?"

She shook her head. The bakery had never been her home, just the house where she grew up. She had promised herself she would never live there again. But where else was she supposed to go? She had spent the last two nights in the poorhouse, where she had to share a bed with the feeble-minded, the drunk, and the insane. She'd tried to find work in Boston and had gone to the hospital to ask for a job even though she had never wanted to work as a nurse again after the horrors of the war. But the war was over now, and the hospital no longer needed so many nurses. Immigrants, fresh off the ship, worked for next to nothing. No one wanted to employ Rika, and Mr. Macauley had gotten her blacklisted, so no other cotton mill would take her in either.

After losing Jo and her job in the mill, there was nothing left for her in Boston. She needed a new start somewhere else. Her fingers closed around the train ticket in the pocket of her worn coat. *What if I traveled to Oregon in Jo's place?* She dismissed the thought as crazy, but once it had taken root, she couldn't forget about it. Not allowing herself to hesitate, she straightened her shoulders. "I'm going west."

Nic nodded but didn't ask for details. "You have a husband?"

Again, Rika shook her head. "The war left me a widow."

"Then you won't make it very far."

Her father had told her the same before she had left home. The hard, patronizing look in Nic's eyes reminded Rika of their father—and it made her even more determined to go to Oregon. She clenched her jaw. "I'll be fine." If she made do with a piece of bread and a bowl of beans a day, she would make it to Oregon with the money Jo had saved for the journey. "Good-bye, Nic. Take care of yourself, and don't become too much like Father."

Without waiting for an answer, she stepped into the crowd and let the noise of the market wash over her, hoping it would drown out her pain.

POST OFFICE
CHEYENNE, WYOMING
MARCH 18, 1868

"*A* LL ABOARD! BOISE, UMATILLA, THE Dalles!" Rika lifted her wrinkled skirts with one hand and ran to catch the stagecoach before it could depart. The train that brought her to Cheyenne had been late, and if she missed the connecting stage to The Dalles, she would be stuck in this busy little town for three days.

She almost collided with a man who was lugging a large sack toward his wagon. A mule brayed next to her, and Rika jumped and dropped her carpetbag. She snatched it up and hurried toward the red and golden stagecoach.

The driver sent her a glare. "Come on, Miss. I don't have all day."

Rika produced one of Jo's tickets. When he nodded, she handed up her carpetbag, climbed into the stagecoach, and squeezed into the only free seat. "Good day," she said to the other travelers.

The well-dressed, portly man next to her tipped his forehead, where the brim of his hat normally rested. "Welcome, young lady. James Kensington at your service."

Instead of introducing herself, Rika asked, "Are you traveling to The Dalles too?"

"Yes. I signed up for the whole four weeks of dust and misery."

Misery? Surely nothing could be worse than the last five days spent in the stuffy passenger car of that box-on-wheels calling itself a train. Her back still hurt from the hard wooden bench, and she couldn't get the coal soot out of her mouth.

"I'm sorry," Mr. Kensington said, "but I didn't catch your name."

There it was, the dreaded question.

Better learn to be convincing now. "Johanna Bruggeman," Rika said and suppressed a shiver. Her father had never talked about God, but surely taking the name of a dead woman was a sin.

Mr. Kensington gave her a friendly smile. "Pleased to meet you, Miss Bruggeman."

Hours later, Rika finally admitted to herself that the stagecoach was indeed worse than the train. The coach's wheels bumped over a rock, and she grabbed the leather strap dangling from the ceiling. Mr. Kensington crowded her from the left, while a mailbag pressed against her feet from the right. Every now and then, her knees collided with that of the traveler facing her in the cramped space.

"You hungry?" Mr. Kensington held out a piece of cold ham.

"Oh, no, thank you." Rika pressed a hand to her belly. Every time the stagecoach lurched, her stomach did the same. She had no memory of the long journey across the ocean when she had been just one year old, but she imagined her parents must have felt like this. With the leather curtains closed to keep out the dust, the inside of the coach was as stifling as the train's passenger car, despite the March breeze outside.

"In a year or two, once the transcontinental railroad is finally done, we'll make it from the East Coast to the West Coast in just seven days," the man opposite her said.

As heavenly as that sounded to Rika, it was of no use to them now. She had been traveling for days and was still nowhere near the Willamette Valley.

The coach slowed, and Mr. Kensington stiffened. His hand crept to the mother-of-pearl grip of his revolver.

"Easy, easy," another traveler said. "Probably just a rest station. No need to worry."

"I'll stop worrying when we arrive in The Dalles," Mr. Kensington said. With the ruts and rocks in the road, his interrupted words sounded as if he had the hiccups. "This is a major route. Bandits and marauding Indians could lurk behind every bush."

The only other woman on the stagecoach gasped.

Surely he's being overly dramatic.

The stagecoach rocked to a halt before Rika could ask, and her backside rejoiced when she climbed off the stage to stretch her cramped legs.

Just a few minutes later, they were on the road again with six fresh horses.

Silence settled over the travelers, though sleep was impossible on the swaying coach.

Rika took the bundle of letters out of her coat pocket and smoothed her finger over the carefully knotted ribbon that held Jo's treasures together. Jo and Phineas Sharpe had been corresponding for six months, and now she held half a dozen letters on her lap.

She undid the knot and slipped the first letter from its envelope. A newspaper advertisement landed in her hands, and she lifted it to her eyes to read the printed text despite the coach's swaying.

A good-natured, hardworking fellow of twenty-five years, six foot height, is heartily tired of bachelor life and desires the acquaintance of some maiden or widow lady not over twenty-five. She must be amiable, loving, and honest. Please respond to Phineas Sharpe, Hamilton Horse Farm, Baker Prairie, Oregon.

Honest. The corners of Rika's mouth drooped as if she tasted something foul. Lying and pretending had always come easy to her. With a father like hers, she'd had ample practice.

She stared at the advertisement. *How strange. What kind of man orders a bride through the mail?* But the answer was clear. *Someone as desperate as you.* She folded the advertisement and straightened her shoulders. This couldn't be worse than marrying Willem. She wanted a house and a secure position, and maybe Jo was right. Few women ever got a house of their own without marrying.

She studied the artful pen strokes on the letter and read some of the sentences. Phineas Sharpe was a simple ranch hand, yet his words had a poetic beauty that surprised her.

Deftly, she put the letter into its envelope. She'd never allowed herself to be blinded by beauty. Her mother's art, though beautiful, hadn't filled her siblings' stomachs when her father was too drunk to work.

When she bundled the letters, her glance fell on the dented tintype Jo had placed between two envelopes.

The small, slightly out-of-focus image showed a blond man sitting stiffly with his hat on his knees. He craned his neck as if he was uncomfortable in his starched shirt, worn only for the occasion of having his image taken. His hair was parted on one side and his handlebar mustache neatly trimmed, probably from a recent visit to the barbershop.

Rika had never cared for mustaches.

With every mile on the bumpy road to Oregon, her doubts grew. Had her desperate decision been foolish? If she found out Phineas Sharpe had misrepresented himself and was neither good-natured nor hardworking, what would she do? What if he discovered she was not the woman who had sent him the letters? Could she take the next stage out of town and go home?

Rika shook her head. She had no home, not for a long time.

No. There's no way around it. She would have to become Mrs. Phineas Sharpe and get used to a mustache.

HAMILTON HORSE RANCH
BAKER PRAIRIE, OREGON
APRIL 18, 1868

"*P*hin?" Amy shoved open the creaking door. Phin flinched and whirled around. His razor dangled from his fingers, and the scent of castile shaving soap filled the small cabin. "Damn it, Amy. If you keep comin' in like this, I'm gonna kill myself one day." He wiped a drop of blood from his throat and turned back around. "Or your father will do the killin' for me. A young, unmarried lady visitin' a bachelor without a chaperone…"

"You're our foreman. How else can we organize our workday if Papa or I don't come to talk to you?"

Phin's blue eyes met hers in the mirror. "Talk about it over breakfast at the main house?"

"With Mama there to try and get me out of the most interesting things? No, thanks."

"Don't know why you bother," Phin said. "Your mama always knows what you're up to anyway. Your parents never keep secrets from each other."

Yes, because they have nothing to hide. Unlike me. She pushed the unwelcome thought aside and fiddled with the edges of a saddle blanket hanging over a chair. "Besides, most people would say I'm not a lady." Not that she cared. If it meant being like the young women in town, Amy wanted no part of being a lady.

"I'd give anyone who said that to my face a good thrashin'." Phin's jaw clenched beneath the shaving soap. Then his expression softened. "You'd better learn to knock or meet me at the main house anyhow. I'm not gonna be a bachelor for much longer."

"What? You're joking, right?" To her knowledge, Phin wasn't courting anyone. She rode stirrup to stirrup with him every day. She would know if he had a sweetheart somewhere.

He turned toward her, and she sensed that he was blushing under the thick layer of shaving soap. Wordlessly, he pointed at the table against one wall.

Amy pivoted. Her fingertips slid over the burned corner of the table where she and her younger sister, Nattie, had toppled over the kerosene lamp years ago, when they fought over something Amy couldn't remember. Traces of flour still lingered in the fine grain of the wood, remnants of countless apple pies Mama had made for Papa when they had lived in the cabin, their first home in Oregon.

Amidst the childhood memories was something new. A stack of letters. On top, the tintype of a young woman looked back at her.

She frowned. "Who's that?"

"My future wife." Phin's chest swelled like that of a rooster.

"You're really getting hitched?" She gave the image on the table a curt nod. "To her?" It wasn't that she was jealous. Not like that. Phin was like a brother to her. She just hated the thought of him moving away or another woman invading her home.

"To her," Phin said. "Johanna Bruggeman. Ain't she pretty?"

She was. Her enchanting smile dazzled Amy even in its black-and-white form. But pretty or not, would she fit in at the ranch? Amy looked around the small cabin. "Papa says the cabin isn't fit for a woman to live in. Not that I think so, but she looks like the kind who'd agree. Didn't you ever wonder why none of the ranch hands has a wife?"

"They're too ugly?"

They broke out in laughter, but it didn't last long.

Amy pressed her fingertips to the table's familiar contours. "You're leaving, aren't you?"

"I can't be a foreman forever," Phin said. "I like workin' for the Hamilton outfit, but I want to have my own place someday. Your father promised to set me up with a few acres of land and some horses."

It was true, and Phin had earned it, but she still bit her lip at the thought of him leaving. Papa would hire a new foreman, and for Amy, the struggle to be accepted and not sent away to the kitchen would begin anew.

"Hey," Phin said. "Why the long face? I'll still be your friend. Seein' how Johanna doesn't know a soul 'round here, she's goin' to need a maid of honor for the wedding. Would you do us the honor?"

Amy slapped her hips. "What's with you and everybody else wanting to see me six inches deep in petticoats?"

Phin eyed her as he would a stubborn filly. "Maybe you should think about gettin' married too."

Not that again. It was why Amy rarely went into town. The whispers and glances made her feel like the only unwed twenty-year-old on the face of the earth. "Where did you meet her?" she asked instead of answering. "She new in town?"

Shaving soap dripped onto Phin's shirt, and he wiped it away. Then he found a few more spatters that needed his attention.

"Phin?"

"I haven't exactly met her yet."

"What do you mean?"

Phin drew in air as if he were about to face a lynch mob. "I put an advert in three fancy eastern papers, and I got an answer from a young lady in Boston."

"You advertised for a wife?" Amy had heard of that but never understood it. What kind of self-respecting woman would sell herself to a complete stranger?

His gaze veered away from hers. "I knew you'd think it tomfoolery, but you gotta understand. There's nary an unwed woman in town and none who'd have me, so..."

"There are a few."

Phin snorted. "Yeah, the likes of Ella Williams and Fanny Henderson. No, thanks."

"So you thought you'd just order yourself a woman from the catalog, like you'd order a new saddle?"

"What's a feller to do if he's aimin' to marry? Since you won't have me."

His grin was contagious. Amy could never stay angry with her friend for long. "So you're marrying Johanna Bruggeman." She risked another glance at the picture of the smiling woman. "Is that a German name?"

"Dutch." Phin's grin grew, as if being Dutch were a great accomplishment.

Lord, he's smitten, and he hasn't even met her. She watched in silence as Phin continued to shave. Somehow, his simple, efficient movements seemed wrong, maybe because he was shaving himself. Amy had watched her parents share this private ritual almost every day for as long as she could remember.

Papa sat in the kitchen, and Mama lathered his face with the shaving soap, sometimes sneaking a kiss when she thought their daughters weren't watching. Amy always watched. She knew she was witnessing something special, something that bound her parents to each other. Trust glowed in Papa's eyes when he let Mama put the razor to his neck.

A sudden longing for that kind of trust overcame Amy. She shook it off and focused on Phin.

For Phin, shaving seemed to be a necessary evil. There was nothing gentle or loving about the way he scraped lather and stubbles off his cheeks and his strong chin.

Maybe he really needs a wife. "So when is she coming here?" Amy asked.

"Well..." He wiped off the rest of the shaving soap and twirled his handlebar mustache. Amy often teased him about it. She liked Papa's clean-shaven look better. "I wanted to talk to you about that. If the stagecoach is on time, she'll get here Monday afternoon."

Meaningful silence spread between them.

"Monday afternoon? But—"

"I'm supposed to leave for Fort Boise with your father on Monday mornin', yes."

This was her chance! Amy hid a grin and tried for nonchalance. "Oh, not a problem. I'll help Papa bring the horses to Fort Boise, and you can pick up your bride from town on Monday afternoon."

He cleared his throat. "That's not what I meant, and you'd have to discuss that with your father."

Who would say no. Not because traveling four hundred miles with a herd of horses was a man's job. Papa never told her something like that. He would say that she wasn't ready for the trip, not while there was unrest among the Shoshoni, and that he wanted her to keep an eye on the ranch while he was gone.

She sighed. "So what did you mean?"

"If it ain't too much to ask, you could put on your Sunday finery and pick up my future wife from town."

That meant wearing a dress and facing the nosy folks in town, not two of Amy's favorite activities. Still, Phin was her best friend.

"Please?" He grinned his most charming smile. "I don't trust any of the boys with her."

Asking her to pick up his betrothed so she would be safe from unwanted attentions... Amy shook her head. Phin didn't understand the irony of it. *It'll be fine. She might be pretty, but she's not Hannah.* "All right," she said. Something occurred to her. "So your courtship consisted of writing letters, right? How did you manage that? You can't write."

"I'm learnin'. Miss Nattie is teachin' me."

"But you always said you'd rather spend winter evenings repairing broken bridles than studying words on a page."

He shrugged. "Changed my mind. Miss Nattie's a great teacher."

"Nattie helped you advertise for a wife?"

"Oh, no." He rubbed his palms over freshly shaven cheeks. "I wouldn't bother her with that. Your mother helped. But Miss Nattie knew."

"Mama and Nattie knew all this time, but no one ever said one word to me?"

"Miss Nattie heard it from the postmaster. The damn gossip told half of Oregon that I'm gettin' letters from a lady in Boston. I thought maybe you'd heard it around town too."

"Not a word." Amy swallowed her hurt feelings. After all, Phin wasn't to blame for her reluctance to visit town. She tried to stay away from Hannah and the other young women who always knew the latest rumors.

Phin scratched his chin. "I thought you weren't interested in affairs of the heart things."

True. She had never given him reason to think otherwise. She and Phin talked about horses but rarely discussed feelings.

When she stayed silent, he ducked to look into her face. "Are you mad at me for not tellin' you sooner?"

"No." She wasn't mad, just a bit hurt and strangely unsettled. Sharing her home with a beautiful young woman could mean trouble.

"Listen up, boys," Luke said. Decades-old habits made her square her shoulders to appear bigger than she was. "Phin and I will leave tomorrow. Amy is in charge while we're gone." She let her gaze sweep over the ranch hands perched on their bunks and standing around the bunkhouse's cast-iron stove. "Anyone have a problem riding for a woman?"

The ranch hands had worked side by side with Amy every day for the past few years, but working with her and working for her were two different things.

Most of the men shook their heads.

"No problem, boss," Hank said.

Adam spat out a stream of chewing tobacco, earning a sharp glare from Luke. If anyone gave Amy trouble, it would be Adam. She stared at him until he looked away.

"Amy's only in charge until you get back, right?" Emmett asked, shuffling his feet. "It's just for two months."

Luke suppressed a grin. They had no idea that they'd worked for a woman much longer than that. To the world, she was Lucas Hamilton—rancher, husband, and father. Only three people knew that she was not what she appeared to be: her wife, Nora, her oldest friend, Tess, and their neighbor Bernice Garfield.

"For now," she said. Maybe one day, Amy would be able to do what Luke couldn't: run the ranch as a woman.

When no one protested, she gave some last-minute instructions and then left the bunkhouse.

Darkness had fallen, and a myriad of stars twinkled down at her. Luke lifted her head and inhaled the tangy aroma of pines, manure, and sage from Nora's herb garden. A horse's whinny cut through the sounds of a gurgling spring and a hooting owl. She wandered across the ranch yard to check on the horses one last time.

The place in front of the corral was already occupied. Amy stood with her elbows on the top rail and one booted foot propped on the bottom rung. She didn't turn around when Luke joined her.

Side by side, they watched the dark shapes of the horses move around the corral.

Midnight wandered over and snuffled Amy's sleeve. She patted the gelding's neck and combed her fingers through his forelock. "Did you talk to the men?"

"Yes. They know you're in charge."

"Good."

Luke turned to look at her and leaned her shoulder against the corral. "You nervous?"

"No," Amy said quickly—too quickly.

"Because if you were, I'd certainly understand. I was about your age when I earned my lieutenant stripes. Suddenly, I was expected to command a troop of soldiers, some of them much older and more experienced than me."

Amy leaned against the corral too so that they were face to face. "Were you nervous?"

"Terrified," Luke said. Not so much about not measuring up, of course. Back then, her worst fear was being injured so badly that surgeons discovered her secret. "There's no shame in being afraid, Amy. The trick is not to let it paralyze you."

The whites of Amy's eyes gleamed in the darkness. Her chaps scratched along the corral post as she shifted. "I'm a bit nervous," she finally said. "But you don't need to worry. I won't disappoint you, Papa."

"I know." Luke wrapped her arm around Amy's shoulders and squeezed, surprised as always to feel sturdy muscles under her hand. When had the little girl who begged her for rides on Measles become this strong young woman? She sighed. She'd miss her family. "Come on." She gave Amy one more pat to the shoulder. "Let's go to bed. We both have a long day tomorrow."

Nora folded strips of cloth and handed them to Luke, who stowed them in her saddlebags. "Put them at the bottom so no one will see," Nora said.

"Not necessary," Luke answered. "If one of the boys finds the rags, I'll just tell them those are compresses should one of the horses get hurt." She winked and leaned down to brush her lips over Nora's.

But even the warmth of the kiss couldn't chase away Nora's worries. She entwined her fingers with Luke's, lifted them to her lips, and kissed the familiar pattern of scars and rope burns on Luke's hand. "I wish you didn't have to go."

Luke stroked the back of her fingers over Nora's cheek. "I wish I could stay, but you know we need the money if we want to invest in draft horses."

"I regret ever suggesting that." If anything happened to Luke on the way to Fort Boise, she would never forgive herself.

"Hey, don't talk like that," Luke said. "You're a clever businesswoman and have never steered us wrong in all these years. Now that the railroad is coming, investing in draft horses is a brilliant idea."

"It's only brilliant if nothing happens to you," Nora said.

"We'll be careful and post guards at night."

"The trip holds more dangers for you than just Indians and horse thieves." Every muscle in Nora's body felt tight, like a rope that was trying to hold a panicked mustang. "You'll have to live in very close quarters with Phin, Charlie, and Kit for over two months. There'll be no outhouse, no bedroom with a sturdy lock, no privacy to change clothes, wash, or take care of private matters."

Luke slid her arms around Nora and held her close. "I admit I haven't had to do that in a while, but I've lived among men for years. People see what they think is true, not what's really there. And I'm the boss, so I can decide when to scout ahead or leave camp under the pretense of hunting for game. I've always been good at slipping away from camp."

"Oh, yeah?" Amusement bubbled up. "Is that why you were shot by our own guard when you slipped away to follow the call of nature?" She brushed her lips against Luke's upper arm, where an old scar reminded of that day seventeen years ago.

Groaning, Luke rubbed her nose. "Thanks for the reminder of that glorious moment."

Nora laughed, then moved back to look into Luke's eyes. The rain cloud gray told her that Luke was as worried as she was; she just didn't want to admit it. "Come on." She tugged on her hand. "Let's go to bed." She wanted to hold Luke and pretend that she'd never have to let go.

Luke walked around the bed and tested the door to make sure it was locked. Only then did she slip out of her clothes.

In the flickering light of the kerosene lamp, Nora watched as Luke unwrapped the bandages around her chest until she revealed small breasts, pale against the darker color of her arms. Nora licked her suddenly dry lips.

When Luke slipped her nightshirt over her head, Nora changed into her own nightgown and pulled the pins from her hair.

Luke reached for the hairbrush. Slowly, tenderly, she trailed the brush through Nora's hair, often pausing to disentangle an unruly strand or massage her scalp.

The first time Luke had reached for the brush and taken over the nightly task had surprised Nora. She knew it had surprised Luke too. Luke's days were spent in the saddle, working with horses or splitting logs to build fences—tasks that were the epitome of masculinity. She spent so much time convincing others she was a man that sometimes it became hard to tell what was a mask and what was real.

But after a few years, with the bedroom door closed behind them, Luke allowed herself the feminine pleasure of trailing the brush through Nora's locks.

Luke set down the brush and lifted Nora's hair.

Warm lips pressed kisses to the nape of Nora's neck, making her shiver. She gasped as Luke nipped her earlobe.

"Turn out the light," Luke whispered. "I want to say a proper good-bye."

Without hesitation, Nora lifted the lamp's glass shade, blew out the flame, and slid into Luke's arms.

Dancer turned his head and whinnied at the horses in the corral, not pleased to leave the protection of his herd.

"I know, boy." Luke wasn't eager to leave her family either. She patted the gelding's neck, and when she felt him exhale, she tightened the cinch.

Hank walked over and handed her a canteen. "Here, boss."

"Thanks." She looped it over her saddle horn. "We're leaving now. You have your instructions."

Hank nodded.

Would he accept Amy's orders as easily? *Only one way to find out.*

Soft steps padded over the veranda, and Luke knew without looking that Nora was watching her. She felt the gaze rest on her like a loving touch. One more tug on the cinch and she stepped away from the gelding.

The dreaded moment had come.

Luke turned, her glance touching everything they had established in nearly seventeen years of hard work: the main house, two large horse barns, a bunkhouse, Phin's cabin, a blacksmith's shop, and a dozen other outbuildings. All that could continue to prosper and grow—if she made the right decisions at this critical time.

In front of the veranda stairs, she stopped and met Nora's gaze. They stood in silence for long moments. Luke didn't need words to know that Nora's heart was aching too. She stepped closer and slipped both arms around Nora, their faces nearly level though Nora stood on the top stair. The brim of her hat bumped Nora's cheek, making them both smile. With a flourish, Luke took it off and set it down on Nora's red locks.

Nora tightened the embrace until she lost her balance.

Luke caught her in her arms. The hat fluttered to the ground, but they ignored it. "I'll miss you," she said, and though new footsteps told her they had an audience, she didn't lower her voice or end the embrace. They had never hidden their love from their daughters. She pressed her lips against Nora's and got lost in her warmth as if it were the last time—and they both knew it very well could be.

A few weeks before, in revenge for the death of a white settler, an expedition of soldiers had attacked an Indian camp on the Malheur River and killed more than thirty Paiutes, including women and children. Who knew whether the road to Boise was safe or teeming with angry warriors?

Luke had thought long and hard before agreeing to deliver a dozen horses to the cavalry at Fort Boise. She preferred staying out of conflicts, but if she wanted to secure a future for the ranch, she had no choice.

One last kiss and they moved apart, keeping their fingers entwined.

When Luke looked up, Nattie stood there with the forgotten hat in her hands.

"Thanks, sweetie." Luke reached for it, but Nattie jumped forward and threw her arms around her, crushing the hat between them.

"Hey." Luke kissed the top of her daughter's black hair and noticed that she didn't have to bend to do it anymore. At sixteen, Nattie was already taller than her mother.

Phin walked over with his spotted gelding. "You want us to bring you back somethin' from Boise, Miss Nattie?"

"I'm not a child anymore." Nattie moved away from Luke and put on a determined expression as she looked at Phin.

"Right." Phin thumbed back his hat and grinned at her. "So if I happen to come across somethin' of that Jane Austen woman you mentioned or a copy of *The History of England*, I should just ignore it, right?"

Nattie's eyes sparkled, bringing out the green flecks in her eyes and reminding Luke so much of Nora that it robbed her of breath. "Ah, well, I'll make an exception for Jane Austen or *The History of England*. But most of all, I want you to come back safely."

"We will," Phin said. He reached out a hand as if to touch Nattie, but then pulled back and just smiled.

Luke wanted to add her own reassurances but knew she couldn't make any promises. She turned toward Amy, who waited silently. "Walk me to my horse?"

Amy fell into step next to her, with Nattie and Nora following. Her older daughter was half a head shorter, but their steps matched in length and rhythm. How often had they walked like this, side by side, with her teaching or instructing Amy?

"I should be back in two months, maybe a little more. I'll try to send word from somewhere along the trail. You take good care of your mother and sister," Luke said. Nora didn't need someone taking care of her, but Amy would feel better about staying behind if she felt she was doing something important.

Red locks bounced up and down as Amy nodded.

"If it continues to rain like this, you'll have to rotate the horses off the east pasture." Luke's gaze swept over the paddocks and corrals and over the far hills. "And depending on how the hay crop is doing, you'll need to bring in the first cutting on your own. Don't wait until—"

"—it's in full bloom, I know." Amy quirked a grin.

"Don't be such a mother hen." Nora caught up with them and kissed Luke's cheek. "Amy knows what she's doing."

She did.

Pride flowed through Luke, and she smiled. Still, she couldn't stop worrying. Amy was a top hand with the horses, but she'd never had to run the ranch on her own.

Seems it's gonna be a time of new challenges for all of us. She turned to Phin. "Ready?"

"Ready, boss."

One last kiss for Nora and hugs for the girls, then Luke swung into the saddle. "Let's go."

Darned thing! The ribbon of Amy's sunbonnet just wouldn't give. She fumbled at it with one hand while holding the wagon's reins with the other. When the knot still didn't come undone, she clamped her teeth around the reins and, using both hands, finally freed herself of the bonnet.

Not that Old Jack needed her to hold on to the reins. The gelding had pulled the buckboard to town so often that he probably knew the way better than she did.

She lifted her face and let the light, steady drizzle refresh her.

"Whoa." A soft tug on the reins brought the buckboard to a halt on the edge of a rocky ridge overlooking Baker Prairie. Below her, the Molalla River, a frothing mountain stream, joined the broad, glittering band of the Willamette River on its journey north.

She sat up taller as she glanced back at gentle hills, lush grass, and groves of Douglas firs. The roots binding her to this land were as deep as those of the ancient firs.

Above her, a flock of Canada geese formed a large V, and a red-tailed hawk glided through the air. Amy watched as he rose and fell with the currents, drifting wherever he wanted, completely free.

She wished she could be like that, riding freely instead of having to spend the afternoon in town. But Phin's bride was bound to have some baggage with her, so riding Ruby to town was out of the question.

With a sigh, she placed the sunbonnet back on her head. The ribbon tightened beneath her chin, and she swallowed. Then she clucked at Old Jack. "Hyah!"

When Amy slung the reins over the hitching rail, the door to the dry-goods store swung open. Hannah and her husband stepped out. Joshua doffed his hat, mumbled a greeting, and escaped to their buckboard with their little boy, leaving the women to talk.

Amy smoothed her hands over the unfamiliar contours of her skirt and tried a smile. "Hello, Hannah."

"Amy." A smile dimpled Hannah's chubby cheeks. "How have you been?"

"We had a lot of work out on the ranch, trying to get a herd together so Papa could drive them to Fort Boise."

"Fort Boise?" Hannah's brow furrowed. "Josh says there have been massacres up there."

"I heard."

The mines in the Boise Basin lured hundreds of new settlers to the area. In reaction to that intrusion, small bands of Indians began sporadic raids on the settlers. The cavalry promptly retaliated. Papa said the Snake War was a conflict between people who both saw the other as a threat to their homes and their way of life.

"My father took Phin and two of our best hands, just in case. I'm sure they'll be fine," Amy said, willing it to be so.

"How are your parents doing?"

Amy stiffened. Most people asked about her parents just so they could gossip about them afterward, but not Hannah. She never criticized Mama for teaching school even though she was a married woman or Papa for letting Amy ride around in pants. When other girls whispered and laughed at Amy, Hannah never joined in.

"They're fine," Amy said.

"Listen, we want to build a new barn before we bring in the first crop of hay this year." Hannah looked at her husband, who waited on the wagon bench. "You think your papa could help Josh lay the foundation when he's back from Fort Boise?"

Amy nodded. Papa never said no when a neighbor needed help. "I'll let him know. If he's not back in time, the rest of the family will be over to help."

"Thank you." Hannah gave her a soft squeeze.

Amy glanced at the hand on her arm. Her skin tingled where Hannah touched her, and she clamped her teeth together, cursing those unwanted feelings. "I'd better go." She pointed at the dry-goods store. "Mama gave me a list as long as my arm."

"Come over and visit soon," Hannah said. "We used to spend so much time together, and now I never see you anymore."

With a noncommittal nod, Amy hurried into the store. The bell over the door jingled as she entered. Familiar smells of licorice, leather, and vinegar tickled her nose.

"Amy Hamilton! Come over here and let me look at you," Jacob Garfield said from behind the long counter. "Haven't seen you in some time. How are you doing?"

"Keeping busy," Amy said.

Jacob pointed outside to where Hannah was now climbing on the wagon. "My daughter says she hasn't seen you in a while either. I remember a time when you two were joined at the hip."

Amy fixed her gaze on racks of sewing thread and embroidery floss. "Things change when you grow up. But I promised to help Hannah and Josh with their barn." Before he could ask more questions, she handed her list over the counter.

Jacob turned and measured out a pound of salt. "You wanna take a look at the dresses while you wait? I hear there's gonna be a wedding at the Hamilton outfit soon."

Word traveled fast in a small town like Baker Prairie.

Amy's gaze skimmed the new skirts and dresses, ribbons, and bolts of fabric laid out on a long table. "No, thank you." A new dress worn only to church was a waste of hard-earned money. Her Sunday dress would do for the wedding.

Jacob heaved a sack of flour onto the counter and piled the rest of Amy's order on top. Finally, he opened a big glass jar and scooped lemon drops into a small paper bag. He'd done that since she had been a little girl, coming into the store with her parents, and she always shared her bounty with Papa.

But now he was gone, and the lemon drops and the responsibility for the ranch were hers alone.

When she reached for the sack of flour to heave it onto her shoulder, Jacob stared at her with wide eyes. "Oh, no, leave that here. I'll have Wayne bring it out to your buckboard."

Amy bit the inside of her cheek. Did Jacob think the Hamiltons were uncivilized, just because her papa never told her she couldn't carry a sack of flour? She liked the freedom her father gave her, but visits to town made her painfully aware of how different she was from other young women.

A few minutes later, she said good-bye to Jacob and left the dry-goods store.

Across the street, two young men left the saddle maker's shop and glanced at her. One of them said something, and the other laughed and looked at Amy again.

Amy swished her skirts and marched away. She gazed at the stage depot, but the street was still empty. The stage hadn't arrived yet, so she was stuck in town.

She shuffled her feet and glanced down. *Damn!* Mud crusted her lace-up boots. Knocking her heels together didn't help. Instead of dislodging mud and manure, she sent spatters all over her skirt.

Every minute that she waited made her more aware of her not very ladylike appearance. At least the rain had finally stopped. She glanced at the sun, half-hidden behind a pile of gray clouds. The stage was late. When working with horses, Amy had her father's patience, but she would rather wait for a horse to trust her than for some woman who married herself off to a stranger.

Grumbling, she popped a lemon drop into her mouth. The sweet sourness prickled along her tongue. Had Mama remembered to hide some candy as a surprise for Papa in his saddlebags? Then, with a grunt, she spat out the candy. The stagecoach would arrive any moment, and it wouldn't do to greet Phin's betrothed with a bulging cheek.

A high-pitched squeal drew her attention toward the livery stable's corral. On their ranch, Amy had never heard a horse make a sound like that.

Her feet moved toward the corral before she could stop to think.

The two men from the saddle maker's shop blocked her view, and Amy shouldered past them. The urge to help the horse propelled her forward.

Half a dozen men drove a trembling grulla—a gray horse with a black stripe on her back—into one corner of the corral. Ropes flew at the horse from all directions.

The mare reared, her eyes white-rimmed with fear. She pranced to the right, and when another man cut her off, she tried to escape to the left.

A loop snaked around one of her legs, and another rope fell down around her neck, choking her. With one quick pull, the horse crashed into the mud.

Men jumped on her and held her down.

The mare squealed and kicked.

One man rammed both knees into her side to keep her from moving while another bit down on the horse's ear.

Amy's fingers clamped around the corral rail. *No, no, no.* Didn't they understand that the mare was fighting for her life? For the mare, this was a vicious attack by a pack of predators. How could they expect cooperation?

Two of the men blindfolded the mare with a cloth while others wrestled a saddle on her and thrust a bit into her mouth. Then a young man climbed into the saddle. With a big "whoop" of excitement, as if it was all great fun, they snatched the blindfold away and sprang back from the horse.

The mare leaped and bucked, reared and twisted, kicked and arched her back. Her front legs slashed through the air, and for a moment, Amy feared she would flip over backward. But her hooves came down. The mare ducked her head and kicked out her hind legs.

The broncobuster catapulted over her head and splashed into the mud.

Part of Amy wanted to rejoice, but she knew this was far from over. If no one else had the courage to climb on the horse, they would hobble the mare to the snubbing post in the middle of the corral, where she might break her leg or choke to death by getting tangled in the rope. They would leave her standing there on three legs, without water or food. Then, hours later, they would untie her and another man would climb on and buck her out until the mare had no fight left in her.

Amy had seen it often on the neighboring ranches and farms. She couldn't stand watching it again. She ducked between two corral rails.

"Hey!" A man gripped her arm. "What are you doing? This is no place for a woman. If you want to watch, do it from outside the corral."

Amy narrowed her eyes and glowered at the hand on her arm. "I don't want to watch."

The man scratched his head. "What are you doing, then?"

"That's Amy Hamilton, Buzz," someone shouted.

The hand withdrew from Amy's arm. "So your father is Luke Hamilton, the horse rancher?" Buzz asked. "You wanna buy the horse?"

Amy started to shake her head, about to tell him she had no money, but then stopped. The two half eagles Phin had given her for his new bride rested in her pocket. After a moment's hesitation, she fished them out and let Buzz glance at the two five-dollar gold pieces.

"The horse is worth at least twice that much," Buzz said.

"If I can ride her, will you give me the mare for the ten dollars?" she asked. It was crazy. The mouse-colored mare was not a beautiful horse. With the dorsal stripe on her back and the faint stripes on her legs, she wasn't fit to be bred to an Appaloosa stallion. Still, Amy couldn't leave the mare to her fate.

Buzz exchanged glances with his friends, including the broncobuster who was now getting up, spitting out mud and one of his front teeth. "All right," he said. "But if you can't ride her, I get the mare and the ten dollars. Deal?"

Amy's lips twitched. She wanted to spit at the hand he held out, but she kept herself in check and shook it instead. "Deal. Now give me some room to work. Please," she added after a moment. Out on the ranch, the boys were used to taking orders from her, mainly because they knew Papa would back them up. But in town, no man would ever accept her as an equal.

The men climbed over the corral rails, and that was the last time Amy looked at them. From then on, nothing existed in the world beyond her and the mare.

The grulla retreated into one corner of the corral. Sweat and rain darkened her gray coat. Her flanks quivered, and her tail was clamped between her legs. She watched Amy with flared nostrils and pricked ears. When Amy strolled over, the mare ran.

Amy followed, walking calmly but without hesitation. She ignored what the mud in the corral did to her lace-up boots.

Again, the mare fled to the other end of the corral.

Hundreds of times, Amy had watched their horses play the same game of catch. Measles and her daughters had been masters at this game. They chased away the other horses, sometimes by threatening a bite or kick, but mostly by stomping toward the horse. In a herd, the mare that could make the others move established herself as the leader.

Amy had learned to do the same. Jutting her chin and squaring her shoulders, she marched toward the mare.

The mare tossed back her head and looked beyond the corral fence for a place to flee.

Wrong move.

As long as the mare paid attention to anything but her, Amy kept driving her around the corral. She switched sides and slapped her thighs, making the startled mare swivel and sprint in the other direction.

After a few rounds around the corral, one of the mare's ears flicked toward Amy. Another lap and the second ear followed.

Amy relaxed her arms and stayed in the middle of the corral instead of moving toward the horse, taking off some of the pressure.

The frantic racing around the corral slowed.

"Come on, Joe," a man shouted to his friend. "Let's go. This is getting boring."

Fools. If the horse isn't terrified and the broncobuster doesn't lose a few teeth, they aren't interested.

The mare's circles around her became smaller and smaller until she turned her head to look at Amy. She chewed on the unfamiliar bit in her mouth.

Good. Chewing signaled that the mare was starting to relax. In response, Amy softened her own body.

Two more rounds and the mare's head lowered, and she sniffed the ground while she walked. It was a sign of her beginning trust in Amy. A horse that dropped its head couldn't look out for predators. Finally, the mare stopped in the corner where she had been when Amy had first seen her.

Her safety spot. Amy made note of it so she could use it to work with her. She stepped back and half turned, showing the mare her shoulder instead of her front. She had seen lead mares do the same when they allowed another horse into the herd.

The mare took a single step but then stopped and snorted at her. Curiosity gleamed in the big brown eyes, but the stiffness in her neck signaled that she wasn't ready to approach Amy.

All right. Crooning soft words, she walked toward the mare's shoulder. She moved slowly, but without hesitation. It wouldn't do to sneak up on the mare like a predator on the hunt.

The mare stood stiff-legged, her ears twitching.

Amy stopped an arm's length away.

With wide nostrils, the mare sucked in her scent.

Calmly, Amy touched the mare's shoulder, just for the length of a heartbeat. Then she took her hand away. "See?" she whispered. "Getting touched doesn't hurt."

When the mare didn't move away, Amy scratched the stiff neck and around the withers, the way she had seen horses groom each other. Her hands slid over the mare's wet flanks, then down to her belly. She flapped the stirrups around, letting the mare know that the bouncing thing on her back was not a mountain lion out to kill her.

After a few minutes of retreating and advancing, the horse relaxed under her hand. Amy reached for the mud-crusted reins. When the mare pranced away, she stayed with her.

"Easy, easy, girl." She smoothed her fingers into the horse's mane and grabbed a strand. When she moved to put one foot in the stirrup, she remembered that she wasn't wearing pants. Mama had even made her wear a dress instead of the split skirt she usually wore to town. In a dress, she could either ride sidesaddle or pull up the skirt and petticoats to straddle the horse—which would give the audience a good, long look at her legs.

Amy shivered. *No, thanks.* She didn't want to give Buzz that kind of buzz. She reached down and, using a tear in the hem of her skirt, ripped the checkered fabric until she had enough freedom of movement.

She slid her left foot into the stirrup and slowly, without bouncing, rose up until some of her weight rested on the stirrup.

The mare snorted and sidestepped.

Amy dropped down. "Everything's fine, beautiful. Let's try that again." She grabbed the reins and a handful of mane and rose up in the stirrup, this time a little longer. After a few more tries, she could do it without the mare dancing away. Gently, Amy swung her leg over and slid into the saddle.

For a few moments, she just sat, keeping her body relaxed. It had been hard to learn—staying calm and relaxed while she waited to see whether the horse would explode under her. The first time she had seen Papa do it, it seemed like magic.

The mare's back felt stiff as a board, but when Amy didn't pierce her with sharp claws or spurs, the grulla bent her head around to send her a startled glance.

Chuckling, Amy patted her neck. "It's all right, girl."

Gray ears flicked back to listen to her voice.

Amy gathered the reins in one hand and squeezed with her legs.

The mare took a startled step, and Amy relaxed her legs, rewarding the horse for reacting to her cues. One more squeeze with her legs and the mare walked around the corral. It took a while, but she finally dropped her head and her back muscles softened.

Tightening her legs, Amy urged the mare into a jog.

Instantly, the mare's head reared up, and she hopped twice before settling down.

Amy grinned as she rode her around the corral. Despite her mousy look, the mare promised to develop a pretty smooth gait.

With light pressure, she reined in the mare and dropped to the ground. When she looked up, she realized she had lost her audience. Only Buzz waited in front of the corral. The other men and women gathered farther down the street, in front of the stage depot.

Oh, no, the stagecoach!

Amy wasn't in town to gentle a horse. Phin's betrothed was waiting for her and had probably been waiting for some time. The stage's horses had already been exchanged for fresh ones, and the stage was pulling out.

She opened the corral gate and led the gray mare toward her buckboard.

"Hey!" Buzz called. "Aren't you forgetting something?"

Amy whirled around. "What?"

"My money." Buzz thrust out his hand, palm up.

The two gold coins felt heavy in her hand. It wasn't her money to spend. *Too late.* She gritted her teeth and handed over the ten dollars.

STAGE DEPOT
BAKER PRAIRIE, OREGON
APRIL 20, 1868

HE STAGECOACH SWAYED TO A halt, and Rika braced herself so she wouldn't be thrown onto the laps of her fellow travelers.

She drew in a breath. This was it, her new home. The stage's leather curtains were drawn shut to protect them from the mud flung up by the horses' hooves, so she hadn't yet caught a glimpse of the town. The two passengers opened the door and climbed down, but Rika was almost afraid to step outside and see what she had gotten herself into.

One of the men offered his hand to help her out of the stagecoach.

With one step, Rika sank ankle-deep into the mud on the main street. She shook out her wrinkled, sooty skirts and stepped onto the boardwalk.

A few dozen buildings dotted the rutted main street. Wooden signs announced the presence of a barbershop, a doctor's office, a blacksmith, and a saddle maker's shop in the little town. In front of the dry-goods store, a brown horse stood hitched to a buckboard.

One of Rika's fellow travelers disappeared into the barbershop; the other climbed onto a buckboard, tipped his hat, and drove off. Now only Rika stood waiting on the boardwalk.

She scanned the faces of the townspeople milling about Main Street, going into and coming out of buildings. The man with the handlebar mustache, her future husband, was nowhere to be seen.

The stage had come in late. Had he gotten tired of waiting and left? What if he changed his mind and no longer wanted a wife? Rika clutched her carpetbag to her chest.

Her gaze darted up and down the street, but no wagon came to pick her up. People hurried across the boardwalk, trying to get out of the rain that had started falling again. Some threw curious glances her way, but no one talked to her. Shivering, she slung her arms more tightly around the carpetbag.

A few young men wandered over from the livery stable. One of them doffed his battered hat. "Can we help you, ma'am?"

"No, thank you." Rika drew her bag against her chest. "I am waiting for Mr. Phineas Sharpe, my betrothed."

"Ah, then you're plumb out of luck, ma'am, 'cause Phin left to drive a few horses up to Fort Boise and won't be back for two months."

The blood rushed from her face, and she swayed. "Two months?"

"Or more." The man shrugged.

Oh, Jo. Good thing her friend would never find out that her beloved Phineas didn't intend to keep his promises. *Riding off to Boise when he knew his betrothed was coming...* She was stranded in an unfamiliar town, forsaken by a future husband who had apparently changed his mind. *What now?*

"I'm sorry I'm late," someone said behind her.

Rika turned.

A young woman stopped midstep.

Rika took in the woman's mud-spattered bodice and the bonnet hanging off to one side, revealing disheveled fiery red hair. Under a skirt that was ripped up to midthigh, flashes of long drawers startled her. Behind the woman, a sweat-covered gray horse pranced around.

What did she do to the poor horse?

When the wild-looking woman reached for the carpetbag, Rika flinched away. "Who are you?"

"Oh." A flush colored the stranger's golden skin. She wiped her hand on her skirt, probably not getting it any cleaner. "I'm Amy Hamilton, a friend of Phin Sharpe's. And who on God's green earth are you?"

The young woman stared at her.
Amy stared back.

"I'm Johanna Bruggeman," the stranger said.

Amy put her hands on her hips. "No, you're not. I've seen the tintype. You're not her."

The fragile beauty of Phin's bride had burned itself into her memory. The stranger, however, was neither fragile nor beautiful. While the tintype hadn't provided colors, Amy could tell that Phin's bride had fair hair. The stranger's brown hair, though, shone with the same coppery gleam as the mahogany coat of Nattie's mare. Her wide brown eyes reminded Amy of a spooked horse.

The woman's gaze flitted around, and she hid behind her carpetbag as if it were a shield. But then she tilted her head and composed her stern features.

Like a mustang. Spooked but unbroken in spirit.

"Of course I am Johanna Bruggeman." Her slight accent made the name sound exotic.

Right. She's Dutch. So was she Phin's bride after all? "Then how come you don't look like the woman in the tintype?"

A muscle in the stranger's face twitched. "Phineas showed you the tintype?"

Amy nodded and dug her teeth into her bottom lip. She hoped she wasn't blushing. Why did she feel like a boy who'd been caught with the picture of a dance-hall girl? It wasn't as if she had ogled the young woman's picture. She raised her chin. "You still owe me an explanation."

The stranger lowered her gaze. "I was too embarrassed to have my picture taken. I know men don't find me all that appealing, so a friend allowed me to send her picture instead."

Amy slid her gaze over her. *She is a bit on the plain side. All the better.* She had been afraid of how a woman who was every bit as beautiful as Hannah might make her react.

"I know it's vain," the young woman said. "But I hope you won't judge me for it."

"None of my business," Amy said. Just to be on the safe side, she didn't plan on having much to do with Phin's bride. Easy to do, since she would be busy with the ranch. "All right, then let's go. I'll take you to the ranch. My family will take care of you until Phin returns." She kept her movements gentle but firm, as if dealing with a young horse, and again reached for the carpetbag.

Finally, the woman handed over her baggage.

"Do you have any other bags?" Amy asked.

A flush stained the young woman's pale skin. "No, just this one."

As far as Amy was concerned, there was no shame in being poor. At least she wouldn't have to drag half a dozen suitcases, bags, and hatboxes to the buckboard and could get back to the ranch sooner.

The ranch and Mama. No doubt Mama would have something interesting to say about Amy's skirt and the mare.

Patches of mist drifted up from the river and mingled with the never-ending drizzle. In the gray light of the fading day, grassland stretched out in front of Rika like the sea beyond Boston Harbor, the wind rippling through the blades. The tang of pine and leather hung in the air.

Rika pushed her sodden bonnet out of her eyes and threw a glance at Amy, who sat next to her on the buckboard. Unlike Rika, she didn't seem to notice the gloomy weather.

Rika glanced at the sinewy hands holding the reins. *What a strange, unusual woman.* Amy Hamilton was unlike anyone she'd ever met in Boston. After the mindless routine in the cotton mill, at least life out west promised to be interesting.

The brown horse in front of the wagon walked steadily, its head bopping up and down as it pulled them through a valley dotted with trees and bushes Rika didn't know. A creek gurgled alongside them, and the horse's harness jangled with every step. Behind them, the gray horse splashed through the mud. It had whinnied and struggled against the rope at first but had then gotten used to being tied to the wagon.

It's so quiet. After the constant noise in the city and the clatter of the looms in the cotton mill, Oregon's silence made her wish Amy would fill it with idle chatter. She looked at her silent companion, and when their gazes met, both glanced away.

Did she believe the lie about the tintype? Rika bit her lip until a coppery taste filled her mouth. She should have thought of that. Since Phineas sent his picture to Jo, of course Jo had to send one back. Rika had assumed Jo would rather use her money to see a doctor than waste it on getting her picture taken. She vowed to be more careful in the future. "A man in town said Phineas would be gone for two months. Surely he was joking?"

Amy flicked her gaze from the road to Rika. "No. Two months. Might be three. He sends his apologies."

"But..." Rika reached into her coat pocket and pulled out the rumpled bundle of letters. "He said that he'd whisk me away to church the moment I stepped foot off the stagecoach, and now he's not even here to greet me." How serious could Phineas Sharpe be about his promise to marry her if he sent this strange young woman to fetch her?

"It couldn't be helped." Green fire sparked in Amy's eyes. "My father needed him to drive a herd of geldings to Fort Boise. Out here, making sure the ranch survives is more important than getting married on time."

Not to Rika. To her, getting married meant survival. "I understand," she said stiffly.

Amy fell silent, leaving her to her own thoughts. Thinking wasn't what she wanted to do. She wanted to let go of the past with all that it held, but her future was unsure and stolen from a dead woman.

The wagon crested one last hill. Below them, sheds and barns lay scattered around a two-story main house. Tall pines and spruce flanked the large veranda, and she imagined them providing ample shade in the summer and lending shelter from the snow in winter. *Do they even get snow here in Oregon?*

Paddocks spread out from both sides of the house, leading to a large, circular corral. Rika couldn't see what lay on the other side of the house, but from somewhere, an herb garden saturated the air with the scent of sage and mint. The carefully tended home seemed like something right out of a fairy tale. *Jo would have loved it.*

When the buckboard rattled into the ranch yard, a large dog charged up the path, growling and barking.

Rika pulled her skirt around her legs, protecting them just in case the dog tried to bite.

"Quit making such a ruckus, Hunter," Amy said. When she stopped the buckboard, the door of the main house swung open and a woman stepped onto the veranda.

Rika blinked, then glanced back and forth between Amy and the woman. With her flaming red hair and her slender yet sturdy build, the woman looked like Amy's twin. When she came closer, a few lines around her mouth and eyes revealed her to be an older version of Amy.

Her mother?

Amy jumped down from the wagon seat and rounded the buckboard. She extended her hand to help Rika down, and after a moment's hesitation, Rika laid her hand into the calloused palm and climbed down to look at her new home.

A grin sneaked onto Nora's face as she watched Amy help the young woman off the high wagon seat. The gesture reminded her of Luke. "You must be Johanna." She directed a smile at the slim woman next to Amy. "I'm Nora Hamilton. Welcome to—" Then her gaze fell onto Amy's dress, and her mouth snapped shut.

Mud clung to the hem of the dress and painted an ugly pattern over the once clean bodice. The skirt and petticoat hung in ripped tatters, and Amy's hair looked as if a flock of birds had tried to nest in it.

Nora hurried down the veranda steps. "Amy! Are you all right? What happened?"

"I'm fine." Amy folded her hands in front of her body, belatedly trying to hide the large rip in her skirt.

Nora eyed the gray horse tied to the buckboard. "What's that?"

"She's a mare, Mama," Amy answered.

"I can see that. What is the mare doing here? She's not yours, is she?" Nora looked at Johanna.

"No," Johanna said.

"I bought her," Amy said, her gaze fixed on the horse.

"Your father just left, risking his life to sell horses, and you go and buy another one?" Nora shook her head. "Where did you get the money anyway?" While Amy had grown up not wanting for anything, she didn't have much spending money in her pocket.

"Um." Amy stared at her mud-crusted boots. "Phin gave it to me."

"Phin?" Their foreman would have given Amy the shirt off his back and vice versa, but with his new bride coming to live with him, he didn't have that kind of money to give away. Nora stared as realization dawned. "You took the money he gave you for his betrothed?"

Sodden locks fell into Amy's eyes as she hung her head. "I'm sorry. I know it wasn't my money to spend. I'll pay it all back somehow." Her head came up, and her eyes glowed. "But I couldn't stand there and watch them torment the mare. I just couldn't."

Will she ever be this passionate about someone or something other than horses? Nora hoped that one day, her daughters would be as happy as she was in her marriage.

"Half a dozen men threw her down. They would have bucked her until she died or had her spirit broken," Amy said. "Buying her was the only way to save her."

Nora sighed, but a small smile replaced her frown. Luke would have rescued the mare too, no matter the damage to her clothes, her body, or her finances. Incredible how much Amy resembled Luke in everything but the way she looked.

Ignoring the rain, Nora walked around the buckboard. She reached out to touch the mare's flank but stopped when she noticed the rope burns and bleeding scratches covering the gray coat. She knew Amy hadn't caused the marks. Someone had tried to break the mare.

In their early years in Oregon, the neighbors had made fun of Luke's gentle horse taming methods. They said if Luke continued to mollycoddle their horses, they would turn out spoiled and unpredictable. Now, years later, every rancher and farmer in the area wanted to own one of the well-trained Hamilton horses.

"You meant well," Nora said. "But taking money that's not yours isn't what your father and I taught you. The money belongs to Johanna. Phin wanted her to buy something to make her feel comfortable—maybe a set of dishes or linen or a new dress."

"I'm sorry." Amy looked at Phin's betrothed. "It might take me a while, but I promise to pay back every penny."

"It's all right." Johanna shrugged it off as if they were talking about ten cents, not ten dollars. "I already own two perfectly good dresses, and I don't need much to be content. I don't mind that you used the money to help the horse."

Amy's mouth slackened.

Except for Hannah Garfield, the girls around Baker Prairie didn't understand or support Amy's passion for horses. Nora's gaze roved over the young woman. *Maybe she could become Amy's friend.*

"Let's get out of the rain and make proper introductions inside." Nora asked one of the ranch hands to unload the wagon and take care of the horses before she herded the two younger women into the house.

She watched Johanna take in the short divan, the armchairs, the china cabinet, and the rolltop desk in one corner of the parlor. What would a woman from back East think of the home they had built for themselves? Nora was proud of her home, even if the young Boston ladies she had known twenty years ago would have frowned upon it.

But with her simple dress and no dowry, Johanna was clearly a working-class girl, not a Boston Brahman. Her serious face revealed nothing. The young woman was hard to figure out. Nora guessed her to be two years older than Amy. In her dark eyes lurked a caution that was absent from her daughters' gazes.

Nora offered her guest a place near the hearth and watched her settle into an armchair. The carpetbag never left the young woman's hands.

That could have been me seventeen years ago. Before meeting Luke, Nora had never trusted anyone, with the possible exception of Tess Swenson, her only friend back then. Her marriage with Luke had started out as unconventionally as Phin's arrangement with a mail-order bride. *One difference, though. I doubt she will discover something so shocking about her new husband.* Nora hid a grin. Now she could laugh about it, but seventeen years ago, she had thought her world had come to an end when she found out her husband was a woman.

"So, you are Johanna Bruggeman," she said. "Phin has told us so much about you."

Johanna's pale face took on an even pastier shade.

Is she nervous about us knowing what she wrote Phin in his letters?

"Please call me Hendrika," the young woman said. "In Holland, where my family comes from, we tend to use our middle names."

Right, she's from Holland. That explained the exotic cadence to the familiar Boston accent.

"I'm Nora Hamilton." She gestured toward Amy. "And you already met my daughter Amy. I hope you won't hold her appearance against her. I promise she doesn't always look like a scarecrow. And we'll work something out to give you back your money."

Amy clutched the back of Luke's favorite armchair.

"It's already forgotten," Hendrika said, and Nora thought she detected a flash of honesty beneath the polite mask.

"You'll meet Nattie, my other daughter, later. She's visiting with the neighbors but will be home in time for supper. It'll be just enough time for you to settle in and wash up."

A nod from Hendrika answered her.

"Amy, I thought she could share your room until she feels more at home here," Nora said.

Now it was Amy who went pale. "Share my room? Why can't she stay in Phin's cabin?"

"That cabin needs a good scrubbin' before it's fit for a woman," Nora said. "And I don't want her to be on her own. I thought it would be nice if she could stay at the main house until Phin gets back. You're out on the range for most of the day anyway, so you won't get in each other's way."

Her suggestion didn't meet with enthusiastic agreement from either of the young women. Hendrika's grip on her carpetbag tightened until Nora thought she might break a knuckle. "I'll be fine in the cabin," Hendrika said. "I don't want to be in the way."

"You're not—"

"The cabin is fine," Hendrika said. "If you could show me the way, I can get my things stowed away and then come back to help with supper."

Ah. Nora recognized the proud glint in Hendrika's eyes. Twenty years ago, Nora would have said the same. Before she met Luke, she had believed she had to pay for everything she received one way or another. Love and friendship had been unfamiliar concepts for her. She hoped that as part of the Hamilton Ranch, Hendrika Bruggeman would become familiar with both.

The cabin's door creaked open.

Needs to be oiled. Rika added the first item to her list of things she could do to help out around the ranch.

The musky smells of wood smoke, damp earth, and linseed oil engulfed her as soon as she entered the cabin. Her boots stepped onto packed earth. After the boarding house's oak floor and stone walls, the cabin's dirt floor and rough-hewn logs would take some getting used to, but Rika knew she would make do with whatever life threw at her.

Amy slipped past her and lit a kerosene lamp. When she turned up the wick, the flickering light revealed a table charred black on one side. *No cook stove.* Very likely, the cooking was done at the main house. Shelves held broken bridles and harnesses the cabin's owner hadn't gotten around to repairing.

A carpet might be nice. And the hearth needs to be cleaned.

In the light of the kerosene lamp, she walked to the bedroom while Amy followed. A brass bedstead warred for space with a low dresser, a chest at the foot of the bed, and a washstand.

Amy's gaze followed hers, and she looked as if she was trying to see the small cabin through Rika's eyes. She cleared her throat. "I know it's not much. It was the first home my father built when we arrived in Oregon, so it's rather simple."

"It's quite all right," Rika said. "I didn't live in a palace in Boston either." Her words brought back memories of a dilapidated house and nights lying awake, listening to rain drip through the leaky roof while Willem was out drinking.

White teeth flashed in the low light when Amy chewed on her lip. "Maybe Mama was right. If you want, you can have my room in the main house and I could sleep over here."

That wasn't what Nora had suggested. Why would Amy give up her room rather than share it with her? Rika drew her brows together. Had she done anything to make Amy dislike her?

"No, thank you," she answered. "If your family lived here once, I'll be fine here too." If she stayed at the cabin, she could at least get used to her new home before having to share it with the stranger who would become her husband.

She set down her carpetbag at the foot of the bed and pulled out her only clean skirt. When she peeked into the pitcher on the washstand, she found that it still held some water that smelled fresh enough. She poured the water into the bowl and looked around for something to wash with.

"Here." Amy, apparently familiar with where things were kept in the cabin, handed her a towel and soap. "I'll go and look in on the horses before supper. The gray mare needs some ointment."

The door closed behind her before Rika could answer.

Rika stared at the ranch hands, who laughed and teased during supper. She watched Amy and her dark-haired sister, Nattie, heap second helpings of chicken and dumplings onto their plates, not afraid of being thought unladylike.

Story after story distracted her, and she paused with her fork halfway to her mouth. In her family, meals had been a silent affair, the children too afraid of angering their father by chattering on and on.

Fear and silence didn't rule this family, though.

"They named her Emeline Anna Buchanan, after her grandmother," Nattie said. "Little Emmy took quite a long time to arrive. Twenty hours of labor! Can you believe it?"

"I sure can." Her mother grinned. "It took you all night to be born too. And we were stuck in the middle of the Blue Mountains, with no neighbors, midwives, or doctors around. Your father was a mess."

Everyone around the table laughed as if it was common knowledge and they had all teased Mr. Hamilton about it a thousand times.

"Twenty hours," Amy mumbled. "Then I'd rather have a foal than a baby. Horses are quick about it. No big fuss."

Her mother looked up with twinkling eyes. "That's what you said when your sister was born too. You asked your father if you could have a filly instead."

"Thanks a lot, Amy." Nattie glared at her sister.

"Everything all right with the food, Hendrika?" Nora asked. "You're not eating."

Rika stared at her food. "Oh, no, the food is wonderful. I'm just a bit worn out from the long journey."

Nattie's probing gaze met Rika. "You've certainly come a long way just to marry a stranger. A ranch in Oregon is a far cry from Boston."

She's testing me. Rika clamped her hand around the fork. "It sure is," she said as evenly as she could. "And I'm looking forward to it."

"But if you are to marry a ranch hand, are you sure you won't come to resent him if you have to live without all the amenities in Boston?" Nattie's brow knitted. "I hear they even have gas streetlamps in Boston."

Rika took a bite of chicken and nodded. "Yes, but that doesn't mean life in Boston is easy. The gas lighting is also used in the cotton mill, making it possible to work until late into the night. Believe me, I'm no stranger to hard work."

"What's gotten into you, Nattie?" Nora shook her head at her daughter. "Stop questioning the poor girl like that. I'm sure she'll make a wonderful wife for Phin." When Nattie lowered her gaze, Nora turned to Rika. "You said in your letters you were born in Holland?"

Rika's throat constricted and made the chicken hard to swallow. *Oh, gracious. She read Jo's letters...and I didn't.* She knew only Phineas's end of the conversation, not what Jo had told him about herself. Her appetite was gone, but she shoved another piece of chicken into her mouth to indicate that she was too busy to give long answers. Again, she just nodded.

"What's Holland like?" Nattie asked, friendlier this time. "Does it look a little like Oregon?"

Jo, whose family had sailed to America when she was ten, would have known, but Rika had been born in Boston, and her father rarely talked about the past. Only sometimes, when he was sober, had he told her stories about her mother and about their home in Holland. She tried to remember but was distracted when she found she couldn't recall her mother's face. The only picture of her mother had stayed behind when Rika had left her family.

Curious gazes rested on her, and she pulled herself together. "It's not like Oregon at all. It's a flat land, with almost no hills." Her mind flashed back to snowcapped Mount Hood, which Amy had pointed out on the way to the ranch. Rika's parents had grown up without ever laying eyes on such a mountain. "There's water everywhere—rivers, canals, lakes, and the North Sea. Windmills pump water out of the polders that keep the land from flooding."

She remembered the drawing in their parlor. Her mother had penciled in an endless sky, rippling water, and numerous green windmills dotting the landscape.

"You miss it," Amy said from the other side of the table. It was the first time during supper that she had addressed Rika directly.

How can I miss what I don't even remember? She looked at Amy, who glanced at her plate. "It was a long time ago. I'm sure I will feel right at home here."

HAMILTON HORSE RANCH
BAKER PRAIRIE, OREGON
APRIL 20, 1868

"Whoo, hoo-hoo." The owl's call greeted Amy when she stepped onto the veranda. She peered into the darkness but couldn't make out the bird. It was probably perched on a branch somewhere, waiting to swoop down on unsuspecting prey. Amy knew it was the male, because she had observed them many times. Owls mated for life. Now he was out hunting food for the female, who sat on eggs in their nest.

Kind of like Papa. Unlike the lady owl, the Hamilton women weren't just sitting around, waiting for him to get back, though. Amy had a ranch to run, and the responsibility of it kept her up at night. She held out her hand and felt soft drizzle touch her fingertips. *If the rain keeps up, I'll have to bring in the herd from the east pasture. And someone needs to check on the yearlings.*

With Kit, Charlie, and Phin gone, they were short on ranch hands. She had to time all the different tasks just right to make sure everything got done. Worry gnawed at her. Papa had taught her well, but would the ranch hands think so too? Hank and Toby would probably go along with her orders, if only out of respect for Papa. But what about Adam? Whenever Papa handed out tasks that required two people to work together, Adam made sure he was already partnered with another ranch hand so he wouldn't need to work with Amy. But now that she was the boss, he couldn't avoid her any longer.

I need to show him that I'm the boss. She glanced at the dark sky. A curtain of clouds hid the twinkling stars, offering no guidance.

The door to Phin's cabin opened, and a ray of light danced across the ranch yard. Hendrika stepped outside.

Quickly, Amy took a step back, seeking refuge in the darkness.

Hendrika directed her gaze at the sky.

Was she seeking guidance too? Or maybe she was just enjoying the fresh air after being stuck in a stuffy stagecoach all day. Amy didn't know. She often found she didn't understand other women at all.

When Hendrika retreated into the cabin, Amy turned and headed inside too. Tomorrow would be a long, hard day, and if she wanted to prove herself to the ranch hands, she needed to get some sleep.

Rika trudged across the ranch yard in the gray light of dawn. After a sleepless night, her eyes burned as if all the trail dust from Boston to Oregon had accumulated in them, but she forced herself to keep moving. Seeking out work instead of waiting for orders had served her well so far. It had gotten her promoted from the dusty roving room to the weave room with its tidy aisles and better light, and it would help her establish herself as a hardworking, reliable woman—good wife material—before Phineas came home.

She rubbed some color into her cheeks and knocked on the main house's door.

It opened, and Nora stood in the doorway, drying her hands on her apron. "Oh, good morning. Come on in." She held the door for Rika. "I hope you slept well."

"Like a baby," Rika answered. *Well, like a colicky baby.* Despite her exhaustion, she had lain awake, worrying about the future and finding it hard to fall asleep in such a quiet place, with no clatter from the street and no mill girls snoring and coughing.

When Rika entered the kitchen, Nattie gave her a quick wave before turning back to the stove.

Bacon sizzled in a frying pan, and the smell made Rika's mouth water. "Can I help in any way?"

Nora pulled a baking pan of golden-brown biscuits from the oven and gestured to the china cabinet. "You could just sit and relax, but if you want to, you could set the table."

Rika took the stack of plates and set them on the table the way she remembered from supper.

"Oh, no, it's just us this morning," Nora said. "One of our neighbors came over half an hour ago to tell us that our fence is down in the western pasture. Amy and the boys already left to mend it, and they won't be back until later."

Amy and the boys. Did Amy really do a man's work around the ranch? Did the Hamiltons think nothing of letting their daughter tame wild horses and mend fences?

"I have to pay a visit to our neighbors today," Nora said when they sat down for breakfast. "I promised Ruth to come see the baby as soon as it was born, but I put it off yesterday because I didn't want you to arrive to an empty house."

A piece of egg almost lodged in Rika's throat. *She stayed home to make me feel welcome?* No one had ever changed her plans because of her. Maybe Nora was just being nice to make up for Phineas's absence.

"I can't put it off again today," Nora said, "but I thought you might like to come with me and meet the neighbors."

Rika clamped her hand around her fork. Meeting the neighbors would mean answering more questions about her past and having to come up with more lies. "Oh, I thought I'd clean the cabin today."

"Are you sure you don't want to wait and have some help with that?"

"I could help her, Mama," Nattie said before Rika could answer.

The offer was polite, but Rika didn't want to be a burden. "That's nice of you, but I'm sure you have your own chores."

Nora tilted her head. "Yes, you do, Nattie. If I'm not back on time, I'll need you to prepare supper. I haven't seen Ruth and Emeline in ages, and if the pastor comes over to see the baby, I'm sure he'll keep me there all afternoon, trying to convince me to take over teaching school again."

Teach school? Since when did married women teach school? Rika had gone to school for four years, and no female teacher ever stayed on after getting married. The West was truly a strange place.

"You could teach if you wanted," Nattie said. Her eyes, which seemed to change color, were now a determined gray. "Amy and I have things at the ranch well in hand. I am not a child anymore, you know?"

"We'll see," her mother said.

When Rika straightened, her knees groaned and pain exploded in her back. She dropped the brush into the bucket of water black with soot. Ashes and lye soap tickled her nose and made her sneeze.

"One more bucket should do the trick." She used her elbow and hip to open the door, not wanting to get the soot from her hands all over the newly cleaned cabin. A soft drizzle still fell outside. *Does it ever stop raining in Oregon?* Still, after she had cleaned the cabin all morning, the cool rain felt refreshing. Her eyes fluttered shut, and she breathed in the clean air. She drew back her hands and flung the dirty water into the direction of the hazel bushes next to the cabin.

"Hell and tarnation!"

Rika's eyes popped open. Her hand flew to her chest, covering her pounding heart.

Instead of seeping into the earth beneath the hazel bushes, the bucket's contents had hit one of the ranch hands.

No. Rika shook her head. Not a ranch hand. The voice was that of a woman. That of—

She gasped. *Amy!*

Drops of black water stained Amy's collarless shirt and ran down strong legs improperly displayed by gray pants and worn leather chaps. The now clinging shirt left no doubt that she wasn't wearing a corset. When she swept off her hat to wipe her brow, a mass of red hair tumbled onto sturdy shoulders. She shook herself like a dog with fleas. "Being around you seems to be hard on my clothes, Miss Bruggeman. What did you throw at me—a pot of ink?"

Had something like that happened at home, Rika's father would have flown into one of his rages, but Amy grinned.

"Just some dirty water. I'm cleaning the hearth." Her heartbeat calmed, but she couldn't stop staring at Amy's strange attire. Was this some Oregon tradition she had never heard of? Did local women think it was perfectly normal to dress in male garb?

"Amy, what about the east pasture? Should we—?" Two of the ranch hands came around the corner and stopped when they saw Amy. "What happened to you?"

"She did." Water dripped off Amy's finger when she pointed at Rika. "Apparently, Phin's future wife thought the rain wouldn't make me wet enough."

"Maybe she thought you needed to be put in your place," the older of the two men mumbled. His gaze clung to Amy's chest the same way that her wet shirt did.

Fire smoldered in Amy's eyes. She crossed her arms over her chest. "What did you just say, Adam?"

Rika's heart jumped into her throat. While she found Amy's way of dressing curious too, she didn't want to cause any trouble for her.

Amy stood in front of the man, her shoulders squared and her gaze fixed on him without flinching.

For a moment, Rika was afraid the man would hit her. She had a feeling that Amy wouldn't back down even then.

"He said the place is probably a mess," the second man said and pointed at the cabin. "Come on, Adam. Let's get the horses off the east pasture."

"No." Amy kept her gaze fixed on Adam. "I need you to fix the corral gate first. It's sagging, and if it continues to rain like this, the wood will swell and we won't be able to open the gate anymore."

"That's darned stupid," Adam said. "While we're dilly-dallying with the damn gate, the horses will trample the grass on the east pasture. Your father would never give such foolish orders, but that's what you get for letting a woman—"

"My father was the one who taught me how to run a ranch." Amy stepped closer to the ranch hand and skewered him with an angry glare. "And I never said we'd let the horses trample through the mud on the east pasture until the grass is ruined. I'll ride out and drive the herd farther up the hills."

"On your own?" the friendlier man asked.

Russet brows lowered like a thundercloud. "I'm perfectly capable of—"

"I know, but it's a big herd, and two riders might be better."

"I could help," Rika said. The hearth was cleaned; the door didn't creak anymore, and the first spring flowers adorned the table, hiding the burn marks. One quick sweep of the floor and Rika wouldn't have anything more to do in the cabin. She wasn't used to sitting around idly, and if she wanted to have a future on the Hamilton Ranch, she knew she'd have to get into Amy Hamilton's good graces.

Three pairs of eyes studied her. The man named Adam snorted.

"Have you ever been on a horse?" Amy asked.

Rika's struggled not to fidget under Amy's skeptical gaze. "Oh, sure." She didn't mention that, at the time, she'd been a three-year-old in her mother's arms. After her mother's death, her father had ordered her to stay away from the family's only saddle horse, and the big draft horses that brought the flour from the mill to the bakery had scared her. But surely riding a horse couldn't be so hard.

"Women don't belong out on the range," Adam said. "If you want to make yourself useful, see if you can help out in the kitchen."

The words were meant for Amy, showing her a woman's place, but they stung nonetheless. Not that Rika minded helping out in the kitchen. But Nora and Nattie had that area of the ranch firmly in hand and didn't need her help. Adam's harsh words only increased Rika's determination to help Amy.

Amy whirled around to face him. "I don't remember my father leaving you in charge. It's not your place to tell Hendrika what she can and can't do." She turned toward Rika. "You want to help me with the herd? Then come on."

Rika set down the empty bucket, wiped her hands on her apron, and hurried after her.

When they entered the barn, muzzles popped up over the stall doors, and somewhere behind her, a heavy horse hoof crashed against a board. Rika jumped. She stayed close to Amy as they walked down the aisle between two rows of stalls.

A white horse with brown spots craned its neck and blew air out of its nostrils. Farther down the aisle, a black horse with a white rump rasped its tongue over a block of salt.

Rika peered into a few more stalls. "They all look like circus horses." As children, she and her brother had slipped under the tent canvas of a circus and spent the happiest afternoon of her childhood watching the clowns and animals. The horses in the circus ring had been spotted, just like these.

"Circus horses?" Amy stared as if Rika had thrown a second bucket of water at her. "We're breeding Appaloosas, not circus horses."

"I meant because of the spots. They are beautiful." Beautiful and intimidating, but Rika kept that to herself.

A smile softened Amy's expression. "Yeah, they are." She stopped in front of a stall at the end of the barn. "I thought you could ride Cinnamon."

Cinnamon? Rika chuckled to herself. *And here I thought I was on a horse ranch, and not in my father's bakery.*

Amy opened the stall door, and Rika's grin faded. Was the horse really that large, or did it just appear that way because she knew she'd have to get up on it?

She understood why they had named it Cinnamon, though. The horse's red coat was dusted with white hairs, looking like the mix of sugar and cinnamon on the rice pudding her mother used to make. Around the cheeks, the forehead, and the legs, the coat was darker and looked like pure cinnamon. A large white blanket with acorn-sized dots covered the horse's rump.

"She's beautiful," she said, knowing it would make Amy smile.

"He," Amy corrected. "Cinnamon is a gelding."

"Sorry," Rika said to the horse and Amy. "Then he is handsome." *But is he also tame?*

The horse rubbed his muzzle on Amy's shoulder. At the moment, he looked rather friendly. "Cinnamon is real gentle." Amy scratched the high spot on the horse's back. "I've had him since he was a foal. He was the first horse I ever trained, and he's so gentle and calm that even the Garfield grandchildren learned how to ride on him. Come on over and say hello to the old boy."

Keeping an eye on the horse, Rika stepped next to Amy.

"Don't stare at him, or it'll make him feel threatened," Amy said.

"Me make him feel threatened?" Rika turned toward Amy and stared at her. *By shaking like a leaf maybe?*

"Yes," Amy said. "Horses may look big and tough, but they get scared easily."

"Don't be scared," Rika murmured to the horse. "I'm not gonna hurt you." *So please don't hurt me.* She lifted her hand and looked at Amy for confirmation.

Amy nodded. "Let him sniff you."

Cinnamon's nose lowered. Warm air brushed against her palm and then the long hairs on the horse's muzzle tickled her wrist. A velvet nose touched her hand.

Oh, he's so soft. She slid her hand up and stroked his neck, admiring the small brownish-red dots on the smooth coat.

"There," Amy said. "Scratch him behind the withers. He likes that."

When Rika hesitated, Amy took her hand and placed it on the ridge at the bottom of Cinnamon's neck. Her body leaned against Rika's so that they could both reach the horse, but then Amy retreated.

Rika scratched with careful nails.

"Look at him." Amy chuckled.

Cinnamon wiggled his nose, clearly enjoying Rika's touch.

Rika's fear of the big animal eased. "He's wonderful. I could do this all day."

"Oh, Cinnamon would love that. But I have to move the herd on the east pasture." Amy glanced at the barn's entrance. "If you promise not to enter the stall on your own, you could stay and keep Cinnamon company."

Not having to get on a horse was a nice thought, but if she backed out now, Rika had a feeling she would sit around for the next two months, waiting for her future husband to come home. "I'd rather come with you."

"Then let's get going." Amy swung the stall door open. "Go get your coat, and I'll saddle Ruby and Cin."

Rika scrambled back when Amy put a halter on the horse and led him out of the stall. She hurried to the cabin and fetched her coat.

When she returned, Amy had tied the horses to the corral rail. She turned and studied Rika. "If you're gonna stay in Oregon, you'll need a new coat."

If I stay in Oregon? Does she think going back is an option? "What's wrong with my coat?" Rika trailed her fingers over the worn wool. The coat might not be the most elegant, but it had served her well on the journey west and it would do for at least another year. She had no money to spend on fancy clothes.

"You need a canvas jacket like this." Amy tugged on her jacket, which reached to just below her hips. "It's coated with linseed oil, so it's waterproof. In your coat, you'll be drenched to the bone before we find the herd."

"A little rain won't kill me," Rika said.

Amy shrugged. "Suit yourself." She turned around and began to brush down the gelding.

"I thought you were in a hurry to move those horses? And now you're cleaning him?"

Never stopping her rhythmic brush strokes, Amy glanced at her. "It's clearly been a while since you've been around horses. This is not because I'm vain and want him to look good when we ride out. If there's a stalk of straw or a clump of dirt caught in his coat, the saddle will rub him raw." She put the brush away and lifted Cinnamon's foot.

The gelding didn't struggle. His hoof rested trustingly across Amy's knees while she scraped dirt out of it.

Rika had never seen a woman do that, but Amy moved as if she cleaned hooves every day of her life. She placed a blanket and the saddle on Cinnamon's back and tightened a leather strap in a complicated pattern of knots and metal rings. When Cinnamon was ready to go, Amy brushed down the second horse. The brush slid along the fiery red coat and over the white rump with its red dots.

The red horse flattened its ears and flicked its tail at Cinnamon, and Rika moved one step back.

"Behave, Ruby, and show our guest that you can be a lady." Amy tapped the horse on the rump.

Guest, Rika repeated. *There she goes again.* She was here to stay, but apparently, Amy had other ideas. If she wanted a life in Oregon, she needed to impress Amy. She was running the ranch right now, as unusual as that was, and that meant she was not just Phineas's friend, but also his employer.

"All right. Let's get going." Amy handed her the reins.

"Um…" Rika looked from Amy to the horse. "It's been a while since I've been on a horse. Can you give me a quick reminder?"

"Oh, for heaven's sake. Come over here, to his left side." Amy took back the reins, and Cinnamon stood still like a statue. "Put your left foot into the stirrup."

Rika rustled her skirt. "Um. How do I...?"

"Oh. I could lend you a pair of my pants. They're really the best thing for riding."

Pants were beginning to look almost right on Amy, but for herself? Rika shook her head. "I'll just bunch up my skirt." No men were around to watch her anyway since the ranch hands had ridden off to tend to their own tasks. Rika bundled up her skirt and tucked the hem into the straps of her apron so that it would stay out of the way.

"Sorry," Amy said, staring off into the distance. Her face glowed with a slight blush. "I should have at least put a sidesaddle on him, but we don't use them for ranch work and I thought my old saddle would make you feel more secure."

It seemed Amy felt accountable for everything and everyone on the ranch, including Rika. No one had ever taken responsibility for Rika, and she wasn't sure she liked it. *Maybe you should have thought about that before you came to Oregon. Very soon, your husband is going to be responsible for you.* She shoved the thought away. "It's all right." She eyed Cinnamon. His back seemed so far away.

Again, Amy checked the fit of the leather strap around Cinnamon's belly. She turned the stirrup and held it in place. "Put your foot in the stirrup."

Lifting her foot up so high was harder than expected. Rika grabbed the saddle horn to keep her balance.

"No," Amy said. "I don't know what they've been teaching you in Boston, but here, we don't pull ourselves up by the saddle horn. Grab a bit of mane and rest your hand on his neck. The other hand goes on the cantle." Amy slapped the back of the saddle.

"Grab his mane? But won't that hurt him?"

"No. You're just holding on, not pulling on the mane. It'll hurt him if you pull on the saddle horn and slide the saddle out of position."

Rika placed her hand on the warm neck and weaved her fingers through the reddish-brown mane.

"All right. Now bounce on your foot, then push off until you stand in the stirrup. Then swing your right leg over the cantle."

Rika glanced from the gelding's neck to the different parts of the saddle, trying to figure out the sequence of movements.

"Don't worry," Amy said. "Cinnamon is very well trained. He won't move an inch."

Rika's heart fluttered, and with one deep breath, she pushed off the ground. All went well until she swung her right leg over the saddle and bumped Cinnamon's rump. She landed in the saddle and grabbed the saddle horn, afraid that the bump would make the horse spook and run.

"Relax," Amy murmured next to her. "Cinnamon is a good horse. We trained him to stand still, no matter what. A little bump won't make him run for the hills with you. Trust him to keep you safe."

Easier said than done.

Amy regarded her through narrowed eyes. "Are you sure you wouldn't rather stay here?"

Rika set her jaw. *I can do this. I already made it up into the saddle.* "I'm sure. I'll come with you."

"Here." Amy handed her the reins. Her warm hand closed over Rika's cold fingers, correcting the position of her thumb. Then she reached down to adjust the stirrup. Rika felt her touch against her leg before Amy backed away with a mumbled apology.

"It's all right," Rika said. Amy's touch had been strangely comforting.

Cinnamon shifted his weight, and she grabbed the saddle horn again.

"Don't stiffen up. Sit up straight, but relax and enjoy the ride. Ruby is the boss in the herd." Amy reached over and patted her own horse. "Cinnamon will just follow her without you having to do much. We won't go faster than a walk until you get used to being on a horse again."

"Ruby is the boss? I thought the stallion is the boss of the herd?" Were the Hamilton horses as unusual and liberal as their owners and appointed a mare herd leader?

Amy slid smoothly into the saddle and pulled her mare around to face Rika. "The stallion protects the herd against predators or other stallions, but the real boss is the lead mare. She knows where the best food and the best route to safety are. The others trust her to make the right decisions."

Rika watched Amy, who sat loosely in the saddle, tall but relaxed. Instead of gripping the reins, her fingers held them so lightly that it seemed she didn't need them to steer the horse. Her legs held gentle contact with the mare, as if they were conversing through their bodies. Sudden longing gripped Rika. She didn't have that easy understanding with anyone, not even an animal.

"Ready?" Amy asked.

Her hand around the reins felt sweaty, but Rika nodded, not wanting to look scared and incompetent in front of the tough Amy.

The red mare started to walk, but whatever signals Amy gave her had been so smooth that Rika didn't see them.

Cinnamon's muscles tensed beneath her, and he arched his neck, but he didn't follow Ruby. *How on earth do I get him to move?*

Amy turned around in the saddle. "You changed your mind?"

"Um, no, I just... I'm a bit rusty. How do I get him to move?"

Ruby pivoted and came trotting back. Amy shook her head. "How can you not remember something that basic?"

"Well, it's been a while since I rode a horse," Rika said. "But if you're patient with me, I'm sure it'll all come back to me quickly." She'd always been a quick learner, so by the time they reached the herd, she should at least be able to stay in the saddle.

Amy rolled her eyes. "Your memory must be as leaky as a sieve. Move your hand with the reins forward to give Cinnamon's head room to move and squeeze his sides with your calves."

Rika thrust her hand forward and squeezed with her legs.

Cinnamon took a step, and Rika clutched the saddle horn.

"Relax," Amy said. It seemed to be the order of the day. "Loosen your legs. If you keep squeezing, Cin will think you believe he's dumb and didn't understand you the first time you told him to walk."

The big body under Rika swayed from side to side as the gelding moved his hind legs. His head bobbed up and down as if nodding to Amy's words.

Amy turned in the saddle and watched her. "You really are rusty. Don't stiffen up. Move your hips with his movements."

It looked so easy and effortless for Amy. She and Ruby moved as one, in perfect harmony. A ray of sunshine slipped between two piles of gray clouds. With her hat dangling on a rawhide string down her back, Amy's hair gleamed the same coppery red as her mare's coat.

Rika slowly relaxed as the horses carried them away from the ranch. The rhythmic cadence of the horses' steps mingled with the creaking of Amy's saddle whenever she turned around to make sure Rika was still all right. A pine-scented breeze played with Cinnamon's mane.

Finally, Rika's gaze lifted from the horse beneath her. She took in the long lines of mountains rising in the distance to the east and the west. Did all this land belong to the Hamiltons?

Every once in a while, they passed little groups of horses, all of them bearing a four-leaf clover brand on their spotted hips.

Rika pointed. "Is that the sign that says they are yours?"

"The Shamrock brand, yes."

"Why the shamrock? Is your father Irish?" Despite his absence, Amy's father seemed present everywhere on the ranch. The ranch hands talked about him with an admiration and respect that Rika had never held for Mr. Macauley or any other employer.

Amy shook her head. "The four leaves represent the four of us—Papa, Mama, Nattie, and me."

It was hard to imagine growing up with a father like that. "What if your parents had another child after the horses were branded?"

"Hm." Amy's brows pulled together. "Guess they were pretty confident that they wouldn't."

The ground beneath the horses' hooves got muddier. The splashing and gurgling let Rika know they were close to a river, and moments later, the glittering band appeared behind a row of trees.

"The water is really high for this time of the year," Amy said, her brow wrinkled. "We could sure use some of your Dutch windmills now to drain the land."

Ribbons of fog swirled along the river and then lifted to reveal the shape of a large, bluish-gray bird standing along the riverbank. Its yellow beak shot out and stabbed into the water.

"A blue heron." Amy reined in her horse to watch the bird fish.

Rika's horse kept walking. "Amy?" she squeaked. "How do I get him to stop?"

"Dammit. You lied to me. You've never been on a horse, have you?" Amy glared at her. "If you stop moving with him and sit deep in the saddle, he'll stop."

"And if he doesn't?" Rika asked as the gelding carried her past Amy.

"Then you help him understand with the reins. Just pick them up a little. Don't yank them back, or the bit will hurt his mouth."

Rika tugged at her reins, and Cinnamon came to a stop. Relief flowed through her. She unclamped one sweaty hand from around the saddle horn and patted his neck. "Good boy."

At their loud voices, the blue heron lifted its long neck and turned its face toward them. With a croak, it pumped large wings and took flight.

"Oh, no. Did we chase it off?"

"Don't worry," Amy said. "He or she's just checking in with his partner sitting on the eggs. Their young ones will hatch soon." She pointed at the bird, following its flight until it landed on top of a tree.

Rika counted half a dozen large nests clustered together in the branches of tall trees along the river. "Oh, they have a whole community up there. We had nothing like this in Boston."

"I don't know what Nattie finds so fascinating about the East." Amy gave a dismissive shrug. "If there are no birds, no rivers, and since you can't ride, apparently no horses, I wouldn't want to live there."

"Of course we have birds and rivers and horses. It's just..."

"Yes?"

Rika looked away. "Oh, nothing." She didn't want to admit that she'd never had the time to study trees and birds or to learn how to ride. Amy wouldn't understand. Rika tried to picture Amy in Boston, tending looms, but the image of her in the weave room, surrounded by clattering machines, just wouldn't come. Amy belonged out here, riding in her improper pants.

"Come on," Amy said. "If the earth is as saturated in the east pasture as it is here, we've got to get the herd into a more hilly area before they ruin the spring grass. We'll talk about you lying to me later."

A lump formed in Rika's throat, and she gripped the reins more tightly. Maybe if she proved she was a quick learner and helped with the herd, Amy would forgive her.

When Amy directed her horse away from the river, Rika squeezed her legs and grinned when Cinnamon fell into step behind Ruby. *Oh, if Jo could see me. I'm riding a horse, all on my own!*

Cinnamon plodded up a hill, and this time, Rika didn't need to grab the saddle horn to keep her balance.

Amy's horse snorted and pawed the ground once, obviously wanting to run, but Amy easily held her back. They continued in a steady walk.

Thudding sounds came from somewhere in front of them. Cinnamon's ears twitched toward the sounds, and after a few seconds of listening, Rika figured out what they were. *Hoofbeats! Did we find the herd?*

But instead of a herd, a single horse thundered toward them.

Not one of the Hamiltons' Appaloosas, though. The horse's sand-colored coat had no dark dots and no white blotches.

When he saw them, he veered to the right and fled at a gallop, his dark mane trailing in the wind.

"Dammit," Amy said, making Rika blink at her language. "It's a mustang stallion. If I don't catch him, he'll steal our mares." A sharp glance from her green eyes hit Rika. "You stay here and don't move a muscle until I get back. And get off the horse."

Before Rika could answer, Amy urged her mare forward, already reaching for the rope tied to her saddle. Mud spattered as Ruby broke into a run.

Cinnamon moved to follow.

"Whoa!" Rika pulled back on the reins. Sweat broke out all over her body and her muscles tensed as pictures of hanging on to a running, out-of-control horse flashed through her mind. But thankfully, Amy was right about Cinnamon's training. He gave a neigh of protest or maybe a good-bye to his friend but stopped walking.

Rika's heart hammered, measuring the time while they waited.

After a while, Cinnamon lowered his head and ripped at tufts of lush grass.

Is he supposed to do that? Can horses eat around that bit in their mouth? She didn't want him to hurt himself, so she tugged at the reins.

Obediently, Cinnamon brought his head up, and she patted his neck. Should she dismount, as Amy had said? But once she got down, she wouldn't be able to climb into the saddle without Amy's help.

Cinnamon's ears flicked forward.

Hoofbeats thudded toward them.

Amy? Rika gazed at the approaching horse.

Instead of Ruby, the sand-colored mustang raced toward them. If the tiny dot in the distance was Amy, the stallion would escape. *He'll steal the mares.*

The stallion's eyes flashed. His hooves thundered over the ground.

Cinnamon pranced beneath her.

Fear leaped up in Rika, but then she repeated what Amy had told her. "Horses look big and tough, but they scare easily." Maybe if she scared the stallion a little, if she shooed him toward Amy, they could still catch him.

Her legs trembled as she pressed them against Cinnamon's sides and squeezed.

Cinnamon hopped forward.

Rika slid back in the saddle and grabbed the saddle horn.

The stallion veered away from them but didn't stop. He was already too close. His squeal drowned out the thumping of hooves.

Cinnamon exploded under her, rearing in panic.

Her hands lost their desperate grip on the saddle horn, and Rika fell.

Amy rejoiced when fast hoofbeats approached. Had the stallion swerved when he came to the river with its high water level, just as she hoped? She slowed Ruby and shook out a loop. One quick flick of her wrist and the rope would settle around the mustang's neck.

But instead of the stallion, Cinnamon raced toward her, his saddle empty and the reins flapping behind him. He thundered past her. Something had scared him badly.

"Hendrika!" Amy's heart leaped. She urged Ruby from a brisk lope into an all-out gallop. Hoofbeats pounded in her ears, or maybe it was her own heartbeat. They raced toward the hill where they had left Hendrika.

There!

Relief shot through her at the sight of Hendrika walking toward them. Ruby slid to a stop next to her, and Amy flew out of the saddle. She gripped Hendrika's shoulders. Her gaze darted up and down her body. "Are you all right?"

Hendrika nodded, her eyes wide. Mud covered her skirt and bodice, and she had lost her bonnet, but otherwise, she seemed unharmed.

Amy let go of her. "What happened?"

"The stallion was running right toward us, and I thought I could block his way, but he reared and then Cinnamon reared too."

"Block his way?" Amy wanted to grab and shake her. How could she think that Cin would march toward a wild stallion that came charging right at him? "I told you to stay and not move a muscle!"

Hendrika wrapped her arms around herself. "But he was getting away."

"The river would have stopped him. But now he did get away and Cinnamon too, thank you very much."

Mud-spattered arms tightened around Hendrika's upper body. Her shoulders hunched.

"Are you hurt?" Amy asked.

Hendrika shook her head. "Just sore."

Long years of practice helped Amy shed her anger and her fear, and by the time she reached for Ruby's reins, she had calmed down. Papa had taught her at a young age that an angry person had no business getting on a horse. She could deal with her emotions and with Hendrika later.

Part of her wanted to leave Hendrika behind while she rode and searched for Cinnamon, but she didn't want to risk something else happening while Hendrika waited here, alone. She mounted and directed Ruby downhill so that she was below Hendrika. "Come on. We need to get help to catch Cinnamon and the stallion." At the thought of slinking back, having to ask Adam and the other men for help, anger sparked again, but Amy forced it down. She reached out her hand and pulled her left foot out of the stirrup, making room for Hendrika to put her foot there. "Climb up behind me."

Still trembling like a scared filly, Hendrika gripped her hand and let herself be pulled onto the horse behind the saddle. When Ruby began trotting, Hendrika's hands slipped around Amy's hips.

Amy's stomach fluttered. *Oh, no. Stop it. Not with her too!* But despite her admonishment, heat suffused her cheeks, and she was glad Hendrika was behind her, unable to see her face. She clenched her teeth all the way home.

When Amy pulled Ruby to a stop in the ranch yard, Adam and Hank were just packing up their tools next to the repaired corral gate.

Hank hurried over and helped Hendrika down. "What happened?"

"Where's Toby?" Amy asked instead of answering. She didn't dismount, knowing she'd have to head out again in a moment.

"He went to check on the yearlings, like you told him," Hank said.

Damn. Now she had no choice but to ask Adam for help. "I need you two to ride out with your lariats. There's a wild stallion down by the Molalla River, and he's heading toward the east pasture. I want him caught before he can steal any of our mares. And keep an eye out for Cinnamon." Very likely, the gelding had calmed down by now and was already on his way back home, but she still worried. She hoped she would find him when she moved the herd from the east pasture.

"Oh, now you're finally sending men to do a man's work." Adam lifted his lip in a sneer.

The anger Amy had held in check since the stallion had gotten away bubbled to the surface. Adam would never dare talk like this to Papa or to Phin.

Ruby shifted beneath her, feeling Amy's tension, and Amy forced herself to calm down. "I'm sending you because I still need to move the herd and I can't get the herd, search for Cinnamon, and catch the stallion all at once."

"Please, help her," Hendrika said, her eyes still wide. "It's all my fault. Please, I don't want Cinnamon to get hurt or the stallion to steal your mares just because of me."

Her gentle pleas did what Amy's order hadn't accomplished. Adam headed to the paddock to catch his horse. It rankled Amy that Hendrika had resorted to a doe-eyed look while she was trying to get the men to accept orders from a woman. She ignored the accidental brush of Hendrika's shoulder against her leg and turned to Hank. "Don't let that stallion get away."

When Papa got home, she wanted him to find the ranch thriving, not half of their mares gone.

Hank tipped his hat. "We won't."

Amy pulled Ruby around and loped toward the east pasture.

HAMILTON HORSE RANCH
BAKER PRAIRIE, OREGON
APRIL 22, 1868

W HEN RIKA CLOSED THE DOOR behind her, Nattie looked up from a bowl of peas.

"Hendrika!" Nattie hurried over. "What happened?"

Rika glanced down at herself. Her bodice was drenched with water and mud. Grass stains covered her skirt. Every muscle in her body hurt, especially those in her thighs, her back, and her backside. She let Nattie lead her toward the warming fire and plucked a blade of grass from her skirt. "I wanted to help, but I fell off the horse and the stallion got away."

"Amy let you ride a stallion?" Nattie looked ready to murder her sister.

"Oh, no. I was riding Cinnamon, and I tried to stop a wild stallion from escaping. I thought if I could just scare him a little and shoo him toward Amy... I didn't think that Cinnamon would be the one getting scared. He always seemed so calm."

Nattie licked her lips as if she didn't know what to say. "You don't have any experience whatsoever with horses, do you?"

Wonderful. Rika pressed grass-stained fingers to her temples. *Now she thinks I'm not fit to marry a rancher.* She forced herself to hold Nattie's gaze. "Not yet, but I'll learn."

"There's no shame in admitting you're not cut out for life on a ranch," Nattie said.

"I'm a quick learner. If you give me a chance, I'll prove myself."

Nattie sighed, but her gaze softened. "Where is everyone?"

"The ranch hands rode out to capture the stallion, and Amy went to bring in the herd from the east pasture," Rika said.

"Then they'll be gone for a while, and I'd better go muck the stalls." Nattie looked at the armchair, where a leather-bound book lay. "Seems the new book Phin brought me from his last visit to Portland will have to wait. And you'd better go change into something dry, or you'll catch your death."

A damp strand of hair fell into Rika's eyes as she lowered her head. She realized she'd lost her bonnet. "This was my last clean skirt. Do you think your mother would lend me her scrubbing board?"

"I'll give you one of Amy's skirts. She's only a bit taller than you."

Rika hesitated. Better not try Amy's patience again. "Are you sure it's all right? Amy won't be angry if we just take it?"

Nattie narrowed her eyes. "She yelled at you, didn't she?"

"Oh, no. It's fine. I—"

"Don't mind her. I love her to death, but sometimes, my sister is just too hotheaded for her own good. She gets along with horses better than with people." Nattie patted Rika's arm. "But she won't mind if you take one of her skirts. It's not like she's wearing them all that often anyway."

She led the way upstairs and opened the door to Amy's room. "Be careful not to step on anything."

Rika looked around. The room resembled Phineas's cabin. Halters hung on the wall, and the metal parts of a bridle were strewn over the quilt on Amy's bed. A long shelf drew her attention. She stepped closer and touched one of the carved figurines. On top of the shelf, a herd of Appaloosas galloped toward a miniature version of the Hamilton Ranch. A shaggy dog was barking at a coyote to keep him away from the hens lined up around the henhouse. At the end of the shelf, a stagecoach with six prancing horses waited for its travelers to board.

"These are amazing," Rika said. "Look at that detail! Did Amy make them?"

Nattie laughed. "Amy sitting still and staying inside long enough to carve them? No. Papa made them when we were little. Everybody says I get my artistic talents from him."

"So you carve too?"

"No. I'm the one who painted them." Nattie slid a fingertip over the rich brown coat and the white splotches of one miniature horse.

"You paint?" Rika thought of her mother's paint box. She'd traded it for a loaf of bread.

"A little. Want to see?"

When Rika nodded, Nattie handed her one of Amy's skirts and led her to the room next door. While the smell of leather and fresh air dominated Amy's room, Nattie's room smelled of old paper. In a way, everything in Nattie's room revolved around horses too. On a small desk in the corner, a book on horse anatomy sat next to sketches of Appaloosa coat patterns. A watercolor painting above the bed showed the view from the Hamiltons' porch during sunset, with white-crowned Mount Hood in the distance and a few horses grazing in the corral.

"My mother painted too," Rika said before she could think about it.

"She doesn't anymore?"

Rika cursed herself. Had Jo ever mentioned her parents in her letters? *Hopefully not.* "She's dead."

"Oh. I'm sorry." Nattie shuffled her feet. "You should try painting sometime. Maybe you have some talent for it too."

"Maybe." Painting was for rich women and dreamers. It didn't feed hungry mouths and wouldn't prove her worth to the Hamiltons or her future husband.

"Oh, and this," Nattie nodded at one of the charcoal drawings above her bed, "is Phin."

Rika studied the picture, took in the carefully drawn face, the strong jaw, and the boyish grin. "Do you know him well?"

"I suppose."

"So what's he like?"

"He's a good man." Nattie sat on the bed and trailed a finger along the edge of the drawing, then jerked her hand away.

She keeps a picture of him above her bed. Was Nattie her competition when it came to becoming Mrs. Phineas Sharpe? Was that why she wanted her to return to Boston? Rika decided to ask. If Phineas's affections lay elsewhere, it was better if she learned about it now. "The two of you...are you...close?"

Nattie stood and stepped away from the bed. "It's not like you think. Phin knew me when I was just a little girl. He still sees me as a girl, an adopted sister, not a woman."

It wasn't exactly an enthusiastic denial of any feelings she might have for Phineas, but it would have to do. "Then he has been working for your father for a long time?"

"Ten years." Nattie glanced at Phineas's picture, then away. "He's part of the family now, and I wish he wouldn't leave."

"I'm sorry—"

"Oh, no." The corners of Nattie's lips moved up, but the smile didn't light up her eyes. "I understand that he wants to build his own place. He deserves it. And he deserves a wife who can make him happy. If that's you, then so be it." She glanced out the window, where the sun crept toward the horizon. "I'd better get started on cleaning the stalls and feeding the horses."

"Can I help?" Rika asked.

Nattie laughed. "If you had ever mucked stalls, you wouldn't volunteer."

"I don't mind."

"Come on, then."

Rika peeked into the first stall.

A brown horse with a few white dots on its rump looked back at her.

Nattie reached over the stall door and patted the horse's neck. "This beauty is Snowflake. She's mine." When the mare sniffed her hair, she laughed, then opened another stall door and maneuvered a wheelbarrow through it.

That stall, like most of the others, was empty. Cinnamon's stall was empty too, and the sight of it made worry gnaw at Rika.

"Grab a pitchfork," Nattie said.

After watching for a moment, Rika joined her in raking horse apples into a pile and scooping up the soiled straw. Her muscles, still sore from riding for the first time and getting thrown off, protested fiercely. Her hands started burning after the first stall, but she tightened her fists around the pitchfork handle and marched to the second stall.

While they worked, Nattie told her of her family's journey west. Unlike Amy, her sister seemed to like talking to people as much as keeping company with horses. "Shall I tell you the story of how Mama almost ended up an Indian bride?"

"What?" On the stagecoach, Rika had heard a lot of gruesome stories from the other travelers about how Indians abducted white women.

Laughing, Nattie swung another forkful of manure into the wheelbarrow. "When we were little, we used to beg Papa to tell it over and over again. It seems a few Indians were fascinated with Mama's red hair and wanted to trade a war pony for her. Mama says that if the chief had offered a spotted horse, she might be cooking for a bunch of Indian warriors now."

If their father was anything like Amy, Rika could almost believe it. She eyed Nattie. "Surely you're joking?"

"Of course I am." A grin brought out the green color in Nattie's eyes. "If you had ever seen my parents with each other, you wouldn't need to ask. I pray to God that I'll find someone I love as much as they love each other." Shadows of sadness flashed across her eyes, turning them gray. Then her smile returned. "Come on. We need to hurry. Seems Mama can't tear herself away from admiring the Buchanans' new baby, so I need to make supper."

"If you want, I can finish the other stalls for you," Rika said. Since she had endangered Cinnamon and let the mustang escape, the Hamiltons had probably lost what little respect they held for her, so she needed to prove her worth anew. Maybe mucking the stalls for Nattie was a good start.

Nattie hesitated. "I don't want you to think I'm unloading the most unpleasant work onto you."

"It's all right." Compared to working in the cotton mill, mucking stalls was harmless. At least she couldn't lose a finger or get scalped.

Finally, Nattie nodded. "You saw the manure pile outside?" She turned and pointed to her left. "That's where you empty the wheelbarrow. And if it gets to be too much, just come over to the house and keep me company while I prepare supper. Amy or I can finish the stalls after supper."

Rika's determination grew. She would finish this task, no matter what. Her well-meaning action had caused more work for Amy, so the least she could do was take over this simple task for the Hamiltons.

Pain pulsed through her back as she cleaned two more stalls. Her arm muscles strained with every lift of the pitchfork. She bit her lip and pushed the wheelbarrow to the next stall.

It was getting too heavy. A trip to the manure pile was in order. Slowly, she rolled the wheelbarrow down the center aisle. It lurched from side to side, so she tightened her grip and tried to hold it steady.

The wheel bumped over the barn's threshold, and the wheelbarrow pitched sideways. A pile of soiled straw and horse apples splattered onto the ranch yard.

"Oh, no." Groaning, Rika straightened the wheelbarrow and forked the manure back into it. This time, she was careful not to load it up too high. It took her two trips, but she safely emptied her load onto the manure pile.

Now on to the next stall. This one wasn't empty, though. She recognized the gray horse that Amy had bought with Phineas's money. When the horse saw her, it hurried to the other end of the stall.

Rika hesitated. "Guess you'll need to stay in a soiled stall for a little longer." The last thing she needed was another horse escaping because of her. She also stepped past Snowflake's stall.

The last stall was empty, and Rika struggled with the heavy pitchfork as she cleaned it. After what seemed like an eternity, she spread fresh straw on the floor, making a soft layer for the horses.

When she returned from her last trip to the manure pile, she noticed that stalks of straw and bits of manure littered the aisle. Her hands felt as if they were on fire, but she ignored the pain and swept the barn.

Finally, she straightened and pressed her hands to her back. Despite her aching muscles, a smile crept onto her face. *I bet the Hamiltons have never seen such a clean barn.* She walked past the rows of stalls, eager to wash up and sit down for a while. Her stomach grumbled.

A soft neigh stopped her. From a stall she had bypassed earlier, a spotted head appeared over the stall door. With its white coat and the reddish dots, the horse really did look like the circus horses Rika had seen as a child, even if Amy didn't want to hear that, and the red-brown patch around one eye made Rika smile.

Slowly, as Amy had shown her, she lifted her hand and let the horse sniff it.

Warm lips rasped over her hand in search of a hidden snack.

"Are you hungry too?" Hadn't Nattie mentioned that she needed to feed the horses? Rika straightened. This was something else she could do to prove herself useful. She had seen Amy give oats to the horses this morning.

At the end of the aisle stood a barrel with oats. Rika walked over, opened the lid, and scooped oats into a bucket.

The horses started stamping and neighing. Even the shy gray mare peeked over her stall door.

They must be hungry. I'd better give them enough.

She grabbed the two feed buckets and carried them to the horse with the spots and the eye patch. Rika stretched her arm over the stall door as far as it would go but realized she couldn't pour the oats into the manger from outside of the stall. When she pulled back her groaning arm with the bucket, the spotted horse snorted in protest and surged forward to shove her nose into the oats.

With a shriek, Hendrika jumped back.

The bucket clattered to the floor, and the horse lowered its nose and gobbled up the oats.

All right, this works too. Now that the horse was distracted, Rika found the courage to open the stall door and sneak past the horse. She filled the manger with oats from the barrel and then proceeded to the next horse.

Finally, Snowflake and the mare with the eye patch had a manger full of oats. Rika didn't want to risk opening the gray mare's stall door, so she just lowered a bucket to the ground. With a nod of accomplishment, she hurried to the main house to help with supper.

The door slammed shut behind Amy, and she stormed into the kitchen. "Where is she?"

Nattie turned away from the stove and sent her a startled gaze. "You mean Mama? She's still with the—"

"Not Mama." Amy barely kept herself from shouting. "Hendrika."

"I sent her up to your room to—"

Amy didn't stay to hear the rest of the explanation. The thought of Hendrika alone in her room added to her inner turmoil; she didn't like having her space invaded. The stairs creaked as she took them two at a time, then strode down the hall and shoved open the door to her room. "What on God's green earth were you—?" At the sight before her, the angry words died on her lips.

Hendrika stood in front of the washstand, clad in only a pair of long underdrawers. Wide-eyed, she flinched away from Amy and jerked her hands up in front of her face instead of covering her body.

For a moment, Amy stared at the creamy white breasts. Heat rushed through her. She whirled around and closed the door behind her. Her body trembled, and her breath sounded like one of the steam locomotives the newspapers talked about. She counted to thirty, then named all the horses in their herd. As a child, she'd used the trick to calm herself, but now it failed to smooth the rough edges of her emotions. "Oh, Lord," she whispered. "Please don't let me feel like this."

She had finally gotten a grip on her reactions to Hannah, and now Hendrika came along and threw her world into chaos. Up until now, she had been able to convince herself that it was just Hannah who made her feel like this, but one glance at Hendrika's body made her experience the same inappropriate feelings. Hendrika wasn't even particularly beautiful, as Hannah was, but there was something about that strange mix of stern features and vulnerable brown eyes...

Amy shook her head. *Stop thinking about her like that. She almost killed two of our mares, remember?* She tried to cling to her anger.

"What's going on?" Nattie called from the bottom of the stairs.

"Stay out of this." Amy turned around and called through the still closed door, "Are you decent?"

"Yes," Hendrika answered, sounding as shaky as Amy felt.

Focusing on her anger and nothing else, Amy inched open the door and marched into the room. A part of her registered that Hendrika was wearing one of her own dresses, but she shoved the thought away. Just one thing was important for now.

"What were you thinking? You almost killed Pirate and Snowflake!" She wanted to grab Hendrika and shake her but was afraid to touch her.

"What?" Hendrika scuttled back and collided with the washstand. "I-I didn't kill anybody. What are you talking about?"

The confusion in Hendrika's eyes seemed real.

Amy rubbed her forehead. "Did you feed the horses?"

"Y-yes. They were hungry, and I thought I'd help out."

"You 'helped' more than enough. You almost killed two of our best mares by giving them oats."

"But..." Hendrika wrung her hands. "But I saw you give them oats too."

"A scoopful, not a whole manger! Horses can get colic or founder when you give them too many oats. If I hadn't come back in time, they could have died."

Tears welled in Hendrika's eyes. "I didn't know that. I didn't know, really."

Part of Amy wanted to say, "It's all right," and wipe away the tears that trembled on Hendrika's lashes. Another part wanted to tell her to leave the ranch before she did even more damage. Caught between two impulses, she whirled around and clattered down the stairs.

The cool air of the April evening felt good on Amy's flushed cheeks. She wrapped her hands around the porch railing and watched the twilight shapes of the horses move around in the corral.

Just when she felt calm enough to return inside, two riders approached. A single horse trailed behind them.

Hank and Adam are back. She stepped off the veranda and hurried over.

When they pulled their horses to a stop in the ranch yard, Amy realized that the horse behind them was not the mustang stallion.

Cinnamon! Thank God. She slid her hands over the gelding's flanks and legs, making sure he was all right. Still, if they brought back only Cinnamon, that meant the stallion had escaped and might be out there, trying to steal their mares.

"You couldn't find the stallion?" Amy asked. "Did you at least find his tracks?" In the mud, his unshod hoofprints were easy to tell apart from those of their horses.

The two men exchanged a glance. Hank dismounted and walked toward Amy. "We found him."

Adam leaned back in his saddle and bit off a piece of chewing tobacco.

"And you let him get away?" Now they had a problem. She'd have to ride out with every available ranch hand and keep watch over their herd. *Oh, Papa. I think I'm making a mess of things.*

"Who said we let him get away?" Adam shoved back his hat with his thumb and grinned.

Amy's glance darted to the corral, but, of course, the mustang wasn't there. "Then where is he?"

"Amy..." Mud squished as Hank shuffled his feet.

Dread clutched at Amy and squeezed the air from her lungs. "What did you do?" She glared at Adam.

Adam shrugged. "I shot him."

"It was the only way," Hank said.

Blood hammered in Amy's ears. She would never believe that killing a horse was the only way. "I told you to catch him, not kill him!"

"It was a stupid order. You women are too sentimental to run a ranch." Adam spat out a wad of chewing tobacco. The brown sludge splattered over Amy's boots. "What would you have done if we had caught him? Tried to tame him?"

Her fingers tightened into white-knuckled fists. Unfortunately, Adam was right. The mustang might have been too old to tame. Even if she had managed to gentle him, he didn't fit into the Hamiltons' breeding program and none of their neighbors would have been interested in buying him either. "I would have taken him as far away as possible before letting him go."

"He would have been back here before you." Adam spat out more tobacco. "If you understood horses at all, you'd know that a bachelor stallion that sees a chance to get mares for his herd can't be stopped."

That much was true. Amy had seen them break down corral fences and free mares tied to hitching rails. "I would have found another way," she said. "At the moment, I am the one giving the orders on this ranch, and if you can't accept that, you'd better leave."

"You can't fire him," Hank said. "We're short-handed as it is."

"She can't fire me," Adam said, "because I'm giving my notice. I'm not letting a damn girl boss me around anymore. Her old man with his mollycoddlin' horse taming methods is bad enough, so I'm not waiting 'til he gets back. I'm going."

Amy's jaw tightened. Part of her wanted to shout "Good riddance!" after him, but what would Papa say when he returned and found Adam gone? She lifted her chin. "All right. If that's what you want." Maybe it was better to end it now than to have a struggle for power every day until Papa got back. "Come over to the main house and we'll settle what we owe you for this week's work."

Another wad of chewing tobacco landed at Amy's feet. "Keep your damn money. I'll find better work elsewhere. Hank, you coming with me?"

Amy's throat constricted as if a loop were tightening around it. She couldn't afford to lose another man, but she refused to beg. Silently, she waited for Hank's decision.

Hank hesitated. His glance flitted from Amy to the ranch that had been his home for years. His bony shoulders straightened under a deep breath. "I'll stay," he finally said.

The tension fled Amy's body.

"Coward." A brown brew of tobacco landed in front of Hank's feet. Adam untied Cinnamon's lead rope from his saddle horn and picked up the reins of his gelding, no doubt preparing to gallop away and spray them with mud.

"Stop." Amy grabbed his reins. "The gelding isn't yours. He belongs to the ranch. Get off the horse."

Disbelief widened Adam's eyes. His face turned the color of his bright red bandanna. "You want me to slink out of here on foot, like a dog with his tail between his legs?"

Most ranch hands like Adam refused to walk even from the bunkhouse to the main house, and asking him to walk all the way to town was an insult. Amy wouldn't have liked it either. She thought about selling him the gray mare she'd named "Mouse" but then mentally shook her head. *Who knows how he would treat her.*

She held his gaze without flinching. "Get off the horse," she repeated.

Adam twisted. Amy thought he was reaching into his vest pocket for more of his disgusting chewing tobacco. But then he swiveled around with a revolver in his hand.

Amy's stomach lurched as the muzzle swung around.

"I wouldn't do that if I were you," a voice echoed across the ranch yard.

Amy looked up from Adam's revolver.

Her mother sat on the buckboard, aiming a rifle at Adam. "If you point that weapon at my daughter, I'll shoot you," Mama said as calmly as if she were discussing supper. "And you know the women on this ranch can shoot. I never miss my target."

"Shooting a man ain't like shooting a rabbit. You don't have what it takes," Adam said, but he didn't lift his revolver any higher.

"There are two men buried in Fort Boise who thought the same thing," Mama answered.

A shiver ran down Amy's spine. Mama had never sounded so cold or so determined. *Is she bluffing, or did she really shoot two men?* Mama's cool gaze and steady grip on the rifle made Amy think she was telling the truth.

Fire flared in Adam's eyes, but finally he lowered his revolver. He slid out of the saddle, jerked the cinch free, and threw his saddle over his shoulder. "You'll regret this."

The barrel of Mama's rifle followed him as he got his possessions from the bunkhouse and then disappeared into the falling darkness.

HAMILTON HORSE RANCH
BAKER PRAIRIE, OREGON
APRIL 22, 1868

"COME HERE AND SIT DOWN," Nora said before Amy could run out to take care of yet another chore. Amy had been keeping busy, avoiding the other women on the ranch since her confrontation with Adam two hours before.

Amy didn't stop. "Not now, Mama. I have to—"

"You have to sit your behind down on that chair and listen to me." Nora steeled her gaze. "You might run this ranch right now, but I'm still your mother."

Amy swallowed. She crossed the room to Luke's favorite armchair, making Nora smile. Both of her daughters had done that since they were tall enough to climb into Luke's armchair on their own. It seemed to be a place of comfort for them.

The tendons in Amy's hands stood out when she sank into Luke's chair and gripped the armrests.

"What happened?" Nora asked.

"I found a mustang stallion by the river today. I told Hank and Adam to capture him. Instead, Adam shot him!" Amy's eyes sparked with outrage. "When I called him on it, he said he wouldn't let a woman order him around."

Nora had seen it coming and knew Luke expected it too. Sooner or later, they would come across a ranch hand who refused to take orders from a woman—not knowing that he had been receiving orders from a woman all along. "Then maybe it's a good thing that he's gone. Because on this ranch, my word has always counted as much as your father's."

A grim smile formed on Amy's lips. "Yeah. Good riddance to him."

"What happened between you and Hendrika?" Nora had already heard most of it from Nattie and Hank, but now she wanted Amy's version of the story. "Nattie said you shouted at her?"

"Of course I shouted!" Amy leaned forward as if she wanted to jump up and pace. "First, she put Cinnamon in danger, now she almost killed Pirate and Snowflake!"

"She didn't do it on purpose, Amy."

Amy snorted. "She filled their mangers with oats. To the brim!"

"Sounds like something a certain Amy Hamilton once did when she was trying to help her father," Nora said.

The muscles in Amy's jaw bunched. "I was six years old!"

"You almost killed poor Measles." Nora forced herself to continue even when Amy blanched. "Your father had to walk her around all night. What did he do when he came back in? Did he hit you?"

"What?" Amy's eyes widened. They both knew Luke had never raised a hand against their daughters. "No, of course not."

"Did he yell at you?"

Amy shook her head.

"He hugged you and held you while you sobbed your little heart out," Nora said what her proud daughter didn't want to admit. "He didn't yell at you, because he knew you meant to help and didn't know any better."

"Hendrika is a grown woman, not a six-year-old," Amy said.

"She's a grown woman who has left behind her home to live with strangers," Nora said. "You of all people should know how it feels not to fit in. Hendrika just wants to earn our respect."

"Almost killing two of our best mares is not the way to do that," Amy grumbled.

"So she made a mistake." Nora reached over and tapped Amy on the knee to make her look at her. "You made a few mistakes too. You reacted completely on impulse, like you often do."

Amy opened her mouth to defend herself.

"Let me finish," Nora said, raising her hand. "That's not a bad thing. Most of the time, it works out well for you because you have a good heart and good instincts. But sometimes you need to stop and think before you act, especially now that you are running the ranch."

The conversation wasn't new. Luke had told Amy the same thing.

"You showed some bad judgment today and based your decisions on all the wrong reasons."

This time, Amy didn't try to interrupt. She hung her head as if Nora had slapped her.

Nora's stomach clenched, but this needed to be said. Her daughter still had a lot to learn, and Nora was as responsible for teaching her as Luke was. "You decided to take Hendrika with you to prove yourself to Adam—just like Hendrika wanted to prove herself to you. You wanted to show him who's boss, so you put an inexperienced girl from the city on a horse without giving her a proper lesson first. For heaven's sake, Amy, she could have been killed!"

"Hendrika lied to me. She told me she'd been on a horse before."

"Having been on a horse and knowing how to ride are two different things, you know that," Nora said. "You're experienced enough to take one look and know that she was lying. But you didn't want to know, did you? You didn't want to take the time to turn around."

Amy pressed her lips together and remained silent.

"Amy..." Nora took a breath and tried to keep her voice calm. "You train horses every day. I've seen you standing patiently in the rain for hours just to teach Pirate to pick up her feet. Why can't you have the same patience with Hendrika? She didn't grow up around horses. How is she supposed to know if you don't teach her?"

Amy looked away. "Why do I have to be the one to teach her?"

"Because you are the best person for it," Nora said. "I was so proud when you taught Bernice's grandchildren how to ride. Why not teach Hendrika?"

"I have my hands full running the ranch, Mama."

True. Still, Nora sensed that there was more to it than just that. "What is it about her that makes you so uncomfortable? When Bernice's oldest grandson stayed with us to help with the roundup last fall, you had the patience of a saint with him. You taught that boy so much he could hire on as a ranch hand if he wanted to. You always enjoy showing others around the ranch and teaching them to ride. Why is it so different with Hendrika? You aren't jealous because she'll marry Phin, are you?"

Amy snorted. "Mama, please."

When Amy and Phin had become friends, Luke had hoped they would end up getting married. Phin was almost like a son, and he would have run the ranch in the future without trying to keep Amy chained to the kitchen. But despite those hopes, neither Amy nor Phin had ever shown romantic interest in each other.

"Then you shouldn't have a problem with her presence here," Nora said.

"I don't."

The lie was obvious, but Nora let it go for now. "Go and talk to her. And take this with you." She pressed a jar of ointment into Amy's hand.

Amy frowned.

"From what Nattie said, Hendrika probably has a few blisters on her hands. She mucked out the stalls almost by herself." From the kitchen, the delicious smell of stew wafted over. "Oh, and bring her some of the stew. I doubt she feels up to having supper with the whole family."

Amy stood and walked to the door. When she reached it, she turned around. "Did you really shoot two men in Fort Boise?"

Nora wanted to forget about her past, but Luke and she had promised each other early on that there would be no unnecessary lies in their family. The necessary ones were hard enough to handle. "Yes." She held Amy's gaze. "I had no other choice. They wanted to kill your father."

"What? Why?"

Nora smiled despite the seriousness of the topic. *She wants to appear so strong, but, Lord, she's got a soft heart. She can't imagine why anyone would want to kill another person.*

"It all started when Luke stopped Emeline's husband from beating up on her again," Nora answered, remembering those days in the distant past.

Amy's brows drew together. "Tom beat up his wife?"

"No, not Tom. Back then, Emeline was married to her first husband, who was...well, let's just say he was as different from your father as a man can possibly be. When he attacked Luke in revenge, I had to shoot him." The scar on Luke's shoulder reminded her of it every day. "Tom took Emeline on as his housekeeper after his wife died. They only got married years later."

"Then Emeline is not really Clay, Zeke, and Ruth's mother? She's not little Emmy's real grandmother?"

The tone of Amy's voice sent goose bumps across Nora's skin. "Emeline stayed at Zeke's bed for a week when he came down with the flu. She convinced Tom to let Clay go and work for the railroad, and she helped Ruth give birth to her first child—guess that gives her the right to call herself their mother."

"Guess so," Amy said but didn't look convinced.

As a horse breeder, Amy was used to thinking that only blood relationships determined parenthood. Nora prayed that she never found out Luke hadn't fathered them—or worse, wasn't even a man.

Amy took one more step toward the door and then hesitated. "Thank you for helping me with Adam. That situation could have gotten ugly." Despite the relief in her voice, the tension never left her shoulders.

"Come here." Nora crossed the room and pulled her unresisting daughter into a tight embrace. "I'm your mother, and I love you. You never have to say thank you for helping you out. You don't need to run this ranch on your own, all right?"

Amy wasn't a little girl anymore. Their embrace made Nora aware that her daughter was now half an inch taller than she. Still, one thing hadn't changed: she would never allow anyone to harm her daughters. If Adam had aimed his weapon at Amy, she would have shot him.

"All right," Amy whispered and stepped back. "Then will you go and apologize to Hendrika for me?"

Nora smiled. "Sorry. You're on your own with that."

Amy's heart pounded as she rapped at the cabin's door. *Don't be ridiculous.* She'd faced wild horses and angry bulls without being afraid. Hendrika was just a woman. But maybe that was the problem. Women were more dangerous for her than wild horses or bulls.

When Hendrika opened the door, Amy forced away her distracting thoughts. "Um," she said. "Can I come in for a minute?" She'd rather not have to humiliate herself in front of her ranch hands should one of them happen to walk by.

Hendrika backed away from the door. "Of course. This is your family's cabin."

Was that how she came across to Hendrika? Like the stallion of a herd, driving all others from his territory? Her reluctance to welcome this stranger with open arms wasn't about ownership, but she couldn't tell her that. "It's your home now. I wanted to tell you that our men found Cinnamon. He's fine."

"Thank God." Hendrika pressed a hand to her chest.

The last remains of Amy's anger faded. Hendrika cared about Cinnamon. *I'd better not tell her about the stallion right now.* She felt guilty enough about it, so she could imagine how Hendrika would feel. "Here." She held out the still steaming bowl of stew. "You're welcome to eat with us in the main house, of course, but Mama thought you might like to stay in and get some rest."

Wordlessly, Hendrika took the bowl.

The silence between them pressed down on Amy. Her gaze darted around the cabin. "The place looks great. Phin never got it to look so homey."

Hendrika nodded.

"Want me to eat a little?" Amy pointed at the stew and offered a hesitant grin. "To prove that I didn't poison it."

A hint of a smile tugged at the corner of Hendrika's lips, but sorrow still reflected in her eyes. "I know you are angry, and you have every right to be," Hendrika said. "Lying to you about knowing how to ride and feeding horses when I know nothing about them was a dumb idea. It's just that I—"

Amy lifted her hands. "No. I mean, yes, it was pretty dumb and I was angry, but for the most part, I was angry at myself and I took it out on you. I'm sorry." Being honest with Hendrika and with herself was a relief, but at the same time, she felt like a heel for acting like that in the first place.

"Angry at yourself?" Hendrika asked. Her eyes still hadn't lost their cautious expression.

"I shouldn't have taken you with me. My papa never lets a green rider leave the ranch yard." Her stomach churned at the thought of how disappointed Papa would be if he knew. Nothing seemed to be going right since Papa had left.

"Can I ask you something?"

"Sure," Amy said, not feeling sure at all.

"Why did your father leave you in charge of the ranch?"

Every muscle in Amy's body stiffened. Having her competence questioned by Adam was hard enough to swallow, but hearing it from Hendrika made her even more defensive.

"You seem to know a lot about horses, but you're a woman and you're still fairly young. Why didn't your father have Phineas take over if he's your foreman?"

Amy hadn't questioned her father's decision. She'd accepted his explanation that he needed his best man to bring the horses to Fort Boise. *Is Papa testing me?* Did he want to show her that she wasn't up to running the ranch and should get married, as everyone else said?

No. Papa had never told her she couldn't do something because she was a woman. He believed in her. Maybe she needed to learn to believe in herself too.

"Maybe he wanted to show me that running the ranch is about more than handling horses. Or maybe he thought I knew that already." Amy sighed. She had disappointed her parents and herself. While Hendrika had made mistakes, the responsibility had been hers.

Hendrika set down the bowl of stew and ran her thumb over the black burn marks on the table. "Then we both learned something today. I'll never feed your horses again, and you'll keep a better eye on me, just to make sure I don't do anything stupid."

Keeping a closer eye on her... Amy wasn't sure that was such a good idea, but she admired Hendrika's calm maturity. Instead of holding a grudge, Hendrika was moving on. Maybe she should do the same. "You can feed the horses. Just ask me or one of the ranch hands first. And please, never leave a bucket with a handle in a stall. The horses might get a hoof caught in it."

"Horses really are vulnerable creatures, aren't they?" Hendrika said, her brown eyes wide with the realization. "They look so big and powerful, but they can be hurt so easily."

"Yes." The shared knowledge formed an almost tangible connection between them. Amy lowered her gaze. "How are your hands?"

"Oh." Hendrika hid them behind her back. "They're fine."

"Let me see," Amy said, using the voice she normally reserved for coaxing a skittish foal from its mother's side.

Reluctantly, Hendrika presented her hands, palms up.

"Ouch." Amy winced at the sight of half a dozen blisters. She also noticed that Hendrika's hands were not as smooth as she'd expected. Those weren't the hands of a spoiled eastern lady. Calluses had formed in different places than on Amy's own hands, but they told a story of familiarity with hard work. "Mama gave me some ointment for the blisters." She dug into her pants pocket and held out the small jar. "Here."

"Thank you." Hendrika dipped a finger into the ointment and spread some of it onto her palms.

A mental image of taking over the task, running her fingers over Hendrika's palms, flashed through Amy's mind. *Stop. Don't start this again. Keep your distance from her.* She took a quick step back and almost stumbled when Hendrika reached out to hand her the ointment. She searched for something to say to cover her awkwardness. "Um, listen, there's a dance at the schoolhouse Saturday night. Nattie is trying to talk Mama into letting her go. You're welcome to attend too."

"Just Nattie? What about you?" Hendrika asked.

"Ah, I'm not much for dancing."

Hendrika nodded. "Neither am I."

Though she hadn't wanted to attend the dance, Hendrika's rejection stung, maybe because she couldn't read her well enough to know if it was a rejection of dancing or a rejection of her family. *You should be glad about it. The less involved she becomes with us, the better.* "All right. Goodnight, then."

"Goodnight," Hendrika answered.

Seconds later, the cool night air embraced Amy. She sucked in a calming breath, but the tension in her shoulders didn't dissipate. Her life was getting complicated. Somehow, being angry with Hendrika had been easier.

BIG LAUREL HILL, OREGON
APRIL 23, 1868

MUD SQUISHED IN LUKE'S BOOTS with every step. Her feet felt like frozen blocks of ice. Her breath condensed in front of her, mingling with the mist in the air, as she struggled up the steep path.

Behind her, the horses in her string marched through the mud and the sleet. Every horse in her little herd was a hardy, sure-footed Appaloosa, but she worried nonetheless. Boulder-strewn ravines and slippery grades didn't make the best road. It was slow going, and they'd already lost hours climbing Laurel Hill.

She had initially wanted to keep going and make it down the other side before they set up camp but realized that continuing on would be more dangerous than stopping for the night. "Phin," she called over her shoulder. "Let's make camp here."

No one objected. Without losing time or words, they put up their canvas to protect them from the rain and hobbled the horses so they wouldn't wander off and eat the poisonous laurel growing everywhere on Laurel Hill.

Finally, Luke used her saddle as a backrest and wolfed down a bowl of cold beans and bread. Chewing, she looked around. To her left, half-frozen water glittered in ruts that had been carved into the road by thousands of wagons crossing the Cascade Mountains over the last decades.

One of those wagons had been theirs, seventeen years ago.

Seventeen years. Luke shook her head in silent wonder. *Where did the time go?* A lot had happened since then, but at the same time, it felt like yesterday. She still remembered the night on Laurel Hill. Somewhere around here, Nattie had been born.

And it was here that Nora and I first made love. The memory of it warmed her cold body.

"Boss?" Phin's voice cut through her daydreams. "Can you come over here and look at Blaze? I think he's favorin' his right hind leg."

The thought of a horse being injured chased the smile off Luke's face. She set aside her bowl and hurried over.

The bay gelding stood on three legs, resting his right hind leg. That in itself wasn't unusual; horses often stood on three legs when they were dozing. Blaze wasn't relaxed, though. His muscles stood out in sharp relief, and he was wringing his tail in tight circles.

"Hey there," Luke murmured and softly touched his nose. "How are you doing, big guy?" Sliding one hand over his back to let him know she was there, she walked around him and ran her other hand down his leg. "There's some heat in his fetlock. This doesn't feel good."

Kit watched over Luke's shoulder. The gelding was part of his string. "Anything we can do?"

"Let's pack some moss around his leg and soak it with cold water," Luke said. "Other than giving him lots of rest, there's nothing more we can do."

"Lots of rest?" Phin stepped next to her. "You want to stay here and not move on tomorrow?"

Kit gathered some moss and secured it around the gelding's fetlock.

Blaze twitched, and Luke winced in sympathy. "No," she said. "We can't leave the herd here for more than a night. If he's still favoring his leg tomorrow morning, we'll have to think of something else."

"Somethin' else?" Phin looked at her as if he trusted her to come up with a solution.

Luke often wondered whether that trust and easy acceptance of her authority would turn into disgust and rebellion if Phin ever learned who his boss really was. "He won't make it to Fort Boise," she said. "Not at the pace we need to deliver the herd on time. And there's no settlement nearby and no place where we can safely leave him until we get back. If he's not better in the morning, one of us will need to take him back home."

Phin glanced at Kit and Charlie, then back at Luke. "Want me to go?"

Luke was tempted to say yes. At least then she'd know her family and the ranch were well taken care of. But it wouldn't be fair to Amy to hand over responsibility for the ranch and then take it away so soon. If Amy wanted to run the ranch one day, she needed to learn how to deal with all of the problems and obstacles people threw in her way because she was a woman. "No," Luke said. "Let's send Kit." As their youngest ranch hand, he wouldn't give Amy any trouble, and it would also put him out of harm's way should anything go wrong on the way to Fort Boise.

"All right," Phin said.

Guilt sneaked up on Luke. "Listen," she said. "I know you want to go see your betrothed, but if I send you, people will think you're taking charge."

Phin's blue eyes zeroed in on Luke and studied her. His jaw tightened. "You're keepin' me away from the ranch to test Amy? You're settin' her up to fail?"

His loyalty to Amy sent a smile to Luke's lips. "No. I want her to succeed in whatever she chooses to do with her life."

"I think it's pretty clear what she wants to do," Phin said.

Amy wanted to run the ranch one day, and Luke had never tried to talk her out of it. But other twenty-year-old women were already married and starting families. One or two of Amy's schoolmates had gone east, and Bernice and Jacob's oldest daughter had even become a lady doctor. Amy had many options, and Luke didn't want her to have any regrets later on.

"She doesn't know what it means for an unmarried woman to run a ranch. She never had to give orders without me there to back them up, never had to do business in town without the townspeople knowing that she was acting on my behalf."

"You don't think Amy can do it?"

"Given enough time and experience, I'm sure she could, but I want her to be sure this is what she wants to do with her life, despite all of the difficulties. If it's not, I'd rather she find out now, when she's still young and can do other things with her life." Luke couldn't see Amy being happy anywhere but the ranch, but being a good horsewoman didn't necessarily mean she was cut out to be a good rancher. "If all she wants is to work with horses, she might want to marry a rancher willing to accept a wife who's not just going to sit at home."

Phin's eyes twinkled. "I don't think that's what Amy wants. I offered."

Her heart leaped as she glared at him. What was that supposed to mean? "You proposed to Amy? Without asking Nora and me first?"

"Easy, boss." He rubbed his blond stubbles, which didn't hide his blush. "I knew she would say no, but I thought I'd give her the option. I never made any advances toward your daughters. I promised you that when you hired me."

Back then, Phin had been little more than a pimple-faced adolescent. Had it been easy for him to keep his promise over the years?

"You don't love Amy," Luke said. She wanted love for her daughters, the same happiness she shared with Nora.

"I like her," he answered. "That's more than many men can say about their wives. It would have been a business deal between friends."

A business deal. The familiar words made Luke grin. Her business deal with Nora had blossomed into love. Maybe it would happen for Phin and his mail-order bride too, but she couldn't see it happening between him and Amy.

She clapped him on the shoulder in a fatherly way. "You're a good man, Phin."

He smiled. "I had a good role model."

Helpless laughter brought tears to Luke's eyes as she tried to suppress it and started to cough. *If only he knew.*

BAKER PRAIRIE, OREGON
APRIL 24, 1868

"A RE YOU SELLING NEWSPAPERS NOW?" Jacob Garfield chuckled and nodded at the stack of paper in Amy's hands.

Amy smiled back and tried her best to ignore two young women who looked up from bolts of fabric to throw curious glances at her. "No. These are just posters Mama made. We're searching for a new ranch hand. Know anyone who might be interested?"

"Buzz Williams has been looking to get away from working in the livery stable," Jacob said.

An image of Buzz whipping the gray mare with the end of his rope flashed before Amy's eyes. She gritted her teeth. *We might be in desperate need of new help, but we're not that desperate.*

"One of your men give his notice?" Jacob asked while he cut off a few yards of fabric from a bolt.

Amy nodded. "Adam."

Jacob's bushy brows crept toward each other like two gray caterpillars. "You're not in trouble now that your father is gone for so long, are you? Maybe Luke shouldn't have taken Phin with him."

Anger boiled up, but she forced it back. Papa didn't need her to defend his honor, and she had her own battles to fight. "We'll be just fine. Can I hang up one of the posters in your store?"

At his nod, Amy handed a handwritten poster over the counter. "Thank you," she said and hurried from the store. She marched through town and left posters at the barbershop, the saddle maker's shop, and the livery stable. *One more place to go.* When she neared Baker Prairie's saloon, she slowed her steps.

From beyond the swinging doors, the clinking of glasses greeted her.

Just as she was about to enter, a man stepped onto the boardwalk and almost collided with her. Amy recognized

Augustus Snyder, the only other horse breeder in this part of the valley and Papa's biggest rival.

"Gosh darn it, girl!" He squinted at her through whiskey-clouded eyes. "Aren't you Lucas Hamilton's oldest girl?"

Amy squared her shoulders. She was twenty years old, not a girl. "I'm his daughter, yes. Good day, Mr. Snyder." She tried to slip past him and into the saloon.

"Not so fast." Snyder grabbed her shoulder. "What are you doing, girl?"

"I have business to attend to." She struggled to keep still under his grip. Mama's admonition not to act impulsively still rang in her ears.

"In the saloon? That's no proper place for a young woman. What kind of business is this?"

Under the pretense of adjusting her bonnet, she swept his hand off her shoulder. "I want to hire a new rider." She gave him a sugar-sweet grin. "So if any of your men are interested in working for the best horse breeder in the valley..."

Augustus Snyder snorted. "Hey, boys," he called over the swinging doors. "Anyone interested in riding for a woman?"

Only the tinny plunking of the saloon's piano answered him.

"That's what I thought." Mr. Snyder tipped his hat. "Good day, Miss Hamilton."

Gritting her teeth, Amy watched him walk away. She stepped toward the swinging doors.

The barkeeper, who had walked over at Snyder's shouting, blocked her way. "That's not a good idea, Miss Hamilton. People are already talking about the Hamilton women without you coming into the saloon."

Amy bit her tongue. "I'm not here to drink. I only want to ask around and see if there's a wrangler willing to work for us."

"Yes, I heard. I'll pass the word," the barkeeper said.

Amy pressed her lips together. *I'd better not hold my breath.* Trying to get into the saloon was a waste of time. A lot of work waited at home. She whirled around and strode down the boardwalk as fast as her split riding skirt allowed.

Ruby stood waiting where she had left her. Amy unbuckled a saddlebag to shove the rest of the posters into it.

"Want me to go in there and hang them up for you?"

Amy turned.

A wiry man leaned against the saddle maker's shop. His wide-brimmed hat couldn't hide Indian features.

"You wouldn't have any more luck getting in there than I did." While he was wearing a cotton shirt and a pair of mud-spattered chaps over denim pants, his parents clearly hadn't been white settlers, and only that counted for the men in the saloon. Amy gave him a polite nod, trying not to take her anger out on him. "But thanks anyway."

"You're searching for a horse wrangler?" His dark eyes studied her impassively.

She met his gaze and nodded. "Know someone who might be interested?"

The man tapped his own chest.

This is crazy. If she hired him, it would start the townspeople's tongues wagging. Papa didn't like that kind of attention. He preferred to lead a quiet life. "Do you have any experience with horses?"

"Enough to know that this is the best mare I've ever seen." He pointed at Ruby.

A pleased grin settled onto Amy's lips, but then she folded her arms over her chest. "Are you trying to flatter me into hiring you?"

"It's not working, is it?" He sighed. "Thought I'd try. There aren't many men around here who'd hire me."

"So you thought you'd try it with a woman?" She wasn't sure whether she should be annoyed or impressed by his logic.

He shrugged. "Thought it couldn't hurt." With a nod and a tip of his hat, he turned and walked away.

Amy watched him, studying the lithe steps and the soft touch with which he untied his buckskin gelding from the hitching rail. "What's your name?" she called after him. *What are you doing?* Was this one of the impulsive decisions for which Mama had scolded her?

No. They needed a new ranch hand, especially now during foaling season, and Augustus Snyder would make sure none of the local men would sign up with the Hamilton Ranch. *Besides, Papa has a soft spot for outcasts.* Years ago, an old, one-armed man had lived in the bunkhouse and taken care of their tack. And Papa had taken in Phin when he was too young to qualify as a useful ranch hand.

The man turned around. "John Lefevre." At Amy's questioning gaze, he said, "My father was a French merchant with the Hudson Bay Company, and my mother was from the Hawaiian Islands. Not that most people care about that."

Amy understood. Just as most people never looked beyond her gender, they took one look at him and decided that they didn't want to hire an "Injun." Since the Snake Wars had started, everyone who looked even halfway Indian had become the enemy.

"One month," she said. "On a trial basis."

His dark features lit up. "You won't regret it."

Let's hope not.

"Mama, please."

Nora looked up from her bread dough. She smiled inwardly when Nattie put her grayish eyes, so much like Luke's, to good use and gave her a pleading look.

"Everyone is going," Nattie said.

"Not everyone." Nora pressed her fingers into the dough. "I'm staying home. Hendrika said she's not going either." She pointed at the silent woman peeling potatoes at the other end of the kitchen table.

Nattie ignored her comment. "Even the Tolridge twins are going, and they're only fourteen."

Nora pounded the dough while she thought about it. "I don't know, Nattie. With Amy not going either and Phin not there to keep an eye on you..."

"I don't need Phin to keep an eye on me! I'm not a child, Mama." Nattie's pouting lower lip didn't make her appear very mature, and Nora suppressed a smile. "I'm about as old as you were when you met Papa and had Amy."

It hadn't happened in that order, of course, but Nora had become pregnant when she had been Nattie's age. One more reason not to let her go unchaperoned. But she had to admit that Nattie was much more mature than she had been at almost seventeen.

While Nora had gone to bed with the first man who told her he loved her, Nattie had learned early on to interact with men without fawning over them. Growing up around Luke ensured that she never thought women should submit to whatever men wanted.

"All right," she said. "You can go to the dance—if Hendrika is going too." *Two birds with one stone.* Nora grinned. Hendrika had been on the ranch for a week now, but she hadn't met any of the neighbors yet. She kept to herself, and Nora had a feeling that it was some unknown fear, not a lack of interest, that made her stay away from people. Maybe she was shy with strangers and needed a little encouragement.

A potato slipped from Hendrika's grasp and skidded across the floor. She shook her head in protest.

"Oh, thank you, Mama." Nattie danced around the kitchen table and hugged her. "Thank you, Hendrika." She hugged the startled Hendrika too and then rushed up the stairs, no doubt looking for her best dress.

Nora chuckled at the pole-axed expression on Hendrika's face. "She can be a force of nature, can't she? I hope you don't mind going to the dance with her. If you really don't want to go, I can probably talk Amy into it." In fact, she should talk Amy into going, no matter what. Amy needed to be around people who didn't think hoof thrush was a perfectly fine topic of conversation over supper.

"It's all right," Hendrika said while she scrambled to pick up the escaped potato. "I'll go with her. If we don't like it, we can come back early."

Oh, that's what you think. Now that Nattie was going to the dance, she wouldn't be home before it was time to milk the cows. Nora smiled warmly. "Of course, dear."

Amy flicked the reins without any enthusiasm, urging the horses toward the schoolhouse. Next to her, Nattie bounced on the wagon seat. "Sit still, or I'll make you walk through the mud in your good dress," Amy said. She peeked around Nattie at Hendrika, who rode along in silence.

She was wearing one of Amy's dresses—one that Amy had never liked anyway. Not that she liked any of them. At least not when she had to wear them. On Hendrika, she loved the dress. The dark blue fabric contrasted nicely with the soft, pale skin and made her eyes look even darker. When Hendrika lifted her head and looked over, Amy snatched her gaze away. *Stop looking. You thought she was rather plain-looking, remember?*

She tugged on her bonnet, aware of the paler patch of skin above the line where her hat's sweatband normally rested. Her hands curled to hide the scars on her palms and the black rims that remained under her fingernails, even after careful scrubbing.

The sounds of an accordion and at least one fiddle drifted down the hill.

"They've already started." Nattie clapped her hands. "Oh, and look! There are Hannah and Josh." She waved wildly, and the small button at the cuff of her dress got tangled in Amy's bonnet.

Nattie struggled to break free.

"Hey!" When the ribbon beneath Amy's chin tightened, she grunted.

Hendrika reached over and freed the button.

Amy's gaze met hers, and she didn't hear the music anymore. She cleared her throat. "Thank you."

"You're welcome," Hendrika answered.

Old Jack and Little Jack slowed when they reached the other horses tied in front of the schoolhouse, jerking Amy out of her daydreams and her gaze away from Hendrika.

She tightened the reins and wrapped them around the brake. Then she jumped down and rounded the buckboard to help Hendrika down. After two steps, she stopped. *What are you thinking?* Women didn't help other women down from the wagon. *You are not her beau. Let her climb down on her own before people start wagging their tongues about your unnatural behavior.*

Nattie hooked her arm through Hendrika's with a familiarity that Amy didn't dare. "Come on. Let's go in." She looked over her shoulder. "You coming, Amy?"

"Go on. I'll take care of the horses and be right in." She took her time making sure Old Jack and Little Jack were comfortable and could reach the tufts of grass next to the school, then greeted the mare she had trained for Bernice Garfield. "Hey there, Rhubarb. How are you doing?"

"Except for that name you gave her, she's just fine," Bernice said from behind her. "I remember you came up with the funniest names for the horses when you were a child. What was the name of that mare of Luke's? Smallpox?"

"Measles."

Bernice chuckled and looked around. "Your mother isn't with you?"

"No. She says that dancing with other men is just not the same as dancing with Papa."

Bernice's lips twitched. "I can imagine," she mumbled. Then her smile returned. "What about you? Are you up for a night of dancing?" She pointed at the schoolhouse. "Alex Tolridge has been on the lookout for you. I think that young man is a bit enamored with you."

Alex Tolridge? The son of the local doctor couldn't even stay on a horse. *Gosh, he's nothing but a big baby.* Once, when they had gone to school together, she had shown him a snake she had caught and he had run away screaming. "I might not stay long enough to dance with him. It's still foaling season and Mama is alone on the ranch, so I might leave early."

An affectionate half smile darted across Bernice's face, and she shook her head. "Sometimes I think you're too much like Luke."

Luke. Bernice never said "your father," as everyone else did. Amy wondered about it since she had first noticed it. "Too much like Papa? That's not possible." Being like Papa was the biggest compliment in her book. Sometimes she envied the tall, dark-haired Nattie for looking so much more like Papa than she did.

"So Luke's a good father, then?" Bernice asked.

Amy furrowed her brow. "Why do you keep asking me that? You're almost like family. You know Papa. He's the best father and a wonderful man."

A strange expression darted across Bernice's face. She coughed, then patted Amy's arm. "Yeah. I didn't want to imply otherwise. It's just that...I worry about you. You're not like all the other girls."

Heat flashed through Amy, followed by an icy ripple of fear. Had Bernice noticed how much time she used to spend with Hannah? She clenched her fingers around a fold of her skirt. "W-what do you mean?"

"Everyone else has been looking forward to the dance for weeks. Some of them have come from thirty miles away—and you would rather go home and check on your mares."

Her tense fingers let go of the skirt. Bernice didn't suspect how different Amy really was. "Why is that bad?"

"It's not. It's just that—" Bernice trailed off. "Forget what I said. Go on. Don't let an old woman's strange worries keep you from dancing. And come by later for a piece of my apple pie." She shooed Amy into the schoolhouse.

"You might want to loosen Rhubarb's cinch," Amy said over her shoulder.

When the door closed behind her, she was engulfed by music. A fiddler drew his bow across the strings, keeping time with an accordion and a mouth harp. Booted feet pounded the polished wood floor in rhythm to the music, and the first couples danced to the catchy tune of "Turkey in the Straw."

Laughter and loud conversations drifted between little groups. Amy hadn't seen so many people in one place for many months. She didn't understand it, but she often heard the women complain about the loneliness out on the ranches and farms. The Hamiltons' nearest neighbors lived miles away, and sometimes they didn't see them for weeks. That was just fine with her; she felt much more isolated standing in the schoolhouse than riding the range with no one else for miles.

The school's benches and desks had been removed except for a few seats along the walls. Young mothers sat, bouncing toddlers on their knees in time to the music and handing out pieces of pie. Laughing children weaved between the dancers.

Amy wanted to cover her ears and walk out into the silent night, but she'd promised Mama she would keep an eye on Nattie and Hendrika. When she craned her neck, she found Nattie talking to the pastor's son, her cheeks flushed with either excitement or embarrassment.

Amy's gaze skipped over the dancers and the women admiring the pies. Hendrika was nowhere to be seen.

Then she discovered her in a quieter corner, talking to... *Oh, no. Hannah.* She couldn't say why, but a feeling of uneasiness settled in the pit of her stomach. It was too noisy to hear what the two women were talking about, but she noticed the easy way Hannah touched Hendrika's arm while she talked. *She used to do that to me.*

Hendrika didn't return the friendly little touches, but she didn't shy away either. She probably didn't even notice. Amy had always been overly aware of those touches. Annoyed, she directed her thoughts away from that topic and focused on the two young women. With their dark hair and brown eyes, they looked a bit alike.

Is that why I'm having the same reactions to her that I used to have around Hannah? But other than their hair and eye color, Hannah and Hendrika had nothing in common. Unlike Hannah, who laughed often and talked to everyone around her, Hendrika didn't search out conversation and she rarely smiled. *She's not comfortable here, among the townspeople. We have that much in common at least.*

Hannah looked up and saw her. "Amy!" She waved enthusiastically.

Now Amy couldn't avoid joining them. She trudged over.

"I thought you wouldn't come." Smiling, Hannah reached out and hugged her.

Heat raced over Amy's skin, more because she knew Hendrika was watching than because of Hannah's warm greeting. "Yeah, well, Mama talked me into it."

"Hello there, little man," Hendrika said next to them.

Amy followed her gaze downward.

Hannah's two-year-old son was clutching Hendrika's skirt. Now he stared at her with wide eyes. His bottom lip quivered, and he let go of Hendrika's skirt to grasp Hannah's.

"Oh." Hannah laughed. "I think he mistook you for me from behind."

Hendrika's lips parted in a smile, revealing a slight gap between her front teeth.

Amy stared, aware that she had never seen Hendrika smile. That smile transformed her face from ordinary to beautiful.

"I'm not your mama, little one." Hendrika bent down to be at eye level with the boy. "My name is Rika."

Rika. Amy tasted the name on her tongue. How nice that sounded. Why was no one on the ranch allowed to call Hendrika by that name?

Hannah's son grinned at Hendrika, losing his shyness under her friendly smile. He reached out his little arms, and Hendrika picked him up and settled him on her hip without hesitation.

"You are so good with him," Hannah said. She ran her fingers through the boy's dark hair.

"I've had a lot of practice." Hendrika bounced him, making the boy giggle. "I helped raise my half siblings."

With shame, Amy realized she had lived with Hendrika for a week yet didn't know anything about her. She was distracted when Hannah's son glanced at her and, after a moment's hesitation, reached out his arms in her direction. "Um, I don't know how to..."

Hannah laughed. "Just imagine he's a young colt, and you'll be fine."

"You want me to halter-break your son?"

This time, even Hendrika laughed, and it softened her stern features and put a sparkle in her eyes.

Amy couldn't help staring.

Elam Cooper, the saddle maker's son, walked over and held out his hand toward Hendrika. "May I have this dance?"

"Oh, I'm afraid I have my hands full at the moment." Hendrika lifted the boy higher in her embrace, hiding behind him.

Hannah stepped forward. "Give him to me."

Within a moment of reluctantly handing over the child, Hendrika was whisked away to the dance floor.

"Why the frown?" Hannah asked.

"Hm?"

"You're frowning." She touched her finger to Amy's forehead. "Everything all right?"

Amy dragged her gaze away from Hendrika and her dance partner. "I'm fine. I just wonder if it's proper for her to dance with Elam. She is Phin's betrothed after all."

"And you think that will stop them?" Hannah pointed at the bachelors who already eyed Hendrika with interest. "There are four times more men in here than women. They'll ask every woman to dance. Even Mrs. Fuller's rheumatism won't stop them from dragging her to the dance floor."

"Sounds like I won't be able to escape unscathed either." Amy sighed.

"No." Hannah grinned at something behind Amy. "No escape before dawn."

When Amy turned around, a grinning Alex Tolridge held out his hand. "May I have this dance?"

Suppressing a groan, Amy followed him to join the other dancers.

Nattie plopped onto a bench next to Rika. "If I have to dance with one more man, I'll kill him." Her eyes were shining, though, and Rika had no doubt that she was enjoying the attention of her admirers.

"Oh, no, you don't." Rika tucked her swollen feet beneath her skirt. "If they throw you in prison for murder, your flock of disappointed admirers will want to dance with me instead and my feet can't take that."

A girlish giggle erupted from Nattie's lips. "It's nice, though, isn't it?"

Rika gave a vague nod. The crowd of people was a bit much for her, but the rhythm of the music sent her heart pounding with joy, and she had to admit that the attention of Baker Prairie's men was flattering. Here in the West, it didn't matter that she was plain, poor, and without a family. If Phineas refused to marry her, she should have no problem finding another husband. But she found no comfort in the thought.

"At home, everyone treats me like a child," Nattie said. "Phin, Amy, and my parents try to protect me all the time. For once, it's nice to be treated like an adult."

Envy flickered alive in Rika. No one in her family had ever protected her. "Be grateful. A family like yours is rare." She couldn't quite keep the sadness out of her voice.

Nattie searched her face.

"Who's that with your sister?" Rika asked to stop Nattie from inquiring about her own family. "Is that her sweetheart?"

Nattie turned and craned her neck. "Oh, no, that's just Gary Snyder, the son of a local horse breeder. Amy doesn't have a sweetheart, and I bet they're talking horses."

Rika watched Amy gesticulate, her cheeks flushed with the heat in the schoolhouse. So far, she had thought Amy wasn't interested in people, but she seemed to get along well with Gary Snyder. *So is it just me she doesn't like?* Being liked had never mattered to her, but for some reason, what Amy thought about her did matter.

Two young girls settled down on the bench next to them. "Are you the mail-order bride?" one of them asked.

Gracious, it seems I'm already famous in town. She gave a hesitant nod. "Hendrika Bruggeman."

One girl arched an eyebrow. "You came all the way from Germany to marry a man you don't even know?"

"She's Dutch, Ella, not German," Nattie said before Rika could answer.

"Oh, don't start with your geography lesson. No one here is interested in that." Ella didn't even deign to look at Nattie. Her gaze was fixed on Rika, who tried not to squirm. "I wonder what self-respecting woman would sail across the ocean to marry a stranger."

"A desperate one, with little backbone," her friend answered.

The words cut deep. *I am desperate, and I am a liar with little backbone.*

"Leave her alone," Nattie said. "We're just sitting here, minding our own business, and you have no right to insult Hendrika."

But the young women from town didn't retreat. Their gazes hit Rika like hail, and she hunched her shoulders.

"Finally!" Amy used the musicians' break to evade two bachelors looking for a dance partner and walked over to Bernice, who was arranging pastries and pies on a table. "Bernice? Can you do me a favor?"

Bernice turned, her smile full of affection. "Of course. What is it?"

"I want to leave now, but Mama told me to keep an eye on Nattie and Hendrika, so..." Amy directed a pleading glance at Bernice. "Do you think you can...?"

"Sure," Bernice said. "You know I always looked after you and Nattie as if you were my own. I'll have Hannah and Josh escort them home safely."

"Thank you." Amy squeezed Bernice's hand and went to let Nattie and Hendrika know she was leaving.

A small crowd of townspeople formed around Hendrika, but this time, it was Ella Williams and her friends, not young men eager for a dance. Were they talking about dresses, marital prospects, and other things Amy didn't understand?

Then she saw the look on Hendrika's face and Nattie's rigid pose. She glared at the silly gooses. As long as Hendrika was living on the ranch, she was part of the family. No one was allowed to corner her. Amy stormed over just in time to hear Fanny Henderson's cutting words, "A desperate one, with little backbone."

"I see you're talking about your favorite topic of conversation, Fanny," Amy said, shouldering past Ella. "Yourself."

A collective gasp interrupted the sudden silence, and somewhere, a girl giggled.

"I-I certainly wasn't!" Fanny sputtered. "We were just wondering why a respectable woman would go and answer an ad in a newspaper."

Amy often wondered too. *Oh, nice. Now I do have something in common with the stuck-up girls in town.* "And? Did you ask her before rushing to judgment?" *Like I did.* She tried to catch Hendrika's eye for a silent apology, but Hendrika averted her gaze. "Or did Ella convince you to come over and harass her because she has something that Ella wants for herself?"

Ella lifted her head up high and grazed Amy with a look as if she were the runt of the herd, not worthy of her attention. "And what, pray tell, might that be?"

"Phin," Amy answered.

A strangled laugh escaped Ella. "Phineas Sharpe? Oh, please! As if I would be interested in a simple ranch hand who is too dumb to even know how to read or write."

Nattie stepped forward, almost nose to nose with Ella now. Her eyes hurled daggers at Ella. "Phin isn't—" she started, but Amy shot her a look.

"Don't bother denying it, Ella," Amy said. "Phin told me all about your attempts to catch his attention." Phin had never been interested in Ella or any of the girls in town, and Amy had been afraid that he was holding out for her, as he often joked. "Of course, he wouldn't be interested in a girl who's too dumb to even know a good man when she sees one."

Nattie grasped Amy's hand, and together, they stared down Ella and her friends.

With a huff, Ella whirled around and marched away, her entourage following behind her.

"Oh, Amy, that was great!" Nattie squeezed her hand and then let go.

Hendrika finally lifted her gaze from the floor. "Thank you."

"They were just jealous because you two were hoarding all the eligible bachelors," Amy said. "Don't listen to them, all right?"

"I won't." A little color returned to Hendrika's pale cheeks.

"Listen, you two, I'm gonna head out now. Don't worry about Ella and Fanny. I doubt they'll bother you again."

Nattie stared at the old clock on the wall. "You want to go home? Now? It's not even midnight. The dance is gonna last for at least another three hours. Hank and the boys said they'd go home early and take over milking tomorrow morning so that we can stay."

"You can stay if you want, but we still got two mares in foal, and Mama can't keep an eye on them both." And besides, Amy had all the dancing and socializing she could take for one night.

"All right," Nattie said, still not looking pleased.

Hendrika rose from the bench. "Actually, I'll come with you if it's all right for Nattie to stay here alone."

"Oh, come on, Hendrika." Nattie tugged at her sleeve. "Don't you hear? They're striking up 'Beautiful Dreamer,' my favorite waltz. Please stay. Don't let these arrogant witches spoil the dance for you."

But Hendrika shook her head. "It's not about them. I'm just not used to staying up all night."

Frowning, Amy directed her gaze at Nattie. "Will you be all right here on your own? Bernice promised to keep an eye on you, and Josh will take you home, but if you'd rather—"

Nattie straightened like a rooster ruffling up his feathers. "Would you stop treating me like a child? Of course I'll be fine. It's not like I'm among strangers. Hannah and Rebecca are still here, and in a minute, Bernice will serve her famous midnight snack."

"All right. We're going, then." With one last glance back at Nattie, Amy led Hendrika out the door. She turned her palm skyward. For once, the mistlike drizzle had stopped. She helped Hendrika onto the wagon seat, telling herself that it was just because Hendrika's dress was tighter than her own.

A sigh of relief flew from her lips when the horses trotted homeward. She hoped this would be the last dance for a while. The silence of the night and the rhythmic clip-clop of hooves were a balm to her soul. Only the occasional brush of Hendrika's arm against her side threatened her equilibrium.

"I know you wonder too," Hendrika said after a while.

"What?"

Hendrika stared straight ahead. "You probably wonder why I answered Phineas's ad for a mail-order bride."

Curiosity was burning in her, but Amy forced herself to answer, "It's none of my business."

"I didn't make the decision to come west lightly, but my life in Boston..." Her gaze touched Amy and then veered away. "After the war, few eligible men remained in Boston."

The war had never touched Oregon, so Amy had a hard time imagining all the death and destruction. "So many have died?"

"Oh, there were enough who survived, but so many of them are wounded, either on the outside or the inside. Some started drinking and gambling and—" Hendrika interrupted herself. "The war brings out the worst in people. This land," her gaze caressed the land half-hidden by the darkness, "your family...you're untouched by that ugliness."

Are we? What about the ugliness, the unnatural feelings that lurked inside of her? She looked at Hendrika and waited, but nothing more was forthcoming. She had a feeling she was getting just half of the reason why Hendrika had come west to marry Phin.

She didn't have the right to ask, though. Not when she was keeping so many things to herself.

They spent the rest of the way home in silence.

HAMILTON HORSE RANCH
BAKER PRAIRIE, OREGON
APRIL 25, 1868

*T*HE BUCKBOARD CRESTED THE HILL, and Amy slowed the horses. She always loved coming back from town and getting her first glimpse of home. Below them, the main house lay in darkness.

"Your mother probably went to bed already," Hendrika said.

Amy shrugged. "Could be that she bedded down with the mares." Her gaze wandered to the stable. She jerked in alarm.

Flames shot through the barn's roof.

Fire! "Hold on, Hendrika! Hyah!" she shouted and flapped the reins.

The buckboard flew down the hill.

Hendrika hung on to the seat but didn't protest the breakneck speed.

In the stable, horses screamed in panic.

Amy's heart clenched. "Mama!"

There was no answer, and her fear increased as she reached the ranch yard, pulled the horses to a stop, and jumped down. Already, the flames were dancing higher along the beams of the roof. She raced across the yard and flung open the barn door. A black cloud billowed around her, making her cough and bringing tears to her eyes.

"Amy!" Hendrika shouted from behind her. "No!"

A high-pitched squeal from inside the stable made Amy's decision. She rushed into the black smoke.

"Amy," Rika yelled. "Amy, come back!"

Only the crackling of the fire answered her. She was alone in the ranch yard, with no idea of what to do.

Fear clutched at her and made it difficult to breathe. She hesitated, trying to see something through the smoke. "Amy?"

Nothing.

Going after her is crazy. Completely crazy. "Darn it." She lifted her arm to cover her face and stepped into the burning stable.

Heat leaped at her. The back of the stable was a sea of fire. Flames licked at the barn's old wood and shot along the floor, consuming the hay.

"Amy?" she called.

No answer.

Somewhere a horse squealed, but the smoke was so thick that she couldn't see. Coughing, she groped her way down the center aisle.

Another piercing scream sounded, and something big stormed past her.

The horses! Amy is getting the horses out.

To her left, the spotted horse with the eye patch kicked a panicked rhythm against the stall door.

Rika hurried over and opened the latch.

The horse reared and jumped forward. Heavy hooves missed Rika by inches.

Her heart skipped a beat. She leaped out of the way and watched the horse flee down the aisle and out the door. Breathing hard, she gripped the bolt of the next stall door.

Pain seared her fingers. With a scream, she let go of the red-hot piece of metal. Ignoring the pain, she wrapped the hem of her skirt around her hand, shoved back the bolt, and jumped out of the way.

The brown horse pranced past her, its eyes wide with fear.

The next stall held the gray mare. One slap of her wrapped hand against the bolt and the door opened.

But this horse didn't storm past her. It snorted and backed away.

"Come on, Mouse." Rika tried to make her voice as soothing as possible. Smoke filled her lungs, and she coughed.

The horse moved, but away from her and the door that led to safety.

Someone grabbed Rika's shoulder. "Get out of here," Amy shouted.

Rika's knees went weak with relief at seeing her. "Not without you. The gray mare is still in there."

Amy walked past her, her movements calm, as if a raging inferno weren't blazing around them. With a gentle but firm touch, she grasped a bit of mane and led the snorting mare out of the stall.

Rika hurried after them, careful not to get too close to the hooves of the panicked mare.

The smoke thinned, revealing the barn door.

Rika jumped across the threshold and sucked in a lungful of fresh air.

"Close the door!" Amy shouted.

Startled, Rika slammed the door of the burning barn behind her, not sure what difference it would make.

When she turned around, Amy hurled herself at her, and they both went down.

Rika groaned as she hit the ground and lay dazed under Amy's body. "What?" She struggled when Amy began to grope and slap at her. "What are you doing?"

"Your skirt's on fire!" Amy batted at the flames with her bare hands. "Hold still."

Finally, they lay still, coughing and wheezing. Smoke drifted up from Rika's skirt.

"Your hands," Rika whispered and lifted one of them to study the red burn marks.

"It doesn't hurt," Amy answered, her voice equally low. "Not right now."

"Amy?" A strangled call drifted across the ranch yard.

Amy shot up. "Mama?"

Nora staggered around the corner. She was holding her head with both hands and stared at their blazing barn.

"Mama! What happened?" Amy caught her mother as she stumbled.

Without hesitation, Rika slung Nora's other arm around her shoulder, ignoring the pain in her hand.

The fire reflected off Nora's wide eyes. "Something... someone hit me from behind when I went back to the house after checking on the mares. I passed out. Next thing I know, you were shouting across the ranch yard."

"Who would do something like that?"

"Adam," Amy said through gritted teeth. "I fired him, and now he's out for revenge."

Fast hoofbeats pounded the earth. At first, Rika thought the panicked horses were coming back, but then she saw that riders clung to the horses' backs. The ranch hands were returning from the dance.

Amy shouted orders, still holding on to her mother.

"Go," Rika said. "I'll take care of her."

Amy hesitated.

"I was a nurse during the war."

"Go," Nora said to her daughter. "Take care of the horses. I'll be fine with Hendrika."

After one more reassuring nod from Rika, Amy hurried away.

"Damn Indian!" Hank grabbed his lariat from the saddle horn and spurred his gelding toward the bunkhouse.

"Where are you going?" Amy called after him. "We have to catch the horses before they head back into the barn." Sometimes, horses became so frightened that they rushed back into the fire, searching out the treacherous safety of their familiar stalls.

Hank didn't listen. In front of the bunkhouse, he slid out of the saddle and disappeared inside. When he exited, he dragged a sleep-drunk John Lefevre on his lariat behind him.

"What the hell? Hank!" Amy stormed across the yard. "What are you doing? Let him go—now!"

Hatred burned in Hank's eyes, flickering hotter than the fire in the stable. "Let him go? He set fire to the stable!"

"What?" John gasped. The loop tightened around his neck.

"Yeah, you were the only one who didn't go to the dance." Hank jerked on the rope.

"You idiot!" Amy grabbed Hank's shoulder and shook him. "He didn't go to the dance because the stupid people in town think anyone whose ancestors didn't drink tea with the people on the Mayflower doesn't deserve to be part of their community!"

Hank continued to tighten the rope.

"Stop it!" She pulled on his arm. "Do you think John would go back to sleep in the bunkhouse if he had set the barn on fire? Let him go, or you'll be out of a job."

Reluctantly, Hank loosened the rope. "But didn't you smell it?" He gestured toward the barn. "Kerosene."

The biting smell of kerosene had stung her nose as soon as she had entered the burning stable. While barn fires could spread quickly, this one had gotten out of control too fast not to be caused by arson. "I smelled it. But we can't afford to jump to conclusions. We need to think this through. Let him go."

Hank wrenched the rope off John, who lay in the mud, gasping for breath.

When Amy helped him up, a fresh wave of pain shot through her hands. "Come on. We have to catch the horses, especially Dotty and Nugget."

A few more tense moments ticked by as Hank and John stared daggers at each other, but they finally hurried away to follow Amy's orders.

"I'm fine, really," Nora said as they entered the main house.

Rika kicked the door closed behind her with her heel. "Let me be the judge of that." The amount of weight Nora put on her told Rika she wasn't fine at all. Nora was as tall as she was, so they struggled to make it to the side table to light a lamp. "Bedroom?"

The arm around her shoulders tensed for a moment before Nora nodded. "All right."

They struggled up the stairs. Nora opened the last door at the end of the hall.

The scent of bay rum and leather hit Rika's nose before Nora lit another lamp. Mr. Hamilton was as present here as in the rest of the house, and she wondered if Nora had applied bay rum to one of her pillows because she missed her husband. *Did Mama ever do that when Father wasn't there?* She couldn't see that happening.

Nora sank into the pillows with a groan. "Oh, finally the room has stopped spinning."

Rika removed Nora's bonnet and probed along her skull. "Do you feel nauseous?"

"No, I—ouch!" Nora flinched. "I'm just a bit rattled."

Rika parted the red locks that held no trace of gray. Would Amy's hair feel this soft too? The unexpected thought startled her. What was she doing, thinking about that when she was supposed to be taking care of Nora? She forced herself to focus on the task at hand, but her thoughts kept drifting back to Amy. Was she fighting the fire, or was she galloping through the darkness, searching for the horses? Finally, she straightened. "You've got a big bump right here, but the skin isn't broken."

"Good." Nora pushed up on her hands to get out of bed.

"Oh, no." Rika pressed her down again. "You need some rest."

"I'll rest later. The whole ranch is in an uproar and—"

"Just imagine how much bigger the chaos would get if Amy had to worry about the horses, the barn, and you all at the same time. Don't do this to her." If Nora was the kind of woman Rika thought she was, only an appeal to her motherly side would stop her from getting up.

Nora sank against her pillow. "You fight dirty." A smile trembled on her lips. "And speaking of dirty, you should change out of that skirt. Go to Amy's room and take one of hers."

Heat rushed through Rika's soot-stained cheeks. "If I keep going at this pace, Amy will run out of dresses."

The faint lines around Nora's eyes crinkled as she smiled. "Oh, Amy would be grateful if that happened. Then she could finally start wearing her beloved pants to town."

"I'm starting to see the advantages," Rika said. By now, seeing Amy wear a skirt seemed more unnatural than seeing her in pants. "At least pants would have been less likely to catch fire." She directed a regretful glance at the hem of her skirt.

"Catch fire?" Nora jerked upright, then groaned and grabbed her head with both hands. Her face blanched. "You went into the burning barn?"

Rika could hardly believe it herself. "We had to get the horses out."

Nora squeezed her eyes shut as if she wanted to avoid the mental image. When she opened them again, they held warm regard. "You are a courageous young woman, Hendrika Bruggeman. Thank you."

The last name made Rika flinch. She didn't feel courageous at all. *I don't even have the courage to tell these people who I really am.* "I'll sit with you for a while," she said, "and then go change into another skirt."

∽

The drenched sleeves of Amy's dress clung to her. Her arms felt heavy, and her heartbeat pounded in her burned palms. "This one should do it." She handed John the last bucket from the well.

John passed it on to Hank. The bucket went from Hank to Emmett and finally to Toby, who used the water to soak the grass next to the barn. The stable was still smoldering, but at least this way, the fire wouldn't reach any of the other buildings or ruin too much grass.

"Amy," Toby called. "Did you see this?"

Cursing her sodden skirt, Amy walked to where he was pointing. In the light of breaking dawn, she saw fresh footprints leading from the hills to the ruins of their barn. Next to the indentations left by the boots, a brownish substance had been baked by the heat of the fire. Amy bent down and rubbed a bit of it between her burned fingers.

"Chewing tobacco." She hurled it away. Only one man in the area was chewing and spitting wherever he went. "I knew it. It was Adam."

"That goddamned bastard!" Hank slapped his fist into his open palm. Then he ducked his head. "Sorry, Amy."

"Don't be sorry for cursing." Growing up around ranch hands, she had heard worse. "Be sorry for almost lynching John. You owe him an apology." She held his gaze until he looked away. "Now would be a good time for that."

Hank's teeth ground together. He had his pride, and apologizing to someone he considered an Indian in front of his friends and colleagues... Amy knew it was a lot to ask. But if she wanted to have a good crew, they needed to establish mutual trust and respect. And the men needed to learn that her orders were not suggestions they could take or leave.

"I'm waiting, Hank," she said.

"Sorry," Hank mumbled.

Amy kept staring at him. He had almost killed John. A halfhearted sorry wouldn't do.

Hank turned away from Amy and finally looked John in the eye. "I'm sorry," he said more loudly.

Charred grass rustled as Toby shuffled his feet. They were all waiting for John's reaction.

"If you show me the trick with the rope that let you catch me so easily, we'll call it even," John answered.

Hank blinked. "Deal," he said after a moment.

Relief weakened Amy's knees. For once, she had made the right decision by hiring John. Instead of starting a hateful feud, he had given Hank an easy way out. She gave him a nod of appreciation.

"All right." Now she had to focus on keeping the ranch and her family safe. "Toby, you take the wagon and fetch Nattie from the dance. I don't want her to run into Adam. Hank, ride to Oregon City and tell the sheriff what happened. I want him out here, searching for Adam, as soon as possible. Until then, we won't be taking any chances. We'll set up guards around the clock. John, you take the first watch. I'll relieve you after I've checked on Mama."

"Something happened to Mrs. Hamilton?" John asked. "Was she hurt in the fire?"

Amy's teeth ground together. "No. I think Adam hit her over the head."

"But she'll be all right?" John fixed his gaze on her. Mama had earned his respect by treating him like any other ranch hand.

"She'll be fine," Amy said, hoping it to be true. *God help Adam if she isn't!*

Amy rushed up the stairs, eager to get to her room. *Better not let Mama see the burn marks on the skirt. It'll only make her worry.* A quick change of clothes, then she would go see how

Mama was doing—and if she still kept Papa's spare revolver in the trunk at the foot of their bed. While her parents didn't like her carrying a revolver and people in town would find it improper, she wouldn't risk facing Adam unarmed a second time. Mama had saved her last time. Now it was her turn to protect the family.

She swung open the door and almost stumbled over the threshold. *Oh, God. Not again.*

A half-dressed Hendrika stood in front of the washstand, looking more afraid than embarrassed.

Amy whirled around. "Sorry."

"No, no, it's fine. Your mother said I should change in here and take another one of your skirts. Hope that's all right?" Hendrika's voice trembled.

Am I scaring her? Amy remembered the first time she had found Hendrika in her room; she had seemed frightened then, too. Had someone hurt her in the past? The thought made her blood boil. "It's fine," she said, making her voice as gentle as she could. "How is Mama?"

"She's got a headache and a big bump on her head, but she should be fine in a little while," Hendrika answered.

Relief numbed the pain in Amy's hands. "Good." She untied her bonnet, which had seen better days.

"Is it really all right for me to take another one of your skirts?" Hendrika asked.

"Sure." Amy stole a glance to the side. The skirt and bodice Hendrika had laid out on the bed were just useless pieces of cloth to her. "I hate how this one looks anyway."

"Oh."

"On me," Amy hastily added, then blushed. She rubbed her hands over her face, but that only made them burn along with her cheeks. *Why don't you come right out and tell her that you like how she looks, idiot?*

"You can turn around," Hendrika said after a while.

Amy did, hoping that her cheeks had taken on a more natural color by now.

Her skirt was slightly too long on Hendrika, and the bodice fit her more snugly than it did Amy.

Stop ogling her, for land's sake! Guilt and shame singed through her. She forced her gaze to remain fixed on Hendrika's face. "You've got a little soot right there..." She gestured. Part of her wanted to take the soft cloth next to the washstand and run it over Hendrika's skin, but she stayed where she was.

Hendrika glanced into the looking glass and then rubbed the soot stain away. "Did you find the horses? Did we get them all out in time?"

"Yes," Amy said. Her heart trembled at the thought of the horses burning in the stable. "We got them all. They're spooked but all right. But the mares were scared so badly that they'll probably hold off foaling for another week or two."

"They can do that?"

"Sure," Amy said. "Mares are good mothers. They don't want their babies to be born into a dangerous situation."

Something flickered in Hendrika's eyes, and Amy wondered what kind of mother she had. "Listen," she said when the silence between them grew. "I wanted to say thank you. I doubt I could have gotten all the horses out on my own."

"You're welcome." Hendrika smiled. "Do you think Snowflake and Pirate will forgive me now for feeding them too many oats?"

"Oh, they weren't angry with you." *I was.* Both of them heard what she wasn't saying. Amy saw it in Hendrika's face. She could admit to herself now that she had overreacted because she'd been scared.

"Has anyone looked at your hands?" Hendrika asked.

Amy hid them in the folds of her skirt. The thought of Hendrika tenderly cradling her burned hands in her own... She shivered. "I'll have Mama take a look later."

"Your mother needs her rest. Let me see." Hendrika's tone left no room for protests.

Slowly, Amy lifted her hands and turned them palm up.

Her hands glowed a bright pink and were a little swollen. A blister had formed on one finger.

"Ouch." Hendrika sucked in a breath. "That must hurt. Do you have some ointment we could put on it?"

"I'm a quick healer," Amy said.

"Ointment?" Hendrika waved her fingers in a "give me" gesture.

So our quiet guest can be assertive too. Amy handed her the small jar she kept next to her bed for rope burns.

Hendrika unscrewed the jar and paused. "You should wash up and change first."

"That's why I came up here."

"I'll wait." Hendrika turned and faced the door.

Amy stared open-mouthed. *She expects me to undress with her right here, next to me?* Shivers raced up and down her spine.

"Oh, how thoughtless of me." Hendrika turned around. "You probably can't open all the tiny buttons on your dress with your burned fingers. Here, let me help you."

Amy jumped back. "No, no, I'm fine. See?" To prove that she needed no help, she lifted her hands to the buttons and started to open the first one. Her fingers trembled, though, and refused to cooperate. She fumbled with the button.

"I see," Hendrika said. "Why are you being so stubborn?"

Their gazes met.

Amy dropped her hands. Her refusal of aid was arousing more suspicions than any reaction she might have if she let Hendrika help her undress. "All right," she murmured through a tight jaw.

Hendrika stepped closer until Amy thought she could feel her body heat. A slight touch to Amy's neck and seconds later, her removable collar fluttered to the bed.

Amy's limbs wanted to follow and lie down too. Her knees felt weak. She stared at Hendrika's fingers as they wandered down the button line and opened each of the eight tiny buttons.

One, she counted, just to distract herself.

The gentle fingers barely touched her.

Two. Three. Four.

On their way to the fifth button, Hendrika's fingers brushed over Amy's bosom. Her breath caught. Her skin felt as if she were once again standing in the middle of the burning barn. She lost her ability to count.

Finally, the last button opened, and Amy pressed her forearm against her chest to keep her dress from flapping open.

"Do you need help with the corset too?" Hendrika asked.

"No!" Amy took two hasty steps back. "I mean...no, thank you."

Hendrika turned her back. "Then I'll wait."

Afraid that Hendrika would want to help her again if she hesitated, Amy wrestled out of her corset and skirt and rolled down her stockings. Her skin sparked with life when she ran the wet cloth over it. She couldn't feel the painful pounding in her hands anymore, maybe because her heart was hammering too loudly.

In record time, she pulled a pair of clean pants, a shirt, and an undershirt out of her trunk and put them on. Again the buttons resisted her trembling fingers, and she bit back a curse. She couldn't stand having Hendrika so close to her, not with her emotions already so close to the surface. Finally, she managed to slip the buttons through their holes. "All done." *Let's get this over with.* She needed to get Hendrika out of her room so she could stick her head into the washbowl and cool off.

Hendrika's gaze wandered up and down her body, starting the fire along Amy's skin again. "You missed one," she said and pointed.

Amy stared at the still open button.

Before she could lift her hands to close it, Hendrika did it for her. "There."

The breath whooshed out of Amy's lungs, and when Hendrika turned around to reach for the ointment, she sucked in two quick breaths so she wouldn't topple over. *It's just buttons. Mama helped you with them a thousand times when you were little.* She wasn't a little girl anymore, though, and Hendrika was definitely not her mother.

Hendrika cradled one of Amy's hands in hers.

"I..." Amy cleared her throat. "I could do that myself, you know?"

But Hendrika dipped her finger into the ointment. Gently, she spread a thin layer of ointment over Amy's palm.

Oh, Lord. Amy's stomach prickled in a strange way. She wasn't sure if this was heaven or hell. *It's surely the straightest way to hell if you keep having these thoughts.* Still, she couldn't look away from the fingers stroking over her palm. "Oh!" The sight of a red mark on Hendrika's fingers pulled her from her stupor. "You got burned too."

Hendrika turned her hand to look at it. "It's not as bad as your hands. It happened when I touched the bolt to open one of the stalls."

A strong wave of guilt drowned out Amy's other feelings. She dipped her finger into the jar and spread a generous layer of ointment over Hendrika's palm. Her fingers tingled, but she told herself it was just the ointment.

Finally, Amy closed the jar. Their gazes met.

"I'll go check on your mother, and then I'll try to get some sleep," Hendrika said. "It's been a long day." As she walked to the door, her movements were slow and filled with the leaden exhaustion that Amy felt too.

The thought of Hendrika alone in the cabin made Amy blanch. John was standing guard, but with Adam still out there, she didn't want to take the risk of something happening to Hendrika. "Stay here," Amy blurted. Heat crept up her neck. "Adam might still be out for revenge. I don't want you to stay in the cabin alone. Use my room."

Hendrika hesitated. "All right."

"I'll go see if Mama needs anything," Amy said and escaped from the room.

INDIAN CREEK, OREGON
APRIL 27, 1868

"*B*oss?"

A hand on her shoulder jerked Luke awake. She lay blinking into the darkness, expecting to feel the soft touch of Nora's lips against hers, the way she'd been awakened many times. Then the hard ground under her blanket reminded her where she was.

"Boss?" A wide-eyed Charlie looked down at her. "Two of the horses are gone."

The blanket went flying when she jumped up. "Gone? How can that happen? You were keeping watch, weren't you?"

"Yes, I was. But it's real dark tonight, and they were wandering around a lot, trying to find some grass."

"You had them hobbled and in a rope corral, right?" That was what they had done every night since leaving the ranch.

Charlie nodded vigorously.

Luke's jaw tightened. She strode across the small camp and forced herself to slow down once she reached the herd. She touched a muscular neck here and a spotted hip there, making sure they were all right and identifying them in the dim light of the campfire to see who was missing. "Midnight and Raindrop."

Two of their best geldings. Luke had trained Midnight for the last three years, and she knew the commander of Fort Boise had his eye on him. She would have kept the horse for the ranch, but with his all-black coat, bare of any spots or white blankets, he didn't fit into their breeding program.

She scanned the area, trying to pierce the darkness. When her foot stepped on something soft, she picked it up and carried it to the fire to see what it was. *The piece of rope we used to hobble them.* The hobble had been loose enough for them to wander some and eat grass, but tight enough so they couldn't lope off on their own.

"Did they manage to get rid of the hobble?" Charlie asked, looking over her shoulder.

"Only if our horses somehow learned to handle knives." Her jaw bunched as she stared at the cut edges of the hobble. "Someone stole our horses, and from the ragged edges, I'm betting the Shoshoni helped themselves to some good horseflesh." Ragged edges meant a stone knife, not one of steel. If she remembered correctly, the creek where they set up camp was in Shoshoni territory. Their reputation as horse thieves preceded the Shoshoni. For their young warriors, stealing horses was a sport.

Not for Luke, though. The horses were the result of several years of hard, patient work. *No one's going to take them from me.* "Wake up Phin. We're going after them."

Heat pounded through Luke's veins. Her feet slipped on a patch of snow, and Phin caught her elbow to steady her. Behind them, their horses scrambled down the hill.

They could have made better time riding, but in almost total darkness, it was too dangerous. Luke didn't want to risk losing another horse, so she and Phin set out alone, with their own horses trailing behind them, while Charlie stayed with the rest of the herd.

They ran side by side, following the trail of hoofprints without talking. They splashed through a small creek and jogged up another hill. Dancer whinnied.

"Hush, boy," Luke murmured.

Behind Phin, Lancelot whinnied a greeting too. "There!" Phin pointed.

Directly below them, a young warrior led Raindrop while an older man with feathers woven into his silver hair sat on Midnight's bare back. Two young women ducked fearfully behind the horses.

Luke lifted her rifle and aimed. Out of the corner of her eye, she saw Phin do the same.

The old warrior pointed his own rifle at them.

Was the old, muzzle-loading musket still functional? Luke didn't want to find out the hard way. "These horses are mine," she shouted, mixing English and the Shoshoni's language. She pointed at Midnight and Raindrop.

The younger warrior shouted an answer and lifted his bow. An arrow was already notched, ready to fly at them.

"He said they found the horses wandering without an owner," Luke translated, not looking away from the Shoshoni.

Phin ground his teeth. "Liars."

"They are offering to give us Raindrop but refuse to hand over Midnight."

At least they had good horse sense. Raindrop was a good horse, but Midnight was worth twice as much.

Luke shook her head. "I get them both, and you get to stay alive," she shouted down the hill.

The warrior's hands tightened around the bow.

Sweat trickled down Luke's back. Her index finger crept around the trigger. "Last chance," she called, again mostly in the Shoshoni's language. "Give me the horses, and I'll give you our saddlebags with our provisions."

The young warrior shook his head. His left arm with the bow inched higher. Now he was aiming directly at Luke.

Midnight pranced forward, snorting beneath the unfamiliar rider. The silver-haired Indian urged him to the younger man and laid a hand on his bow arm. He talked in rapid syllables.

At Phin's glance, Luke shook her head, indicating that she didn't understand either.

The younger man swung up on Raindrop's back. Snow and mud flung to all sides as the gelding loped up the hill.

Luke sighted down the barrel. Her finger tightened around the cold metal of the trigger.

Next to her, Phin cocked the hammer of his rifle.

"Wait," Luke said. "Not yet."

The warrior pulled Raindrop to a halt in front of them. He thrust out his hand.

Phin flinched. "What does he want?"

"I offered them our saddlebags in exchange for the horses," Luke said.

"Our saddlebags?" Phin kept aiming at the warrior.

"The saddlebags with our provisions," Luke said. "Don't you see how thin they are?" They'd probably been hiding out in the mountains all winter, keeping out of the way of the soldiers from Fort Boise so they wouldn't be relocated to a reservation. "Give them your saddlebags." Luke threw hers at the warrior, who had to take one hand off his bow when he caught it.

Phin stepped next to his gelding and untied the saddlebags. At the last moment, he stopped. "Wait." He stuck his hand into the saddlebags.

The warrior squinted, ready to let the arrow fly at Phin should his hand come up with a weapon.

The skin on the back of Luke's neck itched. "Phin," she whispered out of the corner of her mouth.

Phin pulled out his hand. Instead of a revolver, he held a tintype.

Before Phin slipped it into his vest pocket, Luke caught a glimpse of her family. A traveling photographer had taken the picture last summer. She hadn't known Phin kept a copy in his saddlebags. Over the sight of her rifle, Luke grinned at him. "I always knew you had a crush on my wife."

"I don't," Phin said, red-faced. "There are hostile Indians around, so can we discuss this later?"

"Oh, don't worry, he won't tell Nora." Luke nodded at the warrior.

Phin gritted his teeth and handed over the saddlebags.

The young warrior slid off Raindrop's back. Cautiously eyeing Phin and Luke, he put the saddlebags over his shoulder and walked away.

Luke pointed her rifle at the older Indian, who was still on top of Midnight. Would he keep his promise and let the gelding go, or would he try to ride off and hide in the mountains, where they might never find him?

A few tense heartbeats later, the old man dropped to the ground. Midnight, freed of his rider, loped over and joined the other horses.

Luke knotted a rope halter around Midnight's head while Phin did the same with Raindrop. "Come on," Luke said. "Let's go before they change their minds and decide the horses are worth the risk of a fight with two armed white men."

Eager to get some distance between them and the warriors, Luke marched into the darkness. When they were a mile away,

Luke slowed and looked at Phin. "About the tintype. Why do you carry that around?"

Phin sighed. "I swear I'm not in love with your wife, boss." He fished the tintype out of his vest pocket and rubbed his thumb across one of the faces.

Nattie? Luke narrowed her eyes and then told herself she was imagining things.

"It's just that you're the only family I have," Phin said.

"I hope you know we consider you part of the family too."

"Yeah."

Luke reached over and gave Phin a pat to the shoulder. "Thanks for not letting the Shoshoni have the tintype."

"Uh." He put the picture back into his pocket. "You're welcome, boss."

HAMILTON HORSE RANCH
BAKER PRAIRIE, OREGON
APRIL 28, 1868

"*M*AMA?" AMY KNOCKED ON THE bedroom door and waited, as she'd been taught from early childhood.

"Come on in," Mama called.

Amy opened the door. "How's the head?"

"I'm fine. Just a slight headache."

Hesitating, Amy stepped closer. "I know we told you to go lie down and rest..."

Mama sat up in bed and patted the empty space next to her.

Half-forgotten childhood memories resurfaced. With a grin, Amy sat on Papa's side of the bed, letting her booted feet dangle over the edge. The pillows still smelled of Papa and the bay rum Mama applied to his cheeks after shaving. Except for the smell of horses, it was the most soothing scent Amy knew.

"Any news about Adam?" Mama asked. "Did the sheriff catch him?"

"No. The sheriff said that he had his revenge, so he's probably halfway to Canada by now. He would be a fool to stick around until Papa comes home." Amy had told the ranch hands to keep an eye out, just in case, but she wasn't particularly worried about Adam anymore. Even Hendrika had gone back to sleeping in the cabin.

"What is it, then, sweetheart?" Mama picked a blade of grass off Amy's chaps.

Self-doubts wrestled with pride and won. "I know I'm supposed to run the ranch right now, but I need some advice," Amy said.

Mama turned to face her. "Running the ranch doesn't mean you can't ask your old mother for advice."

Amy snorted. "You're not old enough to be put out to pasture, Mama."

A gentle laugh tickled her ears. As a child, she had often lain awake at night and listened to Mama's laughter drift upstairs, mingling with Papa's lower chuckles.

"You think your father makes all the decisions alone? That he knows everything? Never doubts himself?" Mama shook her head. "He's asked me for advice a few thousand times. The first few years here in Oregon, your father and I worked side by side every day. I learned how to split corral rails and drive a hay wagon. Your father was never too proud to ask for my help or my opinion. We make the big decisions together. That's what marriage and family is all about—helping each other."

Amy straightened her shoulders. "We need a new barn. Dotty and Nugget still haven't had their foals, and I'd like to keep Zebra confined to a stall until her leg heals."

Mama nodded for her to go on.

"So we've got two options, both of them bad." Amy worried the edge of the covers between her fingers. "If we split the logs to rebuild the barn ourselves, it'll take us forever. And we can't keep up with the rest of the work at the ranch, so we might lose the first cut of hay."

They couldn't afford that. The hay fed their own animals later in the year, and they also made a nice income by selling hay to the farmers higher up in the Cascades.

"I don't think your father would want us to do that," Mama said.

"No." But Papa wouldn't be too fond of option number two either. "We could order the planks and board for the new barn from the sawmill, but we don't have that kind of money lying around. In fall, once we've auctioned off a few of the foals, we could afford it, but not now."

"Socks already had her foal," Mama said. "We could sell him."

An image of the colt's large white blanket flashed through Amy's mind. "I don't know, Mama. Papa might want to keep him. He's got really nice colors, and in a few years, we're gonna need a new stallion. An untrained foal wouldn't cover the costs for the new barn anyway."

"What about the yearlings?" Mama asked.

Amy had thought about that too. "They're not ready to be sold either. They'll bring more money with a bit more training." Only one option remained. "We could sell one or two of the older horses."

Mama's eyes darkened. As much as she insisted she was not a horse person, she loved each and every one of their horses. "Which ones?"

It had to be a gelding. The mares were too valuable for the ranch's future. "Perceval, maybe, and..." Amy swallowed. "Cinnamon. He's a good horse, but he's getting old."

Gently, Mama squeezed her hand. "Oh, Amy."

Amy forced back tears. Cinnamon had been the first foal she had helped birth and the first horse she had trained. *Don't be stupid. Ranching is a business. Papa told you that from the start. It's a bad idea to get too attached to a horse you might end up selling.*

"When Measles died, your father cried all night even though that mare had a good, long life," Mama said into the silence.

"Really?"

"I know he pretends to be this tough rancher, but it's his soft heart that makes him so good with the animals—and that makes him the person I love. It's all right to be sad, Amy."

A shaky breath escaped Amy's lips. "I am sad. But it needs to be done. We need that new barn, and we can't wait until next year." She kissed her mother's cheek and climbed off the bed. "Get some more rest, all right? I'll handle things."

Rika folded her arms across the corral rail and enjoyed the warming rays of the rising sun.

The sight of the barn's black remains made her sad, so she avoided looking in that direction. Instead, she kept her gaze on the horses wandering around in the corral. Watching them soothed her in a way she had never imagined. While all the names and horses had been a blur to her in the beginning, she was now learning to tell them apart.

The horse rolling around in the mud, adding even more splotches to the spots in her coat, was Nora's mare, Pirate. Snowflake, the brown mare who rubbed her lower lip over another horse's back, belonged to Nattie. Ruby, Amy's fire-red mare, swished her tail at Cinnamon, causing him to trot away from the patch of grass she wanted for herself.

"Hey there," Rika murmured when Cinnamon stopped in front of her and stuck his head over the corral rail. After a moment's hesitation, she slid her palm along his neck and scratched the spot Amy had shown her. He wiggled his lower lip and moved his head as if he wanted to return the gentle rubbing.

Rika combed her fingers through his mane. A few cinnamon-colored strands had been singed by the fire, and she shuddered to think how close he had come to being hurt or worse.

Cinnamon's soft nicker made her look up.

Amy stood next to her, looking at her with a strange expression.

"Oh. I didn't hear you."

Still not saying anything, Amy leaned her arms on the top rail. Together, they watched the foals frolic around the corral under the watchful eyes of their mothers. "I'll probably have to sell him," Amy said.

Rika startled. "Who?"

Amy rubbed Cinnamon's smooth head. "Cin."

Dread gripped Rika. She liked the gentle gelding. "This isn't because he threw me off, is it? That wasn't his fault."

"It's not that. We need the money to build a new barn."

Their gazes slid to the charred beams.

Rika glanced back at Amy, who refused to look at her. Moisture shone in her eyes. *It's breaking her heart, and she doesn't want me to see.* Her own heart ached too. "I wish I had some money."

"I already stole money from you once," Amy said.

"You didn't steal it. You used it to save Mouse." Amy might be a little brusque sometimes, but her love for the horses was pure and unselfish like no love Rika had ever known.

They stood in silence.

The rattling of wagons and shouts of "whoa" made them turn around.

Two wagons loaded with boards, planks, and joists rolled into the ranch yard. Riders on horses crested the hill, and women carrying big baskets walked toward them.

"What's this?" Rika asked.

Amy frowned. "I have no earthly idea."

Hannah, the friendly woman Rika had met at the dance, was the first to reach them. She handed Amy her basket. "Here," she said. "Your favorite pie."

"You're bringing me pie?"

"We're bringing you a new barn." Hannah winked.

Rika's gaze flew to the loaded wagons. *She can't really mean...?*

"We already had the wood ready for our new barn, but when we heard what happened, we decided that the old one will do for another year. The wood is yours if you want it. You can pay us back later in the year. No hurry."

Rika couldn't believe it. All the neighbors had come over, leaving behind their own work and bringing wood and baskets of food—all without asking anything in return. *Maybe,* she dared to hope as she watched the men unload the wagons, *maybe this is a good place to make a home.*

"Isn't that dangerous?" Frowning, Rika shaded her eyes with her hand and stared at Amy, who was hammering away high up in the rafters.

"Don't worry," Nora said. "Amy has been doing this for years."

"Why would the men let her do this kind of work?"

Nora handed her a glass of lemonade. "Because she's the lightest and most agile. And because they remember the temper tantrum she threw when she was ten and they told her she had to stay at the food tables instead of helping her papa."

Next to them, two older men measured and sawed off planks while three of the ranch hands nailed boards to the sides of the frame that had been heaved up with ropes and long poles earlier. Other neighbors cleared away the charred wood of the old barn, which was now behind the new structure. Children ran around, shouting and making a game out of gathering waste wood and piling it up out of the way.

"There are no people like this in Boston," Rika muttered to herself.

Nora filled more glasses of lemonade. "In Hannah and Josh's first year of farming, there was a big flood in the valley. Josh's fields were swamped with debris, trees, and stones. Luke packed up our family and the ranch hands, and we helped Josh clear his fields so that they could plant in time."

"Ah." Rika nodded to herself. Now she understood why they were giving up something as valuable as a new barn. "They have a debt to pay."

"No. They're not doing this because they have to," Nora said. "They're doing it because they want to."

Nattie leaned over the pie she was arranging onto plates and laughed. "It's a strange concept called friendship, Hendrika." She shook her head. "Haven't you ever helped someone just because you wanted to?"

"Oh, yes, of course." Her nose wrinkled when she remembered the smell of blood, sweat, and rotting flesh when she had bandaged the horrible wounds of soldiers. She had cared for others many times, but with the exception of Jo, no one had ever helped her. Not without an ulterior motive.

Nora took a tray of glasses and a pitcher of lemonade and carried it to where Amy and the men were working.

"Are people in the East so different from us?" Nattie asked. "Are they so uncaring that you'd distrust the friendly gesture of a neighbor? Then maybe the East is a place where I don't want to live after all."

"You want to leave and live in the East? But aren't you happy here?"

Sometimes, the ranch seemed unreal to Rika, like an idyllic place out of a fairytale. Sure, the days were filled with hard work too and people like Adam proved that not everyone was as friendly as the Hamiltons, yet still things felt different than in Boston. She could breathe here, and it wasn't just because she didn't need to work in the dust-filled weave room anymore.

"Of course I'm happy," Nattie said. "This is my home and my family."

The certainty in her voice made Rika wonder if she would ever have this kind of happiness and belonging for herself. "Then why would you want to leave?" she asked when only the noise of hammers and saws filled the space between them.

"I love it here, but maybe I could do more elsewhere."

"Do more?"

Nattie pointed at the new barn. "Look at Amy."

Rika did. All day, her gaze had been drawn to the young woman, who now put away her hammer and climbed down from the roof.

"She does things around the ranch that I could never do," Nattie said, admiration mingling with envy in her tone.

"Well, I don't see your mother up there on the roof either, and I'm sure your father would say she contributes a lot to the daily life on the ranch. And so do you. You're mucking stalls, taking care of the horses, milking cows..."

A grateful smile softened Nattie's expression. "Yes, but anyone can do that. It's not that I'm contributing something special. Amy will take over the ranch one day. She's the right person to do it. I love horses, and Papa and Phin say I'm a good rider, but I could never run a ranch."

"Neither could I, yet I still hope to be a good wife for Phineas and prove myself useful. Maybe you'll marry in a year or two, fall in love, and be a wonderful wife just like your mother."

The words were meant to cheer Nattie up, but instead, her lips tightened and she shook her head. "I don't think so."

"What else could you do?" Rika liked the friendly girl and didn't want her to end up working in a cotton mill back East.

"I'm thinking about maybe going to school in the East for a while. I want to find something that I could contribute to life in Baker Prairie. A neighbor studied in Boston to become a lady doctor. Maybe it would be the right thing for me too." Nattie directed an expectant gaze at her. "You were a nurse. Isn't it a good feeling to help others? Why didn't you mention it in your letters?"

Rika looked away, her gaze once more finding Amy, who shook shavings from her hair. Whenever Rika started to feel that maybe there was a place for her on the ranch, something reminded her that it was rightfully Jo's place, not hers. "I don't like to talk about the war," she said. It wasn't a complete lie. "Too many painful memories. When I started working in the cotton mill, I tried to forget about that part of my life."

"Oh." Nattie squeezed her arm. "I'm sorry."

"Yes, helping people felt good, but it can consume you if you're not careful," Rika said. "You spend so much time helping others that there's no time to ask yourself what you really want." It was the story of her life, not just her three years as a Union nurse. Only now, while she waited for Phineas's return, was Rika forced to think about what she wanted in life. Was it really to marry Phineas, a man she would have to deceive for the rest of her life? What else was there for her?

Nattie nodded thoughtfully. "I might not have to worry about it anyway. Maybe my parents won't let me go. They act as if the East is an evil place."

Rika shrugged, not wanting to get in the middle of a family affair. "Well, your mother would know."

A frown carved a furrow into Nattie's smooth brow. "Why do you say that?"

"Isn't she from Boston? I thought I heard a familiar accent when she talks sometimes."

Nattie's frown deepened. "I don't know," she said, as if she had just realized it. "Mama?" She waved to her mother, who returned with a tray of empty glasses. "You're not from Boston, are you?"

The tray rattled as Nora abruptly set it down. "Why are you asking?"

Uh-oh. Answering a question with a question. Rika had mastered that technique early on, especially when her father was drunk and she couldn't do anything right, no matter what her answer was. *Seems I'm not the only one with a secret around here.*

"Is it true?" Nattie asked.

"I could kill for a glass of lemonade." Amy's cheerful voice interrupted. Sweat turned the soft locks sticking to her forehead into dark copper. She looked from Nattie to her mother and then to Rika. "Speaking of killing... Why do you all look as if someone died? What's going on?"

Silence answered her.

Just to have something to do, Rika handed her a glass of lemonade.

"Mama?" Nattie asked. Her gaze remained fixed on Nora.

"Yes." Nora looked from one daughter to the other. "I did grow up in Boston."

"Right where Hendrika did?" Nattie asked.

Rika doubted that. If she wasn't mistaken, the hint of accent in Nora's voice indicated a wealthy family, maybe one with a private tutor. Even if they had been the same age, their paths wouldn't have crossed.

"Why didn't you tell us?" Amy wrapped both hands around her glass of lemonade. "You and Papa never talk about your families or your childhoods. Why's that?"

Oh, good gracious. I think I stirred up a hornet's nest. So the Hamiltons weren't the perfect family they appeared to be. They were good people, though, and if Nora kept her past a secret, she probably had a reason for it. Rika wanted to take back her careless question about Nora's accent, but it was too late now.

"I didn't have the happiest childhood," Nora said, and again Rika sensed that it was the truth—but only half of it. She told the same kind of half-truths when asked about her own childhood. "And I haven't seen or heard from any Macauley for seventeen years, so..." Nora shrugged.

"Macauley," Rika repeated. How many wealthy people with that name lived in Boston? She took in Nora's red hair and her green eyes, then looked at Amy's identical coloring. Neither set of green eyes held Mr. Macauley's cruel expression, but the color was the same. "You're not related to William Macauley, are you?"

Nora's gaze jerked toward her. "He's my father."

"Father?" Rika shook her head. No, that couldn't be. William Macauley was too young to have fathered Nora. A sudden thought occurred to her. "Oh! William Senior was your father." One day, when Rika had complained about their hard-hearted boss, Jo had said he was a saint compared to his father, William Macauley Sr.

"Was?" Emotion colored Nora's voice, but Rika couldn't say which one it was—grief? Sorrow? Bitterness?

Rika wanted to squeeze her hand, but she had no right to be so familiar. "I'm sorry," she said. "I never met him, but I heard that he died about two years ago."

"Oh, Mama. I'm so sorry." Nattie reached for her mother's hand, and Amy wrapped her arm around Nora's shoulders.

"It's all right." Nora returned the soft touches of her daughters. "We weren't close. I left Boston after a big argument with him, and I never looked back. What happened to the rest of the family, Hendrika?"

I wonder what happened between her and her father. Was he anything like mine? Despite whatever might have happened, she sensed that Nora still cared about her family back East. "I don't know about your mother, but your oldest brother, William, owns the cotton mill now." Rika shook her head. *Nora's brother is my former boss. What a coincidence! But then again, the Macauleys own half of Boston.*

"We have an uncle in Boston?" Nattie's eyes shone.

Nora squeezed her eyes shut for a moment. No doubt she didn't want her daughters to meet any of the Boston Macauleys—and Rika understood why. What she had seen of William Macauley and his brothers made it hard to believe that they were related to the friendly Nora and her daughters. In William Macauley's cotton mill, Rika had been little more than a slave. Here on the ranch, she was treated like a family member.

"I'm sorry to say this, but he's not a nice man," Rika said and caught Nora's grateful glance. "All he seems to care about is money and power."

Shadows of the past darted over Nora's face. "Then he's truly his father's son." She turned to her daughters. "I'm sorry you had to find out this way, but I didn't want them to be part of your lives. Your father and I swore to be better parents than our own were."

Nattie exchanged a quick glance with her sister, who stood motionless, the glass of lemonade clamped in her hand. "And you are," Nattie finally said.

"Mrs. Hamilton? Amy? Nattie?" Hannah's husband called from the new barn. "We're hanging the barn door now, just to see if it fits. Do you want to do the honors?"

"Go on," Nora said. "I'll be there in a minute."

The Hamilton sisters exchanged a quick glance. Amy pressed her glass of lemonade into Rika's hands before she hurried to the barn, followed by Nattie.

Rika stared at drops of lemonade spilling over the rim of the glass. "I'm sorry." She lifted her gaze to meet Nora's. "If I had known—"

"It's my own fault, not yours," Nora said. "Lying to your family is stupid and hurtful for everyone. Those lies will keep you prisoner, because you are so afraid that one day, they'll find out. With every day, with every lie, the fear becomes stronger." Her eyes darkened with sorrow.

Nora wasn't talking about Rika, but the words hit home all the same. Fear had guided Rika all her life—fear of her father, fear of the war, fear of Willem gambling their money away, fear of losing her job, and now fear of being sent away from the Hamilton Ranch. Her life was filled with lies, and Nora was right—the lies didn't make the fear go away. They just made everything worse. The truth trembled somewhere deep inside her, wanting to be told, but Rika couldn't.

If she did, she might lose everything, just when she was beginning to feel at home on the ranch.

"Come on," Nora said. The color returned to her cheeks. "Let's go watch them hang the door. We might just have a new barn by the time the sun sets."

THE DALLES, OREGON
MAY 2, 1868

*L*UKE STARED INTO THE SWIRLING waters of the Columbia River. A series of foaming rapids and waterfalls accompanied them for miles as they drove their herd of horses upstream. When she had been stationed at Fort Dalles during the Cayuse War, the waterfalls had tumbled fifteen feet until they hit the rest of the water. Now the river carried so much water that the falls were partially submerged and turned into a long line of roaring rapids.

I hope the rivers at home aren't running so high. Thoughts of her family were with her every mile of the way.

"Boss, look," Phin shouted and pointed.

Before them, wooden platforms dangled on scaffolds over the falls. Indians leaned over the edge of the platforms and dipped nets on long poles into the foaming river. Downstream, where the river was calmer, fishermen in canoes drove spears into the water.

"They're fishing for salmon," Luke shouted over the roaring river.

On the high bluffs to both sides of the river, dozens of lodges had been erected. They were fewer than twenty years ago.

The fort was gone now too. Only a few abandoned buildings remained. The town that had grown around the fort was bustling, though.

When Luke's herd crowded into town, people jumped back from the busy main street.

A big sign hanging from one of the false fronts caught Luke's attention. BATHS, the sign declared in capital letters. Her skin itched in reaction. She hadn't bathed in almost two weeks.

At home, bathing wasn't a problem. Every Saturday night, Luke dragged a tin tub into one corner of the kitchen and filled it with hot water. Nora hung a sheet from the rafters, and then it was bathing time. Luke always bathed last—"Because Papa is the dirtiest," Nora said. The girls never questioned it. When the girls were little, Nora had put them to bed right after their own baths, and now they knew that every person should be given privacy while in the tub.

Her ranch hands had no such restraint. Bathing with them anywhere near her was too dangerous.

Later. She urged Dancer on and drove one of the geldings away from a lovingly tended garden, stopping him from making a meal of some woman's first spring flowers. "Keep them away from the gardens, boys," she called. She had no money to pay for trampled flower beds and vegetable patches.

They drove the herd toward the livery stable, and Luke dismounted to negotiate with the stable owner. With hordes of miners in town, she wanted to hurry before all the baths were reserved for the night.

Luke slung her new saddlebags, full of supplies, over her shoulder and left the dry-goods store. Her boots pounded down the boardwalk as she hurried toward the baths.

A Chinese man carrying a stack of towels opened the door. "We all full," he told her. "You wait outside."

While she waited, she took in the busy town and let her gaze wander to the horizon, where white-capped Mount Hood loomed in the distance. The familiar sight made her feel less separated from her family, but at the same time, it increased the longing to be home.

The door to one of the bathing cabins opened, and a man stepped out, twirling his still damp mustache.

Luke waited while the Chinese man disappeared into the cabin with two buckets of steaming water. Her skin prickled in expectation of sinking into the bath. She hoped the cabin had a sturdy bolt so that she could enjoy her bath without worrying about anyone barging in. She would place a chair beneath the door handle, just in case.

After two more trips with the heavy buckets across his shoulders, the Chinese man gave a nod, allowing her to enter.

She rushed forward—and collided with another man who had his eye on the bath.

They stumbled back and stared at each other.

Her bathing rival was a bit older and smaller than she was, with salt-and-pepper hair sticking out beneath a brown hat. A buttoned coat bulged at the right hip, indicating that the stranger was armed.

Then Luke's gaze traveled upward and found another bulge. Two bulges, to be exact. She blinked. *He...she's a woman?* She forgot about her bath as she stared at the stranger. Years ago, Tess had told her she knew others like her, but Luke had never met another woman who lived her life as a man. Was the stranger living in disguise? If she was, she needed a few lessons. *She should at least wrap her chest and cut her hair shorter.*

"Go ahead," the stranger said. Her voice wasn't that of a man, and she didn't try to make it sound deeper. "I think you were here first." She swept her hand at the bathing cabin.

Luke hesitated. She desperately wanted a bath, but decades of living as a man left her little choice. Nora sometimes teased her about her gentlemanly manners and warned her that one day, a damsel in distress would be her downfall. "After you, ma'am," she said and held her breath, waiting for the stranger's reaction to being called "ma'am."

When the stranger smiled, her features softened, and there was no longer any doubt in Luke's mind. She was dealing with a woman.

"It's not often that I get treated like a lady," the woman said. Her tone revealed that she didn't care. Steely brown eyes told Luke that the stranger could take care of herself. Still, a hint of vulnerability remained around her mouth.

Luke could imagine how hard her life might be. The stranger wasn't welcome in saloons or as the owner of a business, because she was not a man and didn't try to pass as one. But looking like this, she also wasn't asked to participate in needle circles or attend the women's Bible study. She would never fit in, never be respected by anyone, have no family and no friends.

Lord, I couldn't live like that. While she had been a loner in the past, now she would rather die than live without her family.

Keeping her true gender secret and lying to her daughters was the price she had to pay.

"Frankie?" A woman waved at the stranger next to Luke. She stepped down from the boardwalk and opened her parasol before she crossed the street.

Seems I was wrong about her not having any friends. Luke watched the woman approach. Even from this distance, her clothes and movements revealed a lady of some standing. How had she come to be friends with the unusual Frankie?

Luke took in the lady's lithe body and golden hair that held a few silver streaks. Blue eyes looked back at her with gentle interest—and then widened. The parasol fell out of the woman's hand. "L-Luke? Is that you?"

Luke blinked. "Tess?"

Soft arms wrapped around her in a stranglehold.

"Tess," Luke murmured into the ear of the only friend she'd had for many years.

Finally, Tess moved back an inch and brushed her lips against Luke's, saying hello in her usual way as if seventeen days, not seventeen years, had passed since they had last seen each other.

"I can't believe it," Luke said. A part of her had thought she would never see Tess again. They had exchanged many letters over the years, but she couldn't entrust her secrets to a piece of paper. "What are you doing here? Last I heard you were in Montana with that partner of yours, Frank."

"Oh, we were. But when Frankie got sent to Oregon, we decided to pay you a visit. I didn't mention it in my last letter, because I didn't want to disappoint anyone in case Frankie's job took longer than expected. We sent off a letter to you yesterday, but we might make it to the ranch before the letter." Tess's gaze traveled to something or someone behind Luke. A smile formed on her full lips.

Luke turned.

The woman in men's clothes watched them, her head cocked to one side.

Oh. Realization dawned, and Luke found herself staring. *That's Frank? Frankie? Tess's companion, the person who shares her life, is a woman?* So Tess was equally reluctant to entrust her secrets to a letter that might fall into the wrong hands.

"We have some catching up to do," Tess said. "Are you staying in town for a few days? Is Nora here too?" She looked around for her old friend.

"No," Luke said. Nora's absence was like a constant nagging ache. She longed to wrap her arms around Nora and feel the confusing whirl of emotions inside her calm. "Nora is at home, taking care of the ranch, while I'm driving a herd of horses to Fort Boise. I'm just staying in The Dalles until first light tomorrow morning."

Tess rested her hand in the bend of Luke's arm. "Oh, don't worry. We'll have all the time in the world to talk when you get back. We're staying a few weeks if that's all right with you and Nora. We're even thinking about settling down in Oregon."

"Really?" Luke clutched the hand on her arm, grinning broadly. The thought of her old friend living nearby wiped away her exhaustion.

"We haven't made a final decision yet. Frankie has some things to wrap up in town, and then we'll travel west to visit your family. I'm eager to meet Amy and Nattie."

Another heavy weight dropped from Luke's shoulders. Tess could make sure Nora and the girls were all right.

"Boss?" Phin called from across the street. He stopped in front of them and stared at Frankie and Tess with a less than welcoming expression.

Luke's relief waned. Concern stirred in her belly. If her ranch hands saw her with a woman who dressed like a man, they might get a few ideas about her too. Things they had never questioned before would begin to make sense when they compared her to Frankie.

But Phin wasn't looking at Frankie. His gaze was fixed on Tess. "I don't want to interrupt, but..."

"It's all right," Luke said. "This is an old friend of mine, Tess Swenson."

"I'm not that old." Tess gave them a wink.

True. The years had been kind to Tess. She was still a beautiful woman. Only a few wrinkles around her mouth and eyes told the story of her hard life. "This is Phineas Sharpe, my foreman."

After some hesitation, Phin tipped his hat and then turned to Luke. "The livery stable's hay looks moldy to me. I'm not sure we can feed it to the horses. Can you come take a look?"

"Now?"

When Phin nodded, Luke turned a regretful glance at Tess.

"We're staying at the hotel across the street." Tess pointed. "Come over and have supper with us when you're done. Just ask for Tess Swenson and her cousin."

Cousin? Luke almost snorted. But she knew Frankie and Tess didn't have a choice. If they told people they were sweethearts, they'd be run out of town within seconds. At least Luke had spared Nora that kind of hiding when she had decided to keep living as a man.

She followed Phin to the livery stable, her mind still reeling with the sudden reunion. One look at the hay had her glaring at him. "That hay is perfectly fine. Not even a hint of mold, and you knew that."

"I wanted to make sure—"

"Nonsense," Luke said. "I taught you better than that. You never needed me before to decide if the hay is safe for the horses. Why now?"

He shuffled his feet. For a moment, he seemed like the awkward adolescent he had been when he had first come to the ranch.

"I get a feeling you wanted to drag me away from my friend." Old feelings of protectiveness resurfaced. She never allowed others to treat Tess like anything but a lady. But Phin didn't know about Tess's past. To anyone looking at her now, she would appear like a wealthy lady with a strange taste in traveling companions. "What's going on?"

"Nothin'," Phin said. "I just wonder..." He hesitated.

"Yes? Come on. Spit it out, boy!" Luke's patience was running thin. Her time with Tess was short, and she didn't want to waste it.

He looked up and into her eyes. "I wonder what Mrs. Hamilton would think of you meetin' your 'old friend' at the hotel."

Why would Nora have anything against me having supper with—oh! Laughter bubbled up when Luke finally understood.

"Phin," she said. "You know me better than that. In all the years of my marriage, I never even looked at another woman."

"You kissed her," he said, a silent accusation in his voice.

His defense of her marriage and of Nora's feelings warmed her heart, but at the same time, it annoyed her that he questioned her devotion. *Maybe I've upheld my manly image a little too well. Now my men think I'm a philanderer.* "Tess is an old friend."

"But she wasn't always just a friend, was she?"

Impatient to end this line of conversation, Luke wanted to tell him it was none of his business, but she stopped herself. Phin was more than just a ranch hand. He was a part of her family. "That ended decades ago. Now we're nothing more than friends. Nora knows that. She has never doubted my faithfulness, and neither should you."

Phin rubbed his blond stubble that made him look like one of the Vikings from Nattie's books. "Sorry. I didn't mean to accuse you of anythin'. I just never saw you actin' so familiar with a woman other than Mrs. Hamilton. Guess I felt like a son meetin' his father's mistress."

"Tess is not my mistress, and I'm too young to be your father." Luke gave him a playful slap on the shoulder.

A grin chased away the serious expression on Phin's face. "Not by much."

"Then I'd better go visit my friend before I'm too old to take her to dinner," Luke said. But first, she would take that long-awaited bath.

Luke tugged on the sleeves of her cleanest shirt and smoothed her hands over her vest to make sure no hint of her breasts was noticeable beneath her clothes. *Calm down. Tess knows exactly what's beneath your clothes.* But still, if she took Tess out to supper, she wanted to appear the perfect gentleman.

After one final brush over her pant legs, she left her hotel room and knocked on Tess's door.

An elegantly dressed woman opened. It wasn't Tess.

"Oh. I'm sorry." Luke snatched her hat off and squeezed it between her hands. "I must have the wrong room numb—" She stopped and stared. "Frankie?"

Instead of the tough woman in men's clothes, she stood in front of a slender lady with artfully arranged hair. The grin was the same, though. "Yes. Frankie Callaghan. And you must be Luke." She looped her arm through Luke's in a ladylike gesture and led her inside the hotel room. "I had a feeling you were a little uncomfortable when your foreman saw us together, so I thought I'd dress up tonight in honor of meeting you." She blinked long lashes at Luke. They were probably as fake as her piled-up hair.

"Frankie!" Tess's smoky laughter drifted across the room. "Don't embarrass him."

"Him?" Frankie repeated.

She told Frankie about me? Luke stared at Tess. The Tess she had known in Independence hadn't trusted anyone, especially not enough to pass on other people's secrets.

Tess shrugged. "Jumping back and forth between pronouns made me dizzy, so I always tended to use male pronouns. Except, of course, when we were making lo—"

"Tess! Didn't you just tell Frankie not to embarrass me?" The tips of Luke's ears burned.

Laughter shook Tess. "It's good to see you haven't changed. I always found your innocence refreshing." She took Luke's other arm. "Come on, let's go eat."

"I'll retreat to our room now," Frankie said right after supper in the hotel's dining room.

When Frankie stood, Luke jumped up and pulled the chair back for her. "No need to go on my account."

"My cousin," Frankie winked at Tess, "wants some time alone with you." She held up her hand to stop Luke's protests and lowered her voice. "It's all right. I got over my jealousy a long time ago."

Dazed, Luke stared after her as Frankie gathered up her dress and ascended the stairs.

"She's amazing, isn't she?" Tess asked somewhat dreamily.

Luke turned. She had never seen that look of loving affection on Tess's face. Tess had loved Luke in her own way, but not like this. "She is." Luke had watched the dainty bites Frankie took and how elegantly she handled her cutlery. Nothing remained of the pants-wearing woman Luke had met in front of the bath. "Is this all an act to fit in?"

"No," Tess said. "This is who Frankie is."

"Then who was the woman with the pants?" At first, it seemed she had met a kindred spirit, but now she found Frankie confusing.

Tess smiled as if she knew what Luke was thinking. "That's part of Frankie too. It took me some time to understand that Frankie is not really like you. Not all the time. She can handle a needle with the same skill she handles a revolver—and she likes both equally."

Luke's mind was spinning, trying to grasp what Tess was saying. She never thought both were possible at the same time. Early in her life, she had decided to live as a man, and she knew switching back and forth wasn't possible for her. "Now I'm the one starting to feel dizzy." She emptied her beer.

Tess patted her hand. "Just give it some time. If you give her a chance, I'm sure you'll like her."

"It's not that I don't like her," Luke said. "She just... confuses me."

"Oh, she confused me too." Tess laughed. "In a very pleasant way."

Luke studied her old friend, enjoying the warm light in the blue eyes. In the past, Tess hadn't been so carefree. Had Frankie put that glint of happiness in her eyes? "I never thought you'd end up with a woman. I thought you were just dallying."

Tess's smile vanished. "You were so much more than a dalliance to me, Luke." She leaned across the table. "Had you knocked on my door instead of Nora's, the answer would have been yes too."

The blood rushed from Luke's face and made her feel light-headed. "You mean...you...?" Had Tess dreamed of starting a new life at her side—and Luke never gave her that chance?

"Don't worry." Tess chuckled. "I love you, but I was never in love with you. But you were so darned kind and honorable that no woman in my establishment would have said no to a marriage proposal from you."

"They would have said yes to a marriage proposal from Lucas, not from Luke," Luke said. It was a fine but important distinction. Women liked her, but only because they thought she was what she pretended to be—Lucas Hamilton, a man.

"Nora hinted in her letters that she knows exactly who and what you are—and yet she's still at your side."

Warmth spread through Luke, and she smiled. "Nora is special. She accepts the male and the female parts of me equally."

"Then I'm glad you knocked on her door and not on mine," Tess said, her expression sincere.

"What about you and Frankie?" Luke asked. "Does she know about your past? Does she know where we met?" Frankie had indicated that she had been jealous of her, so she knew Luke had once shared Tess's bed.

Tess's eyes remained calm as the sky on a warm summer day. "Frankie knows everything about me. We don't keep secrets from each other."

"Hm." Luke wasn't sure she liked that. Her whole life, she had controlled who knew about her biggest secret, and now Tess had told Frankie without consulting her first.

"I'm sorry," Tess said, reading her expression as easily as she had seventeen years ago. "I wanted to ask your permission first, but I didn't want to do it in a letter, because I never knew if there would be curious young eyes around to read over your shoulder."

And there would have been. Nattie had learned to read at four years old, and she had read anything she could get her little hands on. "Good thinking."

Tess's gaze probed her. "So you never told Amy and Nattie? They still think you're their father, the manliest man this side of the Missouri?"

"Hush!" Luke rubbed the bump on the bridge of her nose and looked around to make sure no one was listening in on their conversation. Luckily, most other guests had already retreated to their rooms. "I am their father in every way that counts."

"So you never thought about telling them?"

"Nora and I talked about it a lot in the beginning. But back then, the girls were still so young. And when they were old enough to understand, I had already let them think for too many years that I'm the man who fathered them." She leaned across the table and whispered, "After all this time, how can I tell them that I'm not their father? That I'm not even a man?"

For long moments, silence lingered between them. Tess didn't tell her she was right to keep the truth from her daughters, nor did she say it was a mistake. She looked deeply into Luke's eyes. "Are you happy with the life you have?"

"Yes," Luke said without hesitation. "I'm happier than I ever thought I deserved to be. I share my life with the woman I love, and I have two wonderful daughters. What more could I want?" The truth of her words warmed her body.

Tess smiled and reached across the table to squeeze her hand. "Then I'm glad. I can't wait to see Nora again and to meet your daughters."

Luke's only regret was that she wouldn't be home for most of Tess's visit. She would have loved to witness Nora's joy at seeing her old friend, and she was curious to see what Nora made of Frankie. But at least Tess could tell Nora and the girls that she had made it safely this far. After she had sent Kit back with the injured gelding, Nora was probably worried about her making the rest of the trip with just two men. "When you get to the ranch, please let Nora know I'm fine."

"Is she worried?"

"She pretends not to be, but I know her better than that."

Concern clouded Tess's eyes too. "And she's right to worry, isn't she? Frankie said with the government trying to relocate the local tribes, the road to Fort Boise could be dangerous."

Luke shook her head. "Mostly it's just a few scattered bands, not whole tribes going on the warpath. We made it safely so far, and I'm sure we'll be fine. Once we've delivered the herd, we'll be able to make better time on the way back. I'm more worried about what's going on at the ranch." While she hadn't wanted to admit it to Phin, confessing her fears to Tess still felt right after all those years.

Golden brows lifted. "Is there trouble at the ranch?"

"Nora says I'm just being a mother hen, but running a ranch is a lot of responsibility. A thousand things can go wrong." Luke knew firsthand. Her first year of running the ranch had been hard.

"A mother hen?" Tess chuckled. "Luke, remember what Nora had been through before you met. She's a survivor. She'll be fine."

Any reminder of Nora's past in the brothel stirred anger deep in Luke's belly. "I'm not talking about Nora. She's there to give advice, but Amy is running the ranch while I'm away."

"Little Amy?" Tess grinned. Her gaze seemed to reach into the past as she remembered the little girl she had known.

Luke laughed. "Oh, you'd better not say that to her face. She's not so little anymore." It was hard for her to accept, but she knew her daughters were almost grown women now.

"So Amy is no longer sneaking out of the house to bring apples to the horses?" Tess asked with an affectionate grin.

Amy's attempt to visit the horses in Independence's livery stable was how Luke had first met her. It seemed almost unreal to her now. She could barely remember a time without Nora and the girls in her life. "Oh, I wouldn't say that." A few times, she had found Amy in the stable, visiting the horses in the middle of the night. She had a feeling Amy confessed her thoughts and fears to the horses just as Luke had done before she had met Nora.

"There's that expression again." Tess pointed at Luke's face.

"What expression?"

"I think it's the mother hen expression."

When Luke carefully schooled her features, Tess laughed.

"I don't have a mother hen expression," Luke said. "If anything, it's a rooster expression."

"Oh, don't bother. I like that expression on you. And I promise to check on your chicks."

"And on the mama hen, please," Luke said.

Tess smiled. "Her too, of course."

HAMILTON HORSE RANCH
BAKER PRAIRIE, OREGON
MAY 4, 1868

*T*HE SMELL OF HORSES, LEATHER, and freshly sawed wood filled Rika's nose when she rolled the wheelbarrow down the new barn's center aisle. Straw tickled her neck, and she tried to get rid of it by lifting her shoulder and turning her head back and forth against it.

The wheelbarrow started to topple over, but she had learned not to load it up too high and easily rebalanced it. She stopped in front of the open barn door to catch her breath.

Outside, Nattie was taking care of Zebra, the mare whose leg had been injured in the fire, but Rika's gaze was drawn to the other side of the ranch yard.

Amy had the gray mare called Mouse tied to the corral rail and slid her hands down the mare's leg. Her shoulder leaned against the horse until Mouse shifted her weight.

What's she doing? Rika tried to understand what Amy was saying to the horse, but her voice was too low. She craned her neck and circled the wheelbarrow to catch a glimpse of Amy's hands. *Is she squeezing Mouse's foot?*

After a few seconds, Mouse lifted her foot off the ground. Amy took hold of the foot and cradled it for a moment before she set it down. She straightened and rubbed Mouse's shoulder, then moved to the next foot.

Rika had thought training horses meant riding them, but Amy spent a lot of time working with Mouse on the ground. Despite her lack of patience with Rika's earlier mistakes, Amy never got frustrated with the horses. She handled them in a calm, confident way that made Rika stop and watch every time she crossed the ranch yard.

I think she's teaching Mouse to hold still while someone puts new shoes on her.

Amy circled the mare and started the same procedure on the other side. When Mouse obediently lifted her hoof, Amy looked up. Her eyes widened when she saw that she had an audience.

Caught, Rika lingered in the barn doorway and gave a wave.

Instead of letting go of Mouse's foot, Amy stood frozen.

Mouse struggled against her grip. Her head whipped around. Big teeth flashed.

"Hey!" Amy jumped back.

Oh, Lord, no! Rika squeezed past the wheelbarrow and hurried across the ranch yard. At the last moment, she remembered to slow down before she reached Mouse and Amy. *No running around horses. They scare easily.* "Did she bite you? Are you bleeding?"

"No." Amy's blush hid her freckles for a moment, and she averted her gaze. "I'm fine. It's my fault. I should have paid attention."

"Or maybe you shouldn't have named her Mouse. Now she thinks she's a rodent and is allowed to nibble on you." Rika grinned, hoping to coax a smile from Amy too. Her stiff posture made Rika feel bad about causing the incident.

A reluctant smile leaked through Amy's tense expression. "Yeah, maybe." She looked away.

Is she angry with me for interrupting her work? "So why name a horse Mouse?" she asked, just to test Amy's mood.

Amy shrugged. "When I was a little girl, I had a liking for unusual names. I named Papa's best mare Measles because of her spots."

"And your father allowed that?" Rika's father hadn't asked for her opinion when he named their horse. And had she suggested that it be named after a contagious disease, he probably would have yelled at her. *Or worse.* Rika shoved the thought away.

"Mama said at first he flinched whenever he called the horse," Amy said, now grinning, "but Papa never objected to the names I gave the horses. And when I got older, I kept up with it, mainly to annoy Nattie. She thinks the horses should have poetic or 'historically meaningful' names like Dancer and Lancelot." She rolled her eyes and looked over at Nattie, who was still in the corral with Zebra. "As if the horses could read Nattie's fancy books."

She and Nattie couldn't be more different if they tried. While the Hamilton sisters both loved horses and had stood together to defend her against the girls at the schoolhouse dance, Rika wasn't yet sure how close they really were.

"Are you mucking stalls?" Amy asked, looking over Rika's shoulder to the barn. "Why aren't you wearing gloves?"

"I was. I found these," Rika pulled a pair of gloves from her apron pocket, "when I helped bring the equipment into the new tack room. But they must belong to either your father or a ranch hand. They're too big for me and started to rub my skin raw, so I took them off."

Amy tugged her own gloves from her waistband. "Here. Try these."

"But they're yours. You'll need them or ruin your hands."

"No, my calluses are in all the right places. See?" She held out her hands, displaying palms covered with calluses.

Reluctantly, Rika took the gloves and pulled them on, finding them still warm from Amy's body heat. She stretched her fingers. While still a bit too loose, these would protect her hands much better than the bigger pair she had tried before. "Thank you. I'll give them back once I'm done with the stalls."

"I think this is yours," a deep voice said behind them.

Rika turned to see Hank pushing the wheelbarrow toward her. "Oh." With flushed cheeks, she hurried toward him. "I didn't mean to leave it behind. I just..." She had allowed herself to become distracted while watching Amy work with Mouse.

"It's all right," Hank said. "I just need to get Old Jack, and the wheelbarrow was in the way."

Amy walked over, leading Mouse on a rope. "Old Jack? You're not going to town, are you? I need every hand to replace the loose rails on the corral and prepare it for the roundup."

"It's not for me," Hank said. "Your mother asked me to get the buckboard ready for her. She wants to go to the saddle maker and get some of the tack replaced that burned in the fire."

A shiver raced along Rika's skin as she thought about that night.

"If you take over Mouse for a minute, I'll get the buckboard ready for Mama," Amy said. "I need to talk to her anyway."

Rika gripped the handles of the wheelbarrow, her hands now protected by Amy's gloves. The simple kindness sat like a piece of lead in her stomach because she had earned it with lies. *You earned it with hard work.* Every blister, every bruise, and every drop of sweat had been earned honestly. She had risked her life to help Amy save the horses from the burning barn. *You deserve their respect.*

Clenching her jaw, she pushed the wheelbarrow toward the manure pile.

Amy fiddled with the reins and finally handed them up to her mother. "When you're in town," she said, keeping her gaze on Old Jack, "do you think you have time to go to the cobbler's?"

"The cobbler's? Why would I go there?" Mama glanced at Amy's boots. "You need new boots so soon?"

"No. My boots are fine. Can you order a new pair of gloves, please?"

"Gloves?" Mama's gaze wandered to Amy's bare hands.

"Not for me. Hendrika needs her own pair. I still owe her money, and it would be a good way to say thank you for helping me save the horses."

A warm smile lit up Mama's face. "That's a nice idea." Then a frown replaced her smile. "But with what the new tack is gonna cost us, it might not be the best time for the extra expense."

She was right. New saddles, bridles, and harnesses would use up most of their savings.

"Maybe the cobbler will agree to trade the gloves for some of our hay?"

"I'll try," Mama said. "Do you know what size Hendrika wears?"

It was amazingly easy to call up a mental image of Hendrika's hands. Along with it came the memory of how good it had felt to have Hendrika take care of her burned fingers. Amy shook her head to get rid of the thought. She looked at Mama's fingers, which had a competent grip on the reins. "If they fit you, they should fit Hendrika too."

"All right, sweetie. I'll see you later."

With a flick of the reins, the wagon rolled up the hill.

When Nora left the cobbler's, the town's pastor and doctor descended on her. "Mrs. Hamilton." Dr. Tolridge tipped his hat and extended his hand to help her cross the street. "How nice to see you in town."

Oh, yeah? Nora eyed them suspiciously. Except for a quick greeting in church, she hadn't talked to either of them since she had told them she wouldn't teach while Luke was away. They had accepted it with an uncaring shrug, acting as if good teachers were a dime a dozen. She said nothing but waited to hear what they wanted.

"Do you have a minute?" the pastor asked.

Nora nodded.

"We know you said that with your husband gone you wouldn't be able to teach, but..." Reverend Rhodes looked at the schoolhouse across the street.

"Oh, let me guess. George has managed to chase off yet another teacher and now you want me to take over the rest of the term." Bitterness and grim satisfaction warred within her. When she had first started teaching years ago, these two men had been her biggest opponents, loudly declaring that a married woman shouldn't be allowed to teach school. Only Jacob Garfield's vote of confidence had convinced the school board to give her a chance.

"No," Reverend Rhodes said. "It's not that."

"Not yet," the doctor said.

Right at that moment, the schoolhouse's door banged shut. A young teacher stormed away, his collar askew.

Nora could easily imagine what had happened. George was a big boy of sixteen—almost too old to still be in school. By now, he should have been helping his father or trying to find work, but hard work didn't have much appeal for him. Spelling, arithmetic, and geography didn't interest him either. He came to school to amuse himself by disrupting class and terrorizing the teacher. Openly, he boasted that no teacher would last a whole term—and no one but Nora ever had. Now that his cousin Hiram had moved to town and joined him in school, it was probably even worse.

"All right." The pastor sighed. "It is as you thought. We need a teacher who won't let herself be chased off by George and his cousin. It would just be for a few weeks, until summer break."

Nora hesitated. The boys wouldn't dare to lay hand on a female teacher, but they had other ways to make teaching unpleasant for her. She reached into her apron pocket and felt the list of things they needed from the saddle maker. It was a long list. *We could really use the money.* With Hendrika willing to help out, Nattie could handle the chores around the house.

"All right." She gave the pastor a grim nod. "You've got yourself a teacher, Reverend."

The schoolhouse's door opened again, and laughing children stepped outside.

"Excuse me," Nora said. "I need to stop them before this gets completely out of hand." She marched to the schoolhouse and reached it just as the last two children headed out the door. "If it isn't George Miller—just the young gentleman I wanted to see. And you must be Hiram." She stared them down, acting unimpressed with the fact that the boys towered over her.

Hiram folded muscular arms across his chest. "But maybe we don't want to see you."

Oh, so he's the boss, not George. Nora gestured at the door, ignoring his comment. "Let's go in and talk like adults." They couldn't dismiss her invitation if they didn't want to be thought of as children.

George shuffled his feet and looked at Hiram.

"Oh, not you, George." Nora patted his arm. "You go on home. I'll talk to Hiram—that is, if he's not too scared to be alone with me."

"Scared?" Hiram snorted. "By a little schoolmarm like you?"

Nora held the door open for him. "Wonderful. Then it's settled. We'll go inside and talk."

When Hiram entered after her, the schoolroom felt much smaller than it usually did. The child-sized benches and desks made him appear even larger. For a moment, old fears surfaced, but Nora wrestled them down. At Luke's side, she had learned to face all kinds of threats, and she wouldn't back down from this young brute who had the body of a man and the brain of an unruly child.

She sorted through her options. The teacher's cane next to the blackboard wasn't her style of teaching, and she knew Hiram could easily take it away from her and use it as a weapon against her anyway. Telling his father to discipline him wouldn't work either. She had tried it with George last year, and whatever punishment his father had handed out, it made him resent her even more.

I need to earn his respect—and just being a good teacher won't impress him. She had to prove herself superior in an area that he didn't expect. A slow smile inched across her face when she remembered something else Luke had taught her. "Let's sit down." She gestured at her desk.

"Sitting around is for womenfolk. I'll go fishing now." Hiram sauntered to the door.

"So you don't want to hear the deal I have to offer?" Nora asked from her desk.

A cautious glance met hers. "Deal? What deal?"

"If I win, you'll come to school every day for the rest of the term and you'll sit quietly and try to learn what I'm teaching."

"Sounds like a bad deal. No, thanks." He took another step toward the door.

Nora continued as if he hadn't interrupted. "If you win, I'll cover for you and tell your father you're studying hard while you spend your mornings fishing with your cousin."

Interest sparked in his eyes when he turned his head, but he quickly hid it. "Win at what?"

"Oh, I thought we could arm wrestle." She gave him her sweetest smile.

Silence filled the schoolroom.

Then laughter exploded from Hiram. "Arm wrestle?" He slapped his thighs. "With you?"

"I considered a spelling bee, but then I thought I should give you at least a hint of a chance to win."

"Are you crazy?" He rolled up his sleeve and flexed impressive muscles. "How could a little woman like you beat that?"

She gestured to a bench at the other side of her desk. "Sit down and find out." Nervousness knotted her insides, but she was careful not to show it. Appearing confident and throwing him off balance was part of the strategy. "Or are you afraid? If I win, I promise not to tell anyone what our deal was about." The school board wouldn't like that kind of teaching method anyway—at least not from a woman.

With a snort, Hiram plopped down on the bench.

Nora put her elbow on the table and gripped his hand.

The difference in their arm size made him laugh, but Nora remained focused. She pressed her feet against the floor to support her upper body and leaned forward. "Ready?"

Still chuckling, he nodded.

"Go!"

Immediately, Hiram tried to push her arm down.

Nora didn't push. She locked the muscles in her belly, shoulder, and arm and focused on keeping her arm upright. She used her entire body, not just her arm, to resist his pressure.

Hiram's face turned red, and Nora wasn't sure whether it was from the exertion or from anger when her arm wouldn't budge. He let out a grunt and doubled his efforts.

The muscles in Nora's shoulder and arm screamed at her, but she held on, not trying to push him down. Her fingertips put pressure on the nerve between his thumb and index finger.

Another grunt was wrenched from Hiram's lips. His grip weakened for a moment.

Nora pulled her elbow slightly toward herself and rotated her arm. Her fingers dug into the soft spot on Hiram's hand again, and in one swift move, she forced his arm part of the way down.

"What the hell?" His gaze darted up as if to make sure it was still a slender schoolteacher sitting across from him, not a muscle-bound giant.

With her feet pressed against the desk leg, Nora shifted her hand and used his distraction to push his hand all the way down.

"Hell and tarnation!" Hiram let go of her hand as if it were on fire. He rubbed his fingers and stared at her.

Nora's insides quivered with joy, but she forced herself not to let her triumph show. An adolescent boy like Hiram would be a sore loser if she hurt his pride.

"How did you do that?" he asked, still staring.

"There's a trick," she said. The same trick enabled Luke to beat some of the much stronger ranch hands and prove her "manliness." "If you want, I can teach you."

Eagerness glimmered in his eyes. He was probably already imagining becoming an unbeatable hero and the envy of the other boys.

"Next year," Nora said. "When you have mastered everything else I have to teach you."

The light in his eyes dimmed.

"Deal?" she asked and held out her hand. Her fingers trembled with exertion, but she hoped he wouldn't notice.

Hiram hesitated. Finally, he wrapped his fingers around hers. "Deal."

When Nora stood, her knees felt weak. She knew by tonight, her muscles would be stiff and hurting and she would long for one of Luke's massages. "All right. Then I'll see you tomorrow morning. And bring your cousin." She ambled out of the schoolhouse, her skirt swishing, before he could answer.

HAMILTON HORSE RANCH
BAKER PRAIRIE, OREGON
MAY 6, 1868

"*W*ANNA TRY BRANDING ONE?" NATTIE asked. The blood drained from Rika's face. She retreated until her back pressed against the corral rails. "Oh, no. I couldn't."

"Sure you can. Come on. Amy can show you. She taught me too." Nattie dragged her to the fire as if she were a lassoed foal. "Amy, can you catch one for Hendrika? I need to go help Toby with the colts in the other corral."

Before Rika could protest, Nattie walked away and Amy shook out a loop in her rope.

"Come on over here," Amy said. "Don't be afraid. It's easy to learn, really."

After a second's hesitation, Rika stepped over to her.

A mare rushed from one end of the corral to the other, her foal sprinting after her.

Amy's loop flew through the air and jerked the foal off its feet. Two of the men who stood next to the fire ran to hold it down.

"Here." Amy took a branding iron out of the fire and handed it to Rika.

Rika stared at the foal's spotted hip. She couldn't imagine pressing the red-hot iron against the foal's vulnerable side. If it felt anything like burning her hand in the stable, she didn't want to cause the little horse the same pain. "No." She hid her hands behind her back. "I don't want to hurt it."

Amy tipped back her hat, allowing Rika to see the soft glow in her eyes. "It's not too bad. And if we don't brand her, anyone can take the filly from us and claim to own her."

That wasn't what Rika wanted. The Hamiltons were good people who treated their horses well. Branding the horses seemed a necessary evil, and if she wanted to become Phineas's wife, she needed to get used to it. "All right," she said, hiding the tremor in her voice. "Can you show me?"

"Come over here." Amy walked to where the two ranch hands were holding down the filly. It struggled but couldn't break free. "Grip the branding iron here. Be careful not to burn yourself."

"Yeah." Emmett, one of the ranch hands, laughed. "Phin wouldn't be happy to find the Shamrock brand on his betrothed."

Slowly, Rika stepped up to the struggling foal.

"Press it against her hip right here." Amy stroked a spot on the filly's hip.

Rika clamped trembling hands around the branding iron. She wanted to tell Amy she couldn't do it, but by now, all the ranch hands were watching. She had something to prove—not just about herself, but also about a woman's place on the ranch. Maybe that was why Amy was so strict with her and seemed ambivalent about her presence on the ranch. Every mistake a woman made told her ranch hands that Amy might not be a good boss.

She swallowed and touched the branding iron to the filly's hip.

"Harder." Amy stepped behind her and put her hands over Rika's. Her warm breath tickled Rika's ear. "Press down harder."

With Amy's strong presence against her back, Rika let her hands be guided down with more force, pressing the branding iron against the filly.

The smell of burning hair drifted up, and the filly's scared whinny made Rika's stomach roil. She tried to focus on something else.

Behind her, in another corral, colts squealed as they were gelded, and mares pranced around, calling for their foals. Men shouted over the din while they drove more horses into the corral.

In the middle of all this chaos, Amy's orders were calm and her hands steady as she guided Rika. "Now step back."

When the two men who held down the filly let go, it jumped up and ran to its mother, who sniffed her daughter's hip.

"See," Amy said. "It's not so bad. It only hurts them for a moment, and then it's over."

"Amy?" Hank shouted from the other corral. "I think we got one of the neighbor's horses mixed in with our herd."

A quick glance to Rika, then Amy strode away to take care of the problem.

Rika watched her go. Two weeks before, she had thought it strange that the Hamiltons let their daughter do a man's work. But Amy seemed at home in the corral as if running the ranch was what she'd been born to do. She inspected the neighbor's horse, helped clean the incision of a newly gelded colt, and wielded a branding iron with the same ease with which Rika had tended her looms.

But there was one big difference. Amy loved working with horses, while Rika's work in the cotton mill seemed more meaningless and dreary with every day she spent out west.

"Miss Bruggeman?" Emmett called. "Wanna brand another one?"

Rika swallowed and then squared her shoulders. "Sure."

Hank shoved his hat back with his thumb and looked at something in the other corral.

Amy got up from her place kneeling next to a yearling they were about to geld. Was something wrong in the other corral? She craned her neck to see over Hank's shoulder.

The branding was going well, with no problem Amy could detect. Most mares already stood laving their foals' hips with a soothing tongue. At one end of the corral, Kit and Emmett flanked Hendrika and nearly fell over themselves to be the one to give her branding advice.

"They're fawnin' over her instead of doing their jobs," Hank said, still frowning. "Womenfolk hanging around the branding crew is a damn distraction, isn't it?"

Amusement curled Amy's lips. "It sure is."

He looked up and blinked as if only now remembering that she was a woman too. "I didn't mean…"

"I know what you meant." And he was right; Hendrika's presence was a distraction. A few days ago, that distraction had nearly gotten her bitten when she forgot to let go of Mouse's foot.

"But she ain't doing half bad for a city girl from back East," Hank said, his expression softening.

That much was true. Despite the fear Amy sometimes saw in her eyes, Hendrika did everything asked of her and took on extra chores without being asked. She was no stranger to hard work.

Loud cursing interrupted Amy's thoughts.

John stumbled past them, gripping his hand. Blood spilled from between his fingers.

"John!" Amy rushed to him. "What happened?"

"I cut myself instead of the colt's—" He interrupted himself.

Amy rolled her eyes. She was familiar with every part of a horse's anatomy. "Let me see." She reached for his bleeding hand.

"Don't bother," John said. "I'll go and have Miss Hendrika take a look. She was a nurse during the war, and she took real good care of your mama too." He walked away before Amy could answer.

"Miss Hendrika, huh?" By the time Phin came home, he might have to fight the other ranch hands for the honor of marrying her. Sighing, Amy knelt down. "Come on, Hank," she said. "Give me a hand, or this colt will never be gelded."

Rika's eyelids felt as heavy as her arms, and she struggled to keep them open. She was used to long days and hard work, but helping with the branding had left her exhausted. She stared at the cat on her lap with tired eyes. "You truly are one lucky cat, Othello." She scratched behind one black ear. "How come he's allowed in the house instead of being sent to the barn for mousing duty?"

Groaning, Nattie took a seat next to Rika on the divan and stretched out her feet. "He was trampled by a spooked horse when he was just a kitten. Everyone said he should be put out of his misery, but I convinced Papa to let me try and nurse him back to health."

Rika wished she'd had a father like that. She hoped Phineas would be like Mr. Hamilton.

With another groan, Nattie prepared to get up. "I'd better go and relieve Amy so she can get something to eat."

"Where is she?" Amy hadn't been at supper, and Rika had assumed she was checking on the colts they had gelded today.

"She's staying with Dotty because she thinks the mare's about to foal."

"Oh." A hot rush of excitement swirled through her at the thought of witnessing a foal's birth and sharing the experience with Amy. "Want me to go? I can watch the mare until Amy has eaten."

Nattie's eyes shone. "That would be great. I can go and help Toby with Nugget, then. She might be close to foaling too. We're keeping her at the other end of the barn so that each of the mares gets some peace and quiet. If you're sure..."

Rika lifted the cat and set him on the divan. "I don't mind. I wanted to say goodnight to Cinnamon anyway."

"Oh, dear. I think you caught the horse fever."

The thought made Rika smile. "I think the pot is calling the kettle black."

Nattie laughed. "I'm a Hamilton. It's in my blood."

It might not be in Rika's blood, but she had grown fond of Cinnamon and the other horses. She wrapped her shawl around her shoulders and crossed the ranch yard. Her tired legs protested, but the thought of seeing a foal being born urged her on. A soft voice led her to the last stall in the stable.

"You just wait and see, Dotty," Amy said inside the stall. "Before the week is over, you're gonna have the prettiest foal anyone has ever seen. Oh, yes, the absolutely prettiest, just like its mother."

Rika pressed her fingers against her lips to stop her laughter. *The tough Amy Hamilton, whispering sweet nothings to a pregnant mare.* She cleared her throat and peeked over the stall door.

When Amy saw her, she pretended to be checking the water in the mare's trough.

A chuckle escaped Rika.

"What?" Amy asked.

"Nothing."

Dotty stretched her neck over the stall door to check out the visitor, and Rika let her sniff her hand before she stroked the velvet nose.

"I see you're not afraid of horses anymore," Amy said.

"A few of them still scare me, but by now, I've learned which horses are real gentle and friendly, and I'm staying away from the rest."

Amy combed her fingers through Dotty's mane. "All our horses are gentle and friendly."

True. Compared to some of the horses she had seen in Boston, the Hamilton horses were well behaved. But still, some were gentler than others. "Your mare is a little..." She hesitated.

"Yes?" Amy drawled.

Rika ducked her head. "She's a tiny bit...bossy."

"You're calling my horse bossy?"

"Not in a bad way," Rika rushed to say. "I mean, she needs to be, right? She's the lead mare, after all."

Amy laughed. "I'm just pulling your leg. Ruby is pretty bossy, yes. But she's also very loyal once you show her who's the boss."

The gentle teasing on the Hamilton Ranch still took some getting used to, but Rika was beginning to enjoy it.

"Supper over already?" Amy asked when silence spread between them.

"Yes. If you want to go and eat, I could watch Dotty until you get back."

Amy shook her head. "That's all right. Hank will relieve me at midnight, and I'll eat something..." A big yawn interrupted her. "...then."

"You must be tired." When Rika had gotten up at sunrise, Amy had already been preparing things in the corral. She worked harder than any of the ranch hands, constantly proving that she could rope a horse, handle a branding iron, and hold down a yearling better than any of them. Now most of the ranch hands had gone to bed, but Amy was still up, taking care of the horses.

"No. I'm not tired." Amy's nostrils quivered as she suppressed another yawn.

"Liar," Rika said. Her hand flew to her mouth. Her father would have rewarded such frankness with a slap to her face. "I'm sorry. I didn't mean to say that, but...you do look pretty tired."

In the light of the kerosene lantern, Amy's face seemed pale. "A little."

"Why don't you go eat something and then lie down for an hour or two?" Rika said. "I'll stay with Dotty."

Amy's eyebrows formed a skeptical arch. "Have you ever helped with foaling?"

"No." The thought of being alone with the mare during labor set Rika's heart racing. She had helped her stepmother when her two youngest half siblings were born, but holding her hand and offering a cool rag wouldn't help the mare. "I wouldn't try to help her on my own. At the first sign of the foal coming, I'd hurry to the house and wake you."

Amy rubbed her eyes. "All right." She shook her index finger at Rika. "But you need to be quick about it. Mares aren't in labor for twenty hours. Once it starts, things go quickly."

"What do I need to watch for?"

"When Dotty becomes restless, paces around, or lies down and gets up again, you need to get me immediately. Think you can do that?"

A simple nod was answer enough.

Amy slid her hands over Dotty's swollen belly before she moved to the stall door. "Thank you," she said, stepping into the corridor and holding the door open.

Her trust settled over Rika like a warm blanket. She entered the stall and looked at Amy over the door. "You're welcome."

Rika yawned and watched Dotty curl back her upper lip in something that looked like the equine equivalent of an answering yawn. "You tired too, girl? I'm not keeping you awake, am I?"

In the last two hours, nothing had indicated that the foal was about to come. Maybe it wouldn't be born tonight after all.

She watched Dotty chew on a mouthful of hay, then walk away. A minute later, the mare returned to the manger and got another bite before she moved away.

Was that what Amy meant by "restless," or was her unfamiliar presence making the mare nervous? If she ran to the main house and woke Amy, only to discover that it was a false alarm, Amy would think she was no help at all.

Dotty crossed to the other end of the stall and settled her large body into the straw.

Is this it? Was the foal coming now, or had Dotty just settled down to sleep? Rika hesitated, one hand on the bolt that kept the stall door closed. She wasn't even sure if horses lay down to sleep. In the corral, she had seen horses doze while standing up.

After a few moments, Dotty rolled to her feet. Sweat gleamed on her dark coat. No sound of pain interrupted the silence, but by now Rika sensed that something was wrong.

The foal is coming! She hurried out of the stall, stopping just long enough to close the door behind her.

Darkness greeted her in the main house. The screen door creaked as she closed it behind her, but otherwise, everything was silent. Moonlight filtered in through the windows, and Rika didn't stop to search for matches to light a lamp. Holding on to the banister, she rushed up the stairs. She forced herself to slow down just enough to not wake the entire house. Her heart thumping against her ribcage, she tapped on Amy's door. "Amy!" She knocked again and then opened the door.

Nothing moved in the darkness of the room. Amy had likely fallen into an exhausted sleep as soon as her head hit the pillow.

"Wake up, Amy!" Rika hurried across the room to shake her awake, but her foot collided with an unexpected obstacle. She stumbled and pitched forward.

The air was squeezed out of her lungs when she landed much sooner than expected—and much softer too.

The warm surface beneath her jerked and groaned. "What...?"

Stunned, Rika stared down into the gleaming white of Amy's eyes.

"Rika?" Amy mumbled, her voice rough with sleep. Her hands slid up Rika's back, as if to make sure she was really there.

Heat flowed through Rika at the touch, freeing her of her frozen state. She rolled off the bed and its inhabitant. "Sorry. I think the foal is coming," she blurted.

Amy jumped out of bed. Apparently, she had gone to sleep fully dressed. Now she shoved her feet into the boots in front of the bed. "Hurry!" She grabbed Rika's elbow and dragged her along.

In the stable, Dotty had lain down again.

"Her water already broke." Amy pointed to the wet straw in the stall.

"What do we do?"

Amy took up position in front of the stall but didn't enter. "Nothing."

"Nothing?" All of this excitement and now Amy did nothing? Rika watched as the mare's neck arched, her legs stiffened, and Dotty let out a low grunt. She felt like a young father, forced to watch helplessly.

"Dotty has been through this before, and all her foals were born without a problem. We're just here in case something goes wrong. If there are complications, every second counts."

The thought sent a shiver through Rika, and she prayed that everything would go smoothly this time too.

Dotty got up, paced a few times, then went down again.

"Oh, no." Amy's brow furrowed.

"What? Is something wrong?"

"She's lying too close to the wall. There's no room for the foal to be born." Amy waited a few minutes, but when the mare didn't get up, she shoved back the bolt and opened the stall door.

Rika slipped into the stall behind her, plastering herself to Amy's side. "What do we do?"

"We've got to get her up," Amy said. "Help me. If I tell you to, push her from behind until she moves."

Dotty didn't look as if she wanted to move. Her legs tensed when another contraction started. Rika stared at the whitish bubble that appeared between the mare's hind legs. The contours of little hooves stretched the white sac and then one tiny leg broke through. It slipped partway back when the contraction ebbed.

"Now!" Amy pushed against Dotty's hip, causing the mare to lift her head to look at her.

With trembling hands, Rika pushed the horse from behind.

Dotty gave a snort of protest, then folded her legs beneath herself and got to her feet.

"Good girl." Amy's voice soothed both Rika and the mare. She weaved her fingers through Dotty's mane and urged her over, more to the middle of the stall.

Rika's knees wobbled when she detected that one little hoof was still sticking out of the mare when she lay down. For a moment, she was afraid that Dotty would crush the foal's leg, but the mare made it down safely.

The second hoof broke through the white sac. A gush of fluid dribbled into the straw, and then a nose appeared.

Rika wanted to clap and shout, but she stood rooted to the spot.

With gentle hands, Amy pushed the membrane from the foal's head.

A white mark sat in the middle of the otherwise dark forehead. Rika had learned that horse breeders called it a "star."

Lord, I hope it's a lucky star for the little one.

Dotty groaned and grunted, trying to push out the foal's shoulders.

Rika realized her hands were clamped around Amy's arm, and she let go. "Sorry."

An understanding smile crossed Amy's face. While she acted calm, her eyes reflected the same tense excitement Rika felt. Amy might have witnessed many foals being born, but she still felt the magic of the moment.

The foal slipped out of the mare little by little. With one final grunt from Dotty, the hips and hind legs slid into the straw.

Amy brushed the white sac away from the foal and wiped it down with a handful of straw, revealing a dark coat and a white blanket on the hip. "It's a filly," she said with the biggest grin Rika had ever seen on her. Then she stepped back, her arm brushing Rika's.

They stood in silence, watching as Dotty turned and snuffled her daughter's face. She nickered and began to clean the foal's coat.

"Oh." Rika exhaled carefully, as if a loud breath would interrupt the bonding between mother and foal. "She's so beautiful."

Amy turned toward her. Their gazes touched and held. "She is," Amy said. "Very beautiful."

Something trembled deep inside of Rika, but she couldn't put a name to the unknown feeling. A part of her wanted to reach out and touch Amy, wanted to bond with her in the silent way the mare established contact with her foal.

Amy looked away, breaking their eye contact. "Papa will be so pleased. Black horses with such a nice, big blanket are rare. This little one will be an important part of our breeding program one day."

Sudden sadness gripped Rika. She wouldn't be there to see the foal grow up. Even if she could convince Phineas that she was his betrothed, they wouldn't stay at the ranch for much longer. In his letters to Jo, Phineas had mentioned that he wanted to establish his own ranch soon.

"Everything all right?" Amy asked.

Rika kept her gaze fixed on the foal. "Yeah. Everything just happened so fast."

"I told you mares don't take twenty hours giving birth."

"Yes." She hadn't meant just the foaling, though. Three months ago, her life had been so different. The routine of the noisy weave room and the bustling activity in the boarding house had formed the pattern of her days and left little room for anything else. Now she was playing midwife to a mare with Amy Hamilton by her side. In a way, it felt completely unreal and absolutely right at the same time.

"Look," Amy whispered.

The filly struggled to get up, but her hind legs wouldn't support her body yet. Dotty nudged her foal with a gentle muzzle, encouraging her to try again.

Finally, the filly stood on wobbly legs. Dotty got up too, breaking the umbilical cord. The filly nuzzled her mother's flank, searching for her teat. Moments later, she started to suckle.

"Oh, dear Lord!" A voice interrupted the moment. When Rika turned, Nattie stood in front \of the stall. "What a beautiful foal. Look at that nice blanket. Good girl, Dotty."

"She did great," Amy said and yawned.

A cloak of exhaustion settled on Rika too.

"Why don't you two head off to bed?" Nattie said. "I don't think Nugget will foal tonight, so I'll keep an eye on Dotty and the little one for a while longer."

Hesitantly, Rika directed her gaze away from the suckling filly.

Amy opened the door, and they walked out into the ranch yard. The drizzle had stopped, and the moon and hundreds of stars were shining down on them.

Rika smiled. *So it was a lucky star for the filly.*

Not saying a word, they walked to the cabin. Rika put one hand on the door and looked back at Amy. "Goodnight," she said.

"Goodnight."

She waited until Amy's steps faded away before she let the door fall closed behind her.

Despite her exhaustion, Rika was up before sunrise. She hurried through the chores she had taken over from Nora. In her eagerness to go to the stable and see the filly, she nearly dropped the eggs she had collected from the henhouse.

"Slow down," she told herself. Now that Nora taught school on most days, the Hamiltons needed her help more than ever, and she didn't want to do a shabby job. Only after feeding the hens did she allow herself to wander to the stable.

The spot in front of the stall door was already occupied.

When Rika walked down the center aisle, Amy turned. Her red locks were mussed, but her green eyes sparkled as if she hadn't been up half of the night.

Their gazes met, and they smiled at each other like two proud parents.

"How is the filly?" Rika asked.

Amy turned around to face the stall. "Hungry, it seems." She chuckled.

Rika stepped next to her.

The black filly had her head bent beneath her mother's belly and was suckling. Dotty stood patiently.

"I could watch all day," Rika said.

"Me too, but I don't think the ranch hands would like it. We need to check on the colts today."

Steps announced the arrival of more visitors come to admire the foal, and soon Nora and Nattie were peeking over the stall door.

"Oh, what a beauty," Nora said. "Luke will hate to have missed this year's foals being born, especially this one. Is it a colt?"

Amy shook her head. "A filly."

"Then I hope you found a good name for her," Nora said. She glanced at Rika. "It's an old family tradition. Nattie gets to name all the colts and Amy the fillies."

"Poor little filly," Nattie said to the foal. "Now you'll get teased by the rest of the herd for having an odd name."

A nudge from Nora silenced her. "So?" She looked at Amy. "Have you picked a name?"

"I thought I'd let Hendrika name her," Amy said. Her gaze wandered to Rika, then veered away.

Rika's breath caught. "Me?" She pressed both hands to her chest. "Name the filly? Oh, no, I couldn't."

"Sure you could. Can't be any worse than the name my sister would pick," Nattie said.

Nora said nothing. Her silence made the importance of Amy's generous offer even clearer.

Rika looked at the filly, studying the graceful arc of her neck and the perfect dots on her white hindquarters. No name came to mind. "I can't think of a name beautiful enough for her."

"Don't think," Amy said. "Just feel and the right name will come to you."

Rika closed her eyes and then looked at the filly and her mother again. *Just feel.* She tried to remember what she had felt when she had first seen the filly last night. "Lucky," she whispered. "Lucky Star."

Despite Jo's death, maybe it had indeed been a lucky star that led her to Oregon and to this place, where she got to witness the birth of a foal. "Well," she said, "with the big star on her forehead and Amy there to watch over her when she was born, Lucky Star just seems to fit."

"It does." Amy smiled.

Nattie clapped her hands, making Dotty nudge her foal away from them. "Oh, finally—a filly with a meaningful name."

"Come on, girls." Nora ushered them away from the stall. "Let's get breakfast on the table."

WILLOW CREEK, OREGON
MAY 10, 1868

*L*UKE LED THE FIRST HORSE of her string into the creek. "Come on, Midnight. Not very far now, then you'll get some grass and rest." After saying good-bye to Tess, she was even more eager than before to make it to the fort and back home, but she knew the horses and men needed some rest. By the time they had herded the last horse through the creek, they were mud-spattered, tired, and hungry. "All right. Let's make camp here and—"

The sound of hoofbeats interrupted her, and she reached for her rifle. A silent signal brought Charlie and Phin to her side. Weapons raised, they waited for whoever was approaching.

The first horse appeared on top of the hill.

Luke lowered her rifle. The rider's blue uniform was familiar. She had worn the same uniform many years ago.

Behind the first rider, a dozen more soldiers reined in their horses. Two of them urged their horses down the hill while the others stayed back. A quick glance at the insignia on their uniforms showed that the young lieutenant was in charge. "Good day," he said. "Lieutenant Moylan with the Eighth Cavalry."

Luke tipped her hat. "Luke Hamilton from the Willamette Valley. We're bringing a herd of horses to Fort Boise. What brings you to Willow Creek? You haven't been sent out to escort us, have you?"

"Afraid not," the young officer answered. "We're searching for a band of Indians who have stolen stock and killed one of our men. Have you had any trouble with Indians?"

Dancer shifted beneath Luke, sensing her tension.

"No," Luke said as calmly as possible. "All of our horses are accounted for."

"So you haven't seen any signs of Indians in the mountains?" the lieutenant asked.

Next to Luke, Charlie cleared his throat but said nothing.

"None," Luke answered. "Maybe your thieves joined the bands at the Owyhee River. The mountains aren't very hospitable this time of year."

Lieutenant Moylan nodded, but the bearded sergeant next to him still stared at her. Had he guessed that she was lying? Only long years of practice kept her mask of casual indifference in place.

"Don't I know you from somewhere?" the sergeant asked.

Every muscle in Luke's body stiffened. Nora and she had feared that question for years. She stared at the man, trying to see more of his features beneath his thick beard. He looked familiar.

"Hamilton..." The sergeant studied her. "You aren't the Luke Hamilton who fought in Mexico, are you?"

The tension fled from Luke's frame. She pictured the sergeant's face twenty years younger, and a name finally came to her. "Pete Johnson?"

The sergeant beamed. "Yes. Lieutenant, this man saved my hide more than once in the Mexican War." He looked at his superior. "Maybe we could return the favor and accompany him and his men safely to Fort Boise. The Injun thieves are long gone anyway."

Lieutenant Moylan hesitated but then nodded. "All right. At least our mission won't be a total failure. I know the colonel is waiting for these horses."

Oh, wonderful. That's what I get for being a war hero. Now instead of just two men, twelve soldiers would be watching her every move. Finding a quiet place behind a bush to relieve herself was going to be a challenge.

"Darn, boss, I didn't know you fought in the Mexican War," Charlie said as they set up camp. "You always said you didn't want to fight in a war that was not your own."

Luke shrugged. "I was young and naive." The war had been the perfect way to join the dragoons without being subjected to careful scrutiny by an army doctor. She had qualified just by being able to ride and shoot. Back then, she had desperately needed the order and discipline the dragoons brought to her life.

"I knew you were a dragoon in the Mexican War," Phin said. "Nattie told me. But I didn't know you were such a good liar." He lowered his voice so that none of the soldiers would hear.

Luke gave him a wry smile. *If only you knew.*

"Yeah," Charlie agreed. "You almost convinced me that we never met any Indians. But why lie? Why cover for the red bastards who took our horses?"

"Easy, Charlie." She sent him a warning glance. "I didn't like them stealing our horses any more than you, but they weren't out for a fight, so I doubt these are the Indians who killed the soldier. The lieutenant won't care, though. He's out to find some Indians and kill them. He won't care that it's just one warrior with an old man and two women. I don't want to be responsible for their deaths." She pinned Charlie with her gaze until he looked away. "All right. Let's set up camp."

As soon as the young lieutenant retreated into his tent, a pack of cards appeared from one of the saddlebags and a bottle of whiskey circulated among the soldiers.

Charlie held out his tin cup too.

Luke didn't stop him. One drink wouldn't matter, and she hoped he had the good sense to refuse more. When a soldier passed her the bottle, she handed it to the man next to her, though. She watched them start a game of cards but didn't join in.

Years ago, she would have joined her companions in a card game and laughed at their bawdy jokes, just to fit in. That kind of entertainment didn't hold much interest for her anymore.

In the past, she had lived her life as a man among other men and had lost touch with her female side. But over the last seventeen years, she had shared her home with three women, and it had changed her. She could still fit in with the men but no longer aimed to be like them in every way. Now she just wanted to be herself, whatever that was.

"You all right, boss?" Phin asked from across the fire. He had refused the soldiers' whiskey too.

"Yeah," she said. "Just thinking."

"Hm, me too." Phin came around the fire and sat next to her. "I wonder how things are goin' at home."

Luke constantly wondered the same thing. "Well, if your betrothed is even halfway helpful, I think Nora might have gone back to teaching by now."

"How can you know that?"

"I know my wife," she said. Nora was a practical woman, and if money got tight, she would leave the chores at the ranch to Nattie and Phin's bride and would return to her teaching duties.

"Do you think Johanna can handle life on a ranch?" In the firelight, Luke saw the concern in his eyes.

A grin made its way onto her lips when she remembered Nora's early attempts at building a fire or baking bread. "She'll have to learn. Don't worry. Even if Nora is back in the classroom, Amy and Nattie will teach her what she needs to know."

"Amy givin' my future wife lessons in how a ranch wife should behave..." Phin laughed. "Now that's a scary thought."

Sharp words hovered on Luke's tongue, but she swallowed them. Phin hadn't meant to criticize Amy. Still, it was true that Amy wasn't the kind of woman most men would want as a role model for their wife. Sometimes, Luke wondered if their upbringing would condemn her daughters, especially Amy, to a life of loneliness.

Phin broke a twig into little pieces.

"If you're so worried about Johanna, why did you propose to a woman you don't even know?" Luke asked. "Why not court one of the neighbor girls, someone who grew up on a ranch?"

"Ah." Phin threw the twig into the fire. "They're silly gooses."

"All of them? There's not even one woman you like in the whole valley?"

Phin licked his lips.

"So there is someone you like." Grinning, she hit his shoulder. "Why not propose to her?"

"I'm not right for her." Phin stared into the fire. "I can't offer her what she deserves."

"I thought the same when I first met Nora," Luke said.

Phin still gazed into the flames. "That's different."

You've got no idea just how different it is.

"Want me to check on the horses?" Phin asked.

Luke got up. "No. I'll go." She needed to find a hidden spot to relieve her screaming bladder anyway.

Protected by the darkness and the sharp ears of the horses grazing nearby, she ducked behind a shrub of sagebrush and relieved herself. When she pulled up her pants and buttoned them, a horse snorted.

Luke peeked through the branches of the shrub while she closed the last button and rearranged the padding in her pants.

Two soldiers headed toward the latrine, one of them carrying a shovel. "The lieutenant shouldn't have agreed with Johnson," the taller man said. "Now we're stuck babysitting a bunch of horse breeders instead of finding the damn Injuns who killed Roy."

"Ah, Moylan is a green officer who hasn't seen any action yet. Every howl of a coyote out here makes him jump." He spat out and hit the sagebrush Luke was hiding behind. "He was just waiting for a reason to return to the fort."

"Maybe we should give him a reason not to return to the fort," the other soldier said.

"How?"

His friend chuckled. "If we drive off a few of Hamilton's horses and tell the lieutenant they were stolen by Indians…"

Heat shot through Luke. No one would use her horses for such a plan. The worn grip of her revolver felt soothing against her palm as she drew the weapon. With a resounding click, she cocked the hammer and stepped out of her hiding place. She smashed her boot onto a few branches.

The two soldiers whirled around.

"If even one of my horses goes missing, I'll shoot the two of you," she said.

"You wouldn't dare," the taller man said. "Our comrades would lynch you."

Luke just smiled at him. She had learned that it unnerved most men more than shouting ever could. "Oh, only if they think it was me who killed you. I'll tell your lieutenant you were killed by the same Indians who stole the horses you drove off."

In the silence of the night, the smaller man gulped audibly. "We were just joking about driving off your horses, really."

"I don't like your brand of humor, Private."

"It's not our problem if you don't have a sense of humor," the taller soldier said.

Luke stared him down, knowing he was the instigator. "Then make sure it doesn't become your problem. If all my horses make it safely to Fort Boise, we'll part as friends. If not, you won't be there to regret it."

The two soldiers stared at her. In the near darkness, she couldn't make out their expressions, but she still didn't look away.

"All right," the tall soldier finally said. "We'll leave the horses alone." He strode off in the direction of the latrine, and his friend followed.

Luke put her revolver away and stared into the darkness. *Great.* Instead of enjoying the safety of a cavalry escort, she'd have to sleep with one eye open. She adjusted her pants and walked back to the camp to let Phin and Charlie know.

HAMILTON HORSE RANCH
BAKER PRAIRIE, OREGON
MAY 14, 1868

*A*MY HEAVED HER SADDLE ONTO her shoulder and carried it out of the stable. When she placed it on Ruby's back, she noticed Hendrika standing in front of the corral where they kept Nugget, Dotty, and the two foals. Her arms rested on the top rail, and her chin leaned on her hands. She stared at the horses as intently as if she had forgotten that anything else existed.

She's really fond of Lucky. And it wasn't just the filly. Hendrika visited Cinnamon every night before bedtime, and the way Ruby nickered when she saw her coming made Amy think even the bossy mare had gotten an apple or two from her.

She'll make a good wife for a horseman like Phin. The thought should have been a joyful one since Phin was her friend, but somehow it wasn't.

"Hey," she said. "How's Lucky doing?"

Hendrika whirled around. "Oh. I didn't hear you come up."

"Mama calls it the 'horse trance.' She often has to drag Papa and me from the stable when we forget about supper." Thinking of Papa made a ball of worry form in her belly. How was he doing, out there on the trail? She leaned against the corral rail next to Hendrika and watched the foals.

Jason, Nugget's golden colt, chased Lucky around the corral. Lucky leaped and bucked. After a while, she trotted to her mother to rest.

"Wanna go in and say hello?" Amy asked, then instantly rebuked herself. *What are you doing? You've got work to do.* But despite her best intentions, she couldn't resist spending a little more time with Hendrika.

"Could we?" Hendrika looked at her with a hopeful glance. "Will Dotty and Nugget let us in there?"

"Sure. We always handle the foals from a very young age, get them used to people before they're turned out with the herd." Amy opened the gate and slipped through, then closed it behind them.

Instantly, Nugget's colt bolted to the other end of the corral. Lucky peeked out from behind her mother.

"Dotty," Amy called and made a clicking sound with her tongue.

Dotty lifted her head. When Amy clicked again, she loped toward them. The filly followed.

"Hey there, Dotty. I brought a guest to admire your daughter." Amy turned to Hendrika. "Come here and pat Dotty. It'll show the little one that there's nothing to be afraid of."

Hendrika reached out a hand and let the mare sniff it, exactly as Amy had shown her weeks ago. She slid her hand down the long neck to scratch behind Dotty's withers.

A little nose appeared from behind Dotty. Lucky pranced forward to see what was going on.

Hendrika held out her hand, palm up. She didn't try to touch the filly or get any closer; she just stood and waited, barely breathing.

Amy's breath caught too. Watching these two look at each other seemed like an endless, magical moment.

Finally, Lucky took one step forward, then another. Her nose touched Hendrika's hand, and something, probably the tickling of little whiskers, made Hendrika smile.

Jason, the palomino colt, followed his mother and trotted over.

"Oh, now you are being brave after a girl showed you how it's done," Amy murmured while she rubbed his withers.

Hendrika chuckled. "It seems your family has a history of breeding strong females."

For the first time, someone from outside the family had commented on how different the Hamilton women were—and made it sound like a compliment, not something to wrinkle her nose at.

Amy smiled. "I guess we do." She gave the colt one last scratch. "Come on. I need to ride out before it gets dark."

"Where are you going?" Hendrika asked as they walked to the gate.

"I need to check on the other foals, the ones who have already been turned out with the herd."

When Amy turned to close the gate, she saw the longing in Hendrika's eyes. The other woman remained silent, however. Hendrika had never again asked to ride with her since the fiasco shortly after her arrival on the ranch. But four weeks had passed since then, and Hendrika was more used to horses and how they reacted now. Nattie and Mama had taken her riding a few times.

Amy hesitated. Another glance into Hendrika's eyes made the decision. "If you're done with your chores, you could come with me."

"I don't want to be in the way," Hendrika said.

"You won't." With no wild mustangs around anymore, she should be safe. "Just promise me that you'll get off the horse and stay out of the way should something unexpected happen."

"You won't even know I'm there," Hendrika said.

I seriously doubt that. Amy was always much too aware of Hendrika's presence, but that was her problem. She couldn't make Hendrika feel unwelcome just because she was having those feelings. "Come on," she said. "You can help me saddle the horses."

Ten minutes later, Amy cursed herself. *Brilliant idea. Why didn't I just saddle the horses and let her watch?*

Now Hendrika wanted personal instructions every step of the way. "Like this?" she asked and rubbed the brush over Cinnamon's back.

Her eagerness to learn and to help was hard to resist.

"Longer strokes," Amy said. "Put some muscle into it. You won't hurt him." She stepped closer and reached around Hendrika to take over the brush. Her body pressed against Hendrika's on every brush stroke, making Amy sweat. "See?" Her voice trembled, and she hoped Hendrika wouldn't notice.

"Yes." Hendrika reached for the brush, and their fingers touched.

Amy pulled back. When she couldn't stand watching the slender fingers slide over Cinnamon's coat anymore, she pointed to the saddle hanging over the top rail. "Now the blanket and the saddle."

Hendrika grasped the blanket and placed it on Cinnamon's back, taking care to slide it back in the direction of the hairs, not against it.

"Who showed you how to do that?"

"Emmett," Hendrika said while she made sure that the blanket covered Cinnamon's withers. "He's nice. All the ranch hands are very nice to me."

Of course they are! They're nice to every young, unmarried woman. Amy bit back her comment, though. The boys would be perfect gentlemen. They knew Papa would never stand for anything else. *And they respect Phin too much to make unwelcome advances to his betrothed.* As Phin's friend, she should do the same, especially because she was a woman. Admiring another woman that way wasn't right.

"Do you want me to try saddling him?" Hendrika asked.

Amy nodded. "Go ahead. Grasp the cantle, the part in the back, with your right hand and the base of the fork with your left hand."

Hendrika swung the saddle down from the corral rail and stumbled with the weight of it.

"Careful." Amy reached around her and helped carry the saddle to Cinnamon.

"Gracious! It's a lot heavier than I thought."

It was. As a child, Amy had often ridden bareback because the saddle had been too heavy for her to lift on her own. "Now place your feet shoulder-width apart, and put your left foot forward."

When Hendrika slid her right foot back to balance herself, her leg brushed against Amy, who was still helping her hold on to the saddle.

Amy swallowed. "Rock your body back and forth three times to gather momentum." She cursed the breathless tone of her voice. "On the third rock, you swing the saddle up with a twist of your hips."

When Hendrika's hips rocked back and forth against Amy, the heat that shot through her almost made her drop the saddle. It landed on Cinnamon's back with more force than planned. He turned his head but otherwise stayed still.

"Sorry, Cin," Amy mumbled and stepped back, away from Hendrika.

"Seems I have to practice that some more," Hendrika said. Did her voice sound a bit scratchy too?

Goose bumps broke out all over Amy's body. *Not with me,* she wanted to shout. Her body screamed something different. "Yeah. Cinnamon would appreciate a softer landing instead of just dropping the saddle onto his back."

She showed Hendrika how to secure the cinch, taking care not to let their hands brush against each other. "All right. Now up you go." She folded her hands to form an improvised ladder. When Rika gathered up her skirt, Amy dropped her gaze to the ground, not wanting to make her think she was staring at her legs. The heat of Hendrika's hand on her shoulder seared through the fabric of her jacket. *Oh, Lord. This is getting worse instead of going away.*

Hendrika finally settled into the saddle, and Amy stepped back and took a deep breath.

One glance at Hendrika's hands clutching the reins reminded her of something. "Oh. Wait." She raced to the tack room, where Mama had hidden the new gloves after bringing them home from town yesterday. Amy had wanted them to be a surprise but hadn't found a quiet moment to give them to Hendrika. *Or maybe you just chickened out.*

When she returned, the gloves held behind her back, Hendrika sat stiffly in the saddle, patting Cinnamon's neck.

Amy stepped up to them. "Here."

Hendrika's fingers slid over the soft leather. "What's this?"

"Gloves."

A tiny smile parted Hendrika's lips and gave Amy a glance at the charming gap between her front teeth. "I can see that. But these aren't yours, are they?"

"They're yours."

Hendrika made no move to take them. "I can't accept these."

"Of course you can." Amy fiddled with the gloves. "They're a thank-you for helping me save the horses from the burning stable."

"You don't need to thank me for that. I would never want anything to happen to Cinnamon or any of the others." Her bare fingers slid over Cinnamon's neck.

"I still want you to have these." Except for Mama and Nattie, Amy didn't have much practice giving presents to women. She had always avoided it, afraid the gesture would be misunderstood. "They're from the whole family, not just from me," she said to make it appear less personal.

Hendrika looked back and forth between the gloves and Amy's face. Finally, with her gaze still resting on Amy, she slipped on the gloves. They were a perfect fit. "Thank you. This is the nicest gift I've ever received."

Amy didn't know what to say to that. She went over to Ruby. "Let's get going."

Cinnamon moved smoothly under her, content to follow Ruby without much direction from his inexperienced rider. Rika looked at her hand holding the reins. The supple leather of the gloves felt good against her fingers.

She couldn't remember ever getting such a nice gift—or any gift at all. Even Willem had never given her more than a bouquet of flowers on their wedding day. What meant even more to her than the gloves themselves was their meaning. Amy accepted her. Her pleasure at the thought mixed with guilt. Every day she spent with the Hamiltons made lying harder.

"Rika," Amy called.

Startled by the use of her nickname, Rika looked up.

Amy pointed toward the river, where a beaver plunged into the water. When it was carried downstream by the current and disappeared from sight, Rika's gaze returned to Amy.

A flush crept up Amy's neck. "I'm sorry. I heard you mention that name to Hannah's son, but it's not proper to use it without permission."

Rika hesitated. Few people had ever been allowed to use her nickname. *And some of them were far less worthy than Amy.* "You can call me Rika if you want."

Amy flushed again. "Really? I didn't want to assume—"

"It's all right," Rika said. "You and your family have been so wonderful to me."

"Oh, yeah. I put you on a horse that promptly threw you off. I yelled at you because you fed the horses too many oats, and you were almost burned to a crisp when you followed me into the burning barn—all within a few short weeks."

Laughter shot up Rika's chest. "Well, considering all of that, maybe you should call me Miss Bruggeman."

Amy blinked at her, then her tense features relaxed into a grin, and finally, she joined in Rika's laughter. Her eyes sparkled with life. When her laughter died down, she looked at Rika for a moment longer. "Phin got really lucky," she murmured.

"What?"

"Oh, nothing." Amy urged Ruby forward. "Did you see the beaver?"

Rika was pretty sure Amy had just paid her a nice compliment. Not used to compliments and unsure of how to handle them from Amy, she decided to let it go. "Just for a moment before the current carried him away. Is the river always this high this time of year?"

"No." A frown replaced Amy's carefree expression. "The mountain snowmelt set in late this year, and with all the rain we had, it adds up to this." She pointed at the fast-flowing river that carried small trees and other debris. "But don't worry. The beaver will be all right. They're great swimmers."

They followed a bend in the river.

Without warning, Amy stopped her mare.

"Whoa!" Rika barely managed to rein in Cinnamon before they barreled into Ruby. "What's going on?"

"Stay back!" Amy shouted and urged Ruby down the bank, leaving Rika to stare after them.

There, in the middle of the river, on a half-immersed island, stood a foal. Water crept up its trembling legs. Its mother pranced back and forth next to it and tried to nudge it into the water, but the foal refused.

They might have been there for hours while the water around them flowed higher and higher. With the debris in the murky stream, crossing to the bank might be dangerous even for the mare.

Rika clutched the reins and watched Amy wrench her lasso from the saddle horn. But the nervous mare was in the way. Even if Amy's rope managed to cross the distance, it couldn't get to the foal.

Without hesitation, Amy directed Ruby forward, and they waded into the brown flood. The current tore at Amy's pant legs. Branches and pieces of wood bobbed on the wild waves, making Ruby toss up her head.

Oh, Lord, please don't let anything happen to her. Rika exhaled a shaky breath when they finally neared the small island.

Just then, a board slammed into Ruby. The mare reared.

The wet saddle provided no hold for Amy. She toppled backward. A splash of water swallowed her.

"No!" Rika pressed her heels to Cinnamon's flanks. At the riverbank, she stopped the gelding. Her gaze darted over the water. *There!*

Amy crawled onto the island. She spat out a mouthful of water and lifted up on her knees.

Thank the Lord. What now? Rika looked around. Ruby had safely made it to the other side of the river, unreachable for Amy and Rika at the moment. The foal's mother waded into the water, scared by Amy's sudden appearance on their little island, but the foal still refused to follow.

Water lapped at Amy's ankles as she got to her feet. She stared at Rika, her arms dangling helplessly.

"Can you swim back?" Rika shouted. "Maybe pull the foal along with you?"

Amy shouted something back, but the roar of the water drowned out her voice.

"What?" Rika cupped one hand around her ear to indicate that she hadn't understood.

"No, I can't," Amy shouted again.

What then? Rika saw no other option. "You got a better idea?"

Frustration carved itself onto Amy's face. "No."

"Then why not try?" With the debris bobbing in the water, it was dangerous, but probably not as dangerous as Rika going after her.

Amy shoved wet locks out of her face. "Because I can't swim."

"Can't swim?" Coldness spread through Rika's limbs. Amy couldn't swim, yet she had ridden into the river to help the foal? A lump of emotion lodged in her throat and prevented her from answering.

"Can you ride back to the ranch and bring help?" Amy shouted.

Rika's thoughts raced. The river was still rising. Water sloshed up the small island, crumbling its edges and causing Amy to take a step back. By the time Rika made it to the ranch and back, the island would have been swallowed up by the torrent—and with it Amy and the foal.

The image of Amy being pulled under by the merciless flood flashed through Rika. If she couldn't swim, she would drown in a matter of seconds. Rika clamped her hand around the reins. "I'm gonna ride over to you."

"No!"

"Yes!"

Amy waved her hands. "This is crazy! What if you get tossed off too?"

"At least I can swim." Unexpected anger made Rika's voice rise over the roaring of the river. She forced herself to calm down, having learned that horses could easily read her emotions and be affected by them. Her feet searched for support in the stirrups, and she pressed her legs to Cinnamon's sides. "Be a good boy now, Cin."

"Start upstream," Amy shouted.

"What?"

"The current will sweep you downstream. Start higher up the river, and let it carry you down to the island."

Rika glanced at a large branch that rushed by on the bobbing waves. *She's right.* Tugging on the reins, she directed Cinnamon upstream.

The gelding pranced along the riverbank, hesitating for a few seconds, but then waded into the water. His hooves slipped on the river bottom, and he scrambled for more secure footing, bringing them into deeper water.

Cold water rose up her legs. Rika gasped. Her hands trembled so much that she almost lost her grip on the reins, but then she glanced at Amy and the foal, and new determination filled her. "Good boy." She patted Cinnamon's neck and urged him onward. Her gaze flitted upstream, keeping watch for any large objects that might slam into them.

The current pulled and tugged at them. Water drenched her up to the hip.

Cinnamon lost his footing, and for a moment, he was swimming. The forces of the river grabbed them and rushed them downstream.

Panic robbed her of breath. She clung to the saddle horn for dear life. *Too fast! We'll be swept past the island!*

Cinnamon stretched his neck, his nose pointing at the island. His muscles worked beneath Rika. As he turned, the water hit them from the side.

Please, please, please, don't let anything hit us now.

Inch by inch, they gained against the forces of the river. Then Cinnamon's hooves found solid ground. He scrambled up the small island.

Amy gripped his bridle with one hand and brought him to a stop.

"Oh, God." Rika's stomach lurched, and she slid from the saddle with numb limbs.

Strong arms caught her and kept her upright. "That was crazy." The hot whisper brushed her ear as Amy pulled her against her equally drenched body.

Words deserted Rika. She clung to Amy for long moments, resting against her body. *How odd.* Here she was, drenched to the bone, standing in the middle of a raging river, and yet she felt safe and at peace. Then cold water crept up her calves. "How are we gonna make it back?" She didn't think for a second that Amy would leave the foal behind. She wouldn't either.

Amy let go and pulled back. "We'll ride double and tow the foal along. I'm pretty sure the mare will follow on her own." She again formed a ladder with her hands. "Hurry."

With trembling knees, Rika heaved herself into the saddle.

Amy took the rope off Cin's saddle, slipped a loop around the foal's neck, and then climbed up behind her.

The foal's scared squeal was nearly drowned out by the noise of the water.

The mare circled them and nudged her foal toward the river as if she understood what they were doing.

Amy's arms slid around Rika to grip the reins. The embrace forced back the panic that clutched Rika's insides. "Give me the rope," Rika said, now calm enough to think. "You take the reins, and I'll take care of the foal."

The drenched leather of Amy's gloves tightened around the rope. Then she handed over the rope and the responsibility for the foal. "Keep it tight."

Rika grabbed it with both hands, trusting Amy to keep her in the saddle.

Cinnamon walked forward. Water splashed and drenched them.

Behind them, the foal squealed as the water tore at it. Its little hooves lost traction, and the wild-eyed foal was forced to swim.

Amy's arms tightened around Rika when they reached the halfway point between the little island and the bank. The water rose up Cinnamon's sides, and then he was swimming too.

The tug on the rope increased. Rika's arm muscles screamed in protest. She glanced over her shoulder. "The foal won't make it to the other side." The little head dipped under water, then resurfaced with a panicked squeal when Rika pulled on the rope. "It's getting weaker."

The mare behind them whinnied as her foal went under again, despite Rika's tight grip on the rope.

Cinnamon's hooves found solid ground, but now they were dragging the foal. It had stopped swimming.

Rika tried to duck beneath Amy's arm and slide out of the saddle.

Amy's arms clutched at her. "No! What are you doing?"

"The foal is drowning," Rika shouted. "Take the rope, and let me go!"

A wild curse wrenched from Amy's lips, but she let go.

Shivering, Rika slid into the water. The torrent gripped her, tearing at her, and she grabbed the rope. Water burned in her eyes and made her cough as she slid down the rope. Her hands found the foal's head and struggled to keep it above water.

Something large appeared in her line of sight.

A fallen tree rushed at them.

Rika kicked with her legs. *No! Get away!* She let go of the rope to grip the foal's neck and drag it with her, away from the tree.

Branches scratched and clawed at her like a wild animal, but Rika never let go. Her skirt, sodden with water, threatened to pull her down.

A powerful surge shoved her head underwater.

Rika let go of the foal, afraid she would drag it down with her. She struggled against the force of the water with hands and feet. Her lungs burned. *Air!*

A strong hand grabbed the back of her dress.

Coughing, she resurfaced. She was pulled against Cinnamon's warm side. Seconds later, her feet touched the ground. She struggled up the bank and sank into the mud.

With a splash, Amy landed next to her. "Rika!" Her hands flew up and down Rika's body as if to make sure she was still in one piece. "Rika!"

She wanted to answer, wanted to tell Amy that she was all right, but all she could do was gasp for breath. Her throat burned, and her arms and legs felt as if they weighed a ton.

Gently, Amy turned her around and knelt over her. When their gazes met, Amy blew out a breath. "Rika," she said again and again. "Oh, God, Rika. When you let go of the rope and were gone, I thought..."

Rika opened her mouth to tell her she was fine but stopped when hot breath brushed over her lips and trembling hands framed her face.

Gulping, Rika stared at Amy, transfixed by the intense green eyes just inches from hers. Thoughts swirled through her head faster than the foaming torrent shot through the riverbed, but she couldn't grasp even one of them.

Then all contact between them was gone. Amy pulled back with a startled cry.

It felt like the moment she had been forced to let go of the rope, and she stared at Amy, disoriented. Again struggling for breath, she sat up. *What just happened?* "Amy? What...?" Her voice was rough with river water and confusion. "Are you all right?"

Amy wiped her face with sodden gloves. "Yes, yes, of course. I'm just glad we all made it out of that damn river alive."

The sound of hooves squishing through the mud pulled Rika out of her jumbled thoughts. "The foal!" She glanced around.

"He's fine," Amy said. "You saved him when that tree almost hit him."

The foal stood farther up the bank, its flanks shaking. His mother ran her muzzle all over him. Cinnamon waited with dragging reins not far from them.

Rika shivered. "What now?"

Amy went to check on the horses. She didn't look at Rika. "You could ride to the ranch and send one of the boys back with a horse for me."

"And leave you here on your own?" Rika didn't like the thought. Her imagination showed her pictures of what might happen to Amy while she was gone. She shivered. "Why don't we ride double? I'm sure Cinnamon can carry both of us if we take it slow."

Without answering, Amy continued to slide her hands over Cinnamon's sides and legs. She checked the saddle before turning back to Rika. "All right. Come on, then." She mounted, pulled her foot from the stirrup, and reached down for Rika's hand.

The damp leather of their gloves met in a strong grasp.

Rika put her foot in the stirrup and pulled up her sodden skirt with her free hand.

Amy's gaze dropped to the saddle horn.

When Rika landed on the horse behind her, Amy urged Cinnamon into a fast walk.

The sudden forward motion made Rika grab Amy's hips to avoid getting tossed off. She felt Amy flinch and let go. "Are you hurt?" Her own body ached and was probably covered with scratches and bruises from her encounter with the tree.

"No." Amy's voice rumbled through her. "It's just... Your gloves are wet, and your hands are freezing."

"Oh." Rika curled her fingers into fists. "No wonder." She laughed shakily. "My whole body feels frozen."

Cinnamon trudged up a hill, jostling Rika and nearly throwing her off. "Um, Amy..."

Amy sighed. "Hold on to me."

Rika threw one arm around Amy, stopping her backward slide. She tugged off one glove, then the other with her teeth and tucked them into the saddlebags before she slid her now gloveless hands around Amy. "Better?"

A shaky breath vibrated through the body under her hands. "Um. Yes."

Amy's jacket was dripping, and her shirt was as wet as Rika's dress, but heat still emanated from her. Rika's arms instantly felt warmer than the rest of her body. She held on for dear life, partly not to be thrown off, partly to share Amy's comforting warmth. "Aren't you cold?"

A snort of laughter escaped Amy. "No. Not particularly."

Rika let her gaze trail over the muddy fields and turned to look back at the river. "Amy, look!" She clutched Amy's sides. "The mare and the foal are following us." She had worried about leaving them behind but thought the foal was too exhausted to make the trip back to the ranch.

"I know. Horses are herd animals. They don't want to be left behind."

"Will the foal be all right?" She watched as he broke into a stiff-legged gallop to keep up with Cinnamon and his mother.

"He'll be fine." Amy's still gloved hand stroked hers for a moment, then retreated. "Thanks to you."

Amy's praise, her gratefulness, warmed Rika's cold body from the inside out.

Finally, after what seemed like hours, Cinnamon stopped in the ranch yard. A buckboard with two horses stood tied to the porch rail.

When Rika slid out of the saddle, the door to the main house opened and Nattie stepped outside, followed by Hannah. "Amy, look who's here to—" Nattie pressed a hand to her mouth when she took in their sodden clothes and the mud-crusted horses. "What happened?"

"Later." Amy slid out of the saddle and pushed past her. "Rika needs to get into some dry clothes first, and I need to go out and find Ruby."

The thought of Amy crossing the river to find Ruby made Rika's heart pound. She hurried after Amy and grabbed her arm. "Send one of the ranch hands."

Amy shook her head. "This is my responsibility."

Anger heated Rika's skin. "Being responsible is one thing, but this is just dumb. Ruby is on the other side of the river, and you can't even swim!" The words were out before she remembered that Amy was running the ranch and she was just a guest. But she refused to take them back. She remembered too well how scared she had been when Amy had tumbled into the raging river.

"You still can't swim?" Hannah asked.

Amy shrugged and freed herself from Rika's grip. "Mama can't swim, and Papa doesn't like to either, so no one ever taught us."

"Then she's right," Hannah said. "Send one of your men."

Not waiting for a decision, Nattie gathered up her skirts. "I'll get Toby and take care of the horses."

Amy's jaw bunched, but she didn't stop Nattie from leading away Cinnamon and the mare. The foal followed them to the stable.

"Come on, you two," Hannah said. "Let's get you into some dry clothes."

Rika pointed at the cabin. "I'll go and change into one of my own skirts."

"Good idea." Amy smiled for the first time since she had seen the foal on the small island. "Because that," she pointed at the dress Rika was wearing, "was my last clean dress."

"You rode into the river, even though you can't swim?" Hannah asked after Amy finished her tale. She had followed Amy into her room, too impatient to hear what had happened to wait until Amy finished changing.

With Hannah's back to her, Amy struggled out of her sodden pants. "What was I supposed to do? Watch the foal drown?" Her shirt followed the pants, and she ran a washrag over the mud spatters on her skin. When Hannah turned to answer, Amy felt her friend's gaze on her body, but this time, it didn't send shivers across her skin. Her heart continued with its steady beat. It no longer sped up at the thought of Hannah looking at her half-dressed body.

Maybe I'm finally getting over this unnatural reaction to women. Then she remembered the feel of Rika's hands on her hips on the way home. And she had almost kissed her down by the river. *Lord, what were you thinking?* She ducked her head and hunched her shoulders. Rika was a woman. And not just any woman, but Phin's future wife. Amy's body didn't listen to that admonishment, though. The thought of Rika's closeness raised goose bumps all over her skin. Her back to Hannah, she trailed her index finger across her lips, which had almost touched Rika's, then shook her head to get rid of the unwanted feelings.

"How did you get back to the bank after Ruby ran off?" Hannah asked.

"Rika rode after me." Amy's nails bit into her palms. The helplessness of those moments gripped her again. "She can barely ride, and she had promised to stay out of the way if something unexpected happened, but she rode into the river just the same."

"What was she supposed to do? Watch you drown?" Hannah asked, repeating Amy's words about the foal.

Amy knew she never would have made it out of the river alive, much less rescued the foal, if not for Rika. But still, watching her struggle to stay in the saddle and then seeing her be pulled down by the river... She shivered.

A soft touch to her arm jerked her back to the present. "Lord, that must have been so hard. I bet it brought back some awful memories for you." Hannah rubbed her hand along Amy's bare arm.

No butterflies. Amy slipped on a dry shirt. "You mean when I was swept away with the Buchanans' house when I was fourteen?" That had been the day she had first realized that she felt for Hannah what other girls felt for their beaus.

"That and the Wakarusa River, when your mother almost drowned," Hannah said.

Images of a bobbing raft on a wild river drifted across Amy's inner eye. Her heart jumped. "It's one of the few things I remember about our journey to Oregon." She barely remembered anything about her early childhood. Mama and Papa didn't talk about anything that had happened before they traveled to Oregon, so she had no way of knowing which of the vague images were real and which were just products of her imagination.

"I was eleven, so you must have been three or four," Hannah said. "You were so sad about losing Rosie."

"Rosie," Amy repeated. A half-forgotten memory resurfaced. Her doll had fallen into the river, and they couldn't replace it on the Oregon Trail. Her gaze veered to the shelf with the carved horses. *That's when Papa started making them for me.*

"Yes." Hannah giggled and poked her in the side. "Once upon a time, Amy Hamilton played with dolls, just like any other girl. Don't worry. I won't tell your ranch hands."

Amy poked her back, and for a moment, their friendship felt like it had years ago, before her confusing reactions made Amy awkward around Hannah. *Maybe these feelings for Rika will go away too.*

A memory of full lips and warm breath flashed through her, and she sighed. *Probably not anytime soon.*

A horse whinnied outside.

Amy rushed to the window. "It's Ruby! She made it back on her own."

Hannah hurried over and hugged her, and for the first time in years, Amy held her without worrying whether it was appropriate.

FORT BOISE, IDAHO
MAY 20, 1868

"THERE IT IS." LUKE POINTED at the wooden palisades. She had never been so glad to reach a fort—not because she felt threatened by Indians and the fort provided safety, but because she could now turn around and go home.

The Hamilton horses streamed in through the gate, and Luke received instructions to herd them to an empty corral. When the last horse loped into the corral, the tension drained from her shoulders.

"Where can I find Colonel Lundgren?" She wanted to receive her payment and be on her way. If Phin and Charlie agreed, they would restock their supplies, give the horses a few hours of rest, and then head out.

"You need to talk to the quartermaster, Captain Kelling." Lieutenant Moylan pointed to a sandstone building. "He's in charge of buying horses."

Luke dismounted and waved at Phin to follow her, leaving Charlie with the horses. She knocked on the door and stepped into the quartermaster's office.

A tall man in uniform sat behind a desk and wrote numbers in a ledger.

"Captain Kelling?" Luke asked.

He looked up and nodded.

"Luke Hamilton. I'm bringing the horses Colonel Lundgren ordered."

The captain flipped a few pages in the ledger. "Ah, yes. A dozen Appaloosa geldings. Thirty dollars per head."

Thirty? Luke rubbed the back of her neck. "There must be a mistake. Colonel Lundgren and I exchanged letters, and we agreed on forty dollars for each of the geldings and sixty dollars for Midnight, his personal mount." She took the last letter from her pocket and slid it in front of Kelling.

He didn't look at the piece of paper. "It says thirty dollars in my ledger."

"Then your ledger is wrong," she said, trying not to lose her patience. Over the years, Nora taught her to read and write, so she knew what price was recorded in the letter. "If you ask the colonel, I'm sure he'll clear up the misunderstanding."

Kelling glanced at the numbers in his book. "There is no misunderstanding, and I don't need to ask the colonel. Thirty dollars per head. Take it or leave it."

Phin exchanged a helpless glance with her.

"Then I'll leave it—and you get to explain to your superior why you couldn't procure the horses he needs." Three hundred and sixty dollars was still a lot of money, but Luke refused to accept less than what the horses were worth. Years of hard work went into breeding, raising, and training them. "Come on, Phin. Let's go." She turned on her heel and strode to the door, hoping he would call her back. What would she do if he didn't? She couldn't return home empty-handed. She reached for the door handle.

"Wait," Kelling said. "Maybe we can compromise. What do you say to thirty-five per head?"

That bastard! She was sure the rest of the money would go into his own pocket and the colonel would never learn about it. "I'm saying no."

"Forty dollars is a lot of money for a horse," he said.

"Not for one of mine. These aren't second-class, untrained colts. They were carefully selected and trained to be cavalry horses. Colonel Lundgren knows their worth, so I'll go and talk to him now." She swung open the door.

"Wait," Kelling said.

Luke turned around.

The captain's jaw muscles tightened. She could almost hear his teeth grind against each other. "Forty dollars is practically daylight robbery," he said. "But fine. If you somehow got the colonel to agree on it..."

"He agreed." She held up the colonel's letter but bit her tongue and forced herself not to say anything else. Making enemies wouldn't help her family or the ranch.

He slammed his ledger shut. "All right. I'll inspect the horses, and if they are as good as you say, I'll get you the money."

Luke gave a terse nod. She followed Kelling out the door and to the corral, where he looked at the horses' hooves, checked their teeth, and slid his hands over their backs.

He might be a son of a bitch, but at least he knows something about horses.

Kelling couldn't hide the gleam of appreciation in his eyes when he looked at the Hamilton horses. "All right," he finally said. "Forty dollars per head."

"Sixty for Midnight." Luke pointed at the black gelding.

A dark glare hit her, but she didn't look away.

"You'll have to sign for the money," Kelling said.

"Not a problem. I'm keeping my side of the agreement." She let the words hang between them as she followed him back to the quartermaster's office.

Captain Kelling walked to his desk and opened a drawer. A key unlocked a wooden box, and he counted out twenty-five double eagles.

Bastard. Just the fact that he had five hundred dollars right there told her he knew about her arrangement with Colonel Lundgren. Sharp parting words lingered on her tongue, but she swallowed them. She had her money. Now she just wanted to get out of Fort Boise and back to her family. She pocketed the money, nodded at Phin to follow her, and walked through the door. "Here." She handed Phin twelve of the golden coins. "It's safer if you hold on to half of the money until we're home." If something happened to one of them, her family would still have half of the money.

Instead of pocketing the coins, Phin stared at them. "That's a lot of money."

"And I have a lot of trust in you."

Their gazes met. Silent understanding passed between them, and then Phin nodded.

"All right." Luke clapped him on the back. "Let's buy some provisions and go home."

"Dammit!" The rough curse drifted through the gray half-light of dusk.

Luke paused outside of the sutler's store.

Muffled groans and grunts came from a dark alley. Boots scraped over the packed ground.

"Hold her still," a man hissed.

Clothing rustled.

Luke dropped the sack of provisions and hurried into the alley to see what was going on. Her eyes adjusted to the darkness, and she stopped.

Two men knelt in the alley and forced the struggling limbs of a Shoshoni woman to the ground. A third man stood over her and fumbled with his pants.

Normally, Luke stayed away from fights that weren't her own, but she couldn't ignore this.

One of the kneeling men looked up. He jerked when he saw her. "Bill!"

The third man, his pants half-unbuttoned, turned, and Luke recognized one of the soldiers who had wanted to drive away her horses and blame the Shoshoni. He studied her with cool eyes. "You can have a turn with her—after we're done."

Blood pounded through Luke's head, and she spat out her words. "Let her go."

"Don't get your feathers in a ruffle," Bill said. "She's just an Injun."

"Let her go," Luke repeated. Her hand rested on the grip of her revolver.

The three men exchanged glances.

Luke tensed. She kept her gaze on Bill, the apparent leader.

"Back off." Bill straightened to his full height. "She's not worth fighting over."

"If she's not worth it, then just walk away," Luke said.

Bill's gaze flickered down to her weapon hand, then back up to her eyes.

The Shoshoni woman took advantage of their distraction. She freed one of her feet and kicked out. Her foot hit the back of Bill's knee.

Mud spattered when Bill crashed down.

One of the other men drew his revolver. A flash from the revolver's muzzle lit up the alley, and a bullet whizzed past Luke. Chips of sandstone sliced her cheek.

Luke swung up her revolver.

Boom!

The man went down, screaming and clutching his thigh.

"Stop," Luke yelled. She aimed her weapon at the second man but didn't fire. If she could help it, she didn't want to shoot anyone else.

Heavy footsteps approached. "What's going on?" Sergeant Johnson shouldered past her.

Relief trickled through her. "These three soldiers," she spat out the word because they didn't deserve the title, "tried to force themselves on a woman."

"What woman?"

She looked around. The woman had disappeared in the chaos. *Maybe that's a good thing.* Luke hoped she would be safe from the soldiers in the future.

"Walters," Sergeant Johnson shouted. "Goddamnit, button your pants!"

The man named Bill flinched and did up his buttons. "We didn't do anything, Sergeant."

"Yeah," his friend said. "No woman here, see?"

The third man groaned and pressed his hands on his thigh to stop the bleeding.

"I'll take Mister Hamilton's word over yours any day of the week, Walters," Sergeant Johnson said. "But I'll let our superiors decide what to do with your useless asses." He waved at two of his soldiers to drag away the injured man. "Come on. I bet Captain Kelling will be happy to throw you in the brig."

Luke groaned. *Oh, wonderful.* Of all the men in the fort, it had to be Captain Kelling who would decide on a punishment for the three would-be rapists. If he heard that Luke was involved, he might decide that there had never been a woman in that alley. She gritted her teeth and prepared for another battle.

Traveling home would have to wait for a while.

HAMILTON HORSE RANCH
BAKER PRAIRIE, OREGON
MAY 21, 1868

S UNLIGHT DANCED OVER THE MOLALLA River as it meandered through the valley, a murmuring rivulet instead of a raging torrent.

Amy stopped at the river's edge to allow Ruby a mouthful of water. While her horse drank, she uncorked her canteen and took a swig. Cool water trickled down her parched throat. She had been in the saddle since sunup—her routine for the past few days. *Since you were stupid enough to almost kiss Rika.* As much as she tried not to think about it, the thought intruded again and again.

She told herself she wasn't really avoiding Rika. Dozens of tasks kept her out on the range: checking springs and waterholes to make sure they weren't clogged with debris after the flood, riding line to keep the horses from drifting off the Hamilton land, and seeing how far along the hay was.

Yeah, sure. Truth be told, the main ranch would have kept her busy too. The shed could do with a new coat of paint, and Phin's cabin needed to have a wood floor installed, but she'd decided to leave that to the boys.

Thinking about Phin's cabin brought back images of Rika. With an exasperated grunt, Amy lifted the reins and directed Ruby away from the river. She rode along the gurgling stream bordering the eastern corner of their land. Something rustled in the hazel bushes ahead, and a squirrel skittered across the path.

Ruby tossed up her head and pranced sideways.

"None of that, girl." She stroked Ruby's neck, then pulled the mare's head around and urged her up a hill.

One of their line shacks lay below. The small cabin held enough supplies to feed a ranch hand for a few days so he wouldn't have to return to the main house. Dusk was settling over the hills; maybe she would stay at the line shack tonight.

She had done it before, so Mama wouldn't worry as long as she came home before breakfast.

She urged Ruby into a gallop, glad to have something to do other than think about Rika. As she neared the cabin, she slowed to a lope, then a walk.

The cabin's corral lay empty, and the grass grew high.

Still, the fine hairs on the back of her neck prickled.

Ruby's ears flicked forward.

"Someone here, girl?" Maybe a traveling man or a wrangler in search of a job. Amy didn't mind. They were welcome to a few of the supplies, as long as they left a coin to pay for what they had taken.

She rode up to the cabin, a greeting on her lips, but something held her back from calling out. This time of year, it was better to be careful and watch out for strangers who were handy with a lariat and a running iron. Around here, even rustlers knew the worth of a Hamilton horse.

A quick glance showed her that the pile of stacked wood in front of the cabin had gotten smaller. *Someone is here. Someone without a horse or Ruby would whinny a greeting.* One name shot through her mind: Adam. Any other traveler would have a horse. *Don't be silly.* She shook her head. Adam was long gone. This was probably just a down-on-his-luck wrangler who had lost his horse.

Nevertheless, she slid her hand down to the revolver at her side. Since the fire, she never rode out without Papa's spare revolver.

Before she could reach her weapon, the click of a hammer echoed through the silence.

Fear stabbed her chest, robbing her of breath. *Steady.* She slid her gaze to the source of the sound and tensed her muscles against the impact of a bullet.

Nothing happened. Not yet.

"I told you you'd regret firing me," someone said from behind her.

Adam. She clenched her teeth until her jaw muscles hurt. "I didn't fire you," she said, trying to keep her voice calm. "You gave your notice because you didn't want to work for me. So let's just go our separate ways without any bad feelings." This wasn't the moment to talk about the barn he'd set afire or his attack on Mama.

He didn't answer. His footsteps circled around until he was facing her. Long stubble covered his cheeks, and the glint in his eyes made him appear even wilder and more dangerous.

Amy flicked her gaze to his weapon. *If I charge him, maybe I can kick away his revolver.*

He waved two fingers toward his chest. "Oh, yeah, come on. Try it." The corner of his mouth twitched. "Don't think I wouldn't shoot a woman. If you wear pants like a man and act like a man, I'll shoot you like a man."

Amy hesitated. He would shoot. But if he didn't kill her now, what would he do to her? What was he planning?

"Get off the horse."

She didn't move, knowing that she would be at his mercy once she was on the ground.

"Get off the damn horse, or I'll shoot her!" His revolver swung down, now aiming at Ruby.

"All right, all right. I'll get down. Don't hurt her." Amy wrapped the reins around the saddle horn and swung her leg over the cantle. If she dropped down, Ruby would be between Adam and her, blocking his view. If she could draw her revolver...

"No." Adam's voice stopped her. "Not on that side. Climb off on my side." The muzzle of the revolver swung back up and pointed at the middle of her chest.

Grinding her teeth, Amy dismounted on Ruby's right side. She sent Ruby away with a clap to her rump. If Adam shot at her, at least Ruby wouldn't be hit.

Ruby trotted to the corral but then stopped and looked back at Amy.

Home, Ruby. Go home and get help. But she knew she was Ruby's herd at the moment. Ruby wouldn't leave unless something scared her off.

"Hands up. Come over here," Adam said.

She had no choice. Her thoughts raced as she stepped toward Adam, but with his revolver pointing at her, she couldn't do anything.

His weapon still aimed at her, Adam used his free hand to reach beneath her jacket. His fingers slid over her body, making her shiver with revulsion. "Get your hands off me!"

"Oh, come on. You're enjoying this." His grin widened. Then his searching hand found the revolver she carried against her hip. "That's what I thought." He took the weapon. "Did no one ever tell you little girls shouldn't play with revolvers?" He tossed it away and prepared to step back.

No! If she wanted to survive, she needed to stay close to him to fight for the revolver. If he stepped out of reach, he could shoot her from a safe distance. She lurched forward and hammered both fists at the spot where his neck met the shoulder of his weapon arm.

Her well-placed blow hit Adam before he could react. It worked, just as Papa had taught her. The revolver dropped from his hand.

With a cry, Amy dived for it.

The tip of Adam's boot caught her in the ribs.

Pain lanced through her, and she fell back. Despite the throbbing pain, she groped for the revolver.

"Oh, no, you don't!" Adam snatched her collar and dragged her to her knees.

Amy struggled, but his grip was too strong. She couldn't break free.

"Thought you could best me, huh?" Adam sneered, bending down.

Had he found the revolver?

As his weight shifted, his grip on her collar loosened.

Amy rammed her head into his stomach.

They fell and rolled. She stabbed her hand forward, trying to shove her fingers into his eyes, but Adam jerked his head to the side at the last moment.

Her blow glanced off his cheekbone.

He grunted. With his greater strength, he rolled them around again.

Agony shot through Amy when his weight pressed down on her. His tobacco breath washed over her face. She tried to hit his eyes, his ears, his throat, but Adam's big hands clamped around her wrists, shackling them to the ground.

Get off me! Under the weight of his body, Amy struggled to suck air into her lungs. She thrust upward with her knee, driving between his legs, as Papa had taught her.

Adam's eyes widened, his body stiffening against hers. An unhealthy flush shot up his neck. His mouth fell open, and he howled.

Yes! Her hands were free. Amy shoved at his chest and crawled out from beneath him. Her heart slammed against her ribcage. *The revolver!* She had to get her hands on a weapon before Adam recovered. Her gaze darted left and right.

All around them, the grass was trampled, but no metal glinted anywhere.

She scrambled to her feet.

Adam grabbed her ankle. With one sharp tug, Amy crashed to the ground. She spat out earth and clawed the grass. Facedown, she flailed her hands, searching for the revolver, a stick, a stone, any weapon at all.

Cold steel pressed against the side of her head.

Amy froze. Somehow, Adam had found either his revolver or hers. Her arms dropped to the ground. Pain flared through her ribs. "Adam," she said through a constricted throat. "Don't be stupid. If you kill me, my father will string you from the tallest tree in Oregon. And that's if Mama doesn't get you in front of her rifle first."

They both knew it was true. No one, not even the law, would stop her parents if Adam hurt her.

Adam grasped her shoulder and pulled her around. He leaned over her, his face crimson and his eyes wild. "Yeah, but I bet Mama's pretty little head is still hurting good. And dear Papa isn't here now, is he?" Adam chuckled. The pressure at her temple increased, and his hate-filled eyes stared at her from just inches away.

"No," an unfamiliar voice said from somewhere behind Adam. "But I am. And so is my Spencer carbine."

Oh, thank God! Amy trembled, this time with relief, not fear.

Adam jerked his head toward the voice, still pinning Amy so she couldn't see her savior.

The voice was female. A hysterical chuckle bubbled up Amy's throat. *Adam being defeated by a woman again.* It was almost as good as knowing she would survive.

"Drop the revolver," the woman said.

When Adam hesitated, another voice came from beside the first one. "Drop the weapon and step back, or you'll be too dead to be sorry." The voice was softer than the first one, but equally determined. The hammer of another weapon clicked.

Cursing, Adam withdrew the revolver from Amy's temple and hurled it away. Moments later, tanned hands dragged him off.

"Careful," Amy said. "My revolver has to be somewhere around here."

"I got it," the softer voice said.

Amy sat up and looked at her saviors. She'd thought the voice of the person with the Spencer carbine was that of a woman, but the hat, the pants, and the short hair told her she was wrong. The man held his rifle on Adam while his female companion hurried over and tied Adam's hands.

When Amy tried to stand, the woman pressed her down. "Stay down until you catch your breath, Amy."

"How do you know my name?" There was something familiar about the stranger, the way the sunlight reflected off her golden-silvery hair, the curve of her lips when she smiled. Had they met before?

"Because you look like your mother. And you fight like your father."

Tess blinked at the young woman. With her green eyes, flaming red hair, and freckles sprinkled over a creamy-golden complexion, the young woman staring up at her looked almost exactly like Nora. *Or at least like Nora did when she first came to work for me.*

Then Tess took the time to study her more closely. Denim pants and mud-spattered chaps covered muscular legs, and Tess caught glimpses of a sturdy body beneath a canvas jacket and a men's shirt. A piece of leather could barely restrain a mass of wind-tangled hair. During the struggle, a few tendrils had escaped and now fell into her face.

"How do you know my parents?" Instead of the wary caution Nora had often displayed, her daughter's face showed dazed curiosity.

Not knowing what Nora had told her daughters about her past, Tess thought it best to keep things simple. "I'm Tess Swenson, an old friend from Missouri. I knew you when you were just a three-year-old girl."

Did Amy remember anything about that time? Did she remember living in the brothel?

Lines of concentration formed on Amy's brow, but no sign of recognition lit up her eyes.

Maybe it's better that way. Tess reached down and offered her hand.

"Are you here to visit Mama and Papa?" Amy asked, accepting the hand and struggling to her feet.

"We're here to see your mother and meet you girls," Tess said. "We already met Luke in The Dalles."

Amy beamed. For a moment, she looked like three-year-old Amy when someone had given her an apple for the horses. "So he didn't run into any problems? All the horses are in good shape?"

"I didn't ask about the horses, but Luke seemed all right. He was only worried about his family and the ranch."

"We're doing just fine." Amy straightened and then clutched her side. An expression of pain rushed over her face.

Tess gripped her elbow. "Oh, yeah. Just fine. I can see that." This young woman was as stubborn as her parents. "Did he hurt you?"

"No. I'm just a little winded," Amy said.

If we hadn't gotten lost searching for the ranch and stopped at the cabin to ask for directions... Tess shuddered. "Come on. Let's get you home." It was time to keep her promise and take care of Luke's "chicks."

Each of Ruby's steps sent waves of pain through Amy, but she struggled not to let it show.

"Who is he?" the man Tess had introduced as Frankie asked, pointing his rifle at Adam. "Why did he attack you?" His voice was oddly soft for a man—so soft that Amy had mistaken it for that of a woman, but the hands holding the rifle looked as if they knew how to fight.

"Adam was one of our ranch hands, but he didn't like working for a woman," Amy said. Everything had been fine with Papa in charge, but so much had happened since Amy had taken over. She longed for Papa's return, but at the same time, she wondered what he would say about all of this. Would he think she wasn't capable of running the ranch on her own?

Tess directed her mare closer to Amy and threw a grim smile over her shoulder. "Oh, don't we know that situation. Most men hate taking orders from a woman."

"Mama had to threaten him with a rifle. She chased him off the ranch, and in revenge, he attacked her and set fire to our barn." A shiver raced down Amy's spine when she thought of that night, the panicked squeals of the horses in the burning stable, Rika's skirt catching fire, and then Mama stumbling toward them, holding her head.

"Nora!" Tess blanched. "Is she all right?"

"She's fine. She always said she's got a hard head." Amy forced a smile. Mama wouldn't want her friend to worry about her.

Tess chuckled as the color returned to her face. "Oh, yes, that she did." Her grin deepened the lines around her eyes and mouth, telling Amy that Tess was probably twice her own age, but Amy still found her beautiful.

"You can't prove it was me," Adam shouted from his place running next to the three horses.

"We can prove that you were about to shoot a defenseless woman," Frankie said. "Now shut up and save your breath for keeping up, or I'll drag you behind my horse all the way to the ranch."

"Let me go, goddammit!" Adam struggled against the rope that bound his wrists together. He spat in their direction. "This is none of your damn business. No one will believe a word you say. I have friends in the area, and you're just some stranger."

Frankie jerked on the rope, almost throwing Adam off his feet.

"Oh, Frankie is not just some stranger," Tess said. "She's a railroad marshal."

"She?" Adam and Amy echoed.

Amy's head jerked around. Pain surged along her ribs, and she barely resisted the impulse to clutch her side. Instead, she looked Frankie up and down.

She wore pants, jacket, hat, and sturdy boots. *But so do I, and I'm not a man.* But not even Amy wore her hair as short as Frankie, and she bowed to convention and wore a dress or a split riding skirt to town.

Frankie swept off her hat and gave a bow. Her eyes twinkled. "Frances Callaghan, at your service."

Why didn't I see it before? Frankie's salt-and-pepper hair was a lick too long, and her coat fit too snugly across her chest to pass herself off as a man. The gentle curve of her hips beneath the worn gun belt said "woman."

"Goddamn women!" Adam cursed. "Has the world gone crazy?"

Another jerk on the rope silenced him.

Amy couldn't stop staring even though she knew it was rude. She had never met a woman like Frankie. "Women can become railroad marshals in the East?" Maybe the East wasn't such a bad place after all.

"Not usually. I'm the only one I know of," Frankie said. "But I had some success as a Pinkerton detective, and that convinced the railroad bosses to hire me."

A few of the stories Nattie read to them in the evenings starred Pinkerton agents. In the stories, they protected people and money transports, tracked down dangerous outlaws, and solved train robberies. Amy never imagined someone would hire a woman to do those things. Even more amazing was that Mama and Papa knew people like Frankie—and had never told their daughters about it.

Amy was still studying Frankie when they reached the ranch.

In the fading light of dusk, Amy made out a figure sitting in the rocking chair on the veranda. She didn't need a second glance to know who it was. Mama often kept a lookout for Papa and her when they were late coming in from the range.

At the sound of hoofbeats, the door opened and Rika and Nattie slipped outside.

The light from Nattie's lantern reflected off the rifle in Mama's hands.

"Mama," Amy called out. "It's all right. It's me."

Frankie stopped her horse in front of the hitching rail and jerked on the rope.

Adam nearly tumbled into the water trough. Gasping for breath, he landed on his knees in front of Mama.

"Oh, look what the cat dragged in!" Hank hurried across the ranch yard and yanked Adam to his feet. "What's that little bastard doing here? I thought he'd be all the way to Canada by now."

"Amy?" Mama jumped up from the rocking chair. "What did you do? You hunted him down?" Her gaze turned to ice when she looked at Adam. "Or did you lurk in the darkness and attack her from behind, like you did me? God help me, if you hurt Amy…"

"I'm fine, Mama," Amy said. "I came across Adam at a line shack. And look who else I met." She pointed at Tess and Frankie, hoping their presence would keep Mama from asking too many questions.

Mama slid her gaze over Amy and then squinted in the dim light. "Who's that?" The barrel of her rifle pointed in Tess and Frankie's direction.

"Don't tell me I've gotten so old that you don't recognize me anymore," Tess said.

Mama's rifle trembled before she put it down. "T-Tess? Tess Swenson?"

"In person." Tess slid out of the saddle.

Then both women flew across the ranch yard and fell into each other's arms.

Amy used the distraction to hide her pained grimace when she dismounted. Holding on to Ruby's bridle, she watched Mama and Tess. Mama got along with everyone, but with the exception of Bernice, she wasn't really close to any of the neighbor women. Years ago, Amy had asked her if she had a best friend—and without hesitation, Mama said that Papa was her best friend. The words touched Amy deeply. She longed for the same thing: a sweetheart who was also her best friend.

The tight embrace looked as if Tess was more than a long-forgotten acquaintance. As Amy watched, another image rose from the recesses of her memory: Mama and a younger Tess standing arm in arm in front of a piano, singing Christmas carols. *Was Tess a neighbor, back in Missouri?* She tried to remember more, but nothing came.

Tess and Mama stepped back to look at each other, but their reunion was interrupted by loud cursing as Adam struggled to break free of Hank's grip.

"Get that man out of my sight before I shoot him," Mama said, her eyes as wild and determined as their dog's when Hunter took on a coyote attacking the hens.

"Is there somewhere to keep him until I can bring him to Oregon City in the morning?" Frankie asked.

Amy again marveled at Frankie's confidence. She spoke as if she didn't expect anyone to object to her actions, as unusual as it was for a woman to transport a prisoner on her own.

"Oh, don't worry about him," Hank said, a growl in his voice. "The boys and I will take damn good care of him. We'll have a nice little reunion, right, Adam-boy?"

Adam fought and cursed, but Hank had a firm grip on his bound arms. He wasn't gentle when he shoved Adam across the ranch yard and toward the bunkhouse.

A glance at the blackened grass where the old stable once stood smothered any compassion Amy might have for him.

"What are you doing here?" Mama turned back to Tess. "I thought you were in Montana, freezing your behinds off." Before Tess could answer, Mama hugged her again. When she finally let go, her gaze fell on Frankie.

Amy held her breath. *Is Frankie an old friend too? Does Mama know Frankie is a woman?*

Frankie dismounted and took off her hat in greeting.

"Oh, you must be Frank." With a friendly smile, Mama stepped closer, then froze and let her gaze travel down her body.

Smiling, Frankie shook the limp hand. "Call me Frankie."

"Frankie is a railroad marshal, Mama," Amy said when she couldn't stand the stunned silence anymore.

"I know," Mama said. "But it seems we have some catching up to do on other topics." She nudged Tess, and the smile finally returned to her face.

Tess chuckled. "That's exactly what Luke said too."

"You met him along the way?" Mama's gaze had been warm and welcoming before, but now she looked at Tess as if she was the most important thing in the world—or brought news of that most important thing.

"Yes. He made it safely to The Dalles and said to tell you not to worry."

New energy filled Mama's steps as she walked to the house, her arm still looped through Tess's. "Let's find a place for you to stay, and then you must fill me in on everything. I've got so many questions."

"We could stay at a hotel in town," Tess said.

"Baker Prairie doesn't have a hotel," Amy said. Besides, she didn't want Tess and Frankie to leave so soon. Never had someone as fascinating as these two strangers visited the ranch, and she wanted to learn more about the woman who was a Pinkerton detective and a railroad marshal.

Mama nodded, not letting go of her friend's arm. "And even if it did, I wouldn't hear of you staying at a hotel. I'm sure we can make room here on the ranch." She glanced to where Rika was silently waiting on the veranda. "Hendrika, I know it's a lot to ask, but do you think you could stay at the main house for a while so that Frankie and Tess could have the cabin? Just until we find another solution."

Amy tensed. She knew what that meant. Her parents' bedroom was their sanctuary and not open to visitors. Nattie's room was small and already doubled as an office where the ranch's books and Nattie's notes on the breeding program were kept. That made Amy's room the only logical choice.

Rika's gaze met hers from across the veranda. Even in the falling darkness, Amy felt the gaze like a touch.

"Sure," Rika said.

Tess seemed to become aware of the other people on the porch for the first time.

"This is Nattie, our younger daughter," Mama said, wrapping her arm around Nattie's shoulder. "And this is

Hendrika Bruggeman. She's gonna marry Phin, our foreman, as soon as he gets back with Luke."

The stab this thought sent through Amy was more painful than Adam's vicious kick. *It's none of your business. Be happy for Phin and stay away from Rika.* She climbed the two stairs to the door. *I think I'll bed down in the stable with Ruby tonight.*

Her daughters and the ranch hands crowded around the table, listening to every word Tess and Frankie said. Everyone was starved for stories of faraway places and wanted to hear about the towns Tess and Frankie had visited.

Everyone but Nora. The questions tumbling through her mind had nothing to do with Tess and Frankie's travels. Her questions couldn't be asked in front of others. She tapped her finger against the rim of her plate as she waited for supper to end, but her curious daughters kept the questions coming.

"Oh, Independence sounds so exciting," Nattie said, her supper forgotten on the plate in front of her. "Why did you leave?"

Frankie and Tess exchanged a quick glance.

"During the war, there were two horrible battles in Independence, and after the first one, Frankie convinced me that it was too dangerous to stay. When the railroad bosses sent her out again, I went with her." New lines formed around Tess's mouth when she smiled at her companion. Clearly, she didn't regret her decision to leave Independence and follow Frankie across the country. "We spent a few years up north, far away from Independence and the war."

"Did you ever go back?" Nattie asked.

"No. Independence was never the same again. There's nothing left for me there."

Nothing left? Not even the brothel? Back when Nora had worked for her, Tess had toyed with the idea of selling the brothel. But her sense of responsibility held her back. Unlike the owners of other establishments, Tess made sure her girls were well fed, had access to a doctor, and got fair wages for their services. "So you sold the livery stable and the restaurant and...all of your other businesses?" Nora asked.

Tess's gaze met hers, and a silent understanding passed between them. "Yes. But don't worry, I left everything in good hands. None of my employees will suffer just because I'm no longer there to see to things. But for me, it was time to start a new life."

Every woman in Tess's brothel had wanted that. But unlike the young girls, Tess had long ago stopped dreaming of white knights charging in to rescue her. Now she seemed more hopeful and full of life than ever before, making her appear years younger than she was.

Nora looked at Frankie, who had changed into a beautiful dress. *Sometimes, white knights come in surprising forms.* She still couldn't figure out Frankie Callaghan, but the affection in Tess's gaze was unmistakable. *Are they really...sweethearts?* Tess's letters indicated it, and in hindsight, all her little hints about how Frank was as special as Luke now made sense. Back when the letters had first arrived, Nora had grinned at how smitten Tess sounded, but she never thought Frank might be Frances, a woman.

"And how did you meet Mama and Papa?" Nattie asked.

Nora tensed. Up until now, Luke and she had managed to answer questions like this one with vague explanations. After a while, their daughters stopped asking. Until now. Nora's stomach churned, and she shoved back her still half-full plate.

But Tess didn't blink an eye. "Oh, I met your papa when he was a dashing, young soldier about to fight in the Mexican War. He protected me from the unwelcome advances of a drunken man. That's how he broke his nose. We became friends when I patched him up."

It was the truth—or at least part of the truth. Luke had told Nora that she had protected Tess from a drunken customer in the brothel.

"And Mama?" Nattie asked. "How did you meet her?"

A half smile played around Tess's lips when she looked at Nora. "Well, I guess your mama was drawn to horse places even back then. We met in the livery stable I owned in Independence, and I offered her a job."

Nora had almost forgotten what a smooth liar Tess was. It was a necessary skill for the madam of a brothel. Tess knew how to tell just enough of the truth to make people believe they knew all of it.

"Is that where you met Papa?" Nattie asked Nora.

"I was the one who introduced them." Tess came to her rescue again. "Your papa was rather shy around women back then. Left to his own devices, he wouldn't have talked to your mother."

Nattie giggled. For her, it was probably hard to believe that Luke, the confident rancher, had once been a shy young man.

Nora, however, vividly remembered the self-conscious expression on Luke's face the first few times she had unwrapped her chest in front of Nora. It had taken many years before Luke became comfortable enough to enjoy her own body as much as Nora did.

A sudden wave of longing gripped her. *Oh, how I wish Luke was here and could share this evening with me.* Everything was so much easier, so much clearer when they were together. She sent a silent prayer, hoping that Luke and the boys had found a good place for the night and had enough food.

Finally, supper ended and the ranch hands filed out of the house, but Nattie and Amy still peppered Tess and Frankie with questions while they cleared the table.

Oh, no. Nora wanted some answers of her own. "Amy, you go up and clear some space in your room for Hendrika. Nattie, please help Hendrika pack a few things she might need."

"But, Mama," Nattie said. "I wanted to ask Tess some more questions."

"You can ask her tomorrow. Now it's my turn to catch up with her," Nora said.

Without further protest, Hendrika and Nattie left the house. Amy trudged up to her room.

Frankie blinked when she found herself alone with Nora and Tess. "Um. I think I'll check on Adam, make sure the ranch hands don't let him escape." One last glance at Tess, then the door closed behind her.

Nora smiled and dragged Tess to the cozy kitchen. "I see she's as good as Luke at avoiding these situations."

"Are we having a situation?" Tess asked. Mirth danced in her blue eyes.

No time to play games. Nattie would be back soon with more questions for Tess. "Your letters sounded like you were in love," Nora said, remembering how happy she had been for her friend when she had first mentioned Frank.

Tess's smile softened. "I am."

"With Frankie?"

"Yes."

The certainty of her answer surprised Nora, maybe because she had struggled for a while when she found herself falling in love with Luke. "Does that mean you're..." She searched for the right words. "...like me?"

Tess grinned. "I wish. You're still so beautiful." She trailed the back of her fingers over Nora's cheek. "And here I thought ranch wives were supposed to look old and careworn."

Nora captured the hand and held it between her own. "Flatterer." She softened her words with an affectionate smile. "You know that's not what I mean."

"If you mean am I a woman who loves another woman with all her heart, then the answer is yes."

Nora had always thought her feelings for Luke were unique. "So you are...?"

Laugh lines deepened as Tess grinned at her. "I am what?"

"Sharing Frankie's bed?" Before she could chicken out, Nora sought refuge in the bluntness of the prostitute she had once been.

"I share everything with Frankie—my life, my dreams, and yes, my bed." Tess's gaze was calm as she nudged Nora. "Don't look so baffled. It's hard enough for an old madam like me to find love. I wasn't about to let this chance at happiness pass me by, just because most people think it's unnatural." She rolled her eyes. "I've done a lot of things in my life that felt unnatural, but loving Frankie isn't one of them."

Nora felt the same way about Luke, but still, she never thought other women would want to share their lives with a woman rather than a man. "Have you ever...? I mean, I know you've been with Luke, but other than her, did you ever...?"

"Once or twice," Tess said.

"And?"

"I liked it." Tess shrugged. "I liked being with some of the men in my life too. But I love Frankie. Just Frankie." Her blue eyes held an expression more loving than any Nora had ever seen on her friend.

They sat in silence, their hands clutched together.

"It feels good to finally say it out loud," Tess said.

"You haven't told Frankie?"

"Oh, she knows." A wicked grin spread across Tess's lips. "Believe me, she knows. But everyone else thinks we're cousins."

Sometimes, the lies she and Luke had built around their lives, around their pasts, felt like a prison, but at least they didn't have to hide their love. Were the lies really a prison if they allowed them to love each other openly? She and Luke could share a bed without having to tell people they were cousins. On Sundays, Luke could hand her down from the wagon and lead her up the church steps without anyone whispering about it behind their backs. And when Luke kissed her good-bye, she didn't have to pretend that her heart wasn't aching.

Gently, she squeezed Tess's hand. "I'm glad you have her in your life, even if it isn't always easy."

The door swung open before Tess could answer. Nattie entered, excitedly chatting with Rika.

Nora groaned. "Ready for more questions?"

"I don't mind. Nattie is a wonderful young woman, curious for all life has to offer. She's exactly like you would have been if your father hadn't been such a cold-hearted bastard."

The truth of her words still cut deeply after all those years.

Tess patted her hand and stood. "We'll talk later."

HAMILTON HORSE RANCH
BAKER PRAIRIE, OREGON
MAY 21, 1868

*R*IKA SLOWLY CLIMBED THE STAIRS, savoring the few seconds alone. Tess and Frankie's arrival unsettled her, and she tried to figure out what it was that made her nervous.

At first, she thought it was Frankie's unusual appearance. Even in Boston, the "cradle of liberty" according to Mrs. Gillespie's magazines, Rika had never seen anyone like this woman.

That's not true. For a moment, she was transported back to the time she'd worked as a nurse in a Union hospital. A young, pale soldier had been rushed into the tent, his foot shattered by a minié ball. Rika's stomach churned when she remembered helping to hold down the soldier while the surgeon cut off the mangled foot. After a day, gangrene set in. Rika would never forget the stench of the rotting flesh.

At death's door, the soldier confessed her true identity to Rika. She was a woman who had donned men's garb and joined the Union army to stay with her betrothed.

But Frankie wasn't like that. She didn't hide her gender; she was simply a woman who dressed in men's apparel and didn't care what other people thought.

Weeks ago, Rika might have been appalled, but after getting to know Amy, she no longer thought wearing pants was improper.

Maybe it was her guilty conscience that unsettled her. Frankie was a marshal after all, and Rika had broken the law by traveling west with tickets that didn't belong to her. Soon, she would trick Phineas into marrying her.

Don't make yourself crazy with thoughts like that. This is your life now, the only life you have. If she was careful, no one would ever find out. Instead of worrying about Frankie and Tess, she should focus on the here and now.

In the beginning, Amy had been adamant about not sharing a room. Was she truly fine with it now? Sometimes, she seemed so friendly and nice, but the next moment, she was distant again. In the five weeks since Rika had arrived at the ranch, they had made it through a few dangerous situations and had experienced Lucky's birth together. At times, she even felt close to Amy but would then find herself pushed away for no reason she could understand.

It scared her. She needed Amy's acceptance because she was Phineas's boss and friend.

But if she was honest with herself, she had to admit that Amy's position on the ranch was no longer the only reason she sought her company. She spent time with her because she liked it. Liked Amy.

When she reached the top of the stairs, she knocked on the door.

A grunt came from inside.

"Amy?" she called through the closed door. "Everything all right?"

"Yeah," Amy answered, sounding out of breath. "Just give me a minute."

Rika waited.

Clothes rustled, and Amy cursed. Finally, she opened the door.

Rika entered and set down her carpetbag before turning to get her first look at Amy. What she saw startled her.

Sweat gleamed on Amy's brow. Her red locks were tussled and her shirt half-unbuttoned. The light golden tan she'd acquired during the past weeks was gone, hidden by her flushed cheeks and the paleness lurking underneath.

"Amy! Are you running a fever?" She held on to Amy's sleeve, remembering too well how Jo had suffered and died. The thought of losing Amy the same way pressed the air from her lungs.

When she lifted a hand to touch Amy's forehead, Amy backed away and collided with the washstand. The pitcher teetered precariously, but instead of catching it, Amy clutched her side.

Rika jumped forward and caught the pitcher before it fell. Holding it in both hands, she froze. Her left side was pressed against Amy, and she inhaled the soothing smell of horse and leather. Amy's body heat engulfed her, and her own cheeks felt flushed too. *Whatever sickness she has, it might be contagious.* "You all right?" she murmured and set down the pitcher to touch Amy's cheek.

For a moment, Amy leaned into the touch, her eyes closing, before she pulled away.

Rika let her hand drop to her side. Her fingers rubbed against each other as if trying to remember the smoothness of Amy's skin. "You feel a little warm, but I don't think you have a fever."

"I told you, I'm fine."

"I don't believe you."

Amy turned and gaped at her.

"You looked as if it hurt when you bumped into the washstand," Rika said. Her eyes narrowed when she understood. "Adam hurt you!"

"It's not so bad," Amy said. "I was just looking at it in the mirror when you knocked."

So that was why Amy's shirt was half-open and her hair tussled. Trying to get dressed made her break out in a sweat, so her injuries had to be painful.

"Did he shoot you?" Something inside her trembled at the thought.

"No, nothing like that. He just got a kick in. That's all."

"That's more than enough," Rika said, her voice sharper than intended. Images of broken ribs and a punctured lung raced through her mind. She stepped closer. "Show me."

"I'm sure it's just a bruised rib. Nothing you can do to help."

Another step brought them almost nose to nose. "Show me." She wouldn't be able to sleep before she made sure Amy was all right.

Amy exhaled sharply, her breath brushing Rika's cheek. "All right." She undid the remaining buttons on her shirt.

It reminded Rika of the night of the fire, when she had helped Amy undress. Instinctively, she wanted to reach out and help Amy unbutton the shirt. *She hurt her ribs, not her hands, Hendrika Aaldenberg.* She pressed her hands together in the pocket of her apron.

Amy's shirt slid down her arms, and Rika caught it before it could fall to the floor. The warmth of the fabric seeped into her fingers as she watched Amy pull her long-sleeved undershirt from her pants and tug it up just enough to reveal her side. Rika gasped. Amy's side was visibly swollen. The skin looked raw and was turning black and blue.

"That bad?" Amy craned her neck to peer down her body.

"N-no." She had seen much worse injuries during the war. But still, seeing the bruises on Amy's pale skin affected her in a way that not even fatal wounds had. "Why didn't you tell us you were hurt? You just sat down at supper and pretended to be fine."

"I didn't want Mama to worry about a few bruises," Amy said. "You know how mothers are."

Rika wished she did. Instead of nodding, she sighed.

Amy's gaze caught hers. "You don't, do you? Your mother... is she...?"

A year ago, Jo had asked her the same, but Rika had been reluctant to answer. She had few memories left of her mother and protected them like a hidden treasure she didn't want to share. But now the compassion in Amy's eyes compelled her to speak. "She died giving birth to my little brother when I was four."

"I'm sorry." Amy's voice was soft.

Rika found that Amy was holding her hand, rubbing her thumb across the knuckles.

Amy's gaze followed hers, and she let go as if she hadn't been aware of her gentle touch.

Rika lifted her hand and rubbed her breastbone. It didn't help to smooth the edges of raw emotion. She took a cleansing breath and changed the subject. "Lie down."

Amy stared at the bed, then at her. "Why?"

"I need to palpate the ribs to see if any are broken."

"I've had broken ribs before. I can tell that nothing's broken this time."

How could she be so cavalier about her health? Rika had half a mind to shove Amy down on the bed, but she didn't want to hurt her. "Lie down and let me see for myself."

Amy sank onto the bed and leaned back until she was lying down, her legs dangling over the edge. She clamped her teeth onto her bottom lip when Rika stepped closer.

"Don't worry," Rika murmured. "I'll be as gentle as possible. I won't hurt you." As she sat on the bed next to her, she felt the tension in Amy's sturdy frame. Her palms were sweaty, and she wiped them on her apron. "Can you," she stopped to clear her throat, "pull the undershirt up a little, please?"

Amy drew the shirt up to just under her bosom.

How vulnerable the fair skin of her belly and sides looked in comparison to the golden glow of her arms and her face. Rika smoothed a gentle finger over the lowest rib.

"Um. He kicked me much farther up and more to the left," Amy said. Her words came out in a rush as if she was holding her breath.

"Well, you know, I…" Rika searched for words to explain her strange need to touch Amy and make sure she was all right. "As a nurse, I was taught to be thorough." Her gaze still rested on the elegant curve of Amy's ribs. Most of the time, Amy appeared so strong and confident, but now Rika marveled at how vulnerable she looked. The body beneath her hands trembled. Rika's touch became soothing, stroking much more than probing.

Goose bumps rose under her fingertips.

What are you doing? She's getting cold, so hurry and get this over with. She slid her hands up, following the arch of Amy's ribs. Heat drifted up from Amy's skin. Everything was smooth under her hands, no bumps to indicate that ribs were broken. Her fingertips wandered higher.

Amy groaned, a sound that vibrated through Rika and stilled her hands.

She looked into Amy's flushed face. "I'm sorry," she whispered. "Did I hurt you? Is this rib—"

"No," Amy said. "The rib is fine. It's just…"

"What?"

"Your hands are cold."

"Really?" They felt as if they were on fire, not cold at all.

Amy nodded, her whole body tense.

"Sorry. I'll hurry." Rika palpated the bruised area, probing with her fingertips to see if the ribs underneath were broken.

This time, Amy didn't groan. She lay stiffly, not moving, barely breathing.

Finally, Rika lifted her hands away and tugged down the undershirt. "I don't think your ribs are broken, but two of them are badly bruised."

Amy shoved the hem of her undershirt into her pants. "I told you that without all this... palpating."

Rika gave her a sidelong glance. "You said that because you wanted it to be true, but ignoring a wound won't heal it." She stabbed a finger at Amy. "You have to stay off your horses for a while until the ribs and the bruises heal."

"I can't do that." Amy shrugged back into her shirt and buttoned it so quickly it seemed she needed its protection. "I have a ranch to run."

White-hot anger exploded in Rika. She jumped up from the bed. "And who will run it when you're dead?"

Amy looked up from her shirt buttons. "Dead? You said I'll be fine."

"Yes, this time. You might not be so lucky next time."

"There won't be a next time. Frankie will take Adam—"

"I'm not talking about Adam," Rika said. "I've been here for less than five weeks, and in that time, you almost managed to get yourself killed three times. First you run into a burning stable, then you ride into a raging river even though you can't swim, and now you get into a fight with an armed, dangerous man."

Amy lifted her hand and opened her mouth to say something.

"And don't tell me it's nothing!" Rika realized she was shouting and lowered her voice before the rest of the family came running to see what was going on. She stared at Amy with burning eyes. "Do you know how lucky you were? If Frankie and Tess hadn't shown up when they did..."

"I know," Amy whispered.

Something in her voice made Rika's stomach roil. "What happened?" Over supper, Amy had given them a short explanation about how she had come across Adam at the line shack and how she had overwhelmed him with the help of Frankie and Tess. She didn't mention a fight or being kicked, and neither Tess nor Frankie corrected her—either because they hadn't witnessed the fight or because they wanted to spare Nora.

"He put a revolver to my head." Amy laid a finger against her temple as if she still felt the cold steel pressed against her skin. "And if Frankie hadn't shown up with a rifle, he would have pulled the trigger."

"Oh, Lord!" The room spun around Rika.

"Hey!" Amy caught her when her knees buckled but couldn't suppress a pained groan.

The sound brought the room into focus again, and Rika stared into Amy's eyes. "Sorry," she mumbled. "Your ribs..."

"It's all right," Amy said. She led Rika to the bed and sat next to her.

The warmth of Amy's shoulder brushing hers soothed Rika, and she found the strength to say the words that made her stomach clench. "He would have killed you. If Frankie and Tess hadn't gotten lost on the way from town, you would be dead now."

"Yes," Amy said in an almost inaudible whisper. "But I can't let myself think like that. It would make me crazy, and Adam doesn't deserve that kind of power over me." Intense green eyes burned into Rika's. "Please don't tell my family. I don't want them to worry."

"I promise," Rika said. "On one condition."

"Which is?"

"That you promise me something in return. Promise that you'll be more careful in the future. I know you want to prove yourself to the ranch hands and to your father, but please..." She stopped and looked into Amy's eyes.

Warmth and understanding shone back at her. More words weren't necessary. Amy nodded. "I promise."

"And next time you get hurt, don't hide it," Rika said. "Even if you don't want your mother to know, let me take a look right away."

"I don't plan on getting hurt again anytime soon, so next time it happens, you might not be around to take care of me," Amy said, finally looking away.

The words clutched at Rika with the cruel claws of reality. Just a few more weeks until Phineas would be back to marry her, and the closer that time came, the less sure she was that she wanted to marry him. *Oh, if only things could stay like this forever.* But she shoved the thought away. It was a childish wish, and she had never allowed herself to dream of things that couldn't come true. She wouldn't start now.

"Come on," she said. "Let's go to bed."

Amy jumped up. "You take it." She gestured wildly to the bed. "I'll bed down with Ruby for tonight."

"You want to sleep in the stable?" The words cut deep. After all these weeks, Amy would still rather share space with a horse than with her? In the past, Rika had been content to keep to herself or talk to Jo. But it was different with Amy. She liked Amy, liked spending time with her—and she wanted Amy to like her too.

"I sleep there quite often," Amy said.

"Not when you are hurt. You have bruised ribs, and sleeping in the stable won't help them heal." She eyed the bed. "Why don't we share?" That way, she could keep an eye on Amy and make sure she was all right.

"S-share?"

"Why not? Haven't you ever shared a bed with your sister or a neighbor girl before?" Growing up with a brother and six half siblings, she'd rarely had a bed to herself. Her father and stepmother didn't believe in "spoiling" their children, so whenever a little one had gotten scared at night, he or she had slipped into bed with Rika. And in the boarding house, she'd shared a bed with Jo.

"Sure, but—"

"Good." Rika searched her carpetbag for her nightgown. "Then let's go to bed. It's been a long day."

Tess knocked on the door.

"Yes?" Amy's voice came out in a squeak.

"Amy, it's Tess. I know it's late, but can I come in for a minute?"

Clothes rustled before the door opened a few inches. Amy peered through the crack. "Rika is changing into her nightgown," she said. Her blush contrasted sharply with her own white nightgown.

Ah, sweet innocence. Tess smiled.

"I'm done," Hendrika called from inside the room.

Amy opened the door wider and let her in.

Like every other room in the Hamiltons' house, love showed in every corner—the small figures on a shelf, probably carved by Luke's patient hand, a warm quilt on the bed, and the mirror over the washstand that must have cost a small fortune to bring out west.

Now that Amy had changed out of her pants and had her hair down, she looked even more like Nora than before, but still, the girl's energy, her whole demeanor, reminded her so much of Luke that it was eerie. *If it was possible for the two of them to have children together, they couldn't be a better mix of them than Amy and Nattie.* Amy's younger sister looked a lot like Luke, but with her kindness and her curiosity she was unmistakably Nora's daughter too.

"I know it's not polite or proper to visit you this late in your room," Tess said. *And thank God I never put much value in what is or isn't proper.* "But I wanted to make sure you were all right after..." The words died on her lips, and she looked at Hendrika.

"She knows what happened with Adam," Amy said.

Tess arched an eyebrow. She would have bet good money that Amy would try to dismiss the danger and hide any injury she might have sustained. She looked from Hendrika to Amy, who blushed under her probing gaze. *The mail-order bride and the stubborn rancher's daughter. What an unlikely pair of friends.*

"Frankie and I were too far away to stop the fight, but we saw it when we crested the hill," Tess said, remembering those helpless seconds. "Adam didn't pull his punches. I know you said you're all right, but are you really?"

"I'm fine," Amy said.

"She will be," Hendrika said. Her gaze met Tess's.

So Amy has at least a few scrapes and bruises, and she let Hendrika take care of them. "Good."

"I appreciate you not telling Mama," Amy said. "You didn't, did you?"

"No." While Tess hoped she was still Nora's best friend, she hadn't seen Nora in seventeen years and had never met the adult Amy. It wasn't her place to interfere. "But you should tell her. She's your mother. She has a right to know."

"I'll tell her," Amy said. "Tomorrow."

"All right. Get some rest, you two." Tess nodded at Hendrika. "And thanks again for letting Frankie and me have the cabin." For once, they'd have all the privacy they wanted. *Nice. Let's go and see if Frankie is back from checking on the prisoner.* Tess grinned as she hurried down the stairs.

Rika pressed her nose into the pillow and smiled to herself. It smelled of leather, grass, and the faint aroma of horse. Weeks ago, she might have thought the combination unpleasant, but now those scents meant comfort and safety.

Still, for some reason, she couldn't sleep. Even though she'd shared a bed with Jo and slept just fine, Amy's presence next to her was distracting. She listened to Amy's breathing. It was too fast for her to be asleep. *Is she in pain?*

Rika lifted her head and tried to make out Amy's form in the darkness. Moonlight filtered in through the window. When her eyes adjusted, she saw Amy lying on her uninjured side, facing away from her. She clung to the edge of the bed. "You're gonna fall out and hurt your ribs," Rika said.

Slowly, Amy rolled onto her back and turned her head. Her eyes gleamed in the near darkness. "I don't want to crowd you."

"Crowd me?" Rika laughed. "With miles of space between us?"

Amy mumbled something but didn't move closer.

"What is it? I don't smell funny, do I?" Rika pulled a corner of her nightgown over her face and took a sniff. She smelled of the Hamiltons' homemade soap.

"No," Amy said. "You smell...um...nice."

Oh. So she likes the way I smell. Rika's cheeks heated. *Then why does she keep her distance as if I had bad breath or pestilence?* "Amy, come on. We're not strangers. We are," she hesitated but then said, "friends, aren't we?" She'd had few friends in her life, but she felt Amy would be there for her when it counted.

Maybe we can stay in touch after Phineas and I move away. She allowed herself the wistful thought.

Amy turned to face her, then sucked in a breath when her weight pressed on her bruised ribs.

"Careful." Rika reached over and stroked Amy's hand as if she could rub away the pain.

Groaning, Amy rolled back off her injured side and squeezed Rika's hand before letting go. "Maybe we are," she said.

They lay in the darkness, this time a little closer together, barely touching.

"Can I ask about your mother? Or is it too painful to talk about?" Amy asked just when Rika thought she had fallen asleep.

Rika smoothed a handful of wrinkles from the covers. "It's all right. It was a long time ago."

"Ignoring a wound won't heal it," Amy said.

A sad smile tugged at Rika's lips. "No, it doesn't." She rarely talked about her family, but sometimes she wondered what kind of person she would be if she had grown up with loving parents like the Hamiltons. "My mother was a wonderful woman," she said and then added, "Or maybe I just think that because in comparison to my father, anyone would look like a good parent."

"He hurt you?" Amy's voice was rough.

"It wasn't so bad after he remarried, but for a few years, it was just him and me and my little brother. He didn't know what to do with children, so he treated us like two of his apprentices. He sent me out to peddle his breads and pastries as soon as I was big enough to carry the basket."

Silence hung between them. Amy gulped.

"I'm not complaining about that," Rika said, not wanting Amy to be sorry for her. "I mean, you probably helped at the ranch since you were a child too."

"Yeah, Nattie and I had our chores, but we always knew we were loved," Amy said. "Did you ever have that in your life?"

Did I? Rika wondered. "I searched for it when I was younger."

"Did you find it?"

"No. All I did was trade in one drunkard for another."

The warm touch of Amy's hand seeped through the sleeve of Rika's nightgown. "What do you mean?"

"My father drank too much. Sometimes he flew into drunken rages and…" She stopped and rubbed her left wrist. Her fingers brushed Amy's hand still resting on her arm. She'd never told anyone about that time in her life, but surrounded by darkness, lying next to Amy, she felt safe. "He yelled and shouted." She flinched as his booming voice echoed through her.

Amy rubbed her arm, anchoring her in the present.

"Sometimes, he shoved me or shook me. When he was particularly angry, he slapped me across the face."

"Why would he do something like that?" Amy's voice was thick with outrage. "You're his daughter!"

Despite all her skills around the ranch, Amy was still so innocent in some ways. Her parents' love had spared her from the heartache Rika had been through. "Sometimes it was my own fault. There were days when I couldn't finish my chores in time or sell enough bread. Once, I tripped and the whole basket of breads and pastries landed in the mud, ruined."

"But that's no reason to hit you!" Amy sat up. The bed trembled under her angry movements, and she groaned in pain. "If my papa hit me every time I did something wrong, I would be dead by now. Once, when I was twelve, I sneaked into the corral at night and forgot to close the gate. By morning, all our horses were scattered across the valley."

Rika shuddered at the thought of her father's rage if something like that had happened to her. "What did your father do?"

"He gave me a lariat and told me to catch Grasshopper while he brought back all the other horses," Amy said.

"Grasshopper?" A chuckle chased away Rika's sadness. "Let me guess—she was a mare."

Amy grinned. "One that didn't like to be caught. Papa knew that. He caught the other horses while I was still out there, trying to get close to Grasshopper. After a while, Papa came and watched. But he didn't help. He didn't take the lariat away from me. He just sat in the grass for hours."

"And Grasshopper? Did you ever catch her?" Rika asked.

"After a while, she got curious to see what Papa was doing. I think that's why she finally allowed me to catch her. Papa just stood, dusted off his pants, and the three of us went home." The memory of her father teaching her a lesson brought a smile to Amy's face.

It all sounded like a fairy tale to Rika. "I wish I had a father like that."

"I wish that too," Amy said. "So you became a mail-order bride to get away from your father?"

"Oh, no, I left home much earlier, as soon as I could."

"Where did you go?" Amy asked.

"When the war broke out, I was sixteen, old enough to be a nurse for the Union army. That's how I met Willem."

"Willem?"

"My late husband."

The bed shook as Amy jerked. "You were married? What happened?"

Rika hesitated. Was it crazy to trust Amy with that part of her life? What if she told Phineas and he didn't want to marry a woman who had already been married once?

"It's all right. You don't have to tell me. I don't want to pry," Amy said when Rika remained silent.

"You're not prying." Rika had been the one to say they were friends, and she had already told Amy too much to refuse to answer now. "It's just not something I'm proud of."

The covers rustled, and then Amy squeezed Rika's hand before retreating. "Does Phin know?"

"No." Rika hoped Jo hadn't told her future husband a lot about her family or her life. Her family was poor and had left her to fend for herself, so Jo rarely talked about her past. "And if you don't mind, I'd prefer to keep it that way for now."

"Of course."

"Thanks." Even though Phineas was Amy's friend and her loyalty might be to him, Rika sensed that Amy wouldn't violate her trust.

"So your husband, what happened to him?"

The memories seemed as if from a lifetime ago. "Willem was one of the soldiers in my care. I tended his wounded arm and listened when he talked about his dreams of what he wanted to do after the war. We both knew he might not survive the next battle, so when he asked me to marry him before he was sent back to the front, I said yes."

Amy was silent for long moments. The bed creaked as she shifted her weight to look at Rika. "Did you love him?"

"He was a good man," Rika said, "and sometimes, he talked to me in Dutch. It reminded me of my mother and of the only time in my childhood when I was happy." After her mother died and her father married an English woman, they had stopped speaking Dutch at home.

"So what happened to Willem? He didn't come home from the war?"

Rika bit her lip. "Oh, yes, he did. But he wasn't the friendly young man he had been...or that I thought he was. The war made him bitter and distant." She had realized then that she was married to a stranger. Neither of them knew how to act around the other. "He started to drink."

"Did he..." Amy stared at her in the moonlight. "Did he hit you too?"

"No. But he often didn't come home for days; he idled away his time and rarely worked. What little money he earned, he spent on brandy. One morning, they brought him home dead. He fell off his horse in a drunken stupor and broke his neck."

Amy sank against her pillow. "I'm sorry."

Rika said nothing. She lay back too and stared at the ceiling, stunned at herself for telling Amy so much about her life. In the burning barn and down by the river, she had trusted Amy with her life, and now that the trust between them was established, it was hard to take it back. She wasn't sure she wanted to take it back. "What about you?"

"Me?"

"Did you ever fall in love? Have a beau?" As long as Rika had been at the ranch, she hadn't seen any man come by to court Amy. She didn't understand it. Why did the men of Baker Prairie have a need for mail-order brides while no one asked for Amy's hand? With her deep green eyes and pretty face, Amy was too beautiful to be overlooked even though she was different from other young women.

"No," Amy said. "I never had a beau. I want nothing short of what my parents have together. I won't settle for less, and I can't see myself having that with any of the men around here."

The careful response piqued Rika's interest. Amy had answered only one of her two questions. "But you've been in love?"

In the silence, an owl hooted in front of the window.

"Amy?" Rika whispered when no answer came. "You asleep?"

"No, I just... I don't know how to answer your question. I had...feelings for someone before, but I don't think it was love."

Rika nodded. She had found out too late that her feelings for Willem hadn't been love either. "I know what you mean."

"I doubt that." Amy's voice was a low murmur, but with Rika lying so close, she could still hear.

"Why wouldn't I understand?" Rika asked. "Do you really think we're so different from each other?"

"You have no idea how different we are."

The words weren't a surprise—Rika had always been an outsider, different and distanced from the other girls. She wasn't beautiful or even interesting. People didn't go out of their way to become close to her. Still, hearing it from Amy hurt, and she turned away.

"Hey." A shy hand touched her shoulder. "I didn't mean it in a bad way. You wouldn't want to be too much like me, believe me."

"Why would you say that?" Why wouldn't she want to be like Amy, who was honest, hardworking, and loyal? At first glance, she had thought Amy's life idyllic and uncomplicated, but now she sensed pain behind the words. She turned and studied the shadowy planes of Amy's face in the near darkness. "Everything all right with you?"

"Of course. All I meant is that we're different people, but we can still be friends."

The knots in Rika's gut loosened. "I'd like that."

"All right, then. Friends it is." Amy nodded at her. Their gazes touched; then Amy rolled around to face the wall. "We should get some sleep now."

Rika closed her eyes and let the murmurs of Amy's breathing lull her to sleep.

Nora jerked open the bunkhouse door. "Where is he?"

Playing cards fluttered to the floor when Kit and Emmett tried to hide them.

Nora ignored it. She knew Luke didn't approve of the ranch hands' gambling, but right now, it wasn't important.

"Who?" Hank rolled off his narrow bunk.

Nora drummed a rapid beat on the door. "Adam, of course."

A sly grin crept over Hank's weather-beaten face. "In the pigpen."

"You left him in the pigpen? Alone?"

"No. Miss Callaghan took first watch. I didn't want to leave her alone with Adam, but she insisted. She has some papers that say she's a railroad marshal or somethin'." Hank shrugged, clearly not sure what to make of Frankie.

The door of the bunkhouse fell closed behind Nora. She gathered her skirts with one hand, lifted the lantern with the other, and marched toward the pigpen.

The circle of light fell on Frankie, who sat on the corral rail and whittled away on a piece of wood.

Luke also did that to while away time or to calm herself. Nora slid her gaze over Frankie and found more similarities: the strength in the tanned hands, the confidence of her movements, and the respect in her eyes when she looked at Nora. *Did Tess fall in love with her because she's a bit like Luke?* Sometimes, Nora suspected that Tess and Luke had shared more than friendship, more than their bodies. Not that she could blame Tess if it were true. She, too, had been helpless to stop herself from falling in love with Luke.

But then Frankie greeted her and slid down from the corral rail. While Luke would have jumped and landed in a wide stance, Frankie climbed down with light-footed elegance. She had changed back into a pair of pants but still moved as if she were wearing a dress.

"You know, you could have let our ranch hands deal with Adam," Nora said. "You must be exhausted after traveling for so long. You don't have to stand guard in front of a pigpen."

"I don't mind. I'm used to it." A grin tugged at Frankie's lips. "Well, maybe not to the pigpen being used as a cell, but I've guarded prisoners many times before."

Nora studied her. She had thought Luke's disguise was what enabled them to live their lives the way they wanted. But Frankie did what she wanted too, without pretending to be a man. "And the men just let you do that?"

Frankie walked closer. "The trick is not to wait for permission. After I've already done it, they can protest all they want."

That meant Frankie went off on her own, without any help if things got out of hand. "And when you investigate a case, you don't take Tess with you?"

"I didn't in the beginning. When we first met, I only saw Tess a few times a year, whenever I got back to Independence. But then…" With a glance at the pigpen, Frankie lowered her voice. "When we grew closer, just visiting every once in a while wasn't enough."

Nora understood. Being separated from Luke for two months left an empty place inside of her that couldn't be filled by focusing on teaching, working the ranch, or helping her daughters. "So Tess goes wherever you go?"

"I tried to leave her behind once, while I went to catch an arsonist. Tess would have none of it. She said if it's too dangerous for her, then it's too dangerous for me." Frankie threw away her piece of wood. "And she's right. She's pretty good with that little revolver of hers, and she can handle a rifle as well as I can. She doesn't panic in dangerous situations, so who am I to tell her to stay behind while I go off risking my life alone?"

"Interesting," Nora murmured, more to herself. "I never thought of accompanying Luke to Fort Boise. Maybe I should have. Maybe we have fallen into our roles as husband and wife too quickly, because that's what people think we are."

Frankie's calm gaze rested on her. "You found a living arrangement that works for you, but Tess and I both live as women, so we have to constantly negotiate our roles and can't take anything for granted."

Nora knew she would lie awake tonight, thinking about her role in life. But for now, she was here and taking care of the ranch was her responsibility—and that included Adam. The lantern in her fist swung back and forth as she pointed at the pigpen. "Adam is in there?"

"It has a sturdy bolt, and Hank said the pigs like to bite."

Nora lifted an eyebrow at her.

Frankie grinned. "All right, all right. We put the pigs in the paddock before we locked Adam in there."

"Good." Nora gave a decisive nod. "Wouldn't want to subject the poor animals to such company. That man hit me over the head, not caring if I lived or died, and set fire to a barn full of horses. Is he still tied up?"

"His hands are bound. Why?"

"Because I want to talk to him." Nora knew she wouldn't be able to sleep before she had faced Adam. Maybe it would help her understand why he had nearly killed her. She laid her hand on the bolt and prepared to slide it back. "Keep that rifle ready, please, in case he gets any ideas."

Maybe living with Tess had taught Frankie not to stand in the way of a determined woman. She nodded and lifted her rifle.

Nora pulled back the bolt and opened the door.

Adam rushed forward, his bound hands raised.

"Nora!" Frankie shouted and cocked her rifle. "Get back!"

Instead of jumping back to let Frankie deal with him, Nora stood her ground. When Adam was almost upon her, she kicked out. Her boot hit Adam between the legs.

With a groan, he fell back and sank into the straw.

Nora stared at him coldly. "You still haven't learned not to mess with the Hamilton women, have you? You should know by now that we can defend ourselves."

"Oh, yeah?" Adam gasped out. He rolled to his side, still clutching himself. "Messing with Amy was easy. I kicked her pretty good. I was this close to putting a bullet in her head."

"What?" Nora whirled around to face Frankie. "What's he talking about? What happened with Amy?"

"Nothing," Frankie said, her voice soothing. "We came along before he could do any serious harm. And she kicked him pretty good too. Right where you just did."

"But if you hadn't been there..." Nora didn't finish her sentence. She didn't want to imagine what might have happened to Amy, alone out there on the range. The gleam in Adam's eyes told her enough. Bile rose in her throat, and she had to swallow before she could talk. "Lock him back up before I take that rifle out of your hands and shoot him. When you bring him to Oregon City tomorrow, make sure you tell the judge every little detail of what he's done."

Dizzy with anger and fear, she somehow made it back to the main house. The silence in the parlor engulfed her, leaving too much room for her own thoughts, for the images of what Adam might have done to Amy. Her footfalls on the stairs thudded along with her heart. With a single knock on the door, she entered Amy's room.

When the light of the lantern fell on two figures in the bed, Nora remembered that Hendrika was staying in Amy's room too.

Amy opened her eyes and blinked into the sudden light. She jumped out of bed as if she had done something wrong. Was she feeling guilty for not telling Nora about Adam attacking her?

Well, she should.

Then Amy clutched her side, and Nora's anger drained away, leaving only concern.

"Amy! You're hurt?" With trembling hands, she directed Amy to sit on the edge of the bed. "Where? How bad is it? Why didn't you tell me?"

Was Amy imitating her father? When Luke was sick or hurt, she hid it or pretended it was nothing. Going to the doctor or letting anyone but Nora see her injuries would threaten Luke's life in a way even most sicknesses couldn't. Was Amy now acting the same way because that's what she had seen from Luke growing up?

"Mama, I'm fine."

"Show me," Nora said.

Hendrika sat up in bed. "She's fine, Mrs. Hamilton. I examined her earlier. Two of her ribs are bruised, but that's all."

So at least Amy had told Hendrika and let her make sure she was fine. Some of the tension in Nora's body faded. Still, it felt strange not to be the one to take care of her daughter's scrapes and injuries any longer. *She's a grown woman now. She doesn't want to come running to her mama every time she gets hurt.*

She didn't miss the grateful glance Amy directed at Hendrika and the gentle smile she received in return. *They're becoming friends.* It was what she had hoped for and why she encouraged them to share a room. Amy had so few friends.

"Let me see, please." She had to see with her own eyes that Amy was fine. When Amy pulled up her nightshirt, Nora's breath caught. Anger simmered until she thought steam would come out of her ears. She wanted to march right back to the pigpen and kick Adam again. Hard.

Careful not to put any pressure on Amy's ribs, she slid her arms around her in a tender hug. Her eyes fluttered closed when she felt Amy's sturdy body rest against her. "You need to be more careful," she whispered. "Your father and I couldn't stand it if something happened to you or Nattie."

Amy trembled against her.

"Are you hurt anywhere else?"

"No, I'm fine. He just kicked me, but I hit him a few times too, just like Papa taught us." Amy stopped trembling. She straightened and looked at Nora with a proud gleam in her eyes. Then she swallowed. "Don't tell Papa, please. I don't want him to worry or think that I can't take care of myself."

"Your father and I promised that we'd never keep secrets from each other," Nora said. "You wouldn't want me to break that promise, would you?" She brushed a stubborn lock out of Amy's face.

Amy shook her head.

"Please promise me you'll never try to keep something like this from me again," Nora said. "I know you just wanted to protect me, but risking your health is not the way to do that."

Bare feet shuffled over the floorboards. "I promise."

"Thank you. I'll let you two get some sleep now, but we'll talk more about this tomorrow." For now, it was enough to know that her daughter was all right. She kissed Amy's cheek, then leaned across the bed and kissed Hendrika's too. "Thank you for taking care of her."

Hendrika blinked up at her. "Uh, you're welcome."

Nora smiled. "Goodnight."

KEENEY PASS, OREGON
MAY 24, 1868

*L*UKE'S GAZE SWEPT OVER THE hills and mountains on both sides of them. Up ahead, two long, parallel lines wound through the straw-colored grass—ruts that thousands of wagons had carved into the ground as they made their way through Keeney Pass.

It was the only sign of humans in the area. Other than the creaking of their saddles and the occasional snort from the horses, nothing interrupted the rustling of the wind through the long grass. They were alone in the pass.

Still, the little hairs on the back of Luke's neck prickled. She kept her right hand close to her rifle.

"You all right, boss?" Phin directed his gelding next to hers. Side by side, the horses marched up the steady incline.

"Yeah." Her gaze wandered over the hills. "But I'll feel better once we have a few more miles between us and Fort Boise."

Phin studied her. "It's been two days since we left the fort. By the time they let those three bastards out of their cells, we'll be long gone."

That was what Sergeant Johnson had promised them. The three soldiers had been in trouble before, and this time, they wouldn't get away with a few extra duties. They'd be facing a formal hearing, and the sergeant would read Luke's statement. "I don't trust Kelling. I have a feeling he's doing a lot of things without the colonel's knowledge, and if he's out to take revenge on me..."

Phin adjusted the scabbard on his saddle, making sure his rifle was within easy reach. "We'd better keep an eye out for trouble."

Warm lips moved over hers and placed little kisses over her cheek; then gentle teeth bit down on her earlobe.

Luke moaned, stretching her neck to give Nora easier access.

A trail of hot kisses wandered down her neck, sending shivers of delight down her body. The caressing lips stopped when they encountered a barrier—Luke's shirt. Dazed, Luke took her hands from the familiar curves of Nora's body and reached up to open the shirt.

"No." Nora's breath brushed over her collarbone. "Lie still and let me do this."

When Luke sank back, Nora opened the top button. She pressed her lips to the bare skin, then moved her fingers to the next button. The fabric of the shirt fell open under her eager fingers.

Teasing nails scraped over the bandages that bound Luke's chest.

Luke arched her back.

"Open your eyes," Nora said. "Open your eyes, Luke."

Luke opened her eyes.

Instead of the enchanting green of Nora's eyes, her gaze found the hazy gray light of dawn. She blinked, then lifted her hands and touched her shirt.

All of the buttons were closed.

She rubbed her hand over her chest, feeling Nora's elusive touch. A breath of longing escaped her. Nora wasn't here. She was still three hundred and fifty miles away.

Going back to sleep was impossible now. She might as well get up and see if Phin had put on some coffee. She was about to throw off her blanket and sit up, but her instincts stopped her. Something didn't feel right. Not moving, she listened to the sounds around her and peered through half-closed lids into the gray light.

Phin, who had the last watch, sat next to the fire, drawing lazy patterns in the ashes with a stick. To her left, a staccato of snores indicated that Charlie was still asleep.

Her gaze wandered to the horses.

Dancer stood with his head held high. His ears flicked in every direction as if trying to pinpoint the source of a sound.

Cold fear gripped Luke.

Someone was out there, watching them.

She slid her hand under the blanket. The worn wooden grip of her revolver felt soothing against her fingers. Without a sound, she slid the weapon out of its holster.

A snort from one of the horses interrupted the silence between two of Charlie's snores.

Phin's head jerked up.

Luke tensed her muscles, ready to jump up. Her gaze darted around.

Shadows moved at the edge of their camp.

A shot shattered the morning's peace.

Luke rolled to her left, away from the fire.

More shots. A bullet scratched along the saddle she'd used as a pillow, raining tiny pieces of leather down on her.

Two men ran up the hill toward her.

Where's Phin?

No time to look around. She got to her feet and squeezed off a series of quick shots, forcing the attackers to stop their fast approach. With her free hand, she grabbed the still half-asleep Charlie and dragged him with her. Her searching eyes found no cover.

Their only chance was to run down the other side of the hill, out of reach of their attacker's weapons, and then shoot them as soon as the two men crested the hill.

"Phin! Charlie! Follow me!" With her head down, she raced toward the crest of the hill.

Another shot rang out.

Next to her, Charlie cried out and fell.

Luke whirled around, her revolver raised. She crouched down next to Charlie and tried to get him up.

"Go!" Charlie waved her away. "Get out of here before they shoot you too!"

"Shut up and—"

A flash from a muzzle lit up the semi-darkness.

Luke dived to her belly and squeezed the trigger, aiming for the shadowy shape behind the flash.

With a gurgling scream, the man went down.

Where's his friend? Luke peered through the gray half-light. *There!*

Behind his fallen friend, the second man swung up his revolver and aimed at her.

She squeezed the trigger again.

Click. The hammer fell on an empty chamber.

Luke looked into the grinning face of Bill Walters. "Bet you wish you hadn't interrupted our bit of fun now," he said, walking closer. The muzzle of his revolver pointed right at her.

"Forcing yourself on a woman is not a 'bit of fun.'" Luke glared at him. "You are a soldier. Where's your sense of honor?"

"I'm no longer a soldier, thanks to you." Hatred blazed in his eyes. He pulled back the hammer of his revolver with a resounding click.

Sweat trickled down her back. She tensed her muscles, even knowing that she couldn't outrun a bullet. She would be dead before she made it to her feet.

The moment when he squeezed the trigger was telegraphed in Walters's eyes.

She rolled to the left, but the booming shot rang out sooner than she expected.

No pain came.

Luke glanced up.

Walters lay facedown in the grass, his right hand still clasping his revolver. Phin stood over him, blood dripping from his arm.

Luke looked around for the third man who had tried to violate the Shoshone woman, but there was no sign of him anywhere. She got to her feet and hurried over to Phin. "You all right?"

Unfocused blue eyes stared in her direction, then at the prone man. "I shot him. I think he's dead." A tremor ran through Phin's tall body.

Luke had seen it before. Phin was a tough man, his body hardened and his reflexes sharpened from working with horses, but he wasn't used to gunfights. This was probably the first time he had even shot at a man, let alone killed one. She knelt and rolled the motionless Walters onto his back. Sightless eyes stared at her, and blood soaked the front of his shirt.

Phin turned away. Retching sounds came from where he crouched behind a shrub of sagebrush.

The part of Luke that Nora called the "mother hen" wanted to rush over, but she had lived among men long enough to know that she would only embarrass Phin. She was his mentor, a father figure, and he wouldn't want her to see him so weak.

Acid burned in her throat as she took the revolver from Walters's stiffening fingers. Then she knelt down next to Charlie.

He was sitting up, clutching his leg.

"Let me see." She slid off his boot and pushed up his pant leg. Blood streamed down his calf. Luke probed with gentle fingers.

Charlie flinched. He stared at his leg, his face pale.

"The bullet is lodged in the fleshy part of your calf. You're lucky it didn't shatter your bone."

"I don't feel lucky," Charlie grumbled. "Is Phin all right?"

Luke nodded and used her bandanna to put a bandage around his calf. It would stop the bleeding until she secured the camp, checked the horses, and made sure the third soldier had stayed behind in Fort Boise, nursing his wounded thigh.

She helped Charlie settle down on his bedroll, then walked over to Phin.

He was on his knees, digging in the earth with frantic fingers.

"Phin," she said. "What are you doing?"

Blood soaked the left sleeve of his shirt, but Phin didn't seem to notice. He continued to shovel earth with his bare hands.

"Phin!"

He looked up, cold sweat beading on his pale face. "I need to dig a grave." He bent and continued to dig.

"Look at me, Phin." Luke used her most commanding voice, the one she had perfected as the boss of half a dozen young men and parent of two adolescent daughters.

His gaze flickered up to her.

"I know killing a man is horrible, even if he wasn't a good man. Taking a life is something you never get over, and that's one thing that separates you from men like Bill Walters. If you hadn't shot him, he would have killed me and then Charlie. You did what you had to, and you saved our lives." She looked into his eyes until the haze cleared. "How is your arm?"

Phin looked at his arm as if he hadn't even realized he'd been shot. "Probably just a scratch."

"Can you go and sit with Charlie while I make sure these two were alone?" She didn't want to send Phin out with a weapon.

His Adam's apple bobbed up and down when he swallowed. He nodded.

"If he can, have him check out your arm." Luke reloaded Walters's revolver, then her own. Dew drenched her pant legs as she walked through the grass, both revolvers at the ready. The horses had fled from the sounds of shots and screams as fast as their hobbled legs allowed. She found them next to two geldings that were tied to a shrub.

A quick check revealed the military brand of the horses. Had they stolen them, or had Captain Kelling helped them take their revenge? As soon as she got home, she would send a letter to Colonel Lundgren.

Just two horses. So the third man stayed behind in Fort Boise. The tension in her body dissipated. *We were lucky. If I hadn't woken up...* The memory of her dream came back to her, and once again she heard Nora order her to open her eyes. It was what had woken her. "Thank you, darling," she whispered.

Luke stared into the darkness, listening for anything out of place. The wind rustled the leaves of a few slender willows. Nearby, the Malheur River gurgled on its way north. Even with two wounded men and the additional horses in tow, she had insisted that they cross the river before resting, just in case someone else was following them and had heard the shots.

Most of the horses were dozing. Phin's gelding bent his head in search of some tender tidbits amidst the valley's coarse grass.

Still, Luke kept her rifle at the ready as she walked over and settled a second blanket over Charlie. The young man groaned in his sleep, then continued to snore even worse than usual. She had given him the last of their whiskey before digging the bullet out of his calf. It dulled his pain, but Phin had still paled at the anguished cries of his friend, and her stomach had roiled too.

Quietly, trying not to startle Phin, she made her way back to the fire. The wound on Phin's arm was little more than a scratch, but she worried about him nonetheless. He stared into the fire, watching the flames devour the dry wood and turn it into ashes.

"Hey." She settled down next to him.

A slight tilt of his head indicated that he was aware of her presence.

"Did I ever tell you about the first time I had to kill a man?"

That pulled him from his stupor. He looked up, his eyes still dull, not the usual sparkling blue. He didn't need to answer; they both knew she hadn't told him. She rarely talked about her life prior to meeting Nora. Still, she waited for him to speak. She wanted Phin to be in the present with her, not retreating into himself.

"No," he said at last, his voice rough. "You haven't."

"It was during the Mexican War. I was barely twenty, and I thought I was really tough." She smiled at the memory of her younger, more naïve self. "I'd made it on my own for a lot of years, worked on half a dozen ranches, and tamed wild horses that no one else could ride."

"Sounds familiar," Phin said. He hadn't been all that different when he had first come to work for her.

"Yeah." Luke grinned. "But instead of doing the clever thing and settling down somewhere, I got it into my head that the dragoons were the right place for me. And maybe they were, for a while, but the war..." She closed her eyes as the old images resurfaced. "There's nothing glorious about killing someone. During my first encounter with the Mexican troops, one of their soldiers galloped right at me, yelling loudly, maybe to scare my horse or to encourage himself. I raised my rifle and fired—but nothing happened. My rifle failed. Back then, most of us still had the old muzzle-loading muskets, and the gunpowder must have gotten wet."

She paused and looked at Phin, who was watching her. The flickering light of the fire pasted shadows across his face. He nodded at her to continue.

"The soldier gave a cry of triumph. He was almost upon me now, and he raised an old revolver." She sucked in a breath.

"I slashed my bayonet across his belly before he could pull the trigger."

"He died?" Phin asked.

"Later, when we searched the battlefield to find fallen comrades, I found him." The image of him clutching his belly, blood staining his once white shirt, had haunted her nightmares for years. "He was just a boy in farmer's clothes, fighting with his father's old revolver. They gave me a medal for fighting in that battle. I didn't want a medal. Killing that boy or any of the other soldiers afterward didn't make me feel proud."

Phin flicked a branch into the fire and nodded.

Sparks rained down around them, and Luke watched them trail down to earth.

"I know you don't feel good about killing Bill Walters, and you shouldn't, even though he was a miserable son of a bitch. But you saved my life and Charlie's. Maybe you can at least feel good about that." She clapped him on the shoulder, knowing it was the only physical comfort allowed between two men. When he looked up from the fire, she added a heartfelt "Thank you."

It wasn't just for her. If she had died, her secret would have been discovered. It would have ended not just her life, but life as her family knew it too.

The shadows lifted from Phin's eyes, and he straightened his shoulders. "I would do it again if I had to."

"I know."

They watched the fire in companionable silence until the blazing flames turned into glowing embers.

HAMILTON HORSE RANCH
BAKER PRAIRIE, OREGON
MAY 31, 1868

"*D*O YOU WANT A MARE or a gelding?" Amy looked over her shoulder at Frankie, who followed her across the ranch yard. While mares were thought to make good mounts for women, most men preferred geldings, saying that mares were too cranky and easily distracted.

What would Frankie prefer? Amy still couldn't figure her out. When she rode with the ranch hands to look at the land, she wore pants and short hair. Most neighbors they met mistook her for a man, and Frankie didn't correct them. But when they went into town on Sunday, Frankie wore a dress, a hairpiece under her elegant hat, and dainty shoes that made Amy's feet hurt just by looking at them. Frankie chatted about the newest fashions back East with the townswomen and seemed as at ease as she was riding the range.

"A mare, please," Frankie said. "I prefer mares, and Sally is getting too old to rush down a hill to rescue damsels in distress." Frankie winked at her.

Amy blushed and wanted to object to being called a "damsel in distress," but Frankie's smile was disarming.

They wandered to the herd in the corral and went from horse to horse in comfortable silence. In a strange way, it reminded Amy of walking with Papa, checking on the horses. *How odd that a woman reminds me of Papa.* Frankie had turned all her assumptions of what a woman's life could be upside down. She wondered what it meant for her. Was she like Frankie in a way? Would it be possible for her to determine her own fate, to make her own decisions without ever getting married?

Next to her, Frankie chuckled. "I'm still confusing you, aren't I?"

Heat stained Amy's cheeks. "No, no, it's just..."

"It's all right." Frankie smiled at her. "I confused myself for a lot of years too."

It was hard to imagine the confident Frankie as a confused young woman. "You like dressing like this, right?" Amy asked.

Frankie ran a hand down the outer seam of her pants. "It's comfortable, yes."

They had that in common. "But you don't dislike dresses, do you?"

"No. I like both, just for different occasions," Frankie said. "A woman doesn't have to wear pants to be strong, Amy."

"Oh, I know." Mama was by far the strongest woman she knew, and Amy had never seen her wear pants.

"I grew up a bit like you." Frankie pointed to the bunkhouse and the corral. "In a man's world. I lived in a mining camp with my father and five brothers. Have you ever seen a mining camp?"

Amy shook her head. "Papa went to Silver City once with a herd of horses, but he said I was too young to come with him."

"And he was right. Mining camps are rough. Except for a few Chinese women, I was the only female for hundreds of miles, and my father dressed me like a boy to protect me from any unwanted advances."

The thought of being courted by a horde of unwashed miners sent ripples of disgust through Amy.

"I enjoyed the freedom it gave me." Frankie leaned her arms on the corral rail and stared off into the distance. "I could roam the area with my brothers instead of staying in the tent. It took me years to figure out that dressing in female apparel is fun too and that being a woman is a wonderful thing."

Is it really? Amy wondered if she would ever see it like that. If she were a man, she could run the ranch without people like Adam questioning her at every turn. *And then my feelings for women wouldn't be wrong.* She suppressed a sigh and forced her thoughts back to Frankie's life instead of her own. "How did you become a Pinkerton detective?"

The smile on Frankie's face vanished. She turned and leaned her left side against the corral, now facing Amy. "My father was killed for a handful of gold."

"I'm sorry." Amy didn't know what else to say. The thought of losing her own father filled her with dread.

Frankie nodded in acknowledgment. A veil of grief still covered the normally clear eyes. "His murderers nearly got away with it. But then a Pinkerton detective hunted them down. I never forgot it. When I came across an advertisement, I applied for a job with the agency."

"They were advertising for female detectives?" Amy shook her head in wonder.

"No." The grin was back on Frankie's face. "They were advertising for a secretary. But I can be very persuasive when I want to be. And my success spoke for itself. I solved a lot of cases by befriending the wives, sisters, and mistresses of suspects in a way no male detective could."

"And your cousin? Was she a Pinkerton too?"

Frankie's lips curled. "No. She helps me get the job done, but Tess was never officially a Pinkerton. She prefers to be her own boss."

They wandered along the corral side by side, again looking at the horses.

"How about that one?" Amy pointed at the dun mare that stretched her head to nibble on a bit of clover growing under the corral rail. A whitish blanket without any spots dusted her hip. "Her name is Zebra. She's not a very tall horse, but she's fast."

Frankie chuckled. "Zebra?"

Amy nodded at the shadowy stripes on the mare's legs. "Yeah, well, Nattie once read a story about zebras. Apparently, they look like horses and they have these stripes too."

"What about her?" Frankie pointed.

"Mouse?" They owned a herd of beautiful, well-trained Appaloosas, and Frankie picked a plain gray mare?

A dark eyebrow rose beneath the brim of Frankie's hat. "Mouse?"

"Well, she's—"

"Gray." Frankie laughed. "And that's why I like her. For my kind of work, I need an inconspicuous horse that no one will remember, not a flashy Appaloosa. So, how much would you want for her?"

"You'll have to talk to my mama about that." Even when Papa was home, Mama always had a say in financial decisions. Then something occurred to her. This was her chance to pay back Rika's ten dollars. "Better yet, talk to Rika. I bought Mouse with her money, so I guess you need to see if she's willing to sell her to you."

"All right," Frankie said. "I'll talk to her."

"Want to try riding her before you decide?" It was a test not just for the mare, but of Frankie's skills as a rider too. Frankie was the cousin of Mama's best friend, but still, Amy wouldn't sell Mouse to her if she didn't have a gentle hand and the experience to handle the skittish mare.

A confident grin tipped up the corners of Frankie's mouth, letting Amy know she suspected the true reason for the offer. "Sure."

Rika swept the soiled straw out of the henhouse and sneezed as dirt and tiny feathers tickled her nose.

The dog shot out from beneath the veranda and raced across the yard, barking.

Rika looked up. Her hands tightened around the broom, ready to defend the hens and the rest of the ranch.

But instead of the coyote she expected, Tess closed the outhouse door behind her.

"Hunter," Rika yelled at the dog. "Quit making such a ruckus. You know Tess isn't an intruder."

Hunter trotted back to her. His wagging tail beat against her skirt, and she reached down to scratch behind his ears.

Slowly, keeping an eye on the dog, Tess walked up to them. "I'm impressed. He listens to you."

"He's gotten used to having me around, and Amy let me feed him a few times, so now he wants to stay in my good graces." Rika weaved her fingers through his shaggy coat. "My first week here, he started barking every time I came near the henhouse too."

"He's defending his home." Tess reached down and let Hunter sniff one of her hands. "Speaking of home, are you really fine about staying with Amy? When you agreed to let us have the cabin, you probably thought we'd stay just a night or two. But now it's been ten days, and I know that's not what you expected. If it's a problem, we can figure out some place else for us to stay."

"Oh, no, it's fine. This way, I can keep a closer eye on Amy." And Amy really needed someone looking after her.

A golden eyebrow arched, and something in Tess's expression made blood rush to Rika's face.

"It's fine," she said again. "If Phineas is anything like the Hamiltons, he wouldn't want it any other way."

Tess's gaze probed hers. "Are you looking forward to meeting him?"

Am I? Part of her was curious about him, but another, bigger part of her dreaded his return. As if acting on a silent pact, she and Amy never talked about her betrothal, so on most days she could forget what had brought her to Oregon. For the first time in her life, she was free to be herself—not the dutiful daughter, the wife, the tireless nurse, or the diligent mill girl. Phineas's return would force her to take on yet another role, that of Jo Bruggeman.

"I don't know." She lifted her shoulders, then let them drop. "I don't know him, so I'm not sure what to expect. I know some people think becoming a mail-order bride is unusual or even immoral, but—"

A soft touch on her forearm interrupted her. "I'm not judging you," Tess said. "God knows, I have no right to judge anyone for her life choices. It's just that you seem," she shrugged, "conflicted about it."

Rika blinked. Was she that easy to read? Dozens of answers ran through her mind, all of them lies that sounded plausible and would get Tess to stop asking questions. But something in those blue eyes made her discard the lies and tell the truth. "I barely made enough for a living in Boston, and I lived in fear of losing my place in the cotton mill every day. I thought marrying a perfect stranger couldn't be any worse than what I'd already been through."

"But?"

Now, after a few weeks at the ranch, she felt as if she had found a place where she wanted to stay and people to whom she might belong some day. The thought of moving away made her heart heavy.

Before she was forced to voice her thoughts, hoofbeats interrupted.

Amy and Frankie swept into the ranch yard and pulled their horses to a stop in a cloud of dust.

At the sight, Rika's heartbeat sped up. *Lord, she's so stubborn.* She had told Amy to stay out of the saddle, and here she was, racing with Frankie. Before Amy could dismount, Rika was at her side.

Ruby flicked her ears in her direction, and she slowed her approach. The mare tugged at the bit. A speck of greenish-white foam landed on Rika's sleeve, and she rubbed it away. *This was not a leisurely ride.* Still in the saddle, Amy towered over her, and Rika craned her neck to glare at her. "Didn't I tell you not to ride for a while?"

Amy shoved her hat back and let it dangle from her back. The temper people usually associated with her hair color sparked in her eyes. "You're not my mother."

Rika pressed her hands to her stomach as if an unexpected punch had hit her. "I thought I was your friend."

The muscles around Amy's mouth and eyes loosened. "You are. I'm sorry. It's just that Frankie wants to buy Mouse, and I wanted to give her a chance to see how far she's come in her training. It's been ten days, so my ribs should be fine."

At the sight of her glowing eyes and wind-reddened cheeks, Rika couldn't hold on to her annoyance.

Tess wandered over and reached out to touch Mouse's neck. Frankie leaned down and kissed her cheek, greeting her cousin in the affectionate way Rika had observed between them since their arrival. Despite having helped to raise her siblings, Rika wasn't that close to any of her relatives.

"They have so many beautiful Appaloosas here, and you decide on this plain little mare named Mouse?" Tess chuckled.

That was how Rika had often felt among her half sisters, the young women in the boarding house, and even here at the ranch. In comparison to all the pretty women, she was plain and uninteresting.

"She's not plain," Amy said.

The passionate fire blazing in her eyes stirred something in Rika. *Does she think that about me too?*

"Look at how she carries herself." Amy gestured to the mare. "With a little more training, she'll be the best horse you ever had—if you want her."

Frankie rested her hand on Tess's shoulder. "Oh, of course I want her." She turned to Rika. "So, how much would you want for her? Is forty dollars enough?"

"Me?"

"I bought her with the money Phin left for you, so she's yours," Amy said.

"But you were the one who did all the work and trained her." Rika didn't want to take Mouse from Amy after the long hours she spent with her in the corral. The ten dollars weren't really hers anyway.

"I promised to pay back your money, and this is the only way I can afford it." Amy lowered her head and looked down at her. "Please, take it."

After a second's hesitation, Rika nodded. At least Mouse would be cared for and could be useful in ways that she wasn't at the ranch.

"Then it's a deal." Frankie swung out of the saddle and looped her arm through Tess's.

A wagon clattered into the ranch yard. "Amy!" Nora called as she pulled Old Jack to a stop. "What are you doing on that horse? Didn't we agree that you would take it easy for a few more days?"

Rika couldn't stop the smirk that spread over her face. "Now she," she nodded at Nora, "is your mother. There's no way you can avoid that dressing-down."

"Thanks," Amy murmured and hastily climbed out of the saddle.

HAMILTON HORSE RANCH
BAKER PRAIRIE, OREGON
JUNE 5, 1868

*R*IKA DRIFTED AWAKE. THE ORANGE light of dawn filtered through her closed eyelids, and she knew she had to get up soon, but for now, she kept her eyes closed. Peace filled her, and a contented hum escaped her lips.

At the tiny sound, something moved against her back, and she became aware of the warm body pressed against her own. Unlike Willem's presence in their bed or her half siblings draping their little bodies over hers, this didn't feel like an intrusion on her space. It felt nice and warm and safe.

Behind her, Amy nuzzled closer in her sleep. Soft locks tickled Rika's neck, and the ebb and flow of Amy's breathing bathed her shoulder and trailed a path of warmth down her body.

Amy murmured something and smacked her lips, making Rika grin. After two weeks of sharing the room and the bed, Amy had finally stopped suggesting she sleep in the stable every night. She still clung to the edge of the bed once they slipped beneath the covers, but after talking for a while, she relaxed enough to sleep.

The nightly conversations were nice. Rika had never shared so much of herself with anyone. She loved how close she felt to Amy when they were huddled together beneath the blankets. Hiding her identity became harder every day.

She was jerked out of her thoughts when a warm hand landed on her hip and slid around to her stomach, then upward toward her bosom.

Lord! Unexpected heat shot through her body. Her smile vanished, and every trace of sleepiness fell off her as her hand shot out to grip Amy's wrist. She craned her neck and looked over her shoulder.

Amy was still fast asleep. Russet lashes rested against golden skin, giving her an appearance of innocence and vulnerability.

Calm down. She's sleeping and didn't mean anything by it. It wasn't Amy's fault if Rika's body reacted in improper ways to an accidental touch. She moved Amy's hand to a safe spot outside of the covers and tried to enjoy a few more minutes in bed, but her body had lost its drowsiness now. Every inch of her skin felt alive after Amy's touch. With a sigh, she slipped out of bed, careful not to disturb her companion.

Amy rolled to her stomach on Rika's side of the bed. Her hands slid over the sheet as if searching for something.

Rika pulled the covers over her shoulders and decided to let her sleep for a few more minutes. With the haying, Amy's day would be long and exhausting enough.

Nora bent and trailed her hand along the wide-bladed grass. A few steps to her right, Hank bit down on a stalk of grass. Nora didn't need to taste it to know that now was the time to bring in the hay crop. If they waited any longer, the stalks would become coarse.

With hardly a cloud in the sky, it was good haying weather. "All right," she said. "Let's get started." She ignored the grumbling from the ranch hands. They detested any work they couldn't do on horseback, and that included haying.

Chains jangled and leather creaked when they put Old Jack and Little Jack in front of the two-wheeled mower. Amy climbed on the seat and gathered the reins, and Nora wanted to race across the field to drag her down from the mower before she could hurt her ribs.

Mowing was not a smooth process. Holes, stones, and stumps lurked beneath the grass, threatening to jerk the breath out of the driver and reinjure Amy's barely healed ribs.

But she held herself back. Amy was a grown woman, a woman who was trying to gain the respect of the ranch hands.

Someone else didn't have that kind of consideration for Amy's authority, though. Hendrika gripped Amy's sleeve and tried to tug her down from the mower. "Let Hank do this."

"I've been handling the team with the mower for years." Amy lifted her chin like a battering ram.

Hendrika didn't let go of her sleeve. "Not with bruised ribs."

They stood caught in a silent battle of wills, until Nora reached them and held out her hand. "How about giving me the reins?"

Amy eyed her. "You want to drive the mower?"

Under her daughter's skeptical gaze, Nora straightened to her full height. "I've been driving that thing since before you were big enough to hold the reins." The first few years in Oregon, they couldn't afford to hire ranch hands, and Nora had helped with every chore on the ranch. When Luke had broken her foot one summer, Nora had been forced to learn quickly. She hadn't handled the mower in recent years and was probably quite rusty, but she couldn't hand the reins to Hank. It would send the message that women shouldn't drive the mower.

Finally, Amy relinquished the reins and climbed down.

The ranch hands stopped their own work to watch. Most of them hadn't seen Nora drive the mower before.

Hendrika gave Nora a nod and helped her up on the seat, perched above the six-foot-long cutting blade sticking out to the right side of the mower. With a deep breath, Nora loosened her grip on the reins and clucked at the horses. "Hyah!"

Old Jack started to pull, and his slightly smaller companion followed.

The mower rattled along the field, jostling her. She kept an eye on the long blade and tried to see through the grass. If she hit a rock or another hidden object, the steel blade might break and would have to be replaced.

Little Jack snorted and tried to veer to the left, away from the whirring blade to his right. Unlike his bigger companion, he was still fairly new to pulling the mower.

"Hey there! None of that, Little Jack." She flicked the reins over his broad back and worked to keep the horses driving in a straight line.

Morning dew was long gone from the field, and the sun was rising. Sweat dripped into her eyes, but she had no time to wipe it away. Next to her, lush stalks fell. Field mice scurried into their hidden holes, and a hawk circled above, waiting for a snack that might be left behind by the rattling blade.

Nora steered the mower around and around until, hours later, the whole field was mowed. If they were lucky enough to get a few days of sunshine, they'd be able to bring in the hay by the end of the week.

Days later, Nora took pitchers of cool water from the wagon and placed them in the shade of a tree while she listened to the preparations going on all around her. Luke said haying reminded her of a battle, and sometimes it was. Some years, they raced against time to bring in their hay before rain could ruin it.

"Hank, you drive the wagon. Emmett, you climb up and pack down the hay," Amy shouted across the field.

If haying is a battle, then Amy is our commander. And she's doing a good job. Nora was filled with pride and sorry that Luke wasn't there to see how well their daughter had adjusted to her responsibilities.

"I'll drive the dump rake," Amy said.

Despite her worries about bruised ribs, Nora let her climb on the rake. She didn't want to undermine Amy's authority in front of the ranch hands a second time. Amy had worked too hard to gain their respect. At least driving the rake wasn't as bad as being jostled around on the mower.

The curved wooden tines of the rake lowered to the ground, and with a shout from Amy, Little Jack started to move. The twelve-foot-long rake quickly filled with hay. When it was full, Amy pushed a lever with her foot. The rake rose and dropped a long pile of hay onto the field. Then the tines dropped down to gather more.

When Amy reached the end of the field, she turned Little Jack and urged him back the other way, next to the piles of hay she had already gathered. Each time she passed them, she pressed the lever and dropped another load of hay next to the one she had made on the previous pass. Long windrows formed until, finally, all the hay was gathered into long rows stretching across the field.

Nora had driven the dump rake a time or two before. She knew it wasn't easy to push the lever at the right moment. The first time she had done it, her windrows had been crooked. Amy's were straight and even, each stalk where it should be.

Tess wandered over, pitchfork already in hand. "She's good at that." She nodded to Amy.

Shading her eyes with one hand, Nora watched as Amy lowered the rake's teeth once again. She didn't try to hide her pride. "Yes, she is."

"Luke mentioned that she's running the ranch until he gets back," Tess said.

"We thought it might be a good test to see if she really wants to take over the ranch one day."

Tess turned away from watching Amy and glanced at Nora. "Luke would love that, wouldn't he?"

"Only if it's what Amy wants for herself."

"What do you think about it?" Tess asked.

"With Luke as her parent, Amy grew up thinking that it's all right for a woman to work with horses, ride the range, and make her own decisions."

"And this was just Luke's influence?"

"No," Nora said. "I wanted this kind of freedom for our daughters too. It's been wonderful to see our girls grow up into strong young women." Her gaze slid to Nattie, who gestured at her pitchfork as she explained something to Frankie.

"So that's a good thing, right?" Tess asked.

Nora looked at her old friend. "Yes, but the rest of the world doesn't think so. You saw what happened with Adam. If Amy chooses to take over the ranch, she won't have an easy life."

"Your life isn't exactly easy either," Tess said. "Just because life isn't easy doesn't mean it can't be happy. Or do you regret your decision to stay with Luke even after you found out about...him?"

"No, of course not."

"But?"

So Tess could still read between the lines. "Sometimes, I wonder if Luke is truly happy."

Blue eyes widened. "You've got to be kidding!"

Never voiced concerns clawed at Nora, finally wanting to be spoken. "The life we built together, it's so fragile. She knows it could be snatched away in a heartbeat, so I wonder if she ever lets herself be completely happy."

"Are you saying you aren't happy?"

"No, God, no! It's just..." Sometimes, she sensed the remaining tension in Luke, and it bothered her that she couldn't give her that complete peace and happiness.

"Sweetie." Tess dropped her pitchfork to clutch Nora's hands. "I've known Luke for many years, and he's never been so at peace as when he's talking about his life with you."

The words eased Nora's worries. "He?" She glanced over her shoulder. They were alone on this part of the field, but Tess kept using male pronouns.

"I know he's...she's a woman," Tess said, her voice low, "but when Luke was with me..." She trailed off and shook her head. "You don't want to hear this."

Part of her wanted to pretend Luke had never been with anyone but her, but the bigger part wanted to learn whatever she could and understand Luke even better than she already did. "I know you and Luke were more than friends for a while." When Tess looked away, she squeezed her hands. "I'm not jealous. I'm grateful you were there for her when she thought no one would ever love her."

"And Luke was there for me when I thought no one would ever love me," Tess said. At the mere mention of love, her gaze left Nora and found Frankie.

Nora smiled. "So, what did you want to say about Luke?"

"When we first met, he...she..."

"It's all right." Nora touched Tess's forearm. "Use whatever feels more natural to you. I know Luke wouldn't mind either way."

"When we first met, he was lonely, cut off from the rest of the world by the need to hide and keep his distance. He was starved for some human touch and affection, yet when he shared my bed..." Tess stopped and looked at her as if to make sure she was still all right with hearing about Luke's past.

Nora's gaze darted left and right. Once she was sure no one was within hearing distance, she nodded at Tess to go on.

"Luke is a wonderful lover, as I'm sure you know." A mischievous smile dimpled Tess's cheeks, and Nora felt heat suffuse her face. "She didn't know what to do with a woman, but she was gentle and attentive. She came into my life at a time when I had already given up on that, so what we had was special. But she rarely allowed me to touch her freely, to touch her as I would another woman. I always got the feeling Luke was more comfortable if I thought of him as a man—so I did."

It had been like that between her and Luke in the beginning too.

"I take it that's not how it is between the two of you?" Tess leaned closer. "Does Luke allow you to caress her breasts, to touch—"

"Lord, Tess!" Blood rushed to Nora's skin, and she knew she was blushing bright red. None of the neighbor women talked about intimate matters so openly. *As a matter of fact, they don't talk about it at all. A lady isn't supposed to enjoy relations with her husband, much less talk about it.*

"What?" Tess chuckled. "You never used to blush about these things."

Her years in Tess's brothel felt like a lifetime ago, and Nora knew she wasn't the same woman anymore. She rubbed the tip of her glowing ear. "Back then, we were talking about the men who touched my body. Luke touches my heart and soul."

Tess pulled her into a quick hug. "I'm so happy for you. And I'm sorry for asking about private matters between the two of you."

"No, it's all right. You can ask. I know you ask because you care about us."

"I do." With one last squeeze, Tess let go. The grin returned to her face. "And you don't need to answer. Your blush speaks for itself."

Again, Nora felt her cheeks grow warm, and she chuckled. "Yeah, well..."

"It's wonderful to know Luke trusts you enough to make herself vulnerable and show you her female side."

It was wonderful. Nora loved the female side as much as the Lucas Hamilton that Luke showed to the world. But old doubts remained, and maybe it was finally time to share them with someone. "Sometimes, I wonder if that kind of trust isn't making things harder for her."

"Harder?" Tess shook her head. "How could that be?"

"Before I met Luke, there wasn't much difference between how she was in private and how she acted around others. The life she lived was that of a man—in almost every way." Seventeen years ago, small children had terrified Luke. She hadn't known how to comfort Amy and had stiffened whenever Amy's little arms wrapped around her in a hug. Back then, Luke had been cut off not just from other people, but from her own emotions. *Good gracious, she didn't even name her horse, just because she thought it was unmanly.*

"And now?" Tess asked.

"And now she enjoys brushing my hair at night. She cries in my arms when one of our horses dies, and sometimes, she comes home with a bouquet of wildflowers and leaves little love notes for me all over the house." Last night, she had found a romantic little note hidden in the drawer that held her chemises. "And," she added with a hint of a blush, "she enjoys it when I make love to her."

A frown deepened the lines on Tess's forehead. "I'd think all of that would make her life happier, not harder."

"Yes, but now she needs to pretend and lie more in the rest of her life to hide that softer side. Now there are two Lukes, where before, there was only one."

A golden-silver lock of hair tumbled from beneath Tess's bonnet when she shook her head. "That part of Luke has always been there. It was just smothered and ignored all those years. Now for the first time, Luke has someone in his life that he trusts enough to show both sides. Your love isn't trapping him. It's freeing him."

"Hey, you two!" A pitchfork of hay rained down on them.

Nora looked up and into Frankie's grinning face.

"Are you here to gab or to help with the haying?" Frankie asked, one hand on her hip.

When Nora let her gaze wander over the field, she found that Amy had finished raking. Now Toby drove the bigger buck rake along the rows of hay and raked them into larger piles.

Tess stuck her tongue out at Frankie, making her look like a little girl despite the gray streaks in her hair. "Gab."

Another forkful of hay hit Tess in the chest. "Help." Frankie returned the playful grin.

Tess picked up her pitchfork and tossed hay in Frankie's direction.

"Hey, what's going on?" Amy strode toward them. "Mama, you did tell them that the hay is supposed to go in the wagon, right?"

Nora laughed. It was good to have Tess back in her life.

"Whoa!" Hank called when the wagon rolled through the big double doors of the barn. It pulled to a stop right under the hay door that went up into the loft.

Amy jumped down from the wagon. Before Emmett could do it, she extended a hand to help Rika down.

Emmett climbed into the hayloft. From a track on the roof of the barn, the hayfork was lowered into the wagon, and Hank guided it to grasp a load of hay.

"Come on." Amy nudged Rika, who stared up into the loft. "You can help me with the horses." Two geldings were already harnessed to the rope that ran through a system of pulleys. "Grab his bridle."

They urged the horses forward, and the hay was lifted into the loft.

Up in the loft, Emmett shouted, "Stop 'em!"

"Whoa!" Amy pulled the horse on her side to a stop while Rika tightened her grip on the other gelding.

They smiled at each other.

Hank pulled the rope that tripped the release, opening the hayfork and dropping its load into the loft. While he directed the fork back into the wagon, Amy turned the horses to heave up the next load.

After several repetitions, the wagon sat empty. A sense of accomplishment swept over Amy, and she shook her head at herself. *It's just the first load. Back to work.* She turned toward Hank. "You and Emmett take the wagon back to the field.

Rika and I will climb up and stack the hay to make room for more."

The two men didn't hesitate to follow her orders. Within a minute, the wagon rumbled out of the barn, leaving Amy and Rika behind.

"You up for it?" Amy pointed to the loft. Stowing away the hay was hard work.

"Of course." Rika never shied away from any task. It was part of what Amy liked about her.

Stifling hot air engulfed Amy as soon as she stuck her head through the open hay door and pulled herself into the loft. The sun had been standing high up in the sky for hours, and heat accumulated under the roof. Sweat trickled down her back, and she hadn't even picked up a pitchfork yet.

"What do I do?" Rika asked, pitchfork already in hand.

The hay had been dropped in the middle of the loft, and Amy pointed at the big pile. "We spread the hay and level it to make room for more. Be sure to fill the corners and edges of the loft." To demonstrate, she stuck her pitchfork into the hay and lifted the first forkful. Two quick steps and she dropped it neatly into one corner of the hayloft.

They worked side by side, sometimes brushing against each other as they walked back and forth between the corners and the big hay pile. Combined with the dusty heat in the loft, the little touches made her blood seem to boil. It was sweet torture, and Amy berated herself but couldn't quite stop.

Finally, she paused and leaned on her pitchfork to wipe sweat from her face. Her gaze swept over what they had accomplished and the shrinking pile of hay in the middle of the loft. Then she looked at Rika, and for a few moments, she forgot the work still to be done.

Beams of sunlight trickled into the loft, bathing Rika in gold. Her skirt and bodice, damp with sweat, clung to the gentle curves of her body. She had removed her bonnet, and now stalks of hay dotted the mahogany hair. A few tendrils had gotten loose from their pins and stuck to the fair skin of her neck. Her face was flushed, and Amy watched as a drop of sweat trailed down her neck. She wanted to step closer and kiss away that bead of sweat.

"What?" Rika set down her pitchfork when she noticed Amy's staring. Her gloved hands flew up to touch her hair. "Something wrong with my hair?"

It's beautiful, Amy wanted to say, but, of course, she didn't. "No. It's just covered in hay dust."

"So's yours." Rika reached out but pulled back before she touched Amy's hair.

Amy cleared her throat. "Let's get something to drink." She walked to the edge of the hayloft, where she'd left her canteen. Maybe cooling off with a sip of water would chase away the inappropriate thoughts swirling through her head. She uncorked the canteen and handed it to Rika first.

With a nod of thanks, Rika lifted the canteen to her lips and tilted back her head. Amy couldn't help watching the graceful arch of her neck as she swallowed. The urge to press her lips to that fair neck raced through her, and she fought it down. Usually, she had much better control over those urges. *Must be the heat up here. It's messing with my head.* She took the canteen back and took a swig. The water was warm, but it still felt good sliding down her parched throat.

A soft hand touched her forearm. Rika had taken off her gloves and trailed her fingers up to the bend of Amy's arm.

The gulp of water in Amy's mouth shot back out.

"Hey!" Rika jumped back when drops of water drenched her.

Coughing and wheezing, Amy stared at her, then at her own arm, which still tingled. "W-what are you doing?"

"Your arms..."

"What about them?" Amy stared at her arms, halfway expecting to see burn marks where Rika's touch had heated her skin. Instead, her forearms were speckled with tiny red marks where hay stalks had pricked her.

"You should roll down your sleeves," Rika said. She wiped a few drops of water from her face. "And thanks for the refreshment."

Dumbfounded, Amy stared at her for a second and then discovered the unexpected twinkle in the brown eyes. When Rika had first arrived at the ranch, she had been earnest and serious all the time. Rarely had Amy seen her laugh or smile, and the good-natured teasing in the Hamilton family had clearly been foreign to her.

But now a mischievous grin parted her lips, giving Amy a glance of the charming gap between her front teeth. The sight of Rika's playfulness filled Amy with a heady feeling. Laughter bubbled up, chasing away her awkward breathlessness. "Oh, you! Since I provided you with a nice cooling bath, how about I help you dry off too?" Not giving Rika time to answer or flee, she picked up a handful of hay and threw it at her.

Rika sputtered and blew stalks away from her face. Then she dived for Amy.

They tumbled into the hay, laughing and trying to stuff handfuls of hay down each other's clothes. Light-headedness gripped Amy, and she felt drunk on Rika's laughter.

They rolled through a pile of hay, stalks raining down on them. A warm touch slid up Amy's belly. She froze. Then hay tickled her skin, and she tried to squirm away. Next to the still open hay door, they rolled to a stop with Rika coming to rest on top of her.

"Careful," Amy whispered, not just meaning the open hatch next to them. She felt on the edge of something dangerous, something she couldn't name. Her breath rattled through her chest, and it wasn't the weight on top of her that made her breathless.

They stared at each other. Then Rika's eyes widened. "Your ribs!" She scrambled back.

Amy sucked in a cooling breath—and almost choked on it when Rika's hands flew over her body.

"Did I hurt you?" Uncoordinated, Rika searched for any sign of injury. "Lord, I'm so sorry. I didn't think about your ribs."

"It's all right. It's fine." Amy gasped when Rika accidentally brushed the outer edge of her breast. Panic warred with the hunger low in her belly and finally won. She crawled backward, trying to escape.

"Amy!" Rika lunged forward, threw her arms around Amy, and prevented her from tumbling through the hay door. "What are you doing? You almost fell!"

What am I doing? What am I doing? Amy had no answer. Her heart thumped so loudly that she was sure Rika could hear it.

"Are you all right?" Rika touched her cheek.

Amy nodded shakily even though she felt anything but all right. "You?"

"I'm fine," Rika said. Her face was flushed from their roughhousing and uncontrolled laughter.

Amy slipped out of her arms, careful not to come too close to the hay door again. "We should finish stowing away the hay before Hank comes back with the next load."

A shower of hay rained down from Rika when she got to her feet and shook herself. She looked around at the scattered piles, her full lips crooking into a half smile. "Oh, we really made a mess of things."

Yeah. That was exactly how Amy's formerly well-ordered life felt. *A complete and utter mess.* Sighing, she shook bits of hay from her shirt and picked up her pitchfork.

THE DALLES, OREGON
JUNE 9, 1868

"*B*oy, I've never been so damn glad to see a town in my life," Charlie said as they rounded the last bend in the river and the houses of The Dalles appeared before them.

Luke halted Dancer next to Charlie's gelding and gave the young man a pat on the shoulder. The last two weeks had been hard on him. His boot and the stirrup leather rubbed against his injured leg with every step his horse took. Every morning, Luke wrapped a new bandage and thick padding around his calf, but the wound still hadn't closed. It would heal once Charlie stayed out of the saddle for a while, and as soon as they got home, she would make sure he did.

"We'll stay overnight," she said. It would give Charlie a chance to rest his leg and her an opportunity for a bath. While taking care of Charlie and making sure Phin was all right, she hadn't been able to slip away for a quick dip in the creek. "Phin, take one of the double eagles. Go to the bank and get silver dollars for it. Board your horses, then buy yourself and Charlie a juicy steak and a drink. Book rooms in the hotel for tonight."

The prospect of a good meal and a soft bed put a smile on Phin's face for the first time in days. By the time they dismounted on the main street with its false fronts, he was joking around with Charlie.

Exhaustion overcame Luke when she led Dancer and Bill Walters's two geldings to the livery stable. Even the trail dust on her clothes seemed to weigh her down. *You're not a young man anymore,* she told herself with a wry grin, then chuckled when she noticed she had used "man," not "woman." After living in close quarters with two of her ranch hands for every minute of the last six weeks, the differences between who she was and who she pretended to be began to blur.

273

She longed to go home and rediscover the closely guarded parts of herself in Nora's gentle embrace. *Soon.* Two more weeks and she would be home. If they hurried, they might make it in ten or eleven days. On the lonely mountain roads, she knew she would count the hours.

She put Dancer up in a stall at the livery stable and took her time brushing his coat until it gleamed. For a few cents extra, the stable owner would do it for her, but Luke preferred to do it herself. It gave her time to bond with Dancer and to check him over for little injuries that might have happened on the trail.

When she left the livery stable, two men were in the corral, looking at a horse.

"Twenty dollars?" One of them laughed. "I won't pay you a dime for that misbehaving devil! Show me another horse."

The harsh words caught Luke's attention. After living with horses for all her life, she knew most misbehaving horses were the owner's fault. She looked at the horse in the corral. *Ah. A Percheron mare.* She was on the lookout for a horse just like that one. With railroads being built in the West, there was money to be made in breeding draft horses, and she liked the gentle giants.

Her gaze slid up and down the horse, trying to figure out what was wrong with her. Strong muscles played beneath the shining black coat. At seventeen hands, the mare dwarfed Luke's Appaloosas. She took in the deep, wide chest, the broad forehead, and the gracefully arched neck. Luke knew the breed to be willing workers, ideal for logging and hard farm work.

This one didn't seem very obedient, though.

The owner directed the mare around the corral with a rope in an attempt to show her off. But it wasn't working. Instead of following every tug on the rope and presenting smooth gaits, the mare pranced around the corral and tried to circle to the right even though her owner wanted her to go in the other direction.

On first glance, not a horse worth buying. But Luke had learned to look beneath the surface. She stepped to the corral. "I'll give you ten dollars for her."

The owner's head snapped around. His eyes lit up. "She's worth more. She's young, strong, and has many good years left."

"Don't let him talk you into it. That horse isn't worth it," the other man said. "You'd have to break her first. When he tried to put a saddle on her earlier, she bucked like crazy."

The mare's owner shot him a glare.

Luke ducked beneath the corral rails and walked up to the mare. Murmuring reassurances, she checked her teeth and slid a hand over the muscular neck, back, and hip. The horse shied away with a violent swish of her tail. "Easy, easy." She waited until the mare calmed, then turned to the owner. "Ten dollars."

"Fool." With a snort, the second man walked away.

Luke didn't look at him. She had learned decades ago not to react to stupid provocations.

"All right. You won't regret it." The owner tried with little success to hide his grin.

"I know."

The young mare wasn't a misbehaving devil that needed to be broken. Luke was fairly sure she had a sore back, probably caused by tack that didn't fit and rubbed against her day in and day out. But instead of looking for the cause of her sudden disobedience, her owner had concluded that she was misbehaving and needed to be sold.

What the mare needed was enough rest and an owner with some horse sense.

Luke vowed that she would get both. She flipped a golden eagle coin into the air and watched as the stable's owner clasped his greedy hand around it. "I'll pick her up before I leave tomorrow. When you bring her in tonight, make sure you put the feeding trough to her right."

"To her right?"

"Yeah. She's got a sore back, and it's uncomfortable for her to bend her neck to the left." Luke walked away without looking back.

WILLAMETTE VALLEY, OREGON
JUNE 21, 1868

"MM, NICE." RIKA LEANED BACK on the wagon seat and enjoyed the sunshine and Amy's warmth against her side. Sunlight danced over the path in front of them and made Old Jack's coat gleam. A light breeze carried the scent of wild roses and freshly mowed grass. At the clip-clop of Old Jack's hooves, a robin fluttered from one tree to the other.

Her gaze wandered over the valley. By now, the hills and the flatland along the river didn't feel foreign anymore. On days like this, she felt stirrings of the love for the land that she saw shining in Amy's eyes.

Reins held loosely in one hand, Amy stretched like a contented cat and reached up to remove her bonnet. Her red locks shone like polished copper in the sun.

After a second's hesitation, Rika took off her own bonnet.

Amy turned her head, and they shared a conspiratorial grin.

It was the first time in the two weeks since that strange moment in the hayloft that they had fully relaxed around each other. How was it that Amy's presence put her at ease yet made her nervous at the same time? What she felt for Amy was different from her friendship with Jo, but she hadn't quite figured out how and why.

"Wouldn't it be nice if we didn't have to sit in church on a beautiful day like this?" Amy tugged at her bodice. "We could admire the Lord's creations much better out here than in a stuffy building."

What a daring thought. If Rika had uttered such a thing at home, her father would have beaten her for her insolence. But she was an adult now, and she was learning not to care what her father would have done. "It would be nice, but your mother and Nattie would worry if we didn't show up for church." The two other Hamilton women had ridden ahead to meet the Garfields before church.

"Maybe we could stop on the way back and pick a few strawberries." A grin chased away Amy's frown. "I know a hidden meadow where the best ones grow."

Strawberries. Rika could almost sense the ripe, sun-warmed taste on her tongue. Her mouth watered. Only once in her life had she gotten to try strawberries. The thought of sharing the juicy treats with Amy sent a shiver of delight up and down her spine. "I'd love that."

On the path ahead of them, a horse neighed.

Amy slowed the wagon, making their approach as silent and cautious as possible. She reached for her rifle. As she had promised Rika, she was more careful not to charge into potentially dangerous situations without being prepared.

Their wagon crested the hill, and Amy pulled on the reins to stop Old Jack before whoever was ahead of them could see them.

Rika craned her neck.

"Mouse," Amy said. "It's just Tess and Frankie." She let go of her rifle.

In the valley below them, the gray mare munched on a tuft of grass. Frankie had gotten out of the saddle while Tess waited, still mounted on her own horse.

"Seems they had the same idea." Amy grinned. "Frankie's picking strawberries."

Tess's laughter drifted over when Frankie returned with a handful of the little red fruits and offered them up. But instead of reaching out, Tess bent and plucked the fruit right off Frankie's hand with her lips.

Rika had opened her mouth to shout a greeting. Now her mouth snapped closed. A sudden image of Amy feeding her strawberries formed before her mind's eye, but she chased it away with a shake of her head.

Before Tess could straighten in the saddle, Frankie reached up and pressed their lips together. It was not a friendly peck between cousins.

Heat swirled through Rika's belly, up her chest, and then crawled up her face. It took her a while to form words. "W-what are they doing? They're cousins! And they...they're both women!"

When no answer came, she turned to see Amy's reaction.

Her friend was staring ahead with a pale face. Her left hand clutched the reins in a white-knuckled grip while her right hand was clamped around her knee.

"Amy?"

Amy flinched and turned toward her. It was hard to figure out what she was feeling and thinking, maybe because she felt so many things at once, as Rika did. "Maybe it was just a kiss between cousins." Her trembling voice made it sound like a question, not a statement.

But Rika knew what she had seen. She had lived her whole life facing reality, no matter how unpleasant it might be. That had not been a gesture of affection between relatives. "You don't kiss your sister like that, do you?"

"No!" Amy's face went from white to deep red. "I'd never—"

Rika touched her arm. "I know."

When Amy's gaze flickered down to the hand on her arm, Rika withdrew. They sat in silence until Old Jack let out a snort.

Frankie and Tess looked up from sharing more strawberries.

"Hello, you two," Tess called when Amy directed the wagon down the hill. "Are you off to church?"

Speechless, Rika nodded.

"We're not coming this time." Tess smiled at them as if nothing had happened. "We decided to enjoy the Lord's creation out here instead."

"Yeah. We're gonna have a picnic with strawberries." Frankie presented her hand that cradled a few more of the berries. "Want some?"

Still pale, Amy shook her head. "No. No, thanks. We better get going, or we'll be late for church."

The wagon jerked forward as if Old Jack felt his owner's agitation.

Rika spent the rest of the ride to town in a daze.

"I'm sorry," Amy said after a long silence.

"You don't need to apologize. You're not the one who goes around kissing other women."

But the look of guilt and confusion didn't leave Amy's face. They drove along in silence the rest of the way.

Back in Boston, Rika had liked going to church since it was the only interruption to long, monotonous workweeks. But now she couldn't wait to leave Baker Prairie's little church. She squirmed on the hard pew while Reverend Rhodes delivered his sermon about sin.

Surely it's a sin to kiss your cousin that way. To kiss another woman.

But still, she knew Frankie and Tess were good people. Nora thought highly of them, and they had saved Amy's life. And there was so much love in the way Frankie had fed the strawberries to Tess. Was this really wrong in the eyes of the Lord while her father's cold, sometimes cruel treatment of her stepmother was considered normal?

She didn't know what to think anymore.

Amy wasn't faring any better. Whenever Rika sneaked glances at her during the sermon, she found Amy staring at her hands as if she didn't want to meet anyone's gaze. Sometimes, she flinched when the pastor promised eternal hell to sinners who didn't repent.

As soon as the pastor gave his blessing and church was over, Rika rushed down the aisle toward the church's exit. With a shy nod, she ducked past the pastor, who stood next to the portal to say good-bye to his parishioners.

Behind her, Amy mumbled a quick greeting and followed her down the church steps.

"Miss Bruggeman," the pastor called.

Rika froze. She felt as if the Lord's lightning had struck her. Slowly, she turned around, shoulders lifted as if to protect her vulnerable neck. "Yes?"

The pastor descended the steps, his gaze never leaving her.

Does he know what Tess and Frankie did? What kind of thoughts I've been having about Amy? She shook off her panic. *He's a pastor, not a mind reader.* She tried to put on the mask that had protected her so well in the past but found it hard to erect the familiar walls.

"You've been part of the congregation for a while now, but I haven't found the time to talk to you," Reverend Rhodes said when he stopped next to her. "How do you like it here in Baker Prairie?"

The knot in her stomach loosened. "I like it just fine. The people here are wonderful." She looked at Amy, who was waiting a few steps away.

When the pastor followed her gaze, he lifted an eyebrow but said nothing.

Words weren't necessary. Rika had read the silent disapproval on people's faces often enough when they'd looked at her, knowing she was the daughter of a drunkard and the wife of a ne'er-do-well husband. *He doesn't approve of Amy, because she's not like the other girls in town.* Her lips pressed together until they felt numb. *He doesn't know Amy's kindness, has never seen her care for the animals, yet he judges her for the way she dresses.*

She waited for him to nod and move on to other parishioners, but the pastor kept looking at her. "Phineas is expected back soon," he said. "It's time to discuss your wedding ceremony."

Oh, no. Rika couldn't deal with that. Not today. "Oh, Reverend, I can't possibly make decisions about wedding plans without Mr. Sharpe and without even having met him. Maybe we can talk some other time, when he's back. Now, would you excuse me, please? The Hamiltons are waiting for me." She pointed at Nattie and Nora, who had joined Amy next to the wagon.

"Come see me as soon as Phineas is back." The pastor's stern gaze drilled into her. "You can't live under the same roof with Phineas and not be married to him."

"I won't," Rika said.

One of the women who sat in the first pew every Sunday waved to get the pastor's attention.

"Until next Sunday, then." With one last glance, he walked away.

"What did he want?" Amy asked when Rika climbed onto the wagon. She fidgeted with the reins as if she, too, wondered whether the pastor somehow knew about Frankie and Tess's improper behavior.

Rika settled the folds of her skirt around her and made sure her ankles were covered. "He wanted to discuss the wedding ceremony."

For the long way home, Nora and Nattie, who rode next to the wagon, talked about what Rika would wear, how they would decorate the church, and what passages the pastor would read from the Bible.

Wedding preparations didn't hold Rika's attention. Five years ago, those things had more meaning for her. She had altered one of her mother's old dresses to fit her slim frame, walked miles to pick a few sprigs of cherry blooms, and obsessed about the way her hair looked. Now she knew those things held no importance. Her marriage hadn't turned out any better because of them.

Over and over, her thoughts slid back to seeing Frankie and Tess kiss. They passed the little bend in the path where the strawberry picnic had taken place. It was deserted now, and Rika wondered if she had imagined it all.

But then she saw Amy's gaze flit to the spot.

Rika sighed. Her life had changed. Everything was different—she was different, and she wasn't even sure how.

"Lord, we thank you for this food. Please bless our family, our friends, and the horses." Mama let her gaze travel over the people at the table. "Amen."

"Amen," Amy mumbled. Her mother had asked the Lord to bless Frankie and Tess. Didn't she know God considered them sinners?

Rika nudged her. "Dumplings?" She held the bowl out to Amy and studied her.

"Thanks." Amy's stomach churned at the thought of eating, but she placed three dumplings on her plate. If she took fewer, Mama would become suspicious.

On the other side of the table, Mama heaped chicken and gravy onto Frankie's plate and offered a slice of bread to Tess. They laughed at something, but Amy's thoughts were whirling and she couldn't follow the conversation. *Mama treats them like cherished friends, not like sinners.* She probably didn't know about their unnatural ways. Or was it possible that she knew and was all right with women loving each other? Amy was afraid to let herself hope.

"You're not eating," Rika whispered. The warmth of her arm penetrated Amy's shirt. "You all right?"

"Just fine." Forcefully, Amy's fork sliced through the dumplings.

"Liar."

Amy blinked. Was this the plain young woman who had arrived here two months ago? If she was honest with herself, she had stopped thinking of Rika as plain weeks ago. Now she saw the strength and the beauty in her stern features. Not knowing how to answer, she pierced a bit of chicken with her fork and swallowed it past the lump in her throat.

HAMILTON HORSE RANCH
BAKER PRAIRIE, OREGON
JUNE 21, 1868

"*N*ORA!"

The urgent whisper stopped Nora on her way to the springhouse. She turned her head.

Tess peeked out of the cabin, waving at her to come over.

Fetching the butter could wait. Except for supper, Nora hadn't seen Tess all day, not even at church. Was something wrong with her friend? She hurried over.

Tess closed the door behind them and gestured to the table, where Frankie was sitting.

"What happened?" Nora took in the serious faces of her friends.

"Please sit down, Nora."

She sank onto a chair and laid her hands on the scarred table. Lovingly, she traced the burn marks in the wood, taking comfort in the old memories the cabin held.

"I think Amy knows," Tess said.

Nora's grip on the table turned desperate. Her heart lurched against her ribs, pounding out a frantic staccato. She had lived in fear of this happening for many years, and now that the moment had come, she found she was utterly unprepared. "Amy knows?"

Her cheeks pale beneath a hint of rouge, Tess nodded.

"But how? Now that Luke's not here, how could she find out?"

"Luke?" Tess frowned, then pressed her hands to her cheeks. "Oh, I'm not talking about that. Luke's secret is safe."

Nora sank against the back of her chair. She clutched her chest and felt her heartbeat settle down. "Lord, Tess, you scared me. What does Amy know, then?"

"She knows about me and Frankie. At least I'm fairly sure she does. I thought I was imagining things at first, but she stared at us all through supper. I bet she knows."

Oh. That was bad—but still better than Amy finding out Luke's secret. Luke and she had raised their daughters to respect other people, no matter how different from them they might be. But as far as Nora knew, Amy had never met a woman who had relations with other women. "How did she react?"

"She and Hendrika both turned whiter than your whitest tablecloth." At the moment, Tess was as pale as a tablecloth too.

Nora rubbed her forehead. "Hendrika knows too?" She was fairly sure Amy wouldn't run to town screaming and lamenting about the abnormal women who lived in their cabin, but she had no idea what Hendrika would do.

"They came across us on their way to church. I'm pretty sure they saw us kiss." Tess exchanged guilty glances with Frankie. "I'm sorry. We shouldn't have been so careless. We never were before. We learned to keep our distance from each other when we're out in public."

Frankie reached over and took Tess's hand. "This," she made a gesture with her free hand that included the whole ranch, "is such a safe haven that we stopped being so careful all the time. I'm sorry too."

"No," Nora said. "You don't have to be sorry. A safe haven is exactly what Luke and I want our home to be." They had hired Toby even though he was becoming too old for ranch work; they took in Phin when he was little more than a homeless boy running away from his father, and Luke brought Hank home when he was down on his luck, nursing a broken leg. "I'm sorry you can't show your love for each other the way Luke and I can. It's not fair that you have to hide."

"We all have a price to pay for happiness," Tess said, her eyes soft and sad.

Frankie rubbed her thumb across the back of Tess's hand. "What do we do now? Should we try to convince Amy and Hendrika that in our hometown, cousins kiss each other like that?"

A tired smile tugged at Nora's lips. "I don't think they'd buy that. And there are already enough lies in our family. I don't want more. I trust Amy not to panic and tell the whole town."

"What about Hendrika?" Tess asked.

That was the big unknown. "I'm not sure," Nora said. "But I hope she'll follow Amy's lead, like she did when they rescued the horses from the burning stable and the foal from the river."

"Then let me go and talk to them," Tess said. "I'm sure they're pretty confused and have a lot of questions."

Frankie rose to follow her.

"No," Tess said. "Let me talk to them alone."

"Why? I was the one who kissed you."

"Yeah, but I'm the one who ate the strawberries right out of your hand."

Nora raised a brow. *Strawberries?*

Frankie looked at Tess. "Together?"

No more words were needed between them. "Together," Tess said.

A quick gesture from Nora stopped them. She trusted Tess, but this was her responsibility. "No. I'll do it."

"Are you sure?" Tess asked. "Frankie and I caused this situation, and I feel bad that now you have to be the one to take care of it."

"I'm Amy's mother, and Hendrika is a guest in my house," Nora said. "I need to make sure they're all right."

Tess squeezed her hand. "Please let them know they can talk to us too. I don't want them to think we're avoiding them now that they know. We haven't changed, and they can still talk to us."

"I'll make sure they know." With her hand on the old table, Nora pressed up from her chair. "Then let me go talk to my daughters."

A frown deepened the lines across Tess's forehead. "Daughters? You mean you want to tell Nattie too?"

Nora nodded.

"Is that wise?"

Nora understood the fear in her eyes. Tess and Frankie had hidden for years. Telling someone was a risk they were reluctant to take. "If Amy knows, Nattie deserves to know too. I don't want Amy to think your relationship is something bad, something she has to hide even from her own sister."

"How will your daughters take this?" Tess worried her lip.

"I'm not sure. I want to believe that they will come to accept it after a while, but we never actually talked about anything like this."

"You never had a reason to."

"There were two widows living together a few years back, but we avoided the subject, mostly because we didn't want to give the girls any ideas about Luke." Maybe being so overly cautious was a mistake. Nora walked to the door. "Let's get this over with." When the door fell closed behind her, she felt as if she were marching into battle.

Nora trudged across the ranch yard while she searched for the right words. What could she say to make her daughters understand that Tess and Frankie's relationship was not a sin but needed to be protected from others anyway?

When she looked up, the ranch yard was no longer empty. Ruby stood tied to the corral rail, swatting flies from her rump with her tail.

"Hey, girl." Nora walked over and scratched beneath the mare's mane. "What are you doing here?"

Creaking leather made her glance up.

Amy, dressed in pants even though it was Sunday, carried her saddle out of the stable. When she saw Nora standing next to the horse, the saddle sagged in her grasp. She paused but then swung the saddle on Ruby's back.

Nora narrowed her eyes at her. "You're not riding out now, are you?"

"I want to check on the yearlings and the foals." Amy turned her back and reached under Ruby's belly for the cinch.

"You can do that tomorrow. We need to talk."

"Papa will be home soon," Amy said. "I want to make sure he finds the herd in good shape." She tightened the cinch with more force than necessary.

Ruby snorted and stepped to the side.

"Sorry, girl," Amy murmured and gentled her touch.

Nora grasped her shoulder, stopping her from circling Ruby to check the saddle from the other side. Gently, she pulled her around. "I think Luke would rather have his daughters in good shape, and you're clearly not. Amy, I understand why you're upset. Seeing Tess and Frankie kiss each other must have—"

"You know about them?" Amy's voice squeaked. "And you still let them stay?"

Little hairs rose on Nora's neck. Where was this disapproval coming from? "They are our friends." She held her daughter's gaze until Amy looked away. "I know this is confusing for you. Come inside with me, and let's talk about it."

Amy's face was pasty under the brim of her hat. "There's nothing to talk about."

"Of course there is!" Nora softened her tone. "Come on. Let's go inside."

Dust whirled when Amy scraped the heel of her boot over the ground. "Can't it wait?"

Nora hesitated. Should she force her to talk about it even though she clearly wasn't ready? Or should she let her go and wait until she calmed down?

"Please, Mama."

When Amy directed a begging look at her, Nora almost expected to see her eyes white-rimmed with panic.

"Mama..." Next to Amy, Ruby pranced as if infected by her owner's agitation.

Luke had taught Nora that it was never wise to get between a scared creature and its escape route. Maybe it was best to give Amy some time alone. "All right." She brushed a speck of dirt from Amy's chaps. "I still think you'd feel better if we talked about it now, but you are an adult, and I trust you to come to me when you're ready to talk about it."

Amy lifted her gaze. "Thank you."

"I also trust you to keep Tess and Frankie safe."

"Safe?"

"Most people wouldn't understand their relationship. Some might even hate them. I hope you won't be one of those people." She paused, hoping Amy would assure her she wasn't, but Amy said nothing. "If you meet Hannah or anyone else, please don't mention Tess and Frankie's relationship. Even people we think we know well can react in unpredictable ways. Some might even try to harm Tess and Frankie."

The color drained from Amy's face. "I won't say a word."

Nora watched as she swung into the saddle. "Don't stay away for too long, and be careful, please."

"If I don't find all of the foals down by the river, I might stay at a line shack," Amy called. Before Nora could answer, she loped away and disappeared in a cloud of dust.

Voices came from inside the house, and Nora identified Nattie's cheerful tone. A more reserved voice answered every now and then. *Hendrika.* She hesitated with her hand on the door. Was Hendrika telling Nattie what she had seen? No, she didn't seem the kind of woman who would blurt out information like that.

She opened the door and stepped into the parlor.

"If you smudge it with your thumb, you can make it look like shadows," Nattie said. She and Hendrika sat at the large table, sheets of paper all around them.

Hendrika's tongue peeked out of the corner of her mouth as she drew a piece of charcoal over the paper in front of her.

"Hello, you two," Nora said.

Nattie looked up. "I finally convinced Hendrika to try her hand at drawing."

"Hm." Nora took a breath. "Can I talk to you?"

Hendrika picked up her stack of papers. "I'll go upstairs and leave you two to talk."

A "wait" was already on Nora's tongue. Her request to talk included both of them, but maybe talking to them separately was a good idea.

"Can I take a piece of charcoal to draw another?" Hendrika asked.

"Of course," Nattie said. "See, I told you you'd like it." She watched Hendrika climb the stairs, then added, "And she's really good at it too. Probably gets it from her mother." She turned a sheet of paper that had gotten mixed up with her own stack.

Nora studied it. Careful strokes of charcoal formed the strong flanks of a horse and the proud bend of its neck. Its ears flicked back to the rider, who seemed one with the horse, drawn in one big sweep. A dented hat hung down the rider's back, and the wind combed through an untamed tangle of hair. The horse's legs were a bit too thin and the rider's torso seemed out of proportion, but the picture clearly portrayed Amy on her favorite mare.

Thinking of Amy out there on Ruby right now made Nora's stomach clench, but she shoved away her worries. Now it was time to focus on her younger daughter. She glanced at the drawing. "She's quite good."

"Yes." Nattie's lips twitched. "Figures she would be better than me at this too."

"You're not jealous, are you?"

"No, it's just—" Nattie stopped and shrugged. "I'm not jealous, just surprised."

They looked down, studying the drawing again. The raw strokes held a simple beauty, and Hendrika had drawn the details with loving attention.

"Frankie mentioned that she saw portraits like this in Paris," Nora said.

Excitement smoldered in Nattie's eyes. She looked ready to run out the door and pepper Frankie with questions. "Frankie has been to Paris?"

"I'm sure she'll tell you all about it tomorrow, but first, I need to talk to you."

Nattie laid down her piece of charcoal. "What's going on? Everyone is acting so strange around here. First, Amy runs off to check the yearlings even though it's Sunday. And Hendrika seems a bit..." She gestured but couldn't find the right words.

"Amy and Hendrika found out something that left them pretty confused." Nora hesitated. Was it fair to put Nattie through that kind of confusion too?

"What?" Nattie glowed with interest. She was always eager to discover the new things life had to offer. One way or another, Nattie would find out, and Nora decided it would be better if she learned it from her.

She swallowed and realized she'd never had to tell anyone something like this. Since Luke lived as a man, they'd been spared that experience. She longed to have Luke by her side, just to hold her hand and give her courage.

"What is it?" Nattie tugged on Nora's sleeve.

"Tess and Frankie..." Nora licked dry lips. "They're not cousins."

Nattie swiped at a lock of dark hair that fell into her eyes, and a smudge of charcoal appeared on her forehead. "They're not? Then why did they tell us that?"

"It's hard to explain."

Eyes calm, Nattie watched her, not judging, just trying to figure it out.

"It's not that they wanted to lie to you, but telling people that they are cousins allows them to share a room without anyone suspecting."

"Suspecting what?"

Nora took a steadying breath. "That they're sweethearts."

Papers rustled when Nattie dropped them. "Sweethearts?"

"They love each other," Nora said.

"Love each other?" Nattie echoed again. "You mean, they—" She shook her head. "What exactly do you mean?"

How could she explain this? Nora thought of Luke. "It means Tess loves Frankie's courage, the way she can be confident without being stuck-up, and Frankie loves Tess for her good heart and—"

"They admire each other." Nattie's expression cleared when she thought she finally understood.

"Yes, but that's not all. Tess also loves Frankie's body and her lips and the expression in her eyes when Frankie looks at her. And Frankie loves the same things about Tess." Nora rubbed her chin. How could she explain passion and desire to her young daughter who had never experienced it?

"They fell in love with each other?" Nattie's lashes fluttered like the wings of a bird caught in a net. "But that's not possible between two women, is it?"

Many years ago, Nora had thought the same. Now she knew it was not just possible, but wonderful. "Why wouldn't it be possible? Love is a miracle, so anything is possible."

"Do you really think so?" Her gaze cast downward, Nattie smoothed her hands over the stack of paper.

The hint of sadness darting across her face made Nora wonder. "I do." She laid a hand on Nattie's cheek and rubbed away the charcoal smudge on her forehead. "Are you all right?"

"Yeah. It's just..." Nattie fiddled with the hem of her apron.

"What? Tell me, sweetie. You know you can talk to me about anything. What is it?"

Red splotches appeared on Nattie's cheeks. "Everybody says a woman is supposed to go to bed only with her husband," she said, her voice barely above a whisper.

Nora couldn't help smiling. So much innocence. "And that's usually how it works out, but if the person you gave your heart to happens to be a woman... Well, Frankie and Tess can't go to the pastor and tell him to marry them."

"Then wouldn't it be better if they let each other go so each of them could have a happy life? If you love someone, aren't you supposed to think of his or her happiness first, even if it breaks your heart?"

"I'm sure going their separate ways would make their lives easier, but it wouldn't make them happy." Even as she said it, Nora finally understood that it was also true for Luke. Living as Nora's husband and the father of their daughters made Luke's life complicated, but it also made her happy. "Sometimes, falling in love doesn't mean you'll have a happily-ever-after. Sometimes, you have to fight for it, compromise, and pay a price for being with the one person you love most. It's hard, but it's worth it. Life's too short to throw away love, no matter what form it comes in."

Nattie's eyes took on the lead gray that indicated she was deep in thought. She brushed a charcoal stain from her apron. "And it's the same, no matter if you're in love with a man or a woman?"

"I don't know," Nora said. "I wonder if any two loves are exactly the same."

"What do you mean?"

"I love you and Amy differently, and that's a good thing, because you're different people. It doesn't mean I love one of you less. Maybe I love Luke differently from how Hannah loves Josh and from how Tess loves Frankie—not because Tess and Frankie are both women, but because each of us is different from the others."

Nattie shuffled her papers, as if sorting them would bring order to her jumbled thoughts. "Why haven't I heard about this before? None of the books I read mentioned two women together."

"Because most people believe what they have and what they think is the right way—and anything else must be wrong," Nora said.

A smile tugged at the corner of Nattie's lips. "Sounds like Amy when she was stomping her feet, refusing to believe that her way of doing multiplications wasn't the best way."

"Kind of like that." Nora laughed. "But instead of stomping out to hide in the barn, adults come up with long explanations about why anything but their way is wrong, unnatural, and sinful."

Nattie paled. "The reverend preached about sin for a whole hour today. Is that why Tess and Frankie didn't join us for church? It must hurt them to hear people talk like that."

The compassion in her eyes filled Nora with pride.

"Does the reverend know?" Nattie asked.

"No." Nora caught her gaze and held it. "No one can know, Nattie. Please keep this to yourself. Frankie and Tess are our friends, and we need to protect them. Some people might not react too well."

Nattie clamped her fingers around the sheets of paper. "You mean someone might hurt Frankie and Tess because they love each other?"

"You never know what people will do, but it's better not to take stupid risks."

"That's why they tell everyone they're cousins."

"Yes." Nora tilted her head and regarded her. "I know this comes as a surprise to you, but do you think you can accept what I just told you? Can you still be Frankie and Tess's friend, without letting your differences stand between you and them?"

"It seems strange to me." This time, Nattie looked her right in the eyes. "But I guess I'll be fine once I have a little time to get used to it. Life's also too short to throw away friendships."

Tears shot into Nora's eyes. *Oh, what a girl. It seems Luke and I did everything right with her.* When she drew Nattie into her arms, a sheet of paper fluttered to the floor.

Phin's image grinned up at her.

Nora lifted her brow. *She's drawing pictures of Phin?*

"It's a wedding gift," Nattie mumbled into her shoulder.

Touched by her thoughtfulness, Nora pulled her closer.

A soft knock on the door startled Rika from her thoughts. She wasn't ready to face anyone, but she opened the door.

Nora stepped in, perched on the edge of the bed, and smoothed her hand over Amy's pillow. "Come sit by me for a moment. I want to talk to you about Tess and Frankie."

Reluctantly, Rika sat next to her. "You know about... them?"

"Of course I know. Tess is my oldest friend. I'm starting to think of you as a friend too, and I don't want you to be uncomfortable staying here."

"Oh, no." Rika shook her head. She didn't want Nora to believe that for a second. "I really like it here. I also like Tess and Frankie. It's just that..."

"What?"

Rika kept her gaze on the tip of her boots. "They shouldn't kiss each other like that. It's wrong. Against nature. They're cousins and—"

"No, they're not."

Rika lifted her gaze. She hadn't thought she could be any more confused, but now she didn't understand anything. "They're not? But they said—"

"I know what they said, but it's not true. Frankie and Tess aren't related in any way, and I know they aren't proud of lying, but it's the only way."

"The only way for what?" Rika asked.

"The only way to travel together and be affectionate without giving people the wrong idea...or in this case, the right idea."

"I don't understand. Do you mean to say that they..." She lowered her voice. "They are..."

"In love with each other, yes."

In love with another woman. Blood rushed through Rika's ears. She rubbed her thumb over her bottom lip as she remembered their tender kiss. "That's... I never heard of such a thing before."

"It's unusual, but it's not something you should hate or fear. It's just love." Nora reached over and squeezed Rika's hand. "Do you understand?"

Rika blinked. She had never truly been in love, so the concept was hard enough to grasp. Love between two women... She couldn't wrap her head around it. "I guess so."

"Mama?" Nattie's voice drifted up the stairs. "The Buchanans are here for a visit."

"Just a minute," Nora answered. She stood and smoothed wrinkles out of her skirt. "I don't expect you to understand all at once. Talk to Tess and Frankie if you want. But please keep this to yourself, or we might all be in danger."

Rika nodded fiercely. Despite her confusion, she knew one thing for sure. She would never allow anything to happen to one of the Hamiltons or their friends.

Nora looked at her for a moment longer, then crossed to the door.

"Mrs. Hamilton?"

She turned around. "Nora, please."

"Nora," Rika said. "Is Amy all right? She seemed awfully upset earlier."

Nora smiled. "You're such a sweet girl, to think about Amy in a moment like this."

How could I not? At times, Amy was all she could think of, and that was as confusing as the love between Tess and Frankie.

"Amy will be fine," Nora said. "She just needs some time." The door clicked shut behind her.

Rika let herself fall back on the bed and stared at the ceiling.

HAMILTON HORSE RANCH
BAKER PRAIRIE, OREGON
JUNE 22, 1868

*T*ESS GLANCED OUT THE CABIN window. "There she is—finally!"

Amy's red mare rounded the corral, the early-morning sun making the mare's coat and Amy's hair glow.

"Nora already left for town," Frankie said behind her.

"I bet Amy timed it that way." Tess drew her brows together. She had kept Nora company late into the night, until Nora finally gave up and accepted that Amy wouldn't be home that night. Tess was as worried as her friend. But with every hour Amy stayed away, anger outgrew her concern. How could Amy worry her mother so? Why had she and Frankie been so careless? And, most of all, why was the world a place where being in love with a wonderful person created such a mess?

"Let's go talk to her," Tess said.

Just as she opened the door, Hendrika hurried across the ranch yard. "Where have you been?"

"Checking on the herd," Amy said. She dismounted and turned away from Hendrika to check her mare's hooves.

"At night?"

Amy didn't turn around. "By the time I found every foal and every yearling, it was too late to head back, so I stayed at a line shack."

"You promised me you'd be more careful."

"I am careful."

Hendrika stiffened. "Staying out alone all night is not being careful."

"She's damn right." Tess marched toward them. "Your mother is worried sick about you."

Amy whirled around. Hendrika turned too. Now both stared as if Tess and Frankie were about to attack them.

Tess gentled her voice. "I know this is a lot to take in, but running away is not the solution. It's incredibly thoughtless—"

295

"Thoughtless?" Amy's voice rumbled like a cornered dog about to bite back. "You mean like you were thoughtless when you acted on those unnatural urges?" The color of her face matched her crimson bandanna. She wrenched her gaze away from Tess and pressed her lips together as if she thought she'd said too much.

Tess ran her hands along the bell-shape of her skirt, calming herself. Now was not the time for a shouting match and mutual accusations. "Let's go inside and talk."

"Not now." Amy gestured to the bunkhouse. "I need to talk to the men and get them started on—"

"Your mother already gave them their tasks for the day at breakfast," Tess said. Nora knew her daughter well. She had predicted that Amy would hide behind her responsibilities, so she had sent the ranch hands off before Amy returned. "Come on, you two. Let's go to the cabin and talk."

Amy dragged her feet, but Tess resisted the urge to grab her elbow and pull her along. She wasn't sure how Amy would react to being touched by someone she now considered an "unnatural" woman. Finally, Amy moved toward the cabin.

Hendrika followed without a word. She wasn't a talker, but Tess had a feeling that a lot happened behind those brown eyes.

The door snapped shut behind them, and Amy flinched as if she were trapped.

They sat at the table. The leather of Amy's chaps brushed Hendrika's skirt, and Amy pulled her legs back, then continued to fidget in her chair. Next to her, Hendrika seemed calm in comparison.

She's good at hiding her feelings, but Amy clearly isn't.

"Listen, I know this is awkward as hell, but we've got to talk about this." Tess tried to catch their gazes, but Amy ducked her head. She glanced at Frankie and received a short nod. "You saw us kiss each other, didn't you?"

Hendrika's gaze veered to Amy, then back to Tess and Frankie. "Yes," she said, her voice a whisper.

A bitter taste spread through Tess's mouth. *My love for Frankie is something that people only whisper about.* She shook off her frustration and tried to keep her voice calm. "What did you think about that?"

"Nora said you're not cousins, but still it's..." Hendrika turned her hand back and forth as if trying to grasp the right word.

Amy lifted her head and stared at her. "You're not cousins?"

"No. People just have an easier time accepting two women being close when they think they're related," Tess said. "I'm sorry we lied to you, but we've learned to be careful over the years."

"D-does that mean...that you are living together like a man and a woman would?" Again, it was Hendrika who found the courage to ask while Amy continued to stare at her hands.

Under the table, Frankie's hand found Tess's.

"No," Tess said. "We're living together the way two women who love each other would."

The tips of Frankie's fingers slid over hers in a tender caress.

When Hendrika and Amy stayed silent, Tess said, "Most people who are lucky enough to find love find it with a person of the opposite sex."

"Like Mama and Papa did," Amy said, her voice low and her gaze still directed downward.

Tess's lips formed a tight line. Luke and Nora weren't the best example, but she couldn't tell Amy that. "Yes," she said after a moment's hesitation. "But every once in a while, there's a girl who grows up and falls in love with another woman. Or, I suppose, a young man who falls in love with another man."

"But..." A few tendrils of brown hair escaped from their pins and fell into Hendrika's face when she scratched her head. "But the pastor said—"

"I know what the pastor and the Bible say." For most of her life, Tess had been branded a sinner because the Bible condemned anyone who was forced to lie, pretend, and sleep with other women's husbands for a living. "But the Bible also says that slavery is perfectly fine, so I'd rather follow my own heart than whatever the Bible says." She waited until she read a hint of understanding in Hendrika's eyes, then added, "I know the church condemns it, and most people find it disgusting and sinful, but my love for Frankie is the purest thing I ever had in my life."

Hendrika nibbled her lower lip. Her gaze flitted to Frankie, and she opened her mouth but then closed it again without saying anything.

With a friendly smile, Frankie leaned forward. "If you have questions, just ask. It's not possible for us to live our lives openly, but I hope we're among friends here, so we'd like to be as open as possible."

The lip nibbling increased, but then Hendrika looked directly at Frankie. "Is that why you sometimes dress in men's clothes? Do you think of yourself as a man?"

Asking that took guts. Tess gave her an admiring nod. She had thought Amy would ask the questions while Hendrika listened timidly. Instead, it was Amy who looked as if the conversation was giving her a bellyache. Hendrika's question made Amy smooth her hands over her chaps as if afraid that her wearing men's apparel would get her lumped in with Frankie.

"No," Frankie said. "I don't think of myself as a man, and when we are together, Tess doesn't pretend I'm a man either."

Thin lines carved themselves into Hendrika's brow. Clearly, she had never before considered the possibility of romantic love between women.

Tess sent her a sympathetic smile. "I know it's hard for you to understand, but part of what I love so much about Frankie is that she's a woman. Women are wonderful." When she gave her a wink and a motherly grin, Hendrika blushed, but a hesitant smile curved the corners of her mouth.

"Most people won't see it like this, though," Frankie said. "If the wrong people learn about our relationship, we could be run out of town, beaten, or worse. So it would be better to keep this to yourselves."

Hendrika nodded.

"I hope we didn't make you uncomfortable," Tess said.

"It's unusual."

"But?" Tess hoped that at least Hendrika would accept them. Maybe instead of Hendrika following Amy's lead, it would be the other way around.

"It's not my place to judge." Hendrika lowered her gaze and peered at black-rimmed fingernails. "From the moment we met, you and Frankie have been very friendly to me. I won't repay your kindness with hatred."

A clearing of her throat drew Tess's attention to Amy. "Mama said she knows about...about you. Does Papa know too?"

"Yes, they both know. I told Luke when we met him in The Dalles and Nora has known since our first evening here."

Russet lashes fluttered. "They know and they still let you stay?"

Defensive instincts rose, but Tess fought them down. Amy didn't sound appalled or judgmental, as if she wanted Nora to kick them out. *There's something in her voice...* She tried to read the young woman's expression. Emotions rushed across Amy's face. *Hope. Relief.* Tess stared for a few seconds longer. *Oh, good heavens! Why didn't I see it before? This is not about us. She's confused about her own feelings.* Tess's grip tightened around Frankie's hand. *Oh, Lord. I think Amy has feelings for women too, and she's scared to death to tell her parents. Now what do I do?*

"Amy?"

Footfalls came closer and stopped in front of the tack room, where Amy had fled after escaping from the cabin.

Amy looked up from a particularly stubborn sweat spot on her saddle. She set down the saddle soap and gritted her teeth. "Yes?" She didn't bother to make her voice friendly. Couldn't she have a moment's peace?

The tack room's door creaked open. Frankie peeked in. She wore pants and a man's shirt. The sight had always made Amy feel at ease around her, but now it was a reminder of how different Frankie was from other women—and how different Amy was too.

"There you are." Frankie's nose wrinkled at the odor of sweaty saddle blankets and horsehair, but she didn't retreat. She leaned in the doorway and studied Amy. "So this is your hideaway."

"I'm not hiding. The saddles need—"

"I had a hideaway too when I was your age." Frankie ignored her protests with a smile. "Whenever I needed time away from my brothers, I slipped into the Chinese laundry. It was just a shack, really, but the couple running it let me stay as long as I didn't get in the way."

Amy nodded. She had seen Portland's Chinatown. Most folks didn't like the Chinese, so they were outsiders, like Frankie.

"I spent many afternoons watching Mei Ling iron the miners' shirts. She was stoop-shouldered from bending over the hot iron all the time, but she had the most elegant neck and eyes like the night. And when she smiled..." Frankie grinned.

She was smitten with the Chinese woman, and she's talking about it as if it was the most natural thing on earth. Amy still couldn't wrap her mind around it. "Did she...?" She didn't know how or even what to ask. There were so many things she wanted to know.

"Did she like me too?" Frankie finished the question for her. "Probably not. Not that way. Back then, even I didn't know I liked her that way. It took me years to figure out what was going on with me."

All the afternoons spent riding with Hannah came back to Amy. Had Frankie watched Mei Ling the way she had watched Hannah? Had she delighted in her company, in the pleasure of her laughter and the occasional touch to her arm? An image of Rika in the hayloft, face flushed and hair tussled, replaced the old memories. *Does Frankie feel the same things I do? And Tess? Am I like them?*

"I think you know what I mean, don't you?" Frankie asked.

The saddle slid out of Amy's hands and thumped to the floor. *She knows! Oh, Lord, how can she know?* She had always been so careful not to give herself away, and now... Her throat constricted.

Frankie stepped across the threshold and firmly closed the door.

With movements that felt clumsy, Amy picked up the saddle and heaved it onto an empty rack. Her muscles trembled, not from the saddle's weight but from fear. If Frankie knew, would she tell Mama? Had she already told her? Her parents loved her, but they wouldn't understand. And how could they, when Amy didn't understand it herself?

Frankie ducked past bridles, halters, and harness pieces hanging from pegs. She turned over an empty bucket and sat on it. "Have you ever admired a woman's body, Amy? Ever found yourself stopping to breathe in the scent of her skin? Wanted to say something witty just to see her smile?"

An image of Rika's gap-toothed grin flashed through Amy's mind. She knew she was guilty of everything Frankie had just described. At night, she often tried to delay falling asleep so she could breathe in Rika's scent a while longer and admire her form in the moonlight while Rika slept.

She had told herself it was just friendship. She admired Rika and her strength; that was all. For a while, she could almost make herself believe it. But then she had seen Frankie and Tess kiss—and it brought home the true meaning of her feelings.

"I don't know what you're talking about," she mumbled, not meeting Frankie's gaze.

The bucket scraped across the floor as Frankie slid closer. "You don't have to talk to me, but please don't lie to me. I've been where you are now. I know what you're going through, and I know that lying to yourself and to your friends will only make it harder."

"Harder than being chased out of town? Harder than my family hating me? Harder than burning in hell?" The long-buried words broke out of her.

"Amy, don't let your fears—"

"Does your family know about...you know?"

Frankie's jaw tightened. "They know."

"And?"

"The last time I saw my brothers, they spat in my face." Frankie didn't look away, didn't lower her head, so the pain in her eyes was plain to see. "Not everyone will accept our kind of love. Most people probably won't. You need to be careful. But that doesn't mean you should give up on love."

Amy shook her head. "As long as I can control these... urges, everything is fine."

"Sure, just like my life was fine before I found Tess." Frankie's voice vibrated with fierce determination, but her gaze was soft. "But now it's complete. There's a big difference, and you'll understand it once you stop hating that part of yourself."

Amy shook her head. She didn't want to hear it. The price was too high.

With a touch to her shoulder, Frankie stood. "All right. I can see that you're not ready to talk about this. Just know that Tess and I are always here to talk." She walked to the door.

"Frankie," Amy called. Every fiber of her being trembled. For the first time, someone knew her deepest, darkest secret. "You'll keep this to yourself, won't you? You won't tell my parents?"

A sad gaze met hers. "I won't say a word, but I wish you'd talk to your mother. She didn't bat an eye when she found out about Tess and me. She won't think less of you either."

Could that really be true? Mama seemed fine with Tess and Frankie, but maybe it was different when it was her own daughter. *I don't know. I don't know anything anymore.*

The door slid closed with an echoing click. Frankie was gone, leaving Amy with her thoughts in turmoil.

HAMILTON HORSE RANCH
BAKER PRAIRIE, OREGON
JUNE 22, 1868

*T*HE BANG OF WOOD CRASHING against wood greeted Rika as she entered the stable.

There she is.

Amy's red curls bounced up and down above a stall door. She hadn't heard Rika enter and was hurling pitchfork after pitchfork of manure into the wheelbarrow. The pitchfork's handle crashed against the wall, and straw flew everywhere, but Amy continued to work like a possessed woman. She stopped just long enough to jerk up her shirtsleeves. The muscles of her forearms bunched. Her shirt clung to her torso, and drops of sweat beaded on her golden-hued skin.

Rika licked her lips.

Women are wonderful, Tess had said. With her unusual strength and her passion for life, Amy certainly was. In moments like this, Rika understood what drew Frankie and Tess to each other. The thought was new and unsettling, but at the same time, it just fit.

She gave a cough to let Amy know she was there.

Amy whirled around, the pitchfork lifted as if to ward off an attacker.

Rika stepped back and raised her hands. "Just me."

Grunting, Amy set down the pitchfork. She rolled down her sleeves and buttoned the cuffs as if feeling exposed under Rika's gaze.

In the sudden silence, a horse snuffled for any food the visitors might have brought.

This is awkward. Before, they had been friends, but learning that Frankie and Tess were sweethearts made Rika aware that women could be more than friends. Could they be more than friends for her too?

She shook her head at herself. *What are you thinking? You're marrying Phineas, remember?*

Amy picked up the pitchfork again. Horse apples landed half in, half out of the wheelbarrow.

"Want me to help?" Rika asked.

"No, thanks."

Rika leaned against the stall door and watched. Clearly, Amy wanted to be alone, but Rika needed to talk. She plucked at a stalk of straw that had gotten caught in her hair. One of her hairpins slipped, and a shock of hair fell into her face. "Why do you think Frankie and Tess love each other and not men?"

"I don't know," Amy said.

"Have you ever met other women like that?"

"It doesn't matter. I don't want to talk about it."

Rika looked up and found Amy glancing at her hair.

Scowling, Amy wrenched her gaze away.

"We are friends, right?" Rika asked. "If I can't talk to you about this, there's no one else that I feel comfortable talking to."

"Why would you want to talk about this at all?" Amy grumbled.

Rika gave up on trying to fix her hair. "Don't you find it riveting? Two women together... I never heard of that. Aren't you curious?"

"No." Amy grabbed a shovel and scooped up urine spots in one corner of the stall so Rika couldn't see her face. The tension in the strong shoulders was unmistakable, though.

"Do you find it disgusting?" Rika asked. Amy sure acted as if she did.

"Do you?"

"No."

Now Amy threw a glance over her shoulder. "You don't?"

"They love each other." It was so evident in their glances and little touches that Rika now wondered how she had missed it for so long. "It's unusual, yes, but..."

"But?" Amy leaned on the shovel, gaze resting on Rika, transfixed.

"They seem happy together, happier than some women are in their marriage," Rika said. "My husband ignored me and hid at the bottom of a bottle instead of sharing his pain with me." The memories hurt, but now she understood that it hadn't been her fault. It hadn't been her plainness that failed to keep him interested. "My father used to shout at my stepmother. I never heard him talk to her with tenderness. And I watched your uncles with their wives when they visited the cotton mill. They treated them like servants. I don't think Tess and Frankie would ever treat each other like that."

Maybe it wasn't for the pastor to decide that their love was a sin while some of the unhappy marriages she had observed, with all their indifference and cruelty, were considered normal.

Amy's hands relaxed around the shovel. She exhaled slowly. "Not all marriages are like that, you know? My papa and mama still behave like newlyweds when they think no one's watching. And sometimes, when I'm out riding line, I see Jacob Garfield picking flowers for Bernice—after thirty-five years of marriage."

A wistful sigh escaped Rika. She wanted that. Not the flowers, but being loved enough that someone would waste an hour of daylight to pick them for her. She had never allowed herself to dream of love, but now she did. "Do you think Frankie and Tess could have that with a husband?"

Amy stared at the dust motes dancing on beams of sunlight. "I don't know." She sounded badly shaken.

"Why is this upsetting you so? You never seemed to care what other people think."

"I don't." Amy turned and scraped at the urine spots in the corner. "And I'm not upset."

Rika shoved back the bolt and pushed through the stall door. Two strides and she grabbed Amy's shoulder and dragged her around. "You know what? You are exactly like your horses." She stabbed a finger at Amy. "You look tough and act all confident, but you scare easily."

"I'm not scared."

"Oh, no? You're shaking like a leaf." Concern soothed Rika's anger, and she gentled her voice. "Why are you so scared?"

Amy shook her head. "Not scared."

"Liar," Rika said with affection. For once, she felt as if she were the horse tamer and Amy the scared creature that needed gentling. She took the shovel from her limp grasp and pulled Amy against her, hoping to ease her fears, whatever they were.

At first, Amy stiffened. Then she struggled and tried to break the embrace.

"Easy, easy." Rika let go. "You don't have to be afraid of me. I'm your friend."

Finally, Amy sank against her, burying her face on Rika's shoulder.

Rika was far too aware of Amy's warmth and the breath on her neck. She tried to ignore the shivers trailing down her body and focused on her friend instead. "Want to talk about what's bothering you?" she asked, slipping into the familiar role of caretaker.

Red locks brushed her face as Amy shook her head.

"All right." She closed her eyes and held Amy until her breathing calmed. Only then did she notice that she was trembling too.

Still holding her loosely, Amy tipped back her head and studied her. "Are you all right?"

Rika wanted to nod but instead found herself saying, "I don't know. I guess so. It's just all so terribly confusing."

"Oh, yes, it is." Amy pulled her closer for another moment, then stepped away and picked up the pitchfork again.

Rika rubbed her arms and shivered. Without Amy's embrace, cold seemed to seep into her bones. She reached for another pitchfork leaning against the wall and began to help.

For a while, they worked side by side without talking.

Then Amy looked at her out of the corner of her eye. "Thanks."

Rika smiled. "You're welcome."

Nora jumped from the wagon seat and pressed the reins into John's hands. "Would you take care of him for me?" On most days, she brushed down Old Jack after returning from school, but today she had just one priority: finding Amy.

"I'll give him a good rub-down," John said.

Without another glance back, Nora hurried into the house.

Noises came from the kitchen. Someone threw logs into the stove.

Amy? She quickened her step.

Tess turned away from the stove and walked to the table, where a plucked chicken waited to be prepared. "Normally, people don't look so disappointed when they see me." Her tone was light and teasing, but the crow's-feet around her eyes didn't dance with laughter.

"I thought you were Amy. Is she back?"

Tess reached into a bowl on the table and took one of the peas. She turned it this way and that, studying it from all sides as if she had never seen a pea. "Yes. Came in and wanted to hurry off to work, just like you said."

The muscles of Nora's shoulders knotted with tension. "How did she seem?"

"We talked to her." Tess lifted her hands. "I know you wanted to talk to her first, but I was angry that she stayed out so long and when she brought up the kiss..."

Nora grasped Tess's hand. Yes, she'd have preferred to speak with Amy first, but it wasn't important now. All that mattered was that Amy was all right. "And? How did it go?"

With a low plop, the pea landed back in the bowl. "I think Hendrika will be fine with it."

The unspoken words hung between them like thunderclouds, heavy with foreboding. "And Amy?"

"She didn't say much, and that surprised me. I thought she'd be full of questions, but if she had them, she was too scared to ask."

"She's still scared?" Nora didn't understand it. Her courageous daughter had rarely been scared of anything in her life. "Why would she be scared?" Surprised, yes. Maybe even shocked. But scared?

Silence answered her.

Nora plucked a missed feather from the chicken, just to have something to do. "She does understand that you and Frankie would never make any advances toward her, doesn't she?"

"She does," Tess said. "I don't think it's about that at all."

Something more was going on with Amy. Time to finally have that conversation—whether Amy wanted or not. When Nora got to her feet, the feather fluttered to the floor. She bent and tried to pick it up, but it eluded her grasp. She sighed. A lot of things eluded her at the moment. Something was going on with Amy, and she was determined to find out what.

HAMILTON HORSE RANCH
BAKER PRAIRIE, OREGON
JUNE 22, 1868

*N*ORA FOUND AMY IN THE middle of the round pen, Cinnamon loping circles around her. On his back sat Hendrika, in a pair of Amy's pants, with the afternoon sun gleaming on her bare head.

"Nice," Amy called. "Remember to keep your body relaxed."

Nora rested her hands on the corral and watched her daughter.

As Amy kept turning so that she faced horse and rider, her movements were confident. A focused expression settled on her face. Her voice sounded gentle but firm, giving out corrections and praise equally.

Is she really so calm? Nora doubted it. But Luke had taught Amy from an early age not to approach horses when she was angry or upset, and by now, stripping off emotions like confining clothes had become a reflex for her. *She's hiding with the horses instead of coming to talk to me. Why is this so hard on her?*

Her daughters knew they could talk to her about anything and everything. What had changed for Amy to hide her feelings behind a façade of confidence?

"All right," Amy said. "Now get him to stop without slowing to a walk first."

Hendrika's glance sought Amy, and she hesitated.

"You can do it. Just like we practiced. And remember to go easy on the reins."

Three hoofbeats later, Cinnamon slid to a stop in a cloud of dust.

Amy walked over, grabbed his bridle with a steady hand, and patted his neck. "Very nice." She looked at Hendrika, then away.

When Amy noticed Nora leaning against the corral, she hesitated but then led Cinnamon over. "Did you see that, Mama? Rika's getting really good."

At the words of praise, a blush spread over Hendrika's face. She pulled her boot from the stirrup and poked Amy's arm with her toes. Her eyes sparkled with pleasure, though.

"I saw." But Nora's attention wasn't on Cinnamon or Hendrika. "Can I talk to you?"

Amy lost her carefree expression. "All right."

The middle of the corral wasn't a good place to have this conversation. "Let's go for a ride," Nora said. Amy was most comfortable on the back of her horse. Maybe it would help her through this difficult conversation.

"Is there time before supper?" Amy asked.

"We'll make the time."

Amy turned to Hendrika. "Wanna come and get some more practice in?"

"Just you and I this time," Nora said before Hendrika could answer. She reached through two corral rails and touched Hendrika's knee. "You're welcome to come next time, all right?"

Wordlessly, Amy held Cinnamon's reins while Hendrika swung her leg over the cantle. When she hopped down, her heel caught on a pant leg that was an inch too long and she stumbled. Amy's arms came up to steady her. The gentleness of her touch reminded Nora so much of how Luke treated her.

With Amy still holding on, Hendrika looked up and met her eyes. "Thank you."

Something about their interaction struck a chord in Nora, but before she could translate it into conscious thought, Amy let go and stepped back.

Half an hour later, Nora rode side by side with Amy. Their horses slowed to plod up a hill. Nora hesitated, searching for the right words. Almost twenty-one years of being a mother hadn't prepared her for this moment. She adjusted her split riding skirt over the saddle. "Tess and Frankie talked to you about—"

"Yes," Amy interrupted as if she didn't want Nora to say the words.

"What did you think?"

Instead of an answer, Amy asked, "And you? You've had more time to think about it."

"Tess and Frankie are my friends." Nora emphasized every word. "Nothing I learn about them could change that."

"Not even...you know?"

"I still respect and love them just as much." Nora wanted her daughters to love Tess and Frankie too—or, at the very least, to respect them and their love for each other. "Did you know Tess was the first person to ever hold you?"

"Tess? Not a midwife or Papa?"

"Your father couldn't be there when you were born. He was the first to hold Nattie, but it was Tess who helped when I gave birth to you. She held my hand and didn't leave my side for the whole eighteen hours." How young, scared, and naïve she'd been back then. She owed Tess her life and that of her children. "Tess is my best friend, and she was a wonderful aunt to you when you were little. That didn't change just because I know she is in love with Frankie."

Amy said nothing. Her gaze wandered over the hills and to the mountains in the distance.

"What are you thinking?" Nora directed her mare closer to Ruby.

"I don't know what to think." Amy's low voice was almost drowned out by the call of a red-tailed hawk overhead. When she shook her head, her hat flew back until the rawhide string caught it. "They shouldn't have kissed. If anyone but Rika and me had seen them..."

"You're right. They made a mistake. But the mistake is not loving or kissing each other. It's not being more careful."

Amy's expression didn't soften. Her brows drew together like thunderclouds gathering.

"Why are you so angry with them?" Nora had expected surprise and confusion, but not this anger.

"If someone had seen them, people might think..."

"What?"

"That we're all..." A muscle in Amy's face jumped. "That I am...like them."

Nattie hadn't seemed worried about that, so it caught Nora by surprise. "Sweetie, Tess and Frankie's love has nothing to do with you."

Amy's gaze drifted up to follow the circling hawk.

A touch of Nora's heel directed Pirate closer to Amy's horse, and she reached over to touch her daughter's shoulder. "This is new for you, but as much as people would like to pretend it's not true, there have always been women who love other women. Most of them were good, hardworking people. You might not be aware of it, but the widows Sutherland and Mills..."

Amy's flinch told her that she remembered.

Oh, no. She heard the townsfolk talk. Has she lived all these years with the rumors and hateful comments about women who love each other, with no one to tell her otherwise? Nora's insides trembled. Her hand tightened around the reins until she realized she was making her mare nervous. She forced herself to relax. "Amy, listen. I know people said a lot of ugly things, but they aren't true."

"They are true." Amy's voice was a whisper. "They weren't just two widows living together."

"Yes, that part is true. But the rest of what you might have heard people say was just hatred and fear talking."

"Fear?"

Nora nodded. "People are afraid of things they don't understand. Instead of thinking for themselves, they allowed Reverend Rhodes and a few other townspeople to make up their minds for them. Suddenly, they started saying how unnatural the two women have always been and how they would burn in hell. They conveniently forgot that it was Mrs. Sutherland and Mrs. Mills who took so many of them in when the big flood swept away their homes. They were good people."

Nora had met the two widows only a few times, never suspecting that another female couple lived in Baker Prairie. The two women were hiding as much as Nora and Luke did, just in another way. When Mrs. Sutherland's brother had found them in bed together, he beat them and ran them out of town with the help of Baker Prairie's God-fearing people. "If your father and I had learned about what had happened in time to prevent it, we never would have let them chase the two of them out of town. That wasn't right."

Amy's brow furrowed. "But having relations with another woman...isn't that a sin?"

"There are people who think so. But I don't." Nora tried a small smile. "I'm sure your father will agree that loving a woman is wonderful."

"But Papa is a man, and I'm—" Amy's gloved hand flew to her mouth. She clicked her tongue and urged Ruby up a hill, away from Nora.

Nora stared after her. "Amy? What...?" Her breath hitched as a sudden realization slammed into her. *Is Amy...?* Blood roared in her ears to the frantic beat of her heart. She pressed her calves against Pirate's side and loped after Amy. "Amy, wait! Talk to me."

Amy didn't. She raced up the hill as if the devil were after her.

And maybe she thinks he is. Oh my God, has she been hiding this all these years? "Amy, stop!" She used her most authoritarian voice.

Amy threw a glance over her shoulder and slowed her mare.

Bits of grass, thrown up by Ruby's hooves, rained down on Nora as she closed the distance between the two horses.

Ruby slid to a stop. Amy's chest heaved as she stared at Nora.

"Amy," Nora whispered. "Please tell me the truth. Are you...? Do you have feelings for women?"

Instead of an answer, Amy hung her head.

Oh, Lord, how can that be? What are the chances of that happening to one of our daughters? Nora's thoughts raced. *What if we caused this? Did we influence her in any way, like Bernice always thought?*

"Mama..."

The silent plea in Amy's voice clutched at Nora's heart. Her daughter had suffered in silence for so long, and Nora hadn't noticed. Frantically, she searched for the best words to ease that pain, to let Amy know it was all right. Never before had she wanted to reveal the true nature of her relationship with Luke, but now she wanted Amy to know that love between two women was possible and beautiful. But how could she, after all those years, reveal Luke's secret without breaking apart Amy's world?

Her temples pounded in rhythm with her frantic heartbeat. She didn't want to reveal Luke's secret, but neither did she want Amy to live with the burden of self-loathing. "Let's dismount for a moment. We need to talk."

Amy's heart galloped against her ribs. *Mama knows. Oh, God, she knows. What do I do now?* She looked around, expecting to see Mama as panicked as she felt.

Mama wasn't crying or yelling at her, but worry lines were etched around her eyes.

Every instinct in Amy's body told her to press her heels to Ruby's flanks and flee. But her mother's gaze pinned her in place. She ducked her head, slid from the saddle, and landed on unsteady legs.

"Look at me, sweetie." Mama dropped to the ground next to her. A gentle touch to her chin forced Amy to lift her head.

Amy stared off to the side, afraid to look into Mama's eyes and see the disappointment there.

"Amy? Look at me."

Slowly, Amy fixed her gaze on Mama. Her stomach lurched when she saw tears brimming in her mother's eyes.

"Is it true?" Mama asked.

The lump lodged in her throat prevented Amy from answering. When she licked her lips, salt burned her tongue. Finally, her shoulders slumped and she nodded.

A tear spilled over and rolled down Mama's cheek. It pooled in the corner of her mouth.

Those tears hurt more than Amy's own. "Mama." Her voice trembled. "Mama, please don't cry." She never wanted to make her parents sad. "Don't cry. I promise I'll do my best to get over these improper feelings."

"No, Amy. That's not what I want you to do." Mama slipped off her gloves and dried Amy's face with her bare hands. She cradled it between warm palms. "I'm not crying because you hurt me. I'm hurting for you. I know you won't have it easy in life, but these feelings are a part of you. They won't just go away."

How could Mama be so sure? "Maybe they will."

"Yes, maybe," Mama said. "You're still young. When I was young, I had no idea about love. I thought I had, but I didn't really know what I needed in my life to make me happy. I only found out when I met Luke."

"Maybe I'll meet a man like Papa too." Even Amy felt that the words were empty, without emotion or belief. Every day she spent with Rika, every night they shared her room and bed proved that her feelings toward women—toward Rika—weren't going away. If anything, they were getting stronger.

"Maybe," Mama said again. "But if the person you meet ends up being a woman, I want you to know I won't love you any less."

Amy stared. Mama had always understood her and supported her, no matter what, but never in a million years had she thought Mama would accept her unnatural feelings for women. *But she does.* The light of love and acceptance burned brightly in her mother's eyes.

"Come here." Mama engulfed her in a tight embrace.

A trembling sigh escaped, and Amy bent her head to rest it against Mama's shoulder. She breathed in the comforting scent—apples and cinnamon, as if she had just taken a pie for Papa out of the oven. "Oh, Mama."

"It's all right." Mama kissed her cheek, then pulled back to look into her eyes. "Promise me one thing."

"Anything." Whatever it was, Amy knew she would do anything to make sure Mama would never look at her with disappointment.

"Promise me you'll try not to think less of yourself for following your heart instead of what other people think is right."

The ball of tension that had knotted Amy's stomach for years dissolved into tears. She hastily wiped her eyes. "I'll try," she said, voice rough with tears and emotions.

"Good." Mama's smile was full of concern, but Amy saw none of the despair she had expected.

She's at peace with this. It was almost as if Mama had suspected all along and had come to terms with it. The thought made Amy blanch. *Did she know about my infatuation with Hannah? Does she know about Rika?* She struggled to form words. "How did you know?"

"Know?"

"Have you known about...me for a while or—?"

"Oh, no, sweetie." The ribbon of Mama's bonnet came loose when she shook her head. "I would have talked to you much sooner had I known. I would never let you suffer in silence." Tears shone in her eyes. "I didn't know, Amy, but I understand how you feel."

"How could you understand?" Mama was so in love with Papa, even after all these years, that it was sometimes almost embarrassing to watch.

Mama retied her bonnet. Her hands trembled, but her gaze was steady. "I've come to think that the love Tess and Frankie share isn't all that different from the love between Bernice and Jacob or Hannah and Josh."

"Not different?" That couldn't be true. Amy had felt different all her life.

"Well, maybe it is different, but it's not less worthy or less true."

The conviction in her voice soothed Amy's fears. Her biggest fear remained, though. "What will Papa think?"

A wistful smile crept onto Mama's face. "He'll worry."

Amy sniffled.

Mama tipped up her chin. "Your father will worry because he loves you, not because he thinks there's anything wrong with you. It'll just take some getting used to. Maybe we should have seen this coming, but we didn't. Except for Hannah, you never even had any close female friends."

Amy lowered her head. "I tried to stay away, tried to ignore it, but..." Staying away from Rika proved impossible.

"Oh, dear Lord!" Mama slapped her forehead and covered her eyes with one hand. She peeked through her fingers. "And I made you share a bed with Hendrika! I'm so sorry. Was that terribly awkward for you?"

Mama's sheepish expression made Amy smile. "It's all right."

"As soon as we get home, I'll ask her to change rooms with Nattie and—"

"No," Amy said, a bit too quickly. "I mean...she's my friend, and we managed just fine so far." Soon, Phin would be home, and he would take away Rika forever. She wasn't ready to give up her company.

Mama seemed to ponder that for a moment. "All right. It's getting late, and I should get started on supper. Should we head back, or do you want some time to yourself, sweetie?"

She knows me so well. Grateful, Amy nodded. "I need some time." She felt vulnerable, as if all her defenses were stripped away and everyone looking could see into her heart, her very soul. She couldn't imagine sitting down to supper with her family, Rika, and the ranch hands. Not while she felt like this. "I'll ride down to the river and let Ruby graze for a while."

"Don't stay out as long this time. It's all right if you don't want to talk right now. Just please don't shut us out."

Amy nodded, overwhelmed with emotions—hers and Mama's.

The scent of apples engulfed her when Mama pulled her into a quick embrace. "Be careful," she whispered. "I love you."

The inside of Amy's nose burned. She sniffled. "I love you too, Mama." Still trembling, she climbed into the saddle. For once, she didn't start with a walk, then a jog or a lope to warm up Ruby's muscles. One squeeze of her legs and Ruby sprang into a gallop. They raced down the hill as if trying to outrun her chaotic thoughts.

MOLALLA RIVER, OREGON
JUNE 22, 1868

*D*ANCER'S HOOVES POUNDED OVER THE bridge across the Molalla River. Luke's heart thudded along with the fast beat. *Home, home, home,* her heart sang with every step. She let her gaze slide over the hills and trees of her land.

In front of them, a horse lifted its nose from the grass and whinnied a greeting.

Luke lifted herself up in her stirrups to catch a glimpse of the rider, who had dismounted.

A familiar hat dangled down the rider's back, and the setting sun made her hair gleam like copper.

"Amy!"

At her shout, Amy whirled around. "Papa!"

The rope between Dancer and Angel, the Percheron mare, tightened as Luke urged her gelding into an all-out gallop. As soon as Dancer slid to a stop, Luke swung out of the saddle.

For once, Amy had no glance for the new horse. She rushed over and fell into Luke's arms, her body trembling.

Luke tightened her embrace. "Everything all right?"

Amy nodded, her face buried against Luke's shoulder.

Something's not right. "What happened?" She combed her fingers through Amy's hair. It had soothed Amy as a child—and it soothed Luke too. She let herself imagine that she could protect her daughter from whatever had upset her. Finally, she moved back a few inches and slid her worried gaze over Amy. "You're not hurt, are you?"

Amy shook her head.

What, then? Normally, Amy would pepper her with questions about the trip and fawn over the new horse. Something was wrong. Very wrong. Fear clutched her. "Is your mother all right? And Nattie?"

"Yes, yes, they're all right. Everything's fine." Amy rubbed gloved hands over her cheeks.

Luke stared. *Has she been crying?*

"I'm sorry," Amy said. "I didn't want to upset you. I'm just so glad you're home."

Phin rode up behind them. "And Johanna?" he asked. "She all right too?"

"Johanna?" Amy's red-rimmed eyes focused on him.

"My betrothed. She's still at the ranch, ain't she? You didn't scare her off?"

Instead of answering Phin's teasing with a grin, Amy's lips formed a tight line. "Rika's still there."

"Rika?"

"Hendrika," Amy said. "She goes by her middle name."

Luke shook her head. She didn't want to talk about Phin's bride. She wanted to know what had put that desperate expression into Amy's eyes. "Come on. Let's go home." Maybe Nora knew what was going on with their daughter.

"What the hell happened?" Luke reined in Dancer and stared down at the blackened earth where her horse barn had once stood.

"It's not that bad," Amy said, face still pale. "No one got hurt, and we have a new barn already. See?"

The door to the main house banged open.

Luke let out a breath. *Nora.* She knew it before she swung down from the saddle and looked across the ranch yard. With the horse between them, she drank in the sight.

Even with a stained apron, a streak of flour across her cheek, and tousled hair, Nora was the most beautiful thing she had seen in two months.

Nora's lips formed a silent word, and Luke knew what it was. Her name.

She dropped the reins and crossed the ranch yard in long strides, meeting Nora at the bottom step of the veranda. They fell into an embrace, and Luke's eyes fluttered shut when she breathed in the familiar scent. "Apple pie," she whispered. She inhaled twice more, then asked, "What happened to the barn? And what's going on with Amy?"

"I'll explain later," Nora said. "When we're alone." Her lips sought Luke's.

Heat exploded in Luke's belly. She forgot about the barn, the tired horses, and the ranch hands, who by now were standing around, watching them. Nothing else mattered, just Nora.

Rika scooped coffee and crushed eggshells into a large pot and set it on the stove. Coffee was the first thing the ranch hands would ask for when they came in from the range. The ranch hands and Amy, who still hadn't returned after riding out with her mother.

"Where did your mother go?" she asked Nattie. "Is that Amy outside?"

"Probably. I'm not sure what's going on, but Mama seems worried about her." Nattie set the last tin cup on the table, walked to the window, and peeked at the riders in the ranch yard. "Oh! It's Papa! And Phin!" She ran outside.

Phineas. He's back. Rika wanted to run too, but in the opposite direction. She had dreaded this moment for the last two months. Slowly, careful not to stumble on unsteady feet, she trudged to the window. She couldn't help taking a peek at the man who would soon be her husband.

The first thing she saw was a man kissing Nora on the bottom step of the veranda. She blinked at the unusual display of passion right there for all to see.

From the distance, Mr. Hamilton didn't look like Amy at all. While Amy's hair gleamed like fire and sunlight, his was midnight dark.

Rika directed her gaze away from Nora and her husband, giving them some privacy. Relief trickled through her when she detected Amy talking to two dust-covered men. There she was, safe and sound.

Then she remembered that one of the men had to be her future husband. Tension returned to her body. Her heart pounding, she took in the man she recognized from Jo's tintype.

With his blond hair, he looked a bit like the painting of her grandfather. His laughter boomed across the ranch yard as he laughed at something Amy said. He seemed friendly, and the tension in Rika's body receded—until he slipped his muscular arm around Amy's shoulders.

Such liberties! Rika pressed her fists to her hips. Watching Amy and Phineas together made her want to rush out and pull them apart. Was there more to his feelings for Amy than friendship? Was that why he had stayed for so long instead of starting his own ranch sooner? The thought twisted her insides with an emotion that could only be jealousy. *Oh, come on, Hendrika Aaldenberg. What do you have to be jealous of? He's not even your husband yet.*

Her jealousy receded when Nattie threw herself into Phineas's arms and then embraced her father. The group started for the main house, still laughing, touching, reconnecting. Would she ever belong to a family like this?

Amy looped her arm through Phineas's. They looked like a courting couple.

Rika shoved her fists into her apron pocket. She realized she wasn't glaring at Amy but at Phineas. She wanted to slap his hand until he took it off Amy's. *What kind of nonsense is this?* Since Tess had revealed that she and Frankie were sweethearts, Rika found her thoughts heading down strange paths.

The door swung open.

Mr. Hamilton was the first one in. He stood with his hat in his hands. His dusty clothes and crooked nose made him look like a ranch hand, but his stance and confident movements told her he was the boss—not in her father's loud, sometimes violent way, though. The ranch hands who followed him in looked at him with respect, not fear. Deep lines around his eyes indicated that he liked to laugh. He was grinning now, glowing with the happiness of being home. His arm was still wrapped around Nora as if he would never let go again.

"Rika." Amy squeezed past her father until she stood beside Rika. "This is my father, Lucas Hamilton. Papa, this is Rika—Hendrika Bruggeman."

The mention of Jo's last name made Rika squirm. She bit the inside of her cheek and forced herself to stand still. The silvery gray eyes studied her. She got the impression that they saw too much.

Rika curtsied, just a bit so that her trembling knees wouldn't give out on her.

Mr. Hamilton lifted her hand and indicated a kiss without touching her skin with his lips. "Pleased to meet you." His eyes twinkled, the gentleness in them reminding her of Amy. "I've heard so much about you. Phin talked about you every step of the four hundred miles to Fort Boise."

"And back," the ranch hand next to Mr. Hamilton added.

Rika's gaze darted to the tall, blond man, who now stepped into the house. Whatever Phineas had told his boss was about Jo, not her.

At Amy's nudge, Phineas snatched off his hat and came closer. "Hello."

"Hello," Rika said.

Phineas studied her through narrowed eyes, and she squirmed. Surely he had noticed that she didn't look like the woman in the tintype at all. She hoped he wouldn't say anything in front of the Hamiltons.

After a few moments, he took off his gloves and held Rika's hand in his. His calluses felt like Amy's. He shifted from one foot to the other, as tongue-tied as Rika.

Amy interrupted the awkward silence by shouldering past them. "Let's go eat before supper gets cold."

The last bite of apple pie melted on Luke's tongue, and she leaned back in her chair at the head of the table. She watched the people around her, drinking them in. Her family. She laid down her fork. Was it just her, or was something different?

Instead of attacking their desserts as they usually did, Nattie and Amy stabbed at their food without eating much. Once, Luke caught Amy glaring at Phin.

What's the matter with her? Did Amy think now that Phin was back she'd lose her position of respect among the men?

Something was going on. Even Nora seemed quiet tonight.

The men made up for their silence with rambunctious laughter. Jokes flew back and forth. The dangers along the way to Boise became heroic adventures in Charlie's and Phin's recountings.

Luke met Nora's gaze. The familiar green eyes saw more than Luke wanted to reveal in front of the girls. Nora knew there was more to the stories than the men let on. She'd want the uncensored story later, and she'd get it, just as Luke would get the truth about what had happened to Amy and their barn.

"Weren't you scared when that Indian pointed his bow and arrow at you?" Nattie asked. Her fork hovered in front of her lips while she stared at Phin.

"Scared?" Phin asked. "There was no time to be afraid. We had to act before they got away with the best horse in our herd."

Oh, yeah, sure. Luke suppressed a smile. Of course Phin had been afraid, but she said nothing. If he wanted to boast in front of his new bride, so be it.

Not that the young lady seemed overly impressed. While Nattie clung to Phin's words, Hendrika nodded in all the right places but didn't fawn over him.

When Nora and the girls finally stood to carry the dirty dishes into the kitchen, Hendrika stayed next to Amy instead of trying for a more private conversation with her future husband.

Maybe she's just shy. She and Phin are strangers—like Nora and I were when we met. Luke had married a stranger and then fallen in love with her wife. She hoped it would turn out the same way for Phin. She would keep an eye out and try to get to know the young woman better. After all, Phin was almost like a son to her, so Hendrika Bruggeman was as close as she would ever get to having a daughter-in-law.

An owl hooted somewhere above them. Was it the same one Rika had heard so many nights when she lay next to Amy?

"Isaac," Phineas said, nodding skyward.

"What?"

"That's what Nattie calls the owl." Phineas took measured steps so he wouldn't leave her behind on their romantic after-supper stroll. "So, do you like livin' on a ranch?"

"Yes," Rika said, and not just because she wanted to convince him she'd make a good wife. "It's a lot of work, but it's worth it to own something like this." She indicated the corrals, the outbuildings, and the barn with the horses. Grass swayed around her ankles. It was getting long again, but Rika wouldn't be there for the second cut of hay.

"Once we start our own ranch, the first few years won't be easy," Phineas said.

"I didn't expect them to be." Nothing in her life had ever been easy, so why should this be any different? She would grit her teeth and make it through the hard times, as she always had.

Phineas stopped under a large pine tree. "You're not at all like I expected." His gaze raked over her.

Rika lowered her head. Would he notice that she wasn't the woman who had written to him? "I hope you're not disappointed with what you got."

"Not at all. You sounded like a romantic dreamer in your letters."

A romantic dreamer. Jo had been exactly that.

"But now I think you're a woman who's got both feet firmly on the ground." His eyes narrowed to slits. "And you don't look anythin' like the woman in the tintype."

"I sent the picture of a friend," Rika blurted. "I thought if I sent mine, no one would want to marry me with the way I look."

His gaze softened. "You look just fine to me."

Heat blossomed in her cheeks. "Thank you." It was the best compliment she could ever hope to get. "You're not upset?"

Phineas rubbed the blond stubbles on his chin. "I don't like being lied to, but I haven't been completely honest with you either."

"No?" He seemed like an honest man, but maybe the frozen blue of his eyes hid his own secrets.

"I can't write." He blushed beneath his beard. "Miss Nattie's teachin' me, but I can't write letters yet, so I asked Mrs. Hamilton to help me with my letters to you."

Ah. So the poetic words about Oregon were Nora's, not his. Rika held back a giggle. *Jo was swooning over a woman's prose.*

"So I guess we're even," Phineas said. "Let's be honest with each other from now on." He paused and tilted his head, clearly waiting for an agreement.

She couldn't hold his gaze. "All right." Her stomach cramped, and she imagined the lies turning to stone in the pit of her belly.

He smiled. "So? Think you can stand spendin' the rest of your life with me?"

A "no" formed in her throat, but what good reason did she have for rejecting him?

The owl hooted again, perhaps calling for its mate.

When silence fell, she whispered, "Yes."

Amy pressed her forehead against the windowpane. The cold seeped into her skin and into her heart. It hurt to see Rika with Phin, but at the same time, she couldn't look away.

Were they kissing out there, under the pine tree? It was too dark to see, but the images in her mind tortured her.

Footsteps stopped behind her, and she jerked away from the window. Turning, she met Nattie's eyes. "Should be good weather to check on the foals tomorrow," she said, pretending to have watched the darkening sky, not Rika and Phin.

But Nattie didn't fall for it, nor did she look at the sky. Her gaze was fixed on the two people under the pine tree. "Do you think they'll be happy with each other?"

As much as it hurt, Amy hoped they would be. "Phin's a good man. And I think Rika is gonna make a good wife for a rancher."

"Yes, but will they ever have that?" Nattie pointed at the fireplace, where Mama and Papa sat, holding hands and talking with their foreheads touching.

She looked at Nattie, really looked at her for the first time in a long while. Her little sister was no longer so little. She was all grown. Shadows of pain and doubt swirled in her eyes, making Amy wonder what had put that expression there. Had she, too, given up on ever finding the kind of love Mama and Papa had? "Are you all right?"

"Don't start being a mother hen too," Nattie said. "Mama and Papa already asked me that twice tonight."

Everyone seemed to have a lot on his or her mind this evening. Even Rika was strangely quiet instead of basking in Phin's attentions.

She sighed and wrapped her arm around Nattie's shoulder, realizing with momentary irritation that she had to reach up. "I hope they'll have that kind of love," she said. "And I hope you'll find it too."

At least for Nattie, there was hope.

HAMILTON HORSE RANCH
BAKER PRAIRIE, OREGON
JUNE 22, 1868

*L*UKE LEANED BACK IN HER armchair and ran her fingers through Nora's hair. Her fingertips searched for any trace of injury. "Adam's damn lucky that he's safely in prison for the rest of his life. Even if they end up hanging him, that's better than what I would do to him if I got my hands on that bastard." Her voice vibrated, and she forced down her anger, not wanting her first night home to be tainted by hateful thoughts.

"Don't worry." Nora curled against Luke's side. Now that everyone else had gone to bed and they had the parlor to themselves, she was sitting almost on Luke's lap. "Frankie made sure he got what he deserves."

"Where is she, by the way? I thought she and Tess would still be here."

"They're staying in town for a while," Nora said. "They said they need to work something out."

"You think they'll be fine in town?" Luke didn't realize she was frowning until Nora smoothed a finger along her brow.

"Why wouldn't they be fine?"

"The townsfolk are not exactly embracing women who dress in men's clothes," Luke said, knowing Amy had earned a few haughty comments for wearing pants when she worked with the horses.

"Tess has enough money to buy half the town, and you know she can twist even the meanest people around her little finger. But just in case, Frankie was wearing a dress when they left."

The ease with which Frankie switched back and forth still astonished Luke. "Frankie is quite the character."

"At first I liked her because she reminded me of you," Nora said.

"She's not like me at all." In a way, it was a relief. Luke could be sure that Tess was with Frankie because she loved her, not because she secretly longed for more than friendship with Luke.

The armchair creaked when Nora leaned over and kissed her cheek. "I know that now. She's a good person in her own right."

"Tess with a woman... Did you see that coming?" Heat rushed into Luke's cheeks. "I mean, she was with me, but..."

"That was different, I know. Tess and I talked about it."

Luke's fingers froze on another pass through the reddish locks.

Nora laughed. "Don't look at me like that. She was reassuring me."

That thought was even more unsettling. Why had Nora needed reassurance? "After all these years, you still don't know that no one, not even Tess, will ever compare to you?"

"I know that." Nora kissed her cheek again and rubbed her nose beneath Luke's chin like a little kitten. "There was just so much going on here, and I know it's stupid, but I halfway talked myself into believing that your life would be easier if you had never met me and—"

"Easier?" Luke sputtered. "Yeah, maybe it was easier. Life's pretty uncomplicated if it's just you and your horse. But it's also very lonely."

Nora nestled closer and asked against Luke's lips, "So Measles wasn't as good a kisser as I am?"

"Ugh. I don't even want to think—" Then she wasn't thinking at all. She was kissing Nora with every bit of love and longing that she had.

Breathing heavily, Nora pulled away and reached for her hand. "Come on. Let's go upstairs."

Luke's heartbeat picked up as she climbed the stairs, her hand still in Nora's. The bedroom door closed behind them, and she stared at a tub full of steaming water. "What's this?"

"If it's been so long that you don't remember what a bath is, I'd say you really need one." Nora gave her a teasing grin, then caressed her fingers. "I thought after you had to rush through your ablutions for two months, I would surprise you with a nice, private bath."

Speechless, Luke pulled Nora against her and kissed her. "When did you have time to do that without me noticing?"

"The boys helped me when you were checking on Dancer," Nora said. "Should be just the right temperature now."

With a groan of anticipation, Luke locked the bedroom door and lifted her hands to take off her clothes.

Nora stepped closer. "Let me do this." She pulled the vest down Luke's arms and laid it on the trunk at the foot of their bed. The shirt was next. Nora's eyes never left Luke's as she opened button after button.

Luke held her breath in expectation.

The last button gave way, and Nora stripped off the shirt. She rubbed her fingers over the red flannel undershirt and then opened the three tiny buttons. "Lift your arms."

Dazed, Luke complied. The timbre of Nora's voice cast a powerful spell over her. She shivered as the fabric of the undershirt brushed across her shoulders, then her arms, a harbinger of Nora's touch.

The undershirt sailed onto the trunk. Nora unbuttoned the pants, trailed her hand up Luke's stomach, and ran her nails across the bandages binding Luke's breasts.

Luke didn't protest when Nora peeled back layer after layer of the bandages, looking as if she were unwrapping a long-awaited present.

When Luke stood before her naked, Nora smoothed her hands over the faint red lines that the bandages carved into Luke's skin.

Luke shivered under the gentle touch. Heat rushed through her, and she barely resisted the urge to throw Nora onto the bed and cover her body with hers. It had been so long.

But Nora's gaze commanded her. She glanced from Luke to the tub. "Get in."

On trembling legs, Luke climbed into the tub. Warm water lapped at her already burning skin.

Nora's gaze wandered over every inch of her body and lingered on her breasts.

Years ago, Luke would have crossed her arms over her naked chest. But now, she sat still under Nora's gaze, arms on the rim of the tin tub, and let Nora look her fill. How could she feel self-conscious when Nora stared at her as if she were the most beautiful thing in the world?

Nora sank onto her knees next to the tub. She grasped a square of soap and looked deeply into Luke's eyes while she lathered up a washcloth.

In the past, bathing had been private for Luke, something that happened behind locked doors, a necessary evil and a danger rather than something to enjoy. Sharing the experience with someone had been inconceivable.

"Close your eyes," Nora murmured.

Luke didn't hesitate. Her eyes closed.

Nora's breath brushed her ear. "Tip your head back for me."

Warm water flowed over her head and then Nora's fingers were in her hair, caressing wet strands and massaging her scalp. Every bone in Luke's body melted, and the tension of the last two months drained from her body. "Lord. This is heaven."

Water splashed as Nora cupped her hands and rinsed the soap from Luke's hair. Her fingertips brushed away suds, protecting Luke from getting soap in her eyes. She used her fingers to wash behind Luke's ears and then picked up the washcloth again.

Luke's skin tingled when Nora ran the cloth up her arm. The soapy touch trailed across her shoulders, then down the other arm. Nora lifted Luke's hand out of the water and kissed each finger before running the washcloth over them.

A tingle ran through Luke. Her body came alive under Nora's hands, as if it had been asleep for the last few weeks.

The cloth dipped under water, washing Luke's feet and calves, then teasing the back of her knees. She gasped when Nora slid the washcloth up the inside of her leg. Her eyes shot open, her chest heaved, and water sloshed, dripping onto the floor and drenching Nora's dress.

"Your dress," Luke said, voice rough. She stared at the bodice that clung to Nora's chest.

Nora looked down at her wet dress. "Maybe I'd better take it off." Her voice was smoky, filled with heat.

Luke lay transfixed as the skirt fell to the floor, followed by the bodice, then Nora's corset and drawers. She struggled to climb out of the tub and into Nora's arms.

A soft touch to her chest held her back and made her sink back into the water. "Not yet," Nora said. She picked up the washcloth again and trailed it down Luke's breastbone. When she reached her navel, she leaned over and kissed the damp hollow between her collarbones.

The washcloth slid up Luke's sensitive side. It circled one breast, then the other. Nora's fingers skimmed the curve of a breast, making Luke arch into the whisper of a touch.

Nora gripped her hand and directed her to stand. She poured a pitcher of warm water over Luke's body, her gaze following the suds down. "You are so magnificent."

"You are the magnificent one, darling." Luke wanted to say more, but Nora wrapped her in a towel, helped her out of the tub, and pulled her into her arms.

Their bodies pressing against each other, Nora walked her backward.

Luke followed blindly until she felt the edge of the bed against her legs. She shook off the towel and slid onto the bed, pulling Nora on top of her. Compared to Nora's warm, smooth skin, the sheets felt rough beneath her. Their breasts pressed together. "Oh. Oh, this is so..." Her heart hammered against her ribs. Or maybe it was Nora's heart. She couldn't tell anymore.

Playful teeth nibbled her earlobe, sending shafts of heat down her body. Nora rained kisses down the side of her neck and licked away drops of water. Soft locks fanned over Luke's chest like a protective curtain, tickling her skin. Nora's tongue caressed her shoulder, and she pressed a tender kiss to the faded scar before trailing kisses down her breastbone. She licked circles around one breast.

Heat followed her touch. Luke's body tingled from head to toe. Tension pooled in her belly. She couldn't take more teasing. She threaded her fingers through the red locks and pulled Nora's mouth to her breast.

Both of them groaned.

Nora caressed Luke's breasts with her hands, her lips, her tongue, licking, sucking, stroking.

Weakly, Luke lifted her head to watch. Seeing how much joy Nora took from her body, from touching it, tasting it, gave

Luke new appreciation for her female form after spending every minute of the last two months hiding it.

Nora rasped her teeth over the tip of Luke's breast.

"God, Nora." Luke let go of her and grabbed the sheet instead. She was so close to the edge already that she felt as if she were falling. She wasn't afraid. Nora would catch her.

Breath fanned over Luke's belly. She writhed and arched when Nora moved lower. Nora slid her hands up Luke's thighs; one came to rest on her hip while the other found her fingers and entwined them with her own.

Nora nudged Luke's legs apart and settled between them. She pressed a kiss to the inside of her thigh and looked up. "I love you."

Hot breath between her legs sent tingles up and down Luke. "Oh, Lord." She groaned. "I love you too."

Then Nora's mouth was on her.

Luke's moan mingled with Nora's contented humming.

Nora's tongue flicked over her, circled, then dipped lower.

"Nora!" Luke raised her knee and ground herself against Nora. Her heart thudded in her throat, along with the pounding pulse between her legs. Feeling the answering tremor in Nora's body made her blood burn hotter.

Then Nora closed her lips over Luke and suckled.

Luke's hips surged up. Her mouth fell open, and she gulped in a mouthful of air. She disentangled her hand from around the sheet and gripped the back of Nora's head. The pressure in her belly ratcheted higher. The first tremors threatened. Her heels dug into the bed.

Nora gripped her hips, holding her in place.

A wave of ecstasy crashed through Luke, washing away sound and sight, leaving just touch. She arched against Nora, stiffened, then fell back onto damp sheets.

Nora crawled up, her curves brushing over every inch of Luke's body, and collapsed into her arms.

With shaking hands, Luke caressed Nora's flushed cheeks. "Lord, Nora," she rasped through a dry throat, "what you do to me..."

Nora kissed her, and Luke surged against her when she tasted herself on Nora's lips.

"Welcome home," Nora murmured.

Luke rolled over and kissed her neck. "Now let me say hello too."

The whisper of Nora's hand trailing back and forth over her bare chest sent shivers down Luke's body. Then Nora paused with her hand on Luke's breastbone.

"So?"

Luke smiled. She folded her hands in the small of Nora's back, chaining her to her body, and kissed her. Nora tasted of salt and passion. "Measles could never hold a candle to you."

"You!" Nora reached beneath the covers and pinched her hip. "That's not what I meant. Now tell me what happened on the way back from Fort Boise. And I don't want the heroic tale Charlie told over supper. He tried to hide it, but he was limping, wasn't he?"

Sighing, Luke let go of her and slipped into her nightshirt. She wouldn't be able to rest and sleep with her body uncovered like that. At least not so soon after returning home. She needed time to reconnect with that part of herself.

"What happened?" Nora reached for her own nightgown and slipped it over her head.

Luke's first instinct was to protect Nora from the harshness of life, but the years had taught her that sharing her troubles was better for both of them. She took her time getting back into bed and settling the blankets over them before she said, "Two men waylaid us in camp one morning. They wanted to shoot us while we were asleep."

Nora sat up.

"Everyone's fine," Luke said. "We were lucky. A bullet grazed Phin's arm, and Charlie took a bullet in the calf, but that's all."

"Lord." Nora rubbed her breastbone and sank back against her pillow. "What did they want?"

"Revenge."

A deep line formed on Nora's brow. "What for?"

"I stopped them from laying hands on an Indian woman in Fort Boise." The memory of the woman in the alley still made Luke tremble in outrage.

A smile that held equal parts concern and pride tugged on Nora's lips. She cradled Luke's face and looked into her eyes. "Still rescuing damsels in distress, like you rescued me from my life in Independence."

"I didn't rescue you. You rescued me."

Nora's smile grew brighter. "We rescued each other. I think Tess and Frankie rescued each other too. I like them together."

Luke hummed her agreement and settled against Nora's warmth. Her eyelids drooped, but she fought to stay awake. "Can we talk about what's going on with Amy and Nattie? They both seemed so unsettled." She had asked their daughters half a dozen times during and after supper, but both had brushed her off.

"Nattie too?" In the light of the kerosene lamp, worry lines carved themselves into Nora's brow. "Now that I think about it... She's probably sad because Phin and Hendrika will leave soon."

"What about Amy?"

"I have to tell you something."

Nothing good, if the expression in her eyes was any indication.

Luke sat up. "Something worse than Adam setting the barn afire, hurting Amy, and knocking you out?"

"Yes." Nora hesitated. "No, it's not really bad, just surprising and confusing. I don't know how to tell you."

"Just say it," Luke said over the pounding of her heart.

"Amy and Rika saw Tess and Frankie kiss."

For several seconds, the lump in Luke's throat didn't allow for an answer. "No wonder Amy is upset. I bet she didn't even know two women could love each other like that."

"She knows more about it than we thought." Nora leaned against Luke's shoulder as if searching for strength. "Amy has feelings for women."

Impossible. Luke shook her head. "Just because Amy hasn't shown much interest in her suitors doesn't mean—"

"She told me today. Or rather, I dragged it out of her through tears. She is so ashamed she couldn't even look me in the eye."

Luke's heartbeat roared in her ears. Their proud daughter ashamed, crying hot tears of anguish... The thought made her ache. "How long?" Her voice sounded much calmer than she felt. "How long has she known about her feelings?"

"I don't know. She was nearly hysterical, so I did most of the talking and she just stammered a few words. But I got the feeling she has known for some time. She remembered what the townsfolk did to Mrs. Mills and Mrs. Sutherland."

"But if she has known for this long, why didn't she ever come and talk to us about it?" The thought of Amy suffering alone stabbed at her heart.

"She thinks I'm in love with the most wonderful man God ever created." A smile smoothed the worry lines around Nora's mouth. "She doesn't think we understand."

Luke's temples pounded. She gripped her head. "Do you think if Amy had grown up with a real—"

Nora pressed her fingers to Luke's lips. "Don't even think that. I grew up with a father and three brothers, yet here I am, loving you. If we start thinking that we are to blame for Amy's feelings toward women, then we're telling Amy that we think it's wrong."

"Right. Right." A trembling breath escaped Luke. "What do we do?" She felt as she had seventeen years ago: not knowing how to treat Amy or how to talk to her, sure that everything she did and said would be wrong.

"I don't know. I already talked to her, told her that the love between Tess and Frankie isn't any less worthy than the love between a man and a woman."

"Do you think she believed you?" If Amy had heard what the God-fearing people of Baker Prairie said about "unnatural women" like Mrs. Mills and Mrs. Sutherland, Luke doubted Nora's reassurances had done much good.

"I'm sure she understood it here," Nora tapped her finger against her forehead, "but I'm not sure if she accepted it here." Her palm pressed against the upper part of Luke's unbound breast.

Luke covered the hand with her own and clutched it to her pounding heart. She knew how self-hatred could grow over the years, brick by brick, until it created a wall around your heart that could not be overcome by rational arguments. "I'll talk to her." She threw back the covers and swung her legs out of bed.

"Not now, Luke." Nora grabbed a handful of her nightshirt and held her back.

"You think Amy is sleeping after a day like this?" Luke knew she wouldn't sleep a wink all night, so surely Amy was still up too.

"No, but she's sharing her room with Hendrika."

Luke stopped halfway out of bed. "Why isn't Hendrika staying at the cabin?"

"Frankie and Tess needed a place to stay, and now that Phin is back, we can't have him and Hendrika both staying at the cabin before they're married."

Oh boy. Luke's cheeks flushed. "And you thought nothing of letting Amy share a bed with Hendrika, now that you know about her feelings? Clearly, you never experienced an attraction to women at that age, or you'd know how confusing and overwhelming it can be."

"It was plenty confusing for me when I found myself falling in love with you," Nora said. "I'll talk to Hendrika tomorrow. Now that Tess and Frankie are staying in town, she can have the cabin and Phin can bed down in the bunkhouse. But I asked Amy about it. It was her choice to continue sharing a room, and I don't want her to think she should stay away from Hendrika. They've become friends."

"That's good," Luke said. "I always worried about Amy not having any women friends. Once she stopped spending time with Hannah..."

"I have a theory about that."

The covers rustled when Luke slid back into bed. She leaned over to peer at Nora's face. Over the years, she had learned to read the expression in Nora's eyes as well as she could now read a book. "You think she was in love with Hannah?"

"Don't know if I'd call it love, but I think she was smitten, and she didn't know how to deal with it, so she stayed away."

It all sounded so familiar. "Are we sure she's your daughter, not mine?" Luke lifted one corner of her mouth into a weak smile.

"She's your daughter in every way that counts." Nora leaned up and pressed a kiss to her lips until the smile turned into a real one.

"Yeah. It seems we have more in common than I thought. When I was younger, I tried to stay away from women too. I joined the dragoons and served in lonely forts, where I didn't get to see a woman for months at a time. I hadn't yet learned that desiring women didn't mean I'd desire all of them."

"Maybe you can explain that to Amy somehow," Nora said.

Luke squeezed the bridge of her nose. "The question is just how. I can only talk to Amy as a man, so what I can tell her is limited."

This time, Nora had no answers.

Sighing, Luke doused the kerosene lamp and settled in for a sleepless night.

Cool morning air greeted Nora as she stepped outside and let the door fall closed behind her. "Oh, there you are."

Hendrika sat on the veranda, the butter churn between her feet. She moved the wooden dasher up and down in a steady rhythm.

"Want me to take over for a moment before I have to leave?" Nora asked. Churning butter was monotonous and tiring work.

"No, it's all right. I don't mind."

Nora leaned against the veranda railing and looked across the ranch yard. A few of their mares wandered through the corral, licking morning dew off the grass. Next to the corral, Amy and Luke were saddling their horses, every movement in perfect harmony, stepping around each other without stumbling or getting in each other's way—like two dancers who had practiced their waltz a thousand times.

Watching them together warmed Nora's heart.

Luke swung her leg over the cantle, and as she settled into the saddle, her gaze met Nora's. She kissed her fingertips and held out her palm as if sending the kiss across the ranch yard.

Smiling, Nora repeated the gesture.

Amy lifted her hand as if to imitate Luke, then curled her fingers into a fist and dropped her hand. She pulled her mare around and urged her into a lope.

When Nora turned back to Hendrika, the up-and-down movement of the dasher had slowed. When the hoofbeats faded away, Hendrika directed her gaze back to the churn and picked up the pace.

Am I imagining things, or has she been watching Amy? Nora wasn't sure. "Tess and Frankie are staying in town for a while. If you want, you can move back into the cabin."

The dasher stopped. "But Phineas—"

"Don't worry about him. He can stay in the bunkhouse with the other boys for a few days."

"Oh." Slowly, Hendrika moved the dasher up and down in the cream. "All right, I suppose."

Nora furrowed her brow. "I thought you'd be glad to have a room and a bed to yourself for a few days before you get married."

"I am glad," Hendrika said, sounding anything but. She bent and lifted the lid off the churn. A golden lump of butter had formed and was now clinging to the dasher.

Like Hendrika is clinging to sharing a room with Amy. It seemed Hendrika was fond of Amy, but was it just the innocent friendship between young women or something more? Nora remembered sharing a bed with Luke for the first time, remembered the feeling of peace and safety even as she had shivered under a damp blanket while rain drummed down on their wagon. Did Hendrika feel the same way?

"Old Jack is ready, ma'am," Hank called from the stable.

Nora glanced at the sun. Her pupils were waiting for their last day of school before summer break. There was no time to figure out what was going on with Hendrika. With one last glance at Hendrika, who was busy fishing the butter from the buttermilk, Nora hurried toward the wagon.

"Look, Papa! There's Nugget with her foal." Amy gestured with childlike excitement, but Luke knew she was no longer a child. So much had changed.

Luke let her gaze wander from horse to horse, but her thoughts were on Amy, who halted her mare next to Dancer. They needed to talk. She had opened her mouth half a dozen times while they rode from one band of horses to the next, but every time, she closed it again without saying anything. After living as a man for the past thirty years, how could she talk to Amy about the joys of love between two women? Was it possible to let Amy know she understood without giving away her secret?

She stared at the horses while seeking a solution. The herd was in great shape. Over the last weeks, the grasses had become richer, and now the horses' bellies were pleasantly rounded, their dotted coats gleaming with good health. A few mares stood dozing beneath a stand of trees while their foals leaped through the grass. In the distance, two yearlings bucked, reared, and squealed at each other in a mock fight.

"They're looking good." She turned in the saddle to look at Amy. "You took good care of them. How did you feel about running the ranch?"

"There were a few tense moments," Amy said, openly meeting her gaze.

Why can't she be as honest about her feelings for women? But, of course, Luke knew why. She had been through the same feelings of shame, guilt, and confusion.

"Sometimes I felt like everyone tried to make things harder for me," Amy said. "Adam went crazy as soon as you left. Guess Mama told you about him burning down the stable and attacking me." When Luke nodded, Amy continued, "Hank tried to lynch John, and the folks in town laughed at me when I wanted to hire a new ranch hand. All of that would never have happened to you."

Luke bit her tongue. She wanted to tell Amy that it was just people's perception that made the difference, not Amy's gender. But she couldn't explain without giving herself away. "I would hope not," she said instead. "I have twenty years of experience. But my first year running the ranch... Lord, I felt like a complete failure. We were snowed in, and a coyote got into the henhouse. We didn't even have enough money to buy you a new doll."

Grinning, Amy shrugged. "I preferred the wooden horses anyway."

Luke laughed. She couldn't imagine loving Amy more, even had she given birth to her herself. "Anything else happen while I was away?"

Instead of confessing her feelings, Amy said, "The foals were born. Did you see Jason, Nugget's colt?"

Of course she had. Amy had already pointed out every foal in the herd—and most of the yearlings too as if Luke had forgotten them in the last two months. Since they had left the ranch, Amy hadn't stopped talking. She commented on every horse they encountered, the length of the grass, the new barn, and the ranch hand she had hired.

Luke got the impression that Amy wanted to keep her too busy to have a serious conversation.

"See that one?" Amy pointed at a filly nibbling the grasses alongside her mother.

"She's a beauty." Luke let herself be distracted for a moment. A black horse with such a large white blanket was rare. "She'll make a wonderful brood mare one day if we're lucky."

Amy laughed. "That's her name—Lucky Star."

"Nice. You picked a good name."

A wave of crimson wandered up Amy's cheeks. "I didn't name her. Rika did."

Rika. Interesting. No one else called Hendrika by her nickname, and now the mere mention of her name made Amy blush. Had she reacted to women that way before, and Luke just hadn't noticed? Had she been so blind to Amy's feelings all those years? Knowing she wouldn't get any answers without asking, she cleared her throat. "I talked to your mother."

Amy's blush darkened to a deep cherry color. She clamped her bottom lip between her teeth.

Luke flinched at the expression in her eyes. Neither of her daughters had ever looked at her that way—as if expecting punishment.

Amy let go of her lip just long enough to ask, "Did she... did she tell you?"

They both knew the answer to that question. Luke and Nora never kept secrets from each other. "Amy, there's no need to worry. I'm fine with it. I don't care who you love as long as you're happy."

The defensive hunch of Amy's shoulders didn't change. By now, her lip probably had permanent teeth marks. Tears filled her eyes, but she didn't let them fall. "You and Mama are so wonderful. No one else has such understanding parents. I'm so sorry to cause you—"

Luke slid out of the saddle and landed between the two horses, giving Amy the advantage of looking down at her. She touched Amy's calf. "You never caused me anything but joy and pride."

Amy's brows crept up her forehead.

"All right." Luke forced a smile. "I wasn't pleased when you were six and nearly broke your neck when you tried to ride one of the yearlings."

"This is worse than riding a yearling," Amy whispered.

"No." Luke kept her voice and her grip on Amy's leg firm. "Both could be dangerous, but jumping on a yearling's back was a decision. A pretty stupid one. But this..." She gesticulated, not sure what the right words were. "Being in love with a woman is not a decision. It just happens."

"Maybe for you. You're a man, after all. But it shouldn't happen to me." Amy's voice trembled.

It was like looking in a mirror. When she'd been Amy's age, she'd been so afraid of her own feelings, of losing control over them, that she had hidden away that part of herself. She hoped Amy wouldn't make the same mistake—but how could she tell her that? She couldn't talk about her own experiences without admitting that she was a woman. "But sometimes, it does happen," Luke said. "It's not a curse or a bad thing, you know? If a woman is what you need or want in your life—"

"I want what you and Mama have together, but it's not possible for two women. I'll never have that kind of love." A sadness as vast and as deep as the Pacific filled Amy's eyes.

Burning pain blazed behind Luke's breastbone. She hated to see her daughter give up hope for personal happiness. "That's not true, Amy. You've seen Frankie and Tess together. They don't have an easy life, but they're happy. Don't give up on—"

"I can't talk to you about this, Papa." Amy fidgeted in the saddle.

While Amy had grown up with more freedom and independence than other girls her age, society had still taught her that young women didn't discuss such delicate matters with men. Luke curled her hand around Amy's stirrup until the leather creaked. Most often, being thought of as a man was an advantage. Now it was her biggest obstacle.

Before Luke could answer, Amy dug her heels into Ruby's sides.

Luke was forced to let go of the stirrup and Amy's leg. As Ruby loped up a hill, Luke hurled a curse across the valley. Why the hell did life have to be so complicated?

She got back on her horse and caught up with Amy. They rode the last mile in silence, Amy brooding and Luke not sure what to say.

Luke dismounted in the ranch yard, and Amy dropped down next to her without her usual ease.

Tess and Frankie came out of the house. Tess's skirts swept across the veranda when she hurried down the three steps. "Hello, soldier." She had greeted Luke that way for many years. She slid her arms around Luke and lifted up on her toes for a kiss.

At the last moment, Luke turned her head, aware that Amy was watching.

Tess's kiss landed on her cheek instead of her lips. "I'm sorry we weren't there to greet you when you came home," Tess said. "But we have good news."

Luke followed them into the house. She could use some good news.

Rika held her hand behind the glass chimney and blew out the kerosene lamp. She slipped into Phineas's bed and closed her eyes.

The silence in the small cabin sounded strangely loud.

She yawned and rolled to her other side. A long day full of work had left her exhausted, but still sleep wouldn't come. When she had shared a room with three other women in the boarding house, she had often wished for just one night of peace and quiet. Now that she had it, why was she lying awake, listening into the darkness?

Last night and the nights before, Amy's breathing had lulled her to sleep, the scent of leather and grass and Amy's soap telling her that she was safe. Home. She'd never felt that before.

I'm just too used to not being alone at night. She shook her head. Her childhood had made her a master at lying to others, but she always tried not to lie to herself. *This isn't simple loneliness. You don't miss company. You miss Amy's company.*

She opened her eyes and stared into the darkness. But she had missed Jo, too, after she had died, hadn't she? Yet she had still slept like a log after an exhausting day. Somehow, missing Amy was very different from missing Jo. Sharing the bed with Jo was like sharing with one of her half sisters. Amy's warmth in bed next to her didn't feel sisterly at all. She had never been as aware of Jo's body as she was of Amy's.

Goose bumps broke out over Rika's skin, even under the warm blanket. She closed her eyes, but the image of Amy, red locks spilling over her pillow, remained.

Thoughts like that were getting more frequent. *Nothing good will come of thinking like this. It has no future.* Maybe it was just Tess's and Frankie's confusing presence. Maybe marrying and moving away would be for the best. Once she married Phineas, she'd have no time to miss Amy at night.

She hit her pillow into submission and squeezed her eyes shut more tightly.

"What's going on with you?" Nora asked when the bedroom door closed behind them. "You barely smiled when Tess and Frankie told us they'll be staying in Baker Prairie to open a hotel."

Luke forced a smile. "That's great news."

"Your talk with Amy didn't go well, did it?"

Luke flopped onto the mattress and stared at the ceiling. "She wouldn't talk to me."

"What?" Nora sat on the edge of the bed and leaned over her. "But she always talks to you, even about things she doesn't want to tell me."

"Not about this. How can we expect her to talk to me when she thinks I'm a man?" Luke kicked off her boots and let them thump against the wall. It didn't help her frustration.

"But there has to be something we can do to help her. We can't let her hate herself, Luke. What can we do?"

The question had been running through Luke's mind for twenty-four hours now. She found just one answer, and she wasn't sure whether it would help Amy or throw her even deeper into chaos. She clamped her fingers around the edge of the mattress. "As long as she thinks I'm a man, she won't talk to me. And she thinks you don't understand because you're married to me, a man."

Green eyes appeared in her field of vision, and Nora put her hands on Luke's shoulders. "What are you suggesting?"

"Maybe..." Luke rubbed her nose. "Maybe we should tell her."

"Tell her what?"

Luke opened her mouth, but the words wouldn't come. She took Nora's hand and pressed it to her own chest, letting her feel the bound breasts beneath the vest and shirt.

Nora pulled back and stared at her. "Do you think that would help? Wouldn't it make things worse?"

"Amy said she wants what we have, but she doesn't think it's possible for two women."

"But Frankie and Tess—"

"Amy doesn't know them as well as we do. And they hide their love. Amy needs to see two women she knows and who have a strong, loving relationship."

Nora sighed. "That's a big risk. Are you sure you want to do that?"

"I'm not sure at all." She wanted to stay Luke Hamilton, rancher, husband, and father. But what if by revealing her gender, she could show Amy that love between two women was good and lasting even if it required some sacrifice?

Nora combed her fingers through the silver-tipped hairs at Luke's temple. "Maybe we should wait and give Amy some time before making a decision like that."

"What if time doesn't help? What if Amy still loathes that part of herself in a week, a month, a year?"

"Then we'll tell her. We can't let her hate herself." Nora lowered her voice to a whisper. "Maybe it's time to tell them."

Their daughters were adults now. They had grown up to be responsible, strong women. Luke breathed in deeply. *I've got to trust them with this. They deserve it.*

"Maybe it's better to do this now, on our terms, not while you are lying somewhere, bleeding." Nora shivered. "If you had been shot by those two scoundrels from Fort Boise, Phin and Charlie would have found out."

Luke searched her face. "Did you ever forgive me for not telling you sooner? For having you find out when you opened my shirt to save my life?"

Nora cradled Luke's face between her hands and lowered herself until they were almost nose to nose. "There's nothing to forgive. Back then, we were strangers—married strangers, but strangers nonetheless. We hadn't learned to love and trust each other yet. But our daughters do. They love you, and we have to trust that in the end, they'll come to understand."

Without words, Luke tugged her down. Her lips found Nora's. Teeth clashed for a moment before Luke tamed her despair and gentled her touch. She slid her tongue against Nora's, wanting to drown in her heat as if it were the last time.

Nora drew back and whispered kisses against the corner of Luke's mouth. "I'm warning you. If you're thinking of doing the honorable thing and keeping your promise to Bernice..."

Many years ago, Luke had promised Bernice that she would never shame Nora by staying around if her secret was revealed. The thought of losing Nora, leaving her family and her home, took away her breath.

"If you run, I'll come after you." Nora pressed her finger to Luke's chest and tapped a few times as if to drive home her point. "I'll follow you to the end of the world if need be."

A lump formed in Luke's throat, and she swallowed it down. "What about the ranch?"

"My home is with you."

It was the same for Luke. Losing the ranch would hurt, but giving up Nora and their daughters would shatter her heart in a million little pieces. "And the girls?"

"That's why I'm telling you not to run. Running away won't let Amy know that loving a woman is all right. Now it's time to face our fears, not to run away from them."

"I'll stay," Luke said, her voice rough. Her promise to Bernice still held true. She would never let Nora and the girls live in shame. But maybe it was time to find other ways to keep her promise. Leaving wasn't the solution.

Her promise to Bernice had been well-intentioned, but it had been made by a younger Luke, who hadn't yet fully trusted Nora's love. Part of her had still believed that Nora might be better off without her. Now she understood that her promise to love Nora forever and Nora's promise to love her was the most important thing in their lives. "What about you? If we tell the girls that I'm a woman, they'll want to know who fathered them."

Nora pressed her lips together until they blanched. "We're both risking a lot, but it'll be all right. It'll be all right," she repeated as if willing herself to believe it.

"Let's wait a while longer," Luke said. "Maybe there's another way. I'll try talking to Amy again tomorrow."

HAMILTON HORSE RANCH
BAKER PRAIRIE, OREGON
JUNE 24, 1868

*L*UKE HESITATED OUTSIDE THE TACK room, one hand extended toward the door. Under normal circumstances, she didn't disturb Amy when she was in her hideaway. This time, she couldn't allow Amy to run or hide from her fears or she'd be running for the rest of her life. "Amy?" she called through the door before she opened it.

Amy sat on a barrel, not looking up from the saddle in front of her. She hadn't heard Luke. She also wasn't alone.

Leaning against the barrel, watching Amy work, was Hendrika.

"You put some saddle soap on the cloth and then work it into the leather," Amy said.

"Like this?" Hendrika took over the cloth.

"Circular motions." Amy covered Hendrika's hand with her own and showed her.

It seemed like yesterday that Luke had taught Amy how to clean tack. She still remembered how she had guided her little hands. Now those hands were all grown up and guiding Hendrika with confidence.

And with tenderness. Pausing in the doorway, Luke watched them.

"Make sure you get the underside of the fenders and the cinch," Amy said, her voice husky.

Oh, no. This isn't good. Was Amy smitten with Phin's bride? Maybe she really was too much like Luke. When she'd been Amy's age, every girl she met had made her blush and her heart race. It took her a while to figure out that physical reactions didn't equal love. If she could teach Amy that, it would spare her daughter a lot of heartache and save her from potential danger. The starry-eyed adoration of youth wasn't worth risking her life if the object of her affection ran away screaming and told the rest of town. It certainly wasn't worth ruining Amy's friendship with Phin.

Luke cleared her throat.

"Papa!" Amy wrenched her hands away from Hendrika's.

"I didn't mean to interrupt, but I'm about to head out and check on Lucky, get her used to a halter. Wanna come?"

Amy slid from the barrel. Her gaze flicked to Hendrika, and she hesitated.

"Can I come too, Mr. Hamilton?" Hendrika asked. "I'd love to see Lucky again. I promise not to get in the way."

That wasn't part of Luke's plan. She wanted to talk to Amy alone, but with the gap-toothed smile directed at her, she found herself unable to say no. "Can you ride?"

A long glance passed between Amy and Hendrika.

"I'm still learning, but Amy is teaching me, and she said I'm doing well," Hendrika said. "I'm trying to spend as much time in the saddle as I can."

"You can come," Luke said. "On one condition."

Hendrika shifted and eyed her. "What?"

"Call me Luke. No one ever calls me Mr. Hamilton."

"Oh." Her wary stance relaxed. "Thank you."

Luke waited for an offer to call her Rika, but it didn't come. Apparently, that privilege was reserved for Amy.

When they saddled the horses, Hendrika nudged Amy. "I'm almost afraid to ride out with you."

"Afraid?" Luke asked, frowning.

"It seems every time we leave the ranch together, something happens," Hendrika said. "First, we cross paths with a wild mustang, then we find a drowning foal." Instead of looking fearful, she was smiling, though.

So much had happened in the nine weeks Luke had been away, and now she was desperately trying to catch up and make sense of what was going on with her daughters.

She watched Hendrika mount. In one of Nora's split riding skirts, the young woman cut a fine figure in the saddle. Her transitions were still a little rough, but her touch on the reins was light. "You taught her well," Luke said.

The compliment stained Amy's cheeks red.

How much time did she spend with Hendrika, teaching her how to ride? Luke had thousands of questions, but no answers—and she knew she wouldn't get answers from Amy as long as Hendrika was with them. *And here I thought being a parent would get easier over the years.*

HAMILTON HORSE RANCH
BAKER PRAIRIE, OREGON
JUNE 25, 1868

*R*IKA DROPPED HER BRUSH INTO the empty bucket of paint. "Done." She stepped back to look at the newly painted line shack.

Amy wiped her hands on a rag. "Looks good. Thanks for helping me." Splashes of reddish-brown paint dotted her shirt, and a broad stripe across her forehead made her look like an Indian on the warpath.

Rika laughed and pointed. "Lord, you're a sight." She lifted a corner of her apron to wipe the paint from Amy's face, but Amy backed away.

"Oh, and you aren't?"

Rika looked down at herself. Reddish-brown dots on her forearms and down the front of her dress made her look like one of the Hamiltons' Appaloosas. "Oh, my. I think we should wash up before we ride back." She glanced at the nearby Pudding River, which sluggishly meandered through the valley next to the line shack. "In fact..." She looked from the river to Amy. "I could teach you how to swim while we're here."

Maybe for once, she could be the one to teach while Amy learned from her instead of the other way around.

"We don't have the time to—"

"Yes, we do. We thought painting the line shack would take all afternoon. No one will expect us back before supper."

Amy hesitated and looked around as if searching for another reason to refuse.

"This is important," Rika said. "You almost drowned because you can't swim. If I hadn't been there..." She snapped her mouth shut, not wanting to finish the sentence. Some nights, she still had nightmares about Amy being swept away by the raging river. She tilted her head and took in Amy's pale face. "You're not afraid, are you?"

Amy lifted her chin. "Of course not."

"Then come on." Rika took a step toward the river. "I promise I won't let anything happen to you." She felt Amy's gaze on her as she slipped off her skirt and petticoat. Standing on the riverbank in just her chemise and long underdrawers, she looked back at Amy, who still hadn't undressed. "Are you shy about undressing in front of me?"

"No," Amy said, but her tone lacked conviction.

"Come on, Amy. We're both women."

The words, meant to encourage, made Amy blush instead.

Heat crawled up Rika's neck as well when she remembered that their gender no longer meant they wouldn't look at each other with desire. Finding out about Tess and Frankie's relationship had changed things Rika had taken for granted. "Let's get into the water." Mud squished between her toes as she waded in. With her back turned, she waited for Amy.

Clothing rustled; then water splashed.

Rika turned.

Amy waded into the river, drenching her thin undershirt until it clung to her body. Droplets of water gleamed on her bare collarbone and ran down her cleavage.

Rika couldn't help staring. *You've seen half-naked women before. This isn't any different.* But somehow, it was. She curled her toes into the muddy river bottom and forced her gaze away. Maybe this hadn't been such a good idea after all. "Push off with your feet and let yourself sink into the water."

Amy tried and immediately started to dog-paddle, barely staying afloat.

"Oh, no, no. Not like that. Watch me." Rika sank into the cool water and swam back and forth in front of Amy. "See? You pull your arms and legs toward your body, then kick them out, like frogs do. Here, let me help you." She stepped next to Amy and put her hands on Amy's hips. Even through the wet undershirt, Amy's skin felt warm to the touch.

"Um..."

"Try again. I'm gonna hold you up," Rika said, forcing herself to focus on the swimming lesson. "Move your arms and legs in a circle and push at the water with your hands and feet."

Amy shifted her weight forward, into Rika's hands, and calmed her frantic paddling. "Don't let go," she sputtered into the water.

"I won't." Rika didn't remind her that the water was only hip-deep. *She trusts me to keep her safe.* The feeling humbled her and made her feel powerful at the same time. She tightened her grip around Amy's hips. "Put your fingers together and push with your legs. Yes, yes, like that."

After a few minutes, Amy found a rhythm with her arms and legs.

"All right, now try on your own." With an encouraging squeeze, Rika let go and stepped back.

As soon as Rika's hands vanished from her hips, Amy began to sink and lapsed back into her dog-paddling technique.

Rika grasped her hands and pulled her close. "I've got you."

Amy's arms instantly wrapped around her neck. Her breath washed over Rika's bare shoulders.

Without thought, Rika slipped her arms around Amy. Their body heat seemed to warm up the water around them. She felt dizzy, as if she would be the one drowning if she let go of Amy. It took her a while to remember that the water wasn't deep and neither of them needed the other to hold her up. "Hold..." Her voice sounded breathless, and she cleared her throat before she tried again. "Hold on to my hands. I'm gonna drag you through the water to let you practice how to move your legs." She shivered when their bodies separated.

Their fingers entwined in a strong grip, and their gazes met. They stood like that for what could have been minutes before Rika remembered why they were there. She walked backward, pulling Amy after her. "Move your legs in circles."

Water splashed as Amy kicked powerful legs.

"Steady. Keep your feet in the water." After a while, Rika slowed and let her momentum propel Amy past her. She put her hands around Amy's hips again. Again, heat seemed to vibrate between them. She cleared her throat. "All right, let's try this again. Ready?"

Amy turned her head and peered up at Rika through copper strands that clung to her forehead in wet ringlets. "Yeah."

This time, when Rika let go, Amy continued to move her arms and legs in circles. After swimming a few feet, she sought the river bottom with her feet and straightened. She stared down her body, then at Rika. Water dripped into her face, but it couldn't extinguish Amy's grin. "I did it. I can swim!"

Managing to stay afloat for a few moments didn't exactly make her a champion swimmer, but Rika didn't say that, not wanting to spoil Amy's joy. She grinned back. "You sure can."

She wasn't sure who moved first, but within seconds, they came together in a fierce embrace.

"Thank you," Amy whispered, then let go and stepped back.

Rika shivered. She could still feel Amy's wet body plastered against her own. Every inch of her body felt alive with the memory of that touch. "You're welcome."

They waded up the riverbank and sat down next to their clothes, waiting for the sun to dry them. From time to time, Rika stole a glance at Amy out of the corner of her eye.

Once, she caught Amy looking at her too.

Their gazes veered away.

What is she thinking? Does she feel this strange…pull too?

Amy got up and struggled into her clothes. "Come on. Let's head back home."

A horse whinnied a greeting, and several Appaloosas in the corral behind Luke lifted their heads and answered.

Luke looked up from the three-year-old gelding she was training.

A gray mare loped down the hill toward the ranch, moving smoothly under Frankie. When the horse stopped in front of Luke, she reached out and let the mare sniff her hand. "So this is the famous Mouse. Nora told me about her."

"Yeah. That's her." Frankie patted Mouse's neck. "Your daughter worked miracles on her."

"Want to come in for a cup of coffee? Nora's in the garden, but I can let her know you're here." Being alone with Frankie still made Luke slightly uncomfortable. She never knew whether she should treat her like a pal or a lady.

Frankie swung down and landed lightly on her feet. "It's all right. I'm actually here to see you. Mouse needs new shoes, and I don't like the blacksmith in Baker Prairie. He's too rough with the horses."

Ah. She could handle this. "I can shoe her for you, no problem."

"Oh, no, that's not necessary. If you would just lend me your equipment, I can do the rest."

"Let's do it together." Luke led her over to the ranch's small blacksmith shop. While she worked the bellows and fired up the forge, Frankie picked up Mouse's left front leg and cradled it between her knees. With practiced movements, she cleaned out the hoof. Then she removed the old shoe and trimmed the hoof walls before smoothing the ragged edges with a file.

"You've done this before," Luke said.

"Many times." Frankie looked up at her. "Surprised?"

Luke shrugged.

"I bet people take it for granted that you can shoe a horse," Frankie said.

"Yeah." No one blinked an eye when Luke shoed a horse, but she knew Frankie got different reactions. A sudden realization came to her. "You enjoy this."

"Shoeing a horse?"

"Surprising people by being unconventional."

"Guilty as charged." Frankie's grin made her look more like a mischievous boy than a middle-aged woman.

Maybe this was the biggest difference between them. Luke had never wanted to stand out. All she wanted was to fit in and be seen as just another rancher.

She heated a new horseshoe and then hammered and shaped it on the anvil until she thought it would fit Mouse's hoof. Mouse held still under Frankie's steady grip as Luke placed the shoe on her hoof.

"I just saw Amy and Hendrika," Frankie said over the sizzling sound.

"Yeah, they're painting one of our line shacks." Luke drove the first nail into the wall of Mouse's hoof.

"Um, no, that's not what they were doing."

With the second nail clamped between her lips, Luke looked up and lifted an eyebrow.

"They were standing in the middle of the river in their underwear, hugging each other," Frankie said.

Luke nearly swallowed the nail and then spat it out. "What?"

Lines of concern appeared on Frankie's brow. "Nora told you about..." She hesitated. "...about Amy, right?"

"Yes, but I didn't think there was anything going on between her and Hendrika. Well, maybe a bit of an infatuation on Amy's side." Did Amy have deeper feelings for Phin's bride? And did Hendrika return those feelings? She couldn't ask Amy. Fathers didn't ask their daughters that kind of thing. How ironic. She was trapped by the lie that had always given her so much freedom.

"Well, I don't think anything really happened," Frankie said. "After a second, they quickly let go of each other and Amy backed away. She's not ready to accept that part of herself."

Luke pounded in the nails, carefully channeling her frustration into the physical work. "Was it easy to accept for you?"

Frankie filed off the nails' sharp edges, set down Mouse's foot, and straightened. "Lord, no. After my father died and my brothers chased me away, telling me they hated me..." She shook her head, her gaze searching the horizon. "For a while, I didn't care if I lived or died."

Luke rubbed a spot above her heart. "I'm sorry. I don't want Amy to go through that."

"She won't have to go through it alone." Frankie patted her shoulder in a comradely way. "I wish I had parents like you and Nora."

"But I can't help Amy much since she thinks I'm a man." Luke clamped both hands around the hammer. "How can I tell her she doesn't have to hate a part of herself when I'm hiding that part of myself from her?"

Frankie's friendly pat softened and became a comforting caress to her shoulder. For the first time in Luke's life, another woman was touching her as if she was just one of her female friends. It felt strange, but she appreciated it anyway.

"You're doing the best you can under the circumstances," Frankie said.

Luke put her hand on Mouse's back as if to steady herself. "But it's not enough." She kicked at the old horseshoe lying on the ground. "I need to do more to help Amy."

"More? What more can you do?"

The words seemed stuck in her throat, and Luke forced them out. "We think it's time to be honest with our girls about who I am."

Frankie pushed back her hat and stared at her. "That's huge, Luke. Are you sure?"

"I'll do whatever it takes to help my daughter accept herself. What kind of parent would I be if I let Amy suffer and kept my secret for my own selfish reasons? Compared to you and Tess, who live your lives as openly as possible, I feel like a coward sometimes."

"A coward? You?" Frankie shook her head. "If you were a coward, you would have left Nora behind in Independence when you first met her. Only you can decide what to do, but please know that Tess and I will be there to support you in any way we can."

Luke stared into her warm brown eyes. While Frankie still confused her, she had a feeling that this woman understood her as few other people did. Maybe they could be friends. "You know, I want to say thank you, but I'm not sure if I should shake your hand or kiss it."

"Lucky for you," Frankie said, grinning broadly, "I have two hands, so you could do both."

Their laughter chased away part of Luke's tension.

In companionable silence, they finished shoeing Mouse.

Dusk settled over the ranch like a blanket. Rika let her gaze sweep over the hills in the distance, then the familiar contours of the ranch buildings until her gaze landed on the old oak next to the main house. A swing dangled from one of the thick branches, and she imagined little Amy flying higher and higher, shouting at her papa to push her faster.

But right now, the swing swayed gently back and forth. Nora sat on it, not holding on to the ropes. She leaned back against Luke, who stood behind her, his arms wrapped around her, swaying with her. Every once in a while, he bent to press a kiss to the top of her head. Their lips were moving, and Rika imagined them whispering words of love to each other.

The creaking of the door made her wrench away her gaze.

Amy stepped onto the veranda but stopped when she noticed Rika. "You waiting for Phin? He's still in the office with Nattie." She pointed over her shoulder.

"They're spending a lot of time with each other," Rika said. While Phineas collected her for a short stroll every night after supper, he spent hours with Nattie every day.

"Just discussing the breeding program. You don't need to be jealous."

"I'm not." It was the truth. While she worried about her future and about Phineas keeping his promise to marry her, her heartbeat didn't pick up at all when she thought about Phineas with another woman. *Unless it's Amy.* Scowling, she pushed the thought away.

Amy nodded and leaned against the veranda post next to Rika. She smiled as she watched her parents. "They look like a courting couple, don't they?"

"They're still in love with each other," Rika said, her voice barely louder than a whisper. All her life, she had thought love wasn't real, just something naïve fools dreamed about. But there was no denying the love between Amy's parents. It radiated off them like heat from a cast-iron stove on a cold winter night. Watching them together made her long for love too, and she knew she wouldn't have it with Phineas.

Quit wishing for what you can't have. You've never done it before, so why start now? She cursed the Hamiltons for making her think about love. It was as if she had suddenly become aware of a hole inside of her after having thought herself complete all her life.

"Sometimes I wonder what makes some people fall in love with the right person while others are never lucky enough to have that," Amy mumbled, staring at her parents.

The misery in her expression hit Rika like a punch to the ribs, robbing her of breath. "I'm sure that one day, you'll be one of the lucky ones too." She wanted that for Amy more than she wished it for herself.

Amy turned her head and met Rika's gaze.

For long moments, Rika looked into eyes that appeared like mossy forest lakes in the falling darkness.

Then Amy looked away. "I don't think it's possible for me."

"Why shouldn't it be?" Surely there was at least one man who could appreciate Amy's gentle strength and her passion for the land and its animals?

Amy sighed. "That's just the way it is for me."

She sounded so sad that Rika wanted to step closer and embrace her, but she held herself back. After the effect their hug in the river had on her, she knew it was better to keep her distance.

Luke pressed a kiss to the skin of Nora's neck and let herself be comforted by Nora's warmth and their gentle swaying.

Humming, Nora leaned back and rested her head against Luke's chest.

Over Nora's head, Luke watched the two young women on the veranda. In the falling darkness, she couldn't make out their expressions, but their bodies were pointing toward each other even while they stared off into the night.

"You all right?" Nora's voice vibrated through her, soothing her like a favorite lullaby.

"Did you ever think Amy might feel more than friendship for Hendrika?"

Nora craned her neck to look at her. "A bit of an infatuation, maybe. Amy's a passionate young woman, after all, and she hasn't been around women her age much. Nothing to worry about, right?"

"That's what I thought too, but I watched them together and now I'm not so sure." She glanced toward the veranda again. Amy and Hendrika looked at each other, keeping eye contact for an intense moment. Was this really just random infatuation that could have been directed at any woman who came along?

"You think it could be love?" Nora asked. "Amy is so inexperienced when it comes to that."

"Just as inexperienced as I was when I met you." Luke settled her hand on the curve of Nora's hip.

"If you're right, Amy will be heartbroken once Hendrika marries Phin," Nora said. "Do you think Hendrika might have feelings for Amy too?"

Luke paused their swaying for a moment. "I'm not sure, but I think there could be something there. Something that could grow into love, like it did for us. But nothing will ever come of it. Amy is so afraid. She'll never tell Hendrika how she feels."

"Would you want her to?" Nora asked. "Hendrika is Phin's betrothed, after all."

Luke clutched Nora more tightly to her body. "I don't know. It's all a mess, and I don't want to see Phin hurt either. But I can't help thinking that maybe Amy needs to take the kind of risk that I did, or she'll forever regret it. What if Hendrika turns out to be her Nora, and she lets her go?"

Nora freed herself from their embrace and turned. She clutched the ropes and leaned across the swing. Her lips found Luke's, and for the length of one passionate kiss, Luke forgot their conversation.

Then Nora drew back and breathed deeply. "And under different circumstances, maybe Amy would turn out to be Hendrika's Luke, but Amy isn't ready. She might one day come to accept her feelings, but not now."

"But Hendrika won't be there one day," Luke said. She clutched the swing's rope until it bit into her hands and struggled to draw air into her lungs. "No more waiting. We need to tell the girls the truth about me."

HAMILTON HORSE RANCH
BAKER PRAIRIE, OREGON
JUNE 26, 1868

*W*HEN RIKA REACHED THE EDGE of the carrot patch, she pulled out a handful of dandelions and threw it into a bucket that was already filled with horsetail, wild clover, and other weeds. Groaning, she straightened and brushed earth off her skirt.

Nattie carried over her own bucket of weeds. "All done. Finally." She plucked a bean leaf from Rika's sleeve.

They emptied their buckets onto the manure heap, and Nattie pulled up a bucket of cool water from the well.

Rika drank deeply, enjoying the coldness of the water as it slid down her parched throat. She looked around for Amy, who might be in need of some water too.

"I'll take some water over to Phin," Nattie said.

Rika flushed. *For heaven's sake, Hendrika Aaldenberg! You're supposed to think of your future husband's needs, not Amy's.* "Let me."

Shrugging, Nattie handed over the water bucket.

Bucket in hand, Rika walked over to the corral, where Phineas was cleaning the hooves of a horse. "I brought you some water."

"Thanks." He took the bucket from her, picked up the ladle, and drank. After setting down the bucket, he gestured toward her face. "You've got some dirt on your face."

She rubbed her knuckles across her cheek. "Gone?"

"Um, no. Wait." He opened the saddlebags hanging over the corral rail. "Here. I bought this for you in Fort Boise. I didn't know you were goin' by Hendrika." He held out a handkerchief with lacy edges and the initials J. S. stitched in one corner.

Rika curled her fingers around the handkerchief and trailed her thumb over the initials. *Johanna Sharpe.* Phin's last name sounded as wrong as the first name. "It was very kind of you to think of me."

Phineas took the handkerchief from her, dipped it into the water bucket, and rubbed it over her cheek, wiping away the speck of dirt. "There."

"Thank you." Stepping back, she noticed Nattie on the veranda, watching them with flushed cheeks.

When Nattie saw her looking, she whirled around and hurried inside.

Is she...jealous?

Phineas handed back the handkerchief. A hesitant smile spread across the lower half of his face, which was freshly shaven and paler than the rest of his face. His smile warmed the ice-blue color of his eyes. "Who knows, maybe one day, we'll have a daughter whose name starts with J. Then you could give her the handkerchief."

Daughter. The thought of having children with him hadn't crossed her mind. *You're being silly. He'll be your husband soon. Of course he wants children.* "Maybe." She stuffed the handkerchief into her sleeve. "Thank you, Phineas."

"Call me Phin." He reached for her hand and rested it in the crook of his elbow, then set them off for a stroll along the corrals. "When you call me Phineas, I feel like my father is standin' behind me."

"And that wouldn't be a good thing?" She already sensed the answer.

"No. My father was a real bastard." He blanched. "Um. Pardon my language."

Rika smiled. Why did men always think women would faint at the mere mention of a cuss word? "My father was a real bastard too."

The jangle of his spurs stopped midstride. He stared at her and then laughed.

"Nattie said you've worked for the Hamiltons for ten years?" she asked.

"Ran away from home as soon as I knew one end of a revolver from the other," he said. The muscles under Rika's fingers tensed, then softened. "The Hamiltons took me in. They're like family to me."

They were starting to be like family for her too. "Aren't you gonna miss them?" Since Phin had arrived, she woke up every day afraid that he would show up with the pastor and this would be her last day at the ranch.

His gaze drifted to the main house. "Yeah. I will."

"Then can't we stay?" She clamped her fingers around a handful of her skirt and held her breath.

Instead of looking at her, he still gazed at the main house. "No. I need to leave."

Rika had rarely cried in her life. Not when her father had broken her arm and not when Jo had died. Now tears stung her eyes.

"We'll still see the Hamiltons in church on Sundays, but I can't be their foreman forever," Phin said. "I stayed longer than I should have already. One day, another man is gonna be the boss, and there won't be a place here for me."

Another man? Is he talking about Amy getting married? The thought stabbed her in the pit of her stomach.

"I asked the pastor to come over later today to talk about the wedding," Phin said. "He said he can get us married on Monday."

"Oh." She had expected it, but still... In three days, she would be a married woman and on her way to a new home, away from Amy and the Hamiltons.

He tilted his head. "Is Monday not good? If you'd rather wait a few more days..."

"Oh, no. It's fine." If she hesitated too long, Phin would find another bride. He seemed determined to start a new life.

He squeezed her fingers that still rested on his arm. "I know we don't know each other well, but if we don't get married soon, people will start waggin' their tongues."

How would Jo have reacted to his businesslike tone? Rika got the feeling that he wasn't any more eager to get married than she was. "Of course," she said.

"Wanna learn how to brush down a horse?" His voice was overly cheerful as if he were trying to make her feel better—or maybe himself. "Lancelot is a sucker for a beautiful woman with a brush."

His grin was kind and charming, but his eyes said something else. He didn't look at her with love.

Not that she had expected it. "Lancelot?" she asked.

He pointed at the dotted horse that was tied to the corral rail. "Nattie named him, and now he thinks he deserves to be treated like a real knight."

Rika already knew how to brush down a horse. Amy had taught her weeks ago, but she didn't want to disappoint Phin, so she nodded.

"Great." He slipped out from under her hand. "Wait here. I'll get the brush."

She leaned against the sun-warmed corral rails, closed her eyes, and drank in the sounds of the ranch. Soft neighs, the patter of hooves, and sounds of horses plucking on clumps of grass drifted over. Hens clucked and fluttered. Behind the woodshed, an ax sang as it dug into the chopping block, and then the split logs clattered to the ground. The low rumble of John's voice came from the paddock, and a woman's calm tones answered him.

Amy. Rika opened her eyes and peered at the paddock.

One booted foot propped on the bottom rail, Amy stood and watched the horses. She pointed out one horse to John, who nodded. They ducked between the rails and climbed into the paddock.

"Here we are."

At Phin's sudden voice next to her, Rika whirled around.

"Here." He handed her a brush. "Try it. Start on his left side."

She slid her left hand down the gelding's neck, letting him know she was there. His familiar horse smell engulfed her, and the rhythmic stroking soothed both of them. She listened to the voices from the paddock while she worked.

"Put some muscle into it," Phin said. "Don't be afraid. You won't hurt him." He stepped closer and covered Rika's hand with his to show her how to brush. Amy had done the same, but her warm, slender body felt different against Rika's back than Phin's. The curve of his biceps rested against her arm, and his muscular chest brushed against her shoulder blades. For a moment, an image of what it would be like to share the marriage bed with him flashed through her mind.

It felt all wrong. His bay rum scent didn't set her blood afire. Not the way being close to Amy did.

Lord, what are you thinking? You can't feel that way about a woman. But she did. "Can you take over?" She let go of the brush and stepped to the side, away from him.

"You all right?" He paused the brush against Lancelot's neck. "You're not afraid of him, are you?"

No, she wasn't afraid. At least not of the horse. Thinking about the future made her shiver, though. She felt as her mother might have on her way to America—adrift at sea, with no past to return to and a future she wasn't sure she wanted. "No, of course not. I'm fine." She moved away another step, her gaze returning to the paddock to see if Amy was still there.

"Watch out!"

A bucket clattered on its side. Water drenched Rika's skirt. She jumped back, slipped on the wet grass, and fell.

Her shoulder smashed against a corral post, and a loud pop rang through her ears. Pain exploded. Someone cried out.

Rika's vision dimmed, and she fought to stay conscious. She realized she was lying on the ground.

"Hendrika!" Phin dropped to his knees next to her. "Hendrika, are you all right?"

"Rika," Amy shouted from somewhere.

Rika groaned. Dark spots danced in front of her eyes, but Amy's voice enticed her to answer. "Yes."

Hands touched her, trying to help her up. A new wave of pain stabbed her shoulder and raced down her arm. "Don't." She breathed through clenched teeth. "Don't touch me." Clutching her arm, she rolled around.

The large hands retreated, and then Amy was there. Her fingertips trembled against Rika's cheek. "What happened?"

"Think I threw out my shoulder," Rika said, then clamped her mouth shut. Nausea pulsed through her, and the pain in her shoulder made her light-headed.

"How could you let this happen?" Amy stared at Phin, hands fisted so tightly that her knuckles looked like jagged mountain peaks.

Phin held out his palms, his face pale. "I didn't know she hadn't seen the bucket."

"Stop it," Rika whispered. "No use arguing now." Her voice trembled despite her effort to keep it even. She clutched her arm, which hung motionless, and sat up.

"Let me see." Amy's shaking fingers slid up her arm.

"Want me to fetch the doc from town?" Phin asked.

Rika shook her head, then stopped when a new wave of pain shot down her arm. "No. We need to pop the shoulder back in right away." The muscles were already stiffening up. The longer they waited, the more painful it would become. Her gaze searched Amy's through a haze of pain. "If I tell you how, can you do this?"

The color drained from Amy's cheeks. "I helped put Toby's shoulder back in once, but I don't know if I can do it with you. I don't want to hurt you."

"Sure you can do it." Pain raged through her shoulder. She knew it would stop as soon as the shoulder popped back into its socket.

Amy let out a trembling breath. "All right. Phin, help me get her to the house." Her arm, warm and steady, slung around Rika's waist while Phin reached for her uninjured arm.

Trembling, Rika got to her feet. Pain pulsed through her with every step she took.

"Want me to carry you?" Phin asked.

Rika shook her head. She couldn't speak. It took all her concentration just to breathe without screaming.

Amy swung back the front door and held it open. The doorway was too narrow for the three of them to enter side by side. One of them would have to let go of Rika.

She and Phin exchanged a long glance over Rika's head.

Phin let go, and Amy helped Rika inside. "We should do this down here and spare you the stairs." Amy directed her to the divan.

When Rika sat and jostled her shoulder, a groan erupted from her throat. Finally, the dark spots stopped dancing before her eyes, and she looked into Phin's and Amy's tense faces.

"Want me to boil some water?" Phin bobbed up and down on his toes.

"We don't need hot water," Amy said, scowling at him. "She's not giving birth. She popped out her shoulder."

Phin scratched his head. "Uh, yeah, I know. I thought maybe a hot compress would help loosen her muscles."

Despite the dizzying pain, Rika had to chuckle. Her body cramped, sending flashes of pain through her. She stopped laughing.

"Easy, easy," Amy murmured. She pulled off her gloves with her teeth and stroked Rika's uninjured arm. "How do we do this? Do you think a hot compress would help?" A tremor ran through her voice.

"Later. I need to look at the shoulder first." The thought of wrestling out of her tight bodice made her dizzy, but she needed to see the shoulder. If it was broken or the head of the bone was behind the joint, trying to put the shoulder back in would make things worse.

"Oh. If you're undressin', I'll leave you ladies alone and go take care of Lancelot," Phin said. Three long steps carried him to the door, where he stopped to look back. "Are you sure you can do this, Amy?"

Eyes that had darkened to pine green searched Rika's. "Yes." Amy never looked away.

"All right. Give a shout if you need me." The door fell closed, and Phin's footsteps faded away.

Amy unwrapped the shawl from around Rika's shoulders and draped it over her lap as if to make sure she wouldn't get cold. Trembling fingers brushed Rika's throat as Amy fiddled with the pin and removed her collar.

Rika watched the path of those fingers as they moved downward and opened button after button. She thought of the day she had helped Amy with her dress when Amy had burned her fingers. It seemed many months ago, yet she still remembered the golden hue of skin that faded to a creamy white the farther down the dress slipped.

Amy paused and looked up.

Their gazes touched.

"You all right?" Amy whispered. "You look flushed. How bad is the pain?"

Rika licked her lips. "It's bearable." And it was. Amy's presence soothed her pain more than a bottle of laudanum could.

"Good." Amy lowered her gaze to the buttons.

With her help, Rika struggled out of her bodice. The sleeves slid down her arms, and Amy carefully freed her right hand of the cuff. She pulled the wide neck of Rika's chemise to the side until it dropped off her injured shoulder.

"There," Amy said, voice rough.

Rika peered over her shoulder, biting the inside of her cheek when she saw the bulb-shaped knot. "It's popped out, all right." Acid burned in her stomach, and she breathed through a wave of nausea.

"What's the best way to do this?" Amy asked. "When I helped Toby, he was in so much pain. I don't want to do this to you."

"I watched the doctors with a soldier once." His screams still echoed in Rika's ears, but she didn't tell Amy that. "He bent the forearm at the elbow and rotated it to the side until the shoulder popped back in. Think you can do that?"

Amy nodded and stepped closer. The warmth of her leg penetrated Rika's skirt, and she leaned against the soothing touch. With cold, damp fingers, Amy reached for her forearm. "Ready?"

"Yes." Rika didn't look at her shoulder. She kept her gaze fixed on Amy's eyes. Her muscles tightened in anticipation of more pain.

Amy rotated her arm. It hung like dead weight, protesting the movement, but for a moment, it didn't hurt. At least not worse than before. Then Amy turned the arm farther to the side, applying constant pressure.

Pain lanced through Rika's shoulder. She clamped her jaw tight to hold back a groan.

The arm turned a bit more.

Rika fell into the dark spots that danced before her eyes. The harsh sound of her own breathing dimmed. "Wait!" She gasped.

Amy paused, her fingers gentle on Rika's arm.

"I need to lie down." If she fainted, Amy wouldn't be able to catch her. Not without further hurting her shoulder. She lay on the divan. Her skirt slid up, and her legs tangled with Amy's as they hung off the short divan. She didn't care. Amy's touch was the only thing anchoring her in a sea of pain.

"Do you want some whiskey?" Amy asked. Her face was as pale as Rika's chemise. "Papa keeps a bottle in the parlor for emergencies."

Numbing the pain sounded like a good idea, but she already felt dizzy enough and she had sworn to herself never to rely on the bottle to get her through a tough situation, as her father and husband had. "No. Just get it over with." With the help of her left hand, she pulled her upper arm against her body.

Amy gripped her forearm. Her fingers stroked Rika's hands, soothing away the pain. Then the pressure returned. Rika's forearm rotated to the side.

With her good hand, Rika gripped a handful of fabric, not knowing or caring what it was.

Amy pulled a bit more.

Rika's muscles spasmed and burned with pain.

"What if this isn't working?" Amy paused, her gaze searching Rika's. "What if I'm making it worse?"

Rika shook her head. If she opened her mouth to answer, she would scream, so she nodded at Amy to continue.

Slowly, Amy rotated the elbow.

The knotted muscles protested, flaring with white-hot pain. Rika screamed.

Then, as her forearm moved an inch farther, the pressure stopped. The pain went from roaring to smoldering. Rika panted through a dry mouth. She unclenched the trembling fingers of her left hand from around Amy's sleeve and cradled her right arm to her chest.

Amy let go of her forearm and rubbed her fingertips over Rika's shoulder, making sure the bulb-shaped knot was gone. The gentle touch made Rika forget the pain for a moment. "How does it feel?"

"Good," Rika said. Her cheeks flamed. "I mean, it's a lot better now."

The door burst open. "Hendrika got hurt?" Luke's voice was higher than usual.

Amy tugged the chemise back into place and took a step forward, blocking Rika's half-dressed body with her own. "I got it, Papa. We put the shoulder back in."

Luke patted Amy's arm. "Well done." He peered past Amy but respectfully kept his gaze on Rika's face. "Anything I can do for you, Hendrika?"

"No, thank you. I'm in good hands."

"Yes, you are." Luke smiled like a rooster proud of his chicks.

"Was there something you wanted?" Amy asked.

Luke hesitated. "Your mother and I wanted to talk to you, but it can wait until later. Go make her comfortable." He backed away before Amy could say anything else.

Frowning, Amy watched his retreating back for a few moments before she turned her attention back to Rika. She took Rika's shawl and knotted it around her shoulder. "Toby had his arm in a sling after we put his shoulder back in."

"What about my bodice?"

"Don't bother." With gentle fingers, Amy placed the injured arm into the sling. "You'd only have to struggle out of it again, 'cause I'm taking you to bed." Red blotches formed on her cheeks. "I-I mean, I'm gonna take you upstairs and make sure you rest."

In the past, Rika would have thought nothing of the innocent comment, but now Frankie and Tess had made her aware that women could take other women to bed. Apparently, Amy had thought about that revelation too. *What would it be like?* Again, she felt Amy's fingers on her bare shoulder, stroking gently, but when she looked up, Amy wasn't touching her. She shook her head at herself. *You're drunk on pain.* On legs that felt weak, she let Amy help her up the stairs.

"You don't have to do that," Rika said when Amy plumped up her pillow for the fourth time in half an hour. "I haven't been in bed past sunrise since I was four years old. I should be up, helping Nattie muck the stalls and taking care of—"

"No." Amy hovered over her. "For once, you're the one being taken care of. Better get used to it."

Better not. The pastor would come over later today, and within a few days, Rika would be away from Amy's caring presence. The thought hurt more than the pain in her shoulder.

Amy sat on the edge of the bed, careful not to jostle it. "How's the shoulder? Does it hurt?"

"It's a lot better now that you put it back in."

A knock interrupted, and Amy hurried to the door like a self-appointed guardian. She inched open the door and peered through the crack.

"How is she?" Phin asked from the other side.

Amy glanced back at Rika. "I put the shoulder back in. Now she needs some rest."

"Can I see her?"

"She's not dressed to receive visitors."

"I wouldn't disturb her, but the reverend is over in the cabin," Phin said. "He wants to talk to Hendrika and me, and I would hate to send him away. He already thinks Hendrika and I are draggin' our feet about the wedding."

Rika stiffened. Her shoulder started to pound. Or maybe it was her heart.

"Wait here." Amy closed the door and turned. Was it just Rika's imagination, or was the helpless desperation she felt reflected on Amy's face? But when she opened her mouth, Amy just asked, "Do you feel up to talking to the reverend? We can send him away if—"

Rika shook her head. *No use in dragging it out.* "It's all right."

"Want some help getting dressed?"

"I think I can manage." Rika slipped out of bed, careful not to bang her shoulder on the washstand. She pulled out of the improvised sling, but when she tried to wrestle her right arm through the sleeve of her bodice, her muscles protested.

"Let me." Amy helped her with the sleeves and then lifted her hands to the buttons.

Rika watched the strong fingers move over her bodice. Her glance took in rope burns, scratches, and old scars across the backs of Amy's hands, and she realized the pattern was as familiar to her as the streets of Boston had once been. It seemed she spent a lot of time watching Amy's hands. "We seem to make a habit out of dressing and undressing each other," she murmured.

Amy paused, hands on the top button. Surely, she could feel Rika's heart hammering away through the fabric of her bodice. Her finger trailed over Rika's collarbone when she lifted her gaze. "Rika, I—"

A loud knock on the door made them jerk apart. "Hendrika?" Phin called through the door. "You decent?"

Rika had forgotten that he stood waiting. "Yes, come in."

Phin stepped into the bedroom, squeezing his hat between his hands. He looked like Rika's brother when he had gotten into trouble and was waiting to be scolded.

He's not your brother. He'll be your husband soon.

"How's the shoulder?" He waved his hat in the direction of Rika's right arm.

"It's fine." She wasn't used to all that fussing over her. "Amy took good care of it."

"Good, good. I feel real bad about it."

"It was my own fault. I wasn't looking where I was going." Watching Amy had distracted her. Heat crept up her chest and suffused her face.

Phin took her left hand and squeezed it. "Don't be embarrassed. Everyone stumbles now and again."

"Here." Amy filled a mug with water from the pitcher and shoved it at Rika.

Blinking, Rika freed her hand from Phin's and took the mug. "Thank you." She gulped down the cool liquid as if it would extinguish the fire in her cheeks.

"The reverend is waitin' in the cabin." Phin shoved one hand into his pocket. "Do you want me to send him away?"

Rika was tempted to say yes and buy herself a few more days at the ranch, but she had always faced reality and never allowed herself to linger on what ifs. She wouldn't start now. "No. Go on ahead and tell him I'll be over in a minute."

Phin nodded and turned on his heel. He strode away as if thankful to escape the room.

"Want to come?" Rika gestured in the direction of the cabin with her chin. The pastor's presence made her squirm ever since she had seen Tess and Frankie kiss, and knowing he was there to talk about her wedding didn't help to calm her.

"No," Amy said so quickly that Rika suspected she wasn't eager to be in the pastor's presence either. "I should go check on the horses."

Distance grew between them, and Rika shivered. She fumbled the improvised sling back around her shoulder and turned to go.

"Rika?"

She turned back.

Their gazes met and pulled them together, across the room. Without a word, Amy stepped closer. The heat of her body warmed Rika. Amy lifted her hands as if about to touch her.

Rika's breath hitched. Her heart hammered, but this time, it had nothing to do with pain.

Amy closed the top button on Rika's bodice. "There." She dropped her hands and stepped back.

"Oh. Thank you." On shaky legs, Rika stumbled down the stairs.

HAMILTON HORSE RANCH
BAKER PRAIRIE, OREGON
JUNE 26, 1868

*A*MY SPLASHED WATER FROM THE washbowl onto her burning face and then rubbed a towel over it. When she looked up and out the window, her gaze fell on the reverend's buggy in the ranch yard. The thought of Rika and Phin in the cabin, talking to the reverend about marriage, made her stomach churn. She groaned into the towel.

After a few more minutes of pacing and fretting, she hurled the towel across the room. *Nothing you can do about it. Back to work.* Being with the horses would distract her.

But when she plodded down the stairs to escape to the horse barn, her whole family had gathered in the parlor. Papa sat in his favorite armchair, his body as stiff and wooden as one of his carved figurines. Mama perched next to him, clinging to his arm.

Amy tensed at the strange scene. She looked at Nattie, who sat on the divan, and tilted her head in a silent question.

Nattie shrugged. She looked just as puzzled as Amy felt.

"What's going on?" Amy barely managed to keep her voice even. They weren't going to make her confess her unnatural feelings to Nattie, were they? Her legs began to shake.

"Please sit down," Papa said. "We need to talk."

Uh-oh. No pleasant conversation ever started like that. Her shaky knees plopped her down on the divan next to Nattie. The mantle clock ticked away. Amy's heart pounded twice for every beat of the clock.

Papa looked at Mama.

Mama looked back, her hands clamped around Papa's forearm. They talked without saying a word, and Amy watched with longing. The connection between her parents filled the room, like a living, breathing, wonderful thing.

Finally, Papa turned his head. The silvery color of his eyes darkened to a rain-cloud gray. He wrapped his arm around Mama as if she were the only thing keeping him from drowning. "Your mother and I talked about it. We didn't make this decision lightly, but we think it's time to tell you."

"Tell us what?" Nattie asked.

Papa swallowed. "It's not easy for me to say this."

Heaviness settled in the pit of Amy's stomach. She wasn't ready to hear more bad news. The thought of Rika being gone soon was enough to keep her up at night.

"What I have to say will confuse you terribly," Papa said, "and you might not love me anymore, but please..." He lifted his hand, palm up, like a beggar pleading for a coin.

Amy shook her head. *Not love him anymore?* "That will never happen."

"Papa, please." Nattie's fingernails scratched along Amy's chaps, searching for some hold. "You're scaring me."

"I never wanted that. I never wanted you to be afraid or disappointed or confused—"

"Luke." Mama slid even closer to him on the arm of his chair. "I think you should just tell them. There's no way to prepare them for this."

Papa bent forward. His breathing came in quick gasps, and he looked as if he might be sick.

Mama laid a hand on his bare neck.

The tension in the room made Amy's stomach roil.

"There's something about me that I kept hidden from most of the world for a long, long time." Papa pressed three fingers to his mouth as if he wanted to hold back the words.

He kept something hidden? It couldn't be something big, could it? After all, Papa was the most honest, most honorable man Amy knew.

"My full name, for one thing," Papa said, circling around the truth like a hawk around a field mouse, getting closer and closer until, finally, he added, "I wasn't born Luke Hamilton."

Nattie clutched Amy's arm. "You're an outlaw?" she whispered.

His mouth twitched and then curved up. "I wish it was that easy." He lowered his lashes and studied the diamond pattern of the Brussels carpet. "My mother named me Lucinda."

"Lucinda?" The name echoed through Amy's head. "But that's a girl's name."

"Yes, it is," Papa said slowly, as if every word hurt. "I was born a girl."

Why was he talking like that? Amy scowled at him. "This isn't funny, Papa."

"I'm not joking."

"This doesn't make sense," Nattie said. "People can't switch bodies."

"True." Papa dragged up his gaze and met Amy's eyes, then Nattie's. "But we can choose what to do with our bodies. Some women choose to live as men."

Amy's thoughts were galloping in a thousand directions at once. "You mean like Frankie?"

"I mean like me," Papa said.

"I don't understand." Nattie's voice shook.

"Oh, sweetie. I wish there was an easier way to say this." Papa rubbed his red-rimmed eyes, then looked up. "I'm not a man. I'm a woman."

"No," Nattie shouted. "You're lying!"

Amy jumped up and shook her head until it pounded. No, this wasn't true. It couldn't be. Her gaze slid over her papa, looking for something, anything... But all she saw was the man she loved and admired. "Impossible!" Pressing her hands together, she looked at Mama and silently begged her to deny it.

But Mama nodded, her lips forming a thin white line.

The sick feeling in the pit of Amy's stomach spiraled out of control.

Mama turned her head to press a kiss to Papa's temple and entwined their fingers.

For the first time, Amy noticed that Papa's hands didn't dwarf Mama's. Not the way Josh's hands looked next to Hannah's. Papa's hands were slender for a man, their backs not dotted with hair.

Her own hands flew to her mouth. "No. No. This can't be true."

Nattie cried and shouted, and Mama said something, but the buzzing in Amy's ears drowned out their voices. Her world spun on its axis, refusing to right itself. She couldn't listen right now. She couldn't stay. She jerked free from Nattie's viselike grip on her forearm and fled.

HAMILTON HORSE RANCH
BAKER PRAIRIE, OREGON
JUNE 26, 1868

*R*IKA CURSED HER INJURED SHOULDER. It condemned her to sit at the table with the pastor. At least Phin got to bustle around, lifting a pot of water onto the hook above the fire, while she faced Reverend Rhodes's stare alone.

She hooked her fingers in her crocheted shawl and lowered her gaze under the pretense of re-adjusting the sling. The smell of leather and grass still clung to the fabric, bringing a mental image of Amy. Her cheeks heated at the thought of Amy dressing her.

"...on Monday," the pastor said, making her head jerk up. "What do you think? I have a beautiful sermon about the sanctity of marriage."

Phin and Rika exchanged a glance. Was he as insecure about getting married as she was?

Shouts from outside shattered the uneasy silence in the cabin.

Rika strained her ears. What was going on?

"Amy," Luke shouted over the din of the other voices.

She'd never heard him shout. Unlike her own father, he seemed like a calm and gentle man. Something was wrong. Something with Amy.

With an apologetic glance at the pastor, Rika hastened to the door, almost colliding with Phin and the coffee pot in his hands. She veered to the side and opened the door.

Amy hurried past the cabin, her strides as long and fast as she could make them without outright running. She disappeared into the stable, not glancing at Rika.

"Please, Amy!" Luke flew down the veranda steps. "Amy, wait!"

Nora caught up with him at the bottom of the stairs. She rubbed her hands up and down his arms.

Rika stuck her head out the door and strained to hear what they were saying.

"We need to give her some time," Nora said, her voice gentle, as if she were talking to a scared child or an injured animal. "She's just confused. Her whole world has been turned upside down."

What happened? Rika's heart slammed against her ribs. She stepped out of the cabin.

"Hendrika?" Phin called.

She glanced back.

Phin gestured at the pastor and the Bible on the table.

If she wanted to have a new life as Phin's wife, she needed to stay and have coffee with the pastor. *This is what you came here for. It's what you wanted. Close the door and sit back down.*

But she didn't move. She sucked in a breath, closed her eyes, and made a decision. Making sure Amy was all right was more important than securing her future as Phin's bride. "I'm sorry," she said. "But something's wrong with Amy."

"Marriage needs to be taken seriously, Ms. Bruggeman," the pastor said. "You can't walk away when we were discussing—"

"Excuse us," Phin said. Three quick steps brought him next to Rika.

Luke stormed toward them, his dark lashes clumped together by... Rika stared. Were those tears?

"What's wrong with Amy?" Phin asked his boss. "Half an hour ago, she was fine."

"Something I said unsettled her. I need to talk to her, to explain..." Luke waved his hands as if to shoo them out of the way.

Nattie stepped onto the veranda, paused, and then walked over to them. Her gray eyes looked like coals in her pale face, the red rims like rings of embers. When her father tried to make eye contact, her gaze veered to the side.

Phin hurried over and gripped her elbow. "You all right?"

"I'm fine," Nattie said, but her lips trembled and she clung to Phin's arm.

"What on God's green earth happened?" Rika asked. Amy had fled to the stable, and even the usually calm Nattie looked as if she'd been through hell.

When no one answered her, something boiled over inside of her. She was fed up with the lies bubbling beneath the surface. The Hamiltons hid their own secrets—and now one of those secrets had hurt Amy. But how could Rika shout at them and demand to know what had driven Amy away when she, too, was lying?

The barn door banged open. Ruby pranced into the yard, led by a grim-faced Amy.

"No!" Her father took a step, then stopped as if coming closer would scare her away. "Amy, please, stay and talk to me."

"Let her go if she wants," Phin said. "She'll stew a little and then be back. That's what she always does."

"This isn't like the other times." Luke's voice vibrated with tension. "I can't explain. It just isn't."

Amy grabbed the reins and prepared to swing onto Ruby's bare back.

"Oh, no, you don't!" Rika flew across the yard. She reached out to grab the bridle. Pain shot through her arm, and she cried out as it fell back into the sling.

"Rika! What are you doing?" Amy dropped the reins to cradle Rika's arm.

"Stopping you from running away again," Rika said. She grasped the bridle with her left hand.

Instead of looking at her, Amy stared over her shoulder to where her parents stood. The vacant expression in her eyes reminded Rika of the soldiers in the field hospital. Those young men looked dazed, numb, as if they were still on the battlefield, with mortar shells exploding all around them. "Get out of the way," Amy said, her voice flat.

Rika tightened her grasp on the bridle. "If you go, take me with you." In her shell-shocked condition, Amy shouldn't be alone.

"You can't ride with your shoulder."

"I'll manage." Rika raised her chin.

When Amy stared at her, the haze finally lifted from her eyes. She sighed and whispered, "It's not fair to stop a panicked horse from running."

Rika let go of the bridle and rubbed Amy's hand until she relaxed her fingers around the strand of mane in her grasp.

"Why are you scared?" Rika lowered her voice too. "What happened?"

"Amy." Luke inched closer, hands at his sides, no hasty moves. "Please come back inside. I know I'm the last person you want to see right now, but please, at least stay and talk to your mother."

"Is she even my mother?"

Luke flinched as if Amy had slapped him. "Lash out at me all you want. The Lord knows I deserve it. But don't hurt your mother."

The bit of mane fell from Amy's grasp. Her shoulders hunched. "I'm sorry, Mama."

"Come inside," Nora said.

Amy handed Phin the reins and slouched back to the house.

When Rika returned to the cabin, the pastor still sat at the table, white-knuckling his Bible. "We'll have the wedding on Monday," he said firmly. "I hope once you are married, you'll start keeping better company."

HAMILTON HORSE RANCH
BAKER PRAIRIE, OREGON
JUNE 26, 1868

*A*MY COULDN'T THINK WHEN SHE sat still. Not that pacing through the parlor helped.

"For land's sake, sit," Nattie said.

The sharp tone stopped Amy's pacing. Nattie had never talked to her like that.

"I'm already feeling sick to my stomach, and you're not helping."

Amy plopped down on the divan and turned to face Papa. *He's not your papa. She. Lord.* She pressed her fingertips to her temples. Nothing made sense anymore.

"It's really true?" Nattie asked, her voice trembling. "Are you really...?"

"A woman," Luke said. "Yes."

Nattie swung her head back and forth. "I don't believe it."

"Please," Luke said, "don't make me show you." The lines of despair in the pale face made Amy's protective instincts flare.

How strange. She'd never needed to protect Papa. *Luke. Lucinda. Not Papa.* Her brain was stuck on that one thought. "It's all a lie. My whole life and Nattie's...all one big lie. How could you do that to us? How could you trick Mama into believing—?"

"Wait a minute, Amy." Mama thrust out her hand. "I'm sorry we didn't tell you sooner, but Luke never tricked me into anything."

"You knew?" Amy asked and then shook her head at herself. Of course Mama knew. She had shared her life and her bed with Luke for decades. The air whooshed out of her lungs. "D-does that mean...?" She glanced at Mama, then at Luke, who again dropped her gaze to the Brussels carpet. "You share your bed with...a woman?"

Mama fanned her fingers over Luke's shoulder. "I share my bed, my body, and my life with the person I love. Her gender doesn't matter."

"Doesn't matter?" Nattie shot up from the divan. "How can you say that? Of course it matters! Suddenly everything is so...so..." Tears sprang into her eyes.

Amy wrapped her in her arms and rocked her as she had when they had been little girls. She didn't know if it helped Nattie, but it had an unexpectedly soothing effect on her.

Mama stood next to Papa...Luke, as she always did, chin up, emerald fire in her eyes. "Luke's gender didn't matter when she led our wagon train to Oregon," Nora said, her voice velvet-lined steel. "Her gender didn't matter when you, Nattie, broke your nose and were crying for Luke to hold you. And it didn't matter when—"

"It mattered when you lied to us," Amy shouted. "You lied to us every day of our lives."

Luke's head jerked up. "No." She took a step toward them, then stopped and held out her hands. "Please don't believe that. I wasn't pretending. It's not an act. I showed you my true self all along. I just let you believe that this true self is male."

"But why?" Nattie asked. She lifted her head from Amy's shoulder and rubbed her eyes.

"Because this," Luke tugged at her shirt, "is who I am. There is no other life for me."

Nattie sniffled. "No, I mean, why lie to us? Why did you let us believe that you're a man and our father?"

"I never wanted to deceive you. I thought I was doing what was best for you."

"Best for us?" Nattie's voice sounded like the squeaking of chalk over a blackboard. "How can all the lies be what's best for us?"

"In the beginning, you were too little to understand and to keep my secret. If you had blurted it out to the wrong person..." Luke pressed her lips together until they formed a razor-sharp line.

Again, Mama threaded her fingers through Luke's. It was a familiar gesture, one that Amy had witnessed a thousand times over the years, but now it looked different. Nothing would ever be the same again. "You need to be careful not to give Luke away," Mama said. "If the wrong person learns her secret, we will all be in danger. The ranch could be burned down or Luke killed over this."

Amy's stomach turned to stone. The panicked squeals of the horses in the burning barn echoed in her ears, and she imagined Mama kneeling in the ashes, crying, clutching Luke's dead body. She dug her short nails into her palms and forced away the image.

"We couldn't risk our lives, our safety on the discretion of a child," Mama said.

"We haven't been blabber-mouthed children for many years." Nattie's eyes flashed like knives. "You could have trusted us."

"This was never about trust," Luke said. "I trust you with my life, otherwise I wouldn't tell you now."

"Why are you telling us now?" Nattie asked.

From across the room, Luke's gaze met Amy's. "Because I'm through ducking my head in shame for who I am."

Like I do. Amy hung her head. The message was intended for her. When she noticed what she was doing, she forced her chin up, looking from Luke to Mama and back again. Everything she had believed in, everything she thought was true turned out to be a lie, but one thing was still clear without a doubt: her parents loved each other, and they wanted her to see how proud they were of their love.

"I always tried to teach you by example, but in this one thing, I failed." Luke's voice rose barely above a whisper. "I hid out of fear. But that's the thing about keeping secrets. The longer you keep quiet, the harder it becomes to tell the truth." Silver-gray eyes met Amy's. It was like looking in a mirror.

Amy swallowed and looked away.

Silence filled the parlor. *What now?* Could their family survive this? Were they still a family?

"If Papa isn't...if he..." Nattie paused and tugged on her hair with both fists. "If she isn't our papa, then where do we...?" She gestured at Amy, then pressed her palm to her own chest. "Who's our father, then?"

Amy's stomach twisted itself into knots. For some reason, that thought hadn't yet entered her mind, but Nattie was right, of course. A woman couldn't father children, no matter how long she'd lived as a man.

"A father is the person who's there to pick you up and make it all better when you fall and skin your knees and who's watching over you for three nights in a row when you're sick," Mama said, eyes alive with passion.

True. Luke had done all of that many times. One of Amy's earliest memories was sitting in front of Luke in the saddle, strong arms keeping her safe. Her throat burned with tears. How could that be an illusion?

"That doesn't answer my question," Nattie said. "Don't we have a right to know?"

Mama rasped her teeth along her bottom lip. Her fingers tightened around Luke's until Amy could no longer tell which fingers belonged to whom. Mama looked at her. "The man who fathered you was a dashing young man I knew in Boston."

"Did you love him?" Nattie asked.

"I thought so at the time." Mama stared off into the distance as if she could see the past. "But I had no idea what love really was. I wasn't as mature as the two of you. My father and brothers ignored or bullied me all my life, so I was starved for attention. Rafe gave it to me."

Rafe. So that was her father's name. Not Luke. "What happened to him?" Amy asked.

Luke wrapped her arm around Mama and drew her against her body.

"He wasn't ready to be a father," Mama said.

He didn't want us. The thought cut like steel. *But Luke did.*

"If he wasn't ready to be a father, how come you had me?" Nattie asked.

Silence stretched through the parlor, interrupted by Mama's ragged breathing. She leaned against Luke's shoulder and looked at her.

Luke nodded. "They deserve the truth. We can't hold anything back now."

There was more? Amy's insides trembled. Her knees felt as if they would collapse under the burden of yet another revelation.

"Rafe is not your father, Nattie, just Amy's."

Nattie stiffened against Amy's side. Her breathing stopped. "What? We're not real sisters? Not even that is true?"

"You are sisters. You just had different fathers."

"Who was mine?"

"I don't know."

"Tell me!"

Mama's mouth tore open in a silent sob. Tears ran down her face faster than Luke could brush them away. "I don't know, sweetie, I really don't."

Amy clutched Nattie more tightly. "You don't know? But, Mama, how can you not know?" A thought slammed into her, robbing her of breath. "You weren't violated, were you?" She sucked in air, but none of it seemed to reach her lungs.

"No, not like you think." Mama laid a trembling hand across her eyes. "When I met Luke, I was working in a brothel."

Amy's knees buckled. She sank onto the divan and dragged Nattie with her. "A brothel?" Mama, forever the embodiment of love and goodness, had worked in a brothel? Had sold her body to strangers?

Nattie pressed her forehead to her knees and groaned. A steady stream of "no, no, no" fell from her lips.

"She had no other choice." Luke no longer looked down in shame. Shoulders squared, she stared at them. "She had no family, no friends, no money. No one offered work to an unwed woman with a child. It was either the brothel or letting you starve to death, Amy."

She did it because of me. Guilt added to the queasiness in Amy's stomach. Images flashed through her, memories she had all but forgotten. Faces of young women. The tinny plunking of a piano. Rough laughter and cigarette smoke drifting upstairs. Had she lived with Mama in the brothel?

"It was a very bad time in my life, and I'm not proud of it," Mama said, her voice a whisper. "But still, a few good things came from it. You, Nattie. And I met Luke." Her tears stopped flowing.

A myriad of thoughts buzzed through Amy's mind. "You met..." She stopped and licked dry lips. "...in a brothel?"

"It's not like you think." Mama brushed her fingers across Luke's shirt. "Luke was never anything but the perfect gentleman."

Nattie lifted her head off her knees. She straightened and clutched her stomach. "And Papa…" Her gaze flitted to Luke, then away. "Luke decided to disguise herself as a man so that you could pass yourself off as a married couple?"

"No, Nattie. I lived as a man long before I ever met your mother. She married me without knowing I was a woman."

"When did you find out? How?" Countless questions tumbled through Amy's mind.

"On the way to Oregon, Luke was shot, and I treated the wound."

A vague image rose from the haze of Amy's memory: her papa huddled under a blanket in a wagon, face bruised and pasty, and Mama crouching next to him, just as pale. She tried to remember what had come before that.

Nothing.

Just a few hazy memories of a busy town full of oxen and horses. She couldn't remember her life before Luke had joined the family.

"And after finding out, you still stayed?" Nattie asked. "I don't understand."

Amy did. *Mama is like me. And Papa…Luke is too.*

"Maybe one day, when you fall in love, you will, Nattie." Mama's thumb caressed Luke's knuckles. "I married Luke to give my daughters the best life possible, but I stayed with her because I love her. You can't just walk away from the person you love." Mama looked at Amy.

Was this another message for her? Did Mama think she was in love with Rika? *Am I?* She kneaded the back of her neck, where a knot of tension sent painful flares to her temples. Her whole life had crumbled, and she had no idea how to crawl from beneath the ruins. She stood on shaky legs and stumbled out of the parlor.

HAMILTON HORSE RANCH
BAKER PRAIRIE, OREGON
JUNE 26, 1868

*A*MY LINGERED IN THE DOORWAY of Nattie's room and watched her sister at her desk. She appeared to be bent over a book, but when she shifted, Amy realized she was staring into a handheld mirror. *What is she seeing?*

Finally, Nattie looked up and turned around.

They stared at each other.

"Are you all right?" Amy asked, still holding on to the doorframe.

"No."

Amy took a step into the room, reaching out a hand, then drew it back. What was there to say or do? Nothing could change the fact that their family lay in shambles.

"Do you think this is why we were never really close?" Nattie's voice sounded sluggish, as if something inside her was numb and frozen. "Because we're only half sisters? Do you think we're so different because I'm like my father?"

The agony on her face made Amy's eyes burn. She walked across the room. "Are we so different?" She no longer knew. Finding out Luke's secret had united them and brought them closer than they had been in years. "We both love horses and the ranch, and we want to be more than just some man's wife."

"If we have so much in common, then how come we've never spent much time together?" Nattie clutched the mirror she still held. "Why do you never really talk to me?"

"We talk all the time," Amy said.

"Not about the important things. You never share your thoughts or feelings."

Why is this suddenly about me? But the pain on her sister's face kept her from harshly denying it. She glanced down at the mirror as if it would give her a glimpse into Nattie's heart and soul. When their gazes met, she understood. *It's not about me. It's about her and where she fits into our family.* "That has nothing to do with you. You're my sister, and I love you."

"Why, then?"

"I guess I never grew out of the habit of seeing you as my annoying little sister who kept me from riding out to the range with Papa."

Nattie lifted her chin. "I'm not a little girl anymore."

"No, you sure aren't." Sometimes, Nattie was more of an adult than she was. But in the last few years, Amy had learned to keep her growing attraction to women to herself, and in the process, she had shut out Nattie not just from that part of her life, but completely. "I'm sorry. I should have talked to you more, asked your opinion on things, and shared my thoughts. It's just that..."

"What?"

Amy pressed her lips together so tightly that she felt the blood drain from them. She didn't want to lie, but neither could she tell Nattie the truth. "I'm not ready to talk about it." She wasn't sure if she'd ever be.

Head tilted, Nattie stared up at her. Her eyes were dark, and her wet lashes clumped together. "I don't want to lose you too."

With one long step, Amy reached her and pulled her into a fierce embrace. "You won't."

When Luke's breathing slowed, indicating that she had finally fallen into a restless sleep, Nora slipped from beneath the tangle of her limbs and got out of bed. Without lighting a lamp, she tiptoed down the hall and opened the first door. "Nattie?"

No answer.

She stepped farther into the room, where a sliver of moonlight showed her that Nattie's bed was empty.

Her stomach churned. Had Nattie run away? *Oh, Lord, please.* She peeked into Amy's room.

That bed, too, was empty.

Without taking the time to dress, she hurried down the stairs.

The front door was open, confirming her fears.

She reached for the screen door but stopped when she saw two people sitting on the veranda's top step, huddled together in the darkness without a lantern.

"Whatever he's done, it can't be as bad as how my old man treated me. Luke's not like that. He'd never hurt you."

Nora recognized Phin's deep voice. His trust in Luke loosened the bands of panic that had tightened around her chest.

"No, but... Oh, Phin, you have no idea." Nattie's voice was choked with tears.

Phin wrapped his arms around her. "Tell me what happened."

Nora tightened her grip on the screen door when she realized Luke's life was in someone else's hands. Would Nattie reveal her secret?

Nattie sighed. "I'm not sure I understand it myself."

"What can I do to help?"

"There's nothing you can do." Nattie's voice was muffled as if she was burying her face against his shoulder. "But you being here, sitting with me, makes me feel better."

Nora tried to tiptoe back, but as she shifted her weight, the creaking of a board underneath gave her away.

"Boss? Is that you?" Phin hastily let go of Nattie and stood.

"No, it's me." Nora stepped onto the veranda, her gaze instantly trying to discern Nattie's expression in the darkness.

Phin averted his gaze from her nightgown-dressed body. "I'll leave you two to talk."

After he disappeared into the night, Nora crossed the veranda on bare feet and sat on the top step next to her daughter.

Isaac the owl hooted in a pine tree behind the house.

For the first time in her life, Nora didn't know how to talk to Nattie, what to say to make everything all right.

"You're in your nightgown, Mama," Nattie said.

Nora tugged the thin fabric over her ankles. Unlike her, Nattie was fully dressed. Had she wanted to run away? "I couldn't sleep, and I worried when I found your bed empty. You weren't about to just up and leave, were you?"

"What? No. Amy's the one who runs when she's scared, not me."

Another knot of worry lodged in Nora's throat. Where was Amy?

"She's in the hayloft," Nattie said as if sensing her thoughts.

The knot in Nora's throat loosened. At least Amy hadn't gone far. "Have you talked to her?"

"A bit. But she's not ready to talk."

Again, silence fell between them.

"Do you think my father was a good man?" Nattie didn't look at her but stared straight ahead into the night, her arms wrapped tightly around her pulled-up knees.

"Your father is upstairs in the bedroom, and yes, she's a good person."

"Mama..."

"I know what you're asking, but I don't have an answer. I don't know who fathered you." She placed her hand on Nattie's cheek and guided her around to face her. "It doesn't matter. You're your own, wonderful person."

Nattie trembled beneath her hand. "But I don't look like you and Amy, and I'm not Papa's...Luke's daughter either. I don't resemble any of you."

"That's not true. You're so much like I was at your age that it sometimes takes my breath away. And you have that little bump," she tapped Nattie on the nose, "just like Luke does. You were so proud of that when you were little. Luke influenced you so much more than the man whose blood you share ever could. She taught you how to ride, where to find the juiciest strawberries, and how to be a good human being. You have always loved her so much, and it breaks my heart to think that it might change now." Tears burned in Nora's eyes, and when she blinked, they spilled over and ran in hot trails down her cheeks.

"It won't," Nattie whispered as if afraid to say it aloud. "I still love him...her, but I'm so confused. I thought you and Papa met and fell in love and then had Amy and me. But now everything is different."

"Not everything," Nora said. "We still love each other, and we love you."

"But doesn't love include trust? In all those years, you never once considered telling us?"

"We thought about it a thousand times. Not telling you had nothing to do with lack of trust. We were afraid that you might not be able to accept it...to accept Luke...and our love."

Nattie rubbed the bump on the bridge of her nose, a gesture that reminded Nora so much of Luke that her heart hurt. "Well, finding out you lied to us all these years sure doesn't help me accept the situation. You were in my shoes once. Weren't you terribly angry with Papa...at...her when you found out she'd deceived you?"

It was hard to remember herself as the young woman who had been so scared to love again. "I wasn't just angry. I was devastated. I thought my plans of a happy family life were ruined."

"But they weren't?"

It hurt that Nattie needed to ask, but Nora understood. After discovering such a fundamental lie, Nattie wouldn't take anything for granted anymore. At least not for a while. "I can't imagine loving anyone—man or woman—more than I love Luke." Nora trailed her fingers through Nattie's shiny black hair. "Luke and I, we did things a little backward, and we're a pretty unlikely pair, but that doesn't mean our love is any less than you thought. It doesn't mean **you** are any less. Luke chose to be your parent because she loves you. Do you understand that?"

When Nattie turned toward her, her knees pressed against Nora's thigh. She sniffled and then nodded. "I think I do."

Rika stepped out of the cabin. Moonlight filtered through the shadows on the veranda. Was there someone sitting on the steps leading up to the main house? *Amy?* She quickly crossed the ranch yard.

"Amy?" Nora's voice cut through the darkness.

Rika lifted her lantern so that Nora could see her face. "No, it's me, Hendrika." When she came closer, the circle of light illuminated Nora and Nattie huddling close on the top step. "Everything all right?"

"Yes," Nora said, but it didn't sound convincing. "Nattie, you best go to bed. I'll look for Amy."

Nattie stood and dusted off her skirt. "Give her some time, Mama. You know Amy. If you climb up in that hayloft now, you'll only chase her away."

After some hesitation, Nora agreed. She said goodnight and followed Nattie into the house.

Rika stared after them. Should she go to bed too and give Amy some time alone, as Nattie had suggested? But she knew she wouldn't be able to sleep. Maybe Amy would have an easier time talking to someone who wasn't part of the family. She walked to the hay barn, opened the big doors, and listened.

Hay rustled.

"Amy?"

Silence.

"Amy? If you're there, please answer me. I'm worried about you."

"I'm fine," Amy's voice came from the hayloft. "Go to bed."

Rika left the lantern on a hook, groped for the ladder, and climbed through the hay door. With her arm in a sling, she struggled, but the thought of Amy alone and hurting urged her onward.

"What are you doing? You'll hurt your shoulder!" Amy hurried over and helped her into the hayloft.

"I just want to make sure you're all right," Rika said.

Amy didn't answer, didn't tell her she was fine. She sank into a pile of hay, wrapped her arms around her legs, and pressed her forehead to her knees.

"What's going on?" Rika walked over, knelt, and touched her shoulder. The muscles under her hand were stiff. "What happened with your parents?"

"I can't tell you. I want to, but I just... I can't." Amy let go of her legs and flopped into the hay.

Not a lot of things had the power to upset Amy like this. For Amy, only her family, the ranch, and the horses mattered. Rika stretched out in the hay next to her. Their arms touched, but Rika didn't move away. "Your father," she said and took a wild guess, "he's not your father, is he?"

Amy scrambled upright.

"I'm right, aren't I?"

"Half right," Amy mumbled. She slung her arms around her knees again and rocked back and forth as if to soothe herself. "How did you know?"

"You asked him if Nora is even your mother. I know you love your parents, and you'd never ask something like that if you hadn't just received shocking news."

Amy blew air through her nose. "You have no idea."

"You know what I would say if someone told me that my father isn't really my father?" Rika didn't wait for an answer. "I'd say, 'Oh thank the Lord!'"

"That's different," Amy said.

"I know. Your father...Luke, he's a good man and a good father."

"No."

"No? Don't be stupid, Amy. You have two parents who love you. Don't you know how precious that is? What difference does it make if he's your father by blood or by choice?"

Hay rustled when Amy lifted up on her knees and loomed over her. "You don't understand." Her voice rose to a growl. "He's not my father. He's not even..."

"Not even what?"

But Amy didn't answer. She dropped back into the hay and pressed her hand against her mouth as if she was sorry she had said anything.

What could be wrong with Luke to throw Amy in such a tumult? Rika pictured Luke: tall, with the wiry strength of someone who had worked hard his whole life. He didn't have her own father's heavy build, though. His gentleness was so much like Amy's, not because they were related, but because they were both—

She sucked in a breath. "He's a woman."

Amy said nothing. Her silence spoke volumes.

"It's true? Are you sure?"

"Who would make up something so crazy?" Amy mumbled.

Rika rubbed her forehead, but it didn't help her think more clearly. What on God's green earth was going on? She thought of the dying soldier who had confessed her true identity to her. Was Luke like that?

No. The soldier had dressed as a man to follow her betrothed into battle, but Luke loved Nora. Even if everything else was a disguise, that part was true. Amy's parents were two women who loved each other. *Lord. How many of them are there? Are there really so many women couples, and I just never knew about it?* Maybe it should have been a shock, but for some reason, it wasn't. When Rika looked at Amy, she understood why Luke preferred life with Nora to life with a husband.

"Nothing makes sense anymore." Amy lay back and threw her arm across her eyes, shutting out the world. "And at the same time, a lot of little details make sense now. Why they taught us to always knock on their bedroom door. Why Papa... Luke never went to see Dr. Tolridge, no matter how sick he... she was."

"Come here." Rika wrestled her right arm out of its sling, lay next to Amy, and opened her arms.

Amy didn't resist. She melted against Rika, resting against her uninjured shoulder as if they had lain that way a thousand times.

Carefully, Rika lowered her sore arm and clutched Amy to her body. Hot skin pressed against her own, and she nearly groaned. She trailed the fingers of her left hand through Amy's locks and down her back, feeling the smooth skin beneath the shirt. For an instant, she imagined continuing on and letting her fingers wander down Amy's buttocks. She shook herself. *Stop that. You can't have such thoughts. And especially not now.* "Did they tell you who your father, the man who fathered you, is?"

"Some man in Boston," Amy said. "Well, at least I wasn't fathered by a stranger in a brothel."

"What? A brothel? Where's this coming from?"

"Mama...she..." A tear splashed onto Rika's skin. Amy wiped it away, her hand lingering on Rika's collarbone.

Rika cleared her throat. Twice. "What about your mother?"

"She worked in a brothel after I was born. She doesn't know who Nattie's father is."

Despite Amy's heat against her, Rika's body went cold. She pulled Amy closer. "That's horrible."

"Why did this have to happen?" Amy whispered. She buried her face against Rika's neck.

Rika's head swam with sensation, but she forced herself to focus on Amy's words, not her body. This was serious. Amy needed her. "Would you rather they never said a word? Keeping so many secrets all of these years..." She shook her head. "That must have been so hard on them."

Amy lifted her head. "On them?"

"You don't honestly think they were out to hurt you? Whatever they did, they did for you and Nattie. Your mother didn't have a choice. You don't understand how it is to be all alone in the world. For all your strength, you're so innocent."

"I'm not innocent." Amy's voice rumbled against Rika's skin.

Rika swirled a handful of Amy's hair between her fingers and smiled. "Oh, yes, you are." It was part of her appeal. "You have a kind heart, and you help any creature who needs you. But back East, in Boston, things are not like that. I saw children with dirty faces and hollow cheeks on the street every day. Once, I gave a loaf of bread to a little boy who was clutching his stomach because he was so hungry. My father got so angry..." She closed her eyes. "He broke my wrist."

"Oh, Rika." Amy trailed her fingers along Rika's right arm and cradled her wrist.

It was the wrong arm, but Rika didn't mind. The touch was soothing. "Between starving and doing whatever it took to keep herself and you alive, your mother didn't have a choice. It doesn't make her a bad person."

"I know. It's just... They should have told us sooner," Amy said.

"They were afraid of losing your love." A ball of emotions lodged in her throat, making it hard to continue. She kept her own secret for the same reason. "Did they?"

When Amy cuddled closer, a few strands of her hair tickled Rika's skin, making her shiver.

"Did they what?" Amy asked.

"Lose your love."

Amy gave no answer. Maybe she didn't have one. She laid her face against Rika's neck, and Rika cradled her head. Once, she had lain that way with Jo during a long night when her coughing wouldn't stop, but holding Amy was different. The feeling in her belly wasn't just the protectiveness of a friend. It was fiercer, but at the same time gentler than what she had experienced before. *Is this what love feels like?*

She gave a shake of her head, nearly displacing Amy from her comfortable spot. *You didn't love Willem and you don't love Phin, so how could you feel love for Amy, a woman?* But when she stroked the red locks, marveling at the vulnerability of this strong woman, she thought, *How can anyone not love her?*

But, of course, there was no future in thinking like that. Rika had spent a lifetime listening to reason, not feelings, and she couldn't afford to change that now. "Ready to climb down?"

Amy shook her head. "Stay with me?"

Sleeping in the hayloft when she had a perfectly good bed was crazy, but Rika nodded and pulled Amy closer, basking in her warmth and her company for as long as she could. Monday, her wedding day, would come all too soon.

Phin slung the reins around the brake and walked around the wagon to help Rika up on the seat.

"You going into town again?" Luke asked.

"No," Phin answered. "Just drivin' around, lookin' for some flowers Hendrika can wear to the wedding tomorrow."

Luke nodded from her place on the veranda.

Her. Rika still found it hard to believe that Amy's father was a woman. During breakfast, her gaze had returned to Luke again and again, searching for any hint of female curves beneath the shirt and vest. She found none. Luke's disguise was perfect. Rika wondered how it might feel to live her life constantly hiding and pretending. *You're about to find out.*

Phin stepped up to her and put his hands on her hips to lift her onto the wagon.

The calluses on his palms snagged on the linsey-woolsey dress just as Amy's did, but his touch felt different. It didn't cause the mix of heat and tenderness.

So what? That feeling isn't necessary to survive and live a content life. But that old, familiar way of thinking could no longer convince her. Something had changed inside of her. Survival was no longer enough. *I don't want to be just content. I want to be happy.* After working hard for months—her whole life, really—she had earned it.

"Wait." She turned in Phin's arms.

"What?" He smiled at her. "You changed your mind and don't want flowers for the wedding?"

Behind her, Old Jack snorted and stamped his hoof, waiting to get going.

Rika gulped a mouthful of air. She opened her mouth, not sure what she would say until she heard the words. "I can't marry you."

His hands jerked against her hips. "What?" He stared at her.

Rika stared back. She had hesitated and argued with herself for days or maybe weeks, but her sudden words surprised her as much as they surprised him. She straightened and said again, "I can't marry you."

"Why? I know people expected us to marry the minute I got back, and I admit I dragged my heels, but—"

"It has nothing to do with you."

His blond brows drew together. "What's the matter, then?"

"When you learn the truth, you'll be the one who won't want to marry me."

"Let me be the judge of that." He supported his elbow on one crossed arm and tapped a finger against his chin. "What's goin' on?"

Blood rushed through her ears. Her lungs couldn't get enough air, no matter how fast she breathed. A thousand thoughts and doubts raced through her mind. Should she tell him? She thought of Amy and the pain in her eyes last night. Did she really want her children to look at her like that one day?

Rika drew in a breath, inflating her cheeks, then let it escape. She turned her head to see if Luke could overhear them, but the veranda was empty. "I'm not Jo," she said, voice low even though they were alone now.

"You go by Hendrika."

"I am Hendrika. Hendrika Aaldenberg."

His hands dropped to his sides. "Hendrika Aaldenberg." He repeated the syllables. "You didn't just send a tintype of a friend. That was a picture of Johanna. You're not Johanna."

Rika dug the tip of her boot into the dust. "No, I'm not."

"Then where is she?" he asked. "If she didn't want to marry me, she could have—"

"She's dead." Rika peeked up through half-lowered lashes, every muscle in her body like stone.

Phin's face flushed. A vein pulsed in his right temple. "What in tarnation...? Dead?"

"I didn't kill her," Rika said, in case his thoughts were running in that direction. Her heart pounded in time with the vein in his temple. "She was my friend. I think she had brown lung disease."

He folded muscular arms across his chest, a solid barrier between them. "And you stole my letters and the train ticket off her cold body?"

"I-I... It wasn't like that." Her legs trembled, and she shrank back against Old Jack's warm flank. She curled her lip inward and bit down on it. "I did it because I had no other choice. I lost my job and my place in the boarding house, and I spent most of my money paying for Jo's funeral. I had nowhere to go but the poorhouse. I didn't have the time to start my own correspondence with a bachelor out west. I'd have starved in the meantime."

"If that's really true, why didn't you just tell me? Why lie?"

"Because you'd have sent me back," Rika said.

"You don't know that." He unfolded his arms and tapped his chest. "I'm not heartless, you know?"

No, he wasn't. But before she had come to Oregon, Rika had found little reason to trust in the goodness of people. "Are you saying you'd have married me anyway?"

"I didn't know Johanna, and I don't know you, so what difference would it have made?"

Thoughts flitted through her head like shuttles hissing back and forth in a loom. "Why are you so intent on marrying a stranger?" She had wondered about it for weeks, but only now did she dare ask. "Why didn't you try to court Nattie?" *Or Amy*, she almost added but didn't want to say it out loud. The thought of Amy with Phin made her vision dim to a hazy red.

Phin stumbled back. "No, that... She..." He rubbed the stubbles on his upper lip. "She'd never have the likes of me."

Her thoughts cleared, the mental shuttles ceasing their flitting as if the end-of-day bell had rung. *Ah.* "Did she say that?"

"She doesn't need to. A blind man could see that she deserves better than a ranch hand without a penny to his name."

That comment stung. Rika took a step back. "I don't have a penny to my name either."

"That's different. A man needs to take care of his wife. If I courted the boss's daughter, everyone would think I'm just doin' it to get the ranch one day. I don't want Nattie to think the land is worth more than she is."

"But why advertise for a wife even though you care for Nattie?"

His lips formed a thin line. "Pinin' away for her has no future. I need to move on." When Rika opened her mouth, he cut her off with a wave of his hand. "Enough of that nonsense. What happens now?"

"I'll try to find work." It wouldn't be easy to find employment as an unwed woman, but once she found work, she'd send Phin money. "I swear I'll pay you back for the train and the stagecoach tickets."

"Not necessary," Phin said.

"But you need the money." For a rancher just starting out, every cent counted.

"I need a wife. And you need a husband." His gaze drilled into her, then softened. "Maybe if I took the time to get to know you—the real you—I'd like you. We could try."

Rika's mouth fell open. When Old Jack swung his tail and she almost tasted horsehair, she snapped her mouth shut and continued to stare at Phin. She had expected shouting and cursing, maybe even a slap to her face, not this calm offer to take her anyway. "You...you still want to marry me?"

"If you promise there'll be no more lies between us." He held out his hand as if he had sold her a horse and wanted to close the deal.

Rika hesitated. *What are you doing?* This was what she had wanted all along, wasn't it? To be married and safe for the rest of her life. Now she could get it without having to spend her life as Jo. She thought of Amy, then shook her head. Those feelings had no future. *For goodness' sake, say yes!*

Phin tilted his head. "So?"

∞

Amy dipped the pen into the ink well and paused with the nib above the paper. "Dear Rika," she murmured as she wrote, trying for her smoothest penmanship. She paused again. Tomorrow Rika would marry Phin, and Amy didn't know what to say to her.

Don't marry him, she wanted to write. But of course she didn't.

"Just wish them all the best for the future," Nattie had said. But if it was that easy, why had Nattie been in her own room for the last two hours, trying to compose a letter of congratulations?

Her fingers trembled. A drop of ink splashed onto the paper, and for a moment, she expected it to be red, as if writing a good-bye letter to Rika had opened a vein. But the ink was as black as her mood.

"Damn, damn, damn." She crumpled the paper and threw it across the room.

It hit Rika in the chest just as she entered. She caught the paper ball and blinked at it. "What's this?" She smoothed the paper and read the two words. "You're writing to me?"

Amy tugged on her earlobe. "For tomorrow. But I'm not good with putting my thoughts down on paper."

"You've got a little..." Rika pointed to Amy's ear.

"What?" Amy rubbed her ear.

"You smeared ink all over your ear, and now you're making it worse." Rika took a rag and dipped it in the washbowl. She laid the hand of her uninjured arm along Amy's jaw and tilted her head. "Hold still."

Amy couldn't move even if she wanted to. The heat of Rika's touch melted her bones. Her eyes fluttered shut.

The rag rubbed over her ear, cold against her overheated skin.

"There." Rika trailed her finger over Amy's ear as if to prove that the ink was gone.

Tingles shot through Amy's body. The touch marked her deeper than any ink stain could.

Then Rika dropped her hand and stepped back.

Amy cleared her throat. "Maybe I should just tell you now."

"Tell me what?"

"What I wanted to write." Her hands trembled too much to put pen to paper.

"Wait. That's why I came up here. I need to tell you—"

"Let me go first," Amy said. If she didn't say it now, she probably never would. "I wish you all the best for the future, and I hope you'll be real happy with Phin." Every word hurt, but she meant it. She wanted Rika to find happiness, and since she couldn't provide it, she had to let her go. "If you ever need anything—anything at all—just let me know."

"Amy..."

Amy held up her hands. "I want to give you Cinnamon as a wedding gift."

"Oh, Amy, I can't."

"I want you to have a part of the ranch to remember us by."

Tears shone in Rika's eyes. "I don't need a horse to remember you. And as much as I love Cin, I can't take him."

"Sure you can—"

"I'm not gonna marry Phin." Rika blurted it out.

Amy's breath exploded from her lungs. "What? Why?" She stared at Rika, searching, asking, hoping. Did Rika have feelings for her after all? Was that why she couldn't marry Phin?

"I have to tell you something," Rika whispered.

Amy rose on unsteady legs and stepped closer. "Yes?"

"I-I'm..."

Hope vibrated deep inside. "Tell me."

Rika bowed her head. "I'm not the woman who wrote the letters to Phin."

True. Staying on the ranch had changed her. She had learned to trust and enjoy the moment. And it was not just Rika who had changed. So much had happened in Amy's life since she'd met Rika in front of the stage depot. The last months had been a journey of discovery about herself and her family. "Yeah, I noticed. I happen to think it's a change for the better."

"Change? No, you don't understand." Rika fiddled with her skirt, rearranging it over her ankles as if she felt exposed. "I'm not the woman who wrote the letters. Never was. My name is Hendrika Aaldenberg, not Johanna Bruggeman."

A lie. Another lie. Was no one in her life what he or she appeared to be? "Why?" Amy's voice trembled, barely getting out the single word.

"I didn't know what else to do. I had lost my job, my room, and my only friend, Jo. She died the week before she could take the train west."

"So you thought you'd honor her by marrying her betrothed and lying to him and to me for the rest of your life?" The words tasted like poison on Amy's tongue.

Rika's lips thinned. "You don't understand. How could you? Whenever you need help, your family is there for you. Your parents would do anything for you and Nattie."

"Oh, yeah, the perfect family life." Amy spat out the words. She shook her head until her temples pounded. "It's all just an illusion. If you look beneath the surface—"

"I looked, and all I see is love. This is killing your father. He's not eating or—"

"He's not my father. She. Lord."

Rika's eyes softened to the mahogany color that matched her hair. She touched Amy's forearm. "I know this is hard on you, Amy. I don't want to fight with you, but I hate to see you throw away your family. I'd give anything to have a father like yours, even if he's a woman. I know he...she will be there for you, but my own father... I couldn't go to him for help."

"He would have said no?" Amy couldn't imagine it. When it really counted, Luke had never told her no.

"Oh, no. He would have welcomed me with open arms—after all, a daughter is cheap labor, and if she doesn't sell enough pastries, you can encourage her to try harder with your fists."

Amy swallowed against a dry throat.

"I know it was wrong to lie to you, but between asking my father to take me back or staying in the poorhouse, using Jo's train ticket seemed like a God-sent gift."

"Then why are you telling us the truth now?"

"I don't want to marry and have children, then make them and Phin hate me for lying to them," Rika said.

Unspoken words hung between them.

"I don't hate Papa," Amy whispered. "I'm just..." She flailed her arms, searching for an explanation, searching for balance.

"I know." Rika squeezed Amy's forearm once again, then let go and turned. She reached beneath the bed and pulled out a piece of paper.

Amy caught a glimpse of a rider on a red horse before Rika rolled up the drawing and placed it in her carpetbag. "What are you doing?"

"I can't stay here. You know that."

"But you don't have to go now. Not right away. I'm sure my parents will let you stay until you find a job." She sounded like a little girl begging Papa for a ride on his horse. The thought added to the churning of her stomach.

Rika closed the carpetbag, fumbling with her left hand, and carried it to the door. "Why drag this out? The longer I stay, the more people will wag their tongues. I'd better go. The stagecoach leaves Baker Prairie in an hour, and if I miss it, I'll have to wait a week for the next one."

"Where will you go? How will you get by?"

"I'll be fine. Phin let me keep the money I got for Mouse. It'll tide me over until I find work."

One hour and Rika would be gone—not just a few miles, to the cabin Phin would build, but gone forever. Should she take a chance and tell her how she felt?

No. Rika had come west to marry, and now she had talked about having children. *She's not like me, and I don't want the last words she ever speaks to me be in anger and disgust.* Amy hunched her shoulders, her hands dangling helplessly at her sides. She wavered between conflicting emotions. Part of her wanted to make the most of every remaining moment, but another part didn't want to help Rika leave. "Want me to take you to town?"

"Phin asked one of the ranch hands to take me," Rika said. "Old Jack is ready to go."

Amy clamped her hands around the back of the chair.

"So I guess this is good-bye." Rika jingled the carpetbag.

"Yeah." Amy held her breath because even breathing hurt.

Rika crossed the room. She paused one step from Amy and searched her face. With a plop, the carpetbag landed on the floor. She threw her left arm around Amy and pulled her close.

Amy squeezed her eyes shut and felt tears leak out. She rubbed her cheek against Rika's uninjured shoulder to hide them. Careful not to hurt her, she pressed their bodies together, letting their shared warmth filter through her shirt and into her heart.

Lips wet with tears brushed her cheek.

"Good-bye, Amy," Rika whispered.

Then her warmth moved away. When Amy opened her eyes, Rika was gone. She plopped down on the bed and buried her face in the pillow. Rika's scent from the pillowcase engulfed her, and she groaned her pain into the fabric.

Luke lifted her hand. When she noticed that her fingers were trembling, she curled them into a fist and knocked on Nattie's door.

"Yes?"

After a steadying breath, she opened the door.

Nattie sat at her desk. At the sound of Luke's footsteps, she swiveled.

They stared at each other from across the room before Nattie turned back around.

Luke bit the inside of her cheek. What should she say? How could she begin a conversation? Her gaze fell on the papers covering Nattie's desk. Paintings of Appaloosa coat patterns littered the desk. "What's that?"

Silence filled the room, then Nattie answered, "I'm trying to figure out what kind of parents produce the best patterns."

Parents. Luke bit her lip. Did Nattie still consider her a parent? At least she was still interested in their breeding program. They still had that in common. She took a hesitant step, then another, inching closer. "Can we talk?"

Nattie nodded but didn't turn around.

"Look at me." Luke's voice trembled, and she tried to steady it. "Please."

Slowly, Nattie turned and looked up with red-rimmed eyes.

Luke's heart clenched. "Nattie."

"I haven't told Mama yet, but I want to go east this fall, study there for two years."

Luke stumbled back and pressed a hand to her chest. Nattie wanted to leave the ranch, wanted to get away from her. Pain sliced through her, but she said nothing. She was too afraid to ask Nattie to stay—afraid that Nattie would shout at her, would tell her she wasn't her father and had no right to tell her what to do.

"That is, if we can afford it," Nattie added when Luke stayed silent.

"We can." Every year after roundup, Luke and Nora put away some of the money to invest in a good education for Amy and Nattie. She had always wanted to give her daughters that chance, but now it seemed the money would help Nattie to leave her forever.

Nattie's gaze flickered from the paintings on the desk to Luke's face. "There's a college for veterinary surgeons in New York. It's a two-year curriculum that focuses on the study of horses."

"Horses?"

Nattie rubbed the bump on the bridge of her nose and smiled. "What else?"

Wild hope shot through Luke. Was it possible that Nattie wasn't running away from her? Did she still want to be a part of the ranch, of Luke's life, and just needed to find her own way? "They take women students?"

"No." Nattie's gray eyes sparked like tinder. "But I'm not letting that stop me. That's what you taught us, right?"

Tears burned Luke's throat. She nodded numbly.

"Frankie and Tess know one of the professors. He's willing to teach me privately." Nattie hesitated. "If Mama and you allow it."

"Do I still have the right to allow or forbid it?" Luke asked.

Instead of answering, Nattie jumped up and threw her arms around Luke, burying her face against Luke's shoulder and soaking her shirt with tears.

Luke swallowed tears of her own. She stroked Nattie's hair with trembling fingers and held her close, for the first time in her life unafraid to let one of her daughters press too close against her chest.

Finally, Nattie hiccupped and looked up.

"Is that a yes?" Luke whispered.

Nattie pressed her face back against her shoulder. "Y-yes. So, will you allow me to go?"

"I'll miss you." For once, she could openly admit her feelings without being afraid others would think her unmanly. "But I'm so proud of you for doing this. The first woman veterinary surgeon... I'd love that."

When Nattie finally let go and moved back to blow her nose, Luke studied her. "I know telling you who I am was a big shock for you girls—for you especially. I don't want you to think badly of yourself or your mother, just because of the circumstances of your conception."

Nattie sniffled and averted her gaze.

"I know how you must feel."

Now Nattie lifted her gaze. Anger glinted in her eyes for a second. "How could you know that?"

Luke swallowed. She had wanted to forget about that part of her life, but to help her daughter, she would reveal another truth about herself. "Because my mother worked in a brothel too, and my father was one of the men who paid to share her bed."

With a gasp, Nattie stumbled back and sank onto the desk chair. She stared up at Luke with teary eyes.

"But there's one big difference between you and me, Nattie. My mother tried to drown her shame in a bottle of whiskey. I remember sitting on the backstairs, sometimes all night, waiting for her to tell me it was all right to come back in. Sometimes she forgot, and I still sat there when the sun came up." With the old images, feelings of loneliness and despair resurfaced, and she shoved them away. She was an adult now and no longer alone. "My mother stopped caring—about me, about herself, about trying to get out. Your mother never did. She's not a bad mother or a bad human being. And neither are you."

For the second time, Nattie threw herself into Luke's arms. "Oh, Papa."

A knock on the door interrupted them.

Nattie moved back and wiped her cheeks. "Yes?"

The door inched open. "Miss Nattie?" Phin stood in the doorway, not entering. "Can I talk to you for a—?" When his gaze fell on Luke, he stopped. "Um. Didn't know you were in here, boss. This can wait until later."

"Phin, wait! What happened?" Nattie asked.

"Just wanted to let you know Hank is gonna take Hendrika into town," Phin said.

"Into town?" Luke frowned at him. Was it just her imagination, or was Phin paler than the snow on Mount Hood? "I thought you were gonna look for flowers for the wedding?"

"The wedding is off."

"What?" Nattie grabbed his sleeve and pulled him into the room. "What happened?"

"She lied about who she is," Phin said.

The words made Luke flinch. *Damn, not this too.* How would her daughters take Hendrika's deception on top of everything else? Her gaze sought out Nattie, searching for forgiveness, but Nattie was focused on Phin.

"What do you mean?" Nattie asked.

"She didn't write the letters. When Johanna died, Hendrika took the tickets I sent her friend to start a new life out west."

"Johanna is dead? Oh my. I'm so sorry." Nattie squeezed his arm. "Are you all right?"

"Yeah. Maybe it's for the best. I haven't even built a cabin yet, so I can't provide for a wife."

The words were familiar. Luke smiled tiredly. "When I married Nora and came to Oregon, I thought the same way. But let me tell you something that I learned about women, Phin. Women are strong." In the past, she had needed her male identity to feel strong and capable. Now she started to believe that her family would love her and come to trust in her strength even though they knew she was a woman.

Nattie met her gaze. A hint of a smile darted across her face.

"They don't need us to treat them like fragile china or to provide the perfect life," Luke said. "If you find a good woman, she'll want to be your partner and take care of you too."

"Papa's right," Nattie said, still holding on to Phin's sleeve.

The ease with which she said "Papa" lifted a heavy weight from Luke's shoulders.

"Yeah, well, obviously, Hendrika doesn't want that with me," Phin said. "When I offered to marry her anyway, she refused."

Luke studied him. He didn't look heartbroken, just bewildered. Hendrika had hurt his ego, not his heart.

Another knock sounded on the door. Hendrika peered around the doorframe. Her eyes were red-rimmed, but she straightened her shoulders and locked her jaw like a condemned woman preparing for the inevitable. "Sorry to interrupt. I just wanted to say good-bye." Her gaze slid over to Phin, then back to Nattie and Luke. "If you're still talking to me?"

How could Luke judge her for hiding her identity when she was doing the same? "Are you sure you want to leave, Hendrika? If that's really your name."

"It is." Hendrika clutched the carpetbag against her chest. "Thanks for being so kind, but what else is there to do? I've got no reason to stay under the circumstances."

No? What about Amy? Luke wanted to ask. But even if she had dared to ask Hendrika about her feelings, she couldn't do it in front of Nattie and Phin. Not knowing what to say or do, she watched the door close behind Hendrika.

Amy wasn't sure how much time had passed when someone knocked on the door. Time had lost its meaning. She lifted her head from the pillow. "Go away," she shouted and dropped her head back down.

The door creaked open, and lithe steps crossed the room. The bed dipped. A warm hand settled on Amy's shoulder, and a familiar mix of aromas drifted to her nose. Leather, horse, bay rum, and fresh air—scents that meant safety and comfort.

Papa. Amy rolled around and stared into the familiar face. Dark smudges circled Luke's eyes. Pain darkened her eyes to gunmetal gray.

So much pain. Amy couldn't stand it anymore. She threw her arms around Luke's slender hips and buried her face against a firm thigh. Sobs shook her body. Her nose burned, her throat burned, her heart burned. She thought she might be sick.

Luke's hands came up and combed through her hair, the touch as soothing as it had been since Amy was a little girl. As her queasiness ebbed, she quieted and finally looked up.

Tears glittered on Luke's cheeks. She rubbed her hands over her face, hastily wiping them away.

"Rika is gone, Papa," Amy whispered and then stopped, struck by how much had changed between them—and by how much stayed the same. "Can I...can I still call you that?"

Luke laid a hand over her eyes and nodded. "I'd be honored." Her voice shook.

Amy sat up, their knees still resting together.

They sniffled at the same time and then smiled at each other.

"Did you tell her how you feel before she left?" Luke asked.

Amy's gaze flew up. "You...you know? H-how do you know?"

Luke smiled. "I was in your shoes once."

For the first time in many years, Amy was understood completely. Luke knew what was going on inside of her even when Amy struggled to fully understand it herself. This was why Luke had revealed her secret—so that she could be there for her. A wave of gratefulness washed over Amy. Her voice shook when she asked, "What did you do?"

"Same thing you're doing now—I almost let her go. I told your mother I wouldn't stand in her way if she found happiness with a real man." Luke lifted one side of her mouth into a smile. "It took me years to understand that she doesn't want a 'real man.' She wants me."

New tears burned in Amy's eyes. Her parents' relationship was even more special than she had known. "But Hendrika doesn't want me. Otherwise, she would have stayed."

"Did you tell her you want her to stay?"

"What right do I have to do that?" Amy rubbed her burning eyes. "She didn't marry Phin so she wouldn't have to live a lie. Even if she did like me, I couldn't offer her a life without lying and hiding. She wouldn't want that kind of life."

Luke gripped her shoulders and looked her in the eyes, almost nose to nose. "Let Hendrika make that decision. Yes, living your life forced to lie every day is hard," she said, voice low. "But you know what? Lying to townsfolk, letting them believe what they want... I don't mind that. If I could live my life over again, I'd make the same choices—with one exception."

"What?" Amy asked.

"I'd tell you and Nattie sooner. The lies that hurt are the ones you tell yourself and the people you love. Everyone else..." Luke made a move as if tossing something over her shoulder. "They can go to hell if they stand in the way of your happiness."

"You really think someone like me can find happiness?"

Luke tapped her finger against Amy's temple. "Get this thought that you don't deserve love just because you're different out of your head. I let myself believe the same thing for too many years, and only your mother taught me otherwise. There's nothing wrong with you or me. If God didn't want me to love Nora, why did he make me like this? Why didn't he make me fall in love with, say, Hank?"

The thought made Amy wrinkle her nose. She shook herself like a dog trying to get rid of fleas.

Luke laughed. "See? It seems wrong to you too. My heart belongs to Nora, and yours might belong to Hendrika—and hers to you."

Amy shook her head. "She's not...that way. Rika was married once."

"Sweetie, that doesn't mean anything. Your mother's first sweetheart was a man too. And now she's in love with me." Luke's red-rimmed eyes glowed with happiness.

"But what if Rika doesn't love me? What if she hates me once she finds out?"

"She doesn't look at you as if she would hate you. I know this is scary, but sometimes you have to take a chance for love," Luke said.

Just like Papa has. Luke had taken a big risk by telling Amy and Nattie who she was. She'd risked her safety, her life, and her family's love. She had taken that chance out of love, because she wanted to show Amy that happiness was possible for two women together.

Amy vaulted off the bed and stumbled to the door. "What time is it?" she shouted over her shoulder.

"Almost one," Luke answered and snapped her pocket watch closed.

Amy wrenched the door open. "Damn." By the time she reached Baker Prairie, the stagecoach with Rika would be gone.

WILLAMETTE VALLEY, OREGON
JUNE 27, 1868

*R*IKA'S SORE SHOULDER POUNDED EVERY time the stagecoach hit a stone or a hole in the road. At least the ache in her shoulder distracted her from the pain in her heart.

The leather curtains were pulled back to let in fresh air. Outside, the green hills and fields of the Willamette Valley glided by. Every bend of the Molalla River, every dip of the land was familiar now. To her left was the place where Amy and she had pulled the foal out of the raging river. And on that hill over there, they had seen Tess and Frankie kiss.

Then the Molalla River joined the Willamette, and the stagecoach headed away from the Hamilton land. Rika craned her neck, hoping to catch one last glance, until the pain in her shoulder forced her to stop. She felt as if she was leaving behind her home and her heart. Leaving Boston hadn't felt like this.

"Here." The older man who was the only other passenger offered her a sympathetic smile and his handkerchief.

Rika realized that tears were running down her face. "Thank you." She took the handkerchief and dabbed her eyes.

"I'm Jacob Garfield. I own the dry-goods store in town," he said. "I've seen you at church with the Hamiltons, and I think you know my daughter Hannah, but we haven't been introduced."

"Hendrika Aaldenberg," she said from behind the handkerchief. Using her own name should have been a relief, but it wasn't. Hendrika Bruggeman had a home, maybe even a family. Hendrika Aaldenberg didn't.

"It wasn't right of him to have you come here and wait for him and then refuse to marry you," Mr. Garfield said when he took back his handkerchief.

"What?"

"I'm talking about what Phineas Sharpe did to you," he said in a disapproving tone. "That's not how a gentleman acts."

She flinched. So gossip had already started. "You're mistaken, sir. That's not what happened."

"No?" He leaned forward and tilted his head.

She didn't owe him an explanation, but this was her last chance to protect Phin's reputation. Hannah's father was a friend of the Hamilton family, and she didn't want him to think badly of Phin. "I decided not to marry him."

His eyebrows jerked up. "But why? Phineas is a good, hardworking man."

"I know." Rika fiddled with the sling around her arm. "I just..." She shook her head. She couldn't tell him she had feelings for someone else. Not when that someone was a woman. She hardly understood it herself. "I don't love him."

Mr. Garfield smiled as if she were a child who had said something foolish. "I've seen many good marriages in my time that didn't start with love."

Just a few months ago, she would have nodded, but now she said, "I want love. And if I can't have it, then I would rather stay alone. I don't need a husband to be happy."

His eyebrows nearly disappeared in his gray hair, but his smile was still kind, not disapproving. "You sound like the Hamilton girls. My youngest son tried to court Nattie, but she refused to see him."

Before she could answer, the stagecoach picked up speed, jostling her from side to side.

"Hold on," the driver shouted.

Mr. Garfield almost tumbled into her lap. He grabbed the leather strap dangling from the stagecoach's roof. "Have you gone insane?" he yelled at the driver.

"Someone's after us!"

Rika's heart hammered against her ribs. The stagecoach didn't have an armed guard, so if outlaws stopped them, they'd be fair game. Not that she had much to lose. She had already left behind everything that mattered to her.

The stagecoach flew up a hill. The sack of mail tumbled from beneath the front seat and slammed into Rika's shins. Pain flared through her legs and her shoulder.

Hoofbeats drummed behind them, quickly coming closer.

Mr. Garfield pulled his revolver and pointed it out the window, his face grim.

The rider was almost upon them now.

Rika caught flashes of red—a red horse galloping at full speed, red locks flying in the wind.

Mr. Garfield drew back the hammer of his revolver.

"Rika," the rider shouted.

Amy! It's Amy! "No!" Rika threw herself at Mr. Garfield's weapon hand.

A shot drowned out the hammering hoofbeats.

Amy ducked over Ruby's neck as a shot rang out, but no bullet zipped past.

The four stagecoach horses slowed at a bend in the road.

Ruby stretched beneath Amy, her powerful muscles catapulting them past the stagecoach. "Billy," she shouted up to the driver. "Stop! It's just me, Amy Hamilton."

Billy squinted at her, then pulled at the reins between his fingers. "Whoa. Whoa I said, you sons of bitches."

The stagecoach rumbled to a stop in a cloud of dust.

"Goddammit, Miss Hamilton!" He slapped his hat against his thigh and glared at her. "What's gotten into you? You damn near made my horses bolt for the hills. Jacob almost shot you."

"Sorry. It's real urgent." Amy swung out of the saddle. Her legs felt numb as she took the three steps to the stagecoach. She flung open the red and gold door.

Rika sat across from Jacob, slumped over.

Lord! Amy's pulse raced in her throat. Had Rika been shot?

But then Rika straightened. Tiny burn marks dotted the front of her dress, but she seemed unharmed. The bullet had gone through the leather curtain next to her. She coughed at the gunpowder and looked at Amy, who still hung in the stagecoach's doorframe, clutching it with both hands. "Amy? What are you doing?"

Amy hesitated. Her one thought had been stopping Rika before she was gone for good. She hadn't thought about what she would say after that. "I'm stopping you from leaving."

"Amy…"

"Ladies, I got a schedule to keep," Billy shouted. "Either get out now or say good-bye."

Jacob Garfield, the only other passenger, looked from Amy to Rika, no doubt listening to every word they said.

Ignoring him, Amy set one foot inside the stagecoach. "Rika, please. I want you to stay. We all want you to stay. Please come home with me."

Home. The word echoed between them.

Amy extended her hand, palm up.

"You've got five seconds," Billy shouted. "Then I'll be on my merry way."

Leather creaked. Amy knew Billy was straightening the reins, prepared to slap them across the horses' backs. "Rika, please."

Rika gripped her hand.

The breath whooshed from Amy's lungs. Dizzy with joy, she pulled and stumbled backward, out of the stagecoach. At the last moment, she remembered Rika's shoulder and stopped them from tumbling into the dust by pulling her into an embrace.

Jacob closed the door behind them and waved.

"Hyah! Hyah, you sons of bitches," Billy shouted. The stagecoach jerked forward and rumbled down the road, leaving Amy and Rika behind.

"My carpetbag," Rika said. "It's still in the stagecoach."

A smile trembled on Amy's lips. "Seems you'll have to borrow one of my skirts again."

Rika stared at the rapidly disappearing stagecoach, then glanced into Amy's eyes. Emotions darted across her face like clouds drifting across the sky. "What now?"

Amy wanted to pull her even closer and never let her go, but she didn't dare. The dusty road was deserted, but they still needed to be careful. She shrugged and shuffled her feet. "I don't know. I just know that I want you to stay." She gathered her courage. "With me."

Rika's eyes widened.

For a few heartbeats, silence spread between them.

"You mean...?"

Was that hope in Rika's eyes, or was that just wishful thinking? Amy remembered what Papa had said. *Sometimes you have to take a chance for love.* "I like you, Rika," she said. Her voice shook so much that she barely understood her own words. "I mean I really like you." She peeked at Rika through half-lowered lids.

A whisper of a smile darted across Rika's face. "I like you too."

Amy's knees threatened to give out. "You like me? The way Frankie and Tess...or my parents like each other?"

Rika nodded. "I think so." She pulled Amy closer. "Oh, Amy, please don't cry."

Cry? Amy reached up and touched her cheeks. Wetness met her fingertips. She hadn't realized she was crying.

Rika leaned forward and brushed her lips over Amy's cheek, kissing away the tears. Then, as if remembering they had to be careful, she pulled back.

Dazed, Amy stared at her. "I hoped you would like me that way, but I never really thought..."

"I never thought so either. But it feels right." Rika's dark eyes were lit up by the surety of that knowledge.

"You seem so calm." How on earth had Rika come to terms with her feelings so fast when Amy had been running from her own for years?

"You know how the horses always go faster on the way back, when they sense that their stable is close?"

Amy nodded but furrowed her brow. She wanted to talk about horses now?

"I felt like that when I saw you open the stagecoach door. I knew home was close, so I should run toward it, not away from it."

Amy's hands trembled with the need to cup Rika's face, draw her close, and kiss her. *No. Not here.*

The same need made Rika's eyes seem to smolder. She brushed a few tangles out of Amy's hair but otherwise kept her distance. "We need to be careful. If anyone finds out... Not everyone will be as accepting as your family."

Amy peered left and right. Dust swirled around them, but otherwise, nothing moved on the lonely road. They were alone. Still, Rika was right. Amy dug her teeth into her lip. So the lying and hiding had already begun. How long would Rika be willing to deal with it?

"Hey." Rika squeezed her hand. "Why are you looking like that? Do you regret—?"

"No, it's just... It's not gonna be easy for us to be together. Are you sure you want that kind of life?"

Rika entwined their fingers. "We'll find a way. Don't you dare run away from this."

"I'm done running," Amy said. It was time to grow up and fight for what she wanted in life.

"Good. But I can't go back to the ranch. Not with Phin living there. Is there any other way for us to be together?"

"I have no earthly idea." Amy's shoulders slouched for a moment, but then she consciously straightened them. "I just know that I want to figure it out together." She reached for Ruby's reins, helped Rika into the saddle, and climbed up behind her, not yet sure where to direct her horse. Maybe going to town to see if they could get a refund on the stagecoach ticket would be a good first step. Now that Rika had to survive without a husband, she needed every cent.

BAKER PRAIRIE, OREGON
JUNE 27, 1868

*R*IKA HAD NEVER SEEN BAKER Prairie's main street so busy. Several wagons were hitched in front of a building, and half a dozen men were unloading their sacks of supplies or trying to maneuver furniture through the door. Two more men had climbed up on the roof to replace the big "feed and seed" sign with one that said "hotel."

People on the boardwalk stopped to watch.

Tess stood in the middle of the street, waving her arms at the men on the roof like a general instructing his troops. "No, no, more up on the right side." She turned to two men carrying a brass bed. "That one goes to the second floor. Please be careful on the stairs."

Amy clutched Rika's hips as she directed her mare toward Tess. "The new hotel!"

"What about it?"

"Maybe Frankie and Tess need some help." Amy's voice vibrated with excitement.

Rika turned her head. "You think they'd still hire me after they find out I lied to all of you?"

Amy reined in Ruby, and they slid out of the saddle. "They will, even if I have to go down on my knees and beg them."

Proud Amy, ready to beg...for me. A lump formed in Rika's throat. She hurried after Amy, determined to spare her the humiliation. If anyone did any begging, it had to be her.

When the men finally had the sign in place, Tess gave them a satisfied smile and directed her gaze down from the roof. "Oh, Amy, Hendrika! Are you here to see how the hotel is coming along, or are you busy with wedding preparations? Monday's the big day, right?"

Rika glanced at Amy, who looked back with big eyes.

Tess had no idea what had happened since she and Frankie had left the ranch. How could Rika explain, especially with all the men listening? Nervously licking her lips, she glanced around.

Tess looked back and forth between them. "All right, gentlemen. Time for a break," she called and clapped her hands. "Why don't you head over to the saloon and get yourself something to eat? My cousin and I will settle the bill."

The men didn't have to be told twice. Within seconds, Tess, Rika, and Amy were alone on the hotel's veranda.

"Come in." Tess led them toward the parlor, where Frankie was looking up from polishing silverware. "Take a seat and tell us what happened."

With shaky knees, Rika sank onto the divan next to Amy. When Amy opened her mouth, Rika stopped her with a quick touch to her forearm. She needed to do this. "There won't be a wedding on Monday—or on any other day."

Tess frowned. Then a smile crinkled the skin around her eyes. "Because the two of you...?"

Heat shot up Rika's neck. She nodded without looking at Tess. Out of the corner of her eye, she saw Amy blushing just as furiously.

"Don't tell me you ran away from home," Frankie said.

Amy squared her shoulders. "We might if that's what it takes to—"

"No, Amy," Rika said. "I can't imagine you without the ranch and your family. Don't throw that away." She turned back toward Tess and Frankie. "But I need a place to stay and a way to earn a living."

Tess and Frankie exchanged a quick glance. "You have it," Tess said.

Amy beamed. "Thank you."

But Rika didn't want to start her new life based on a lie. "There's something you need to know before you make that decision." The comforting warmth of Amy's knee touching hers gave her the courage to say it. "I'm not the woman who exchanged letters with Phin and accepted his proposal. She... Jo was my friend, but she died shortly before she could travel west." The pressure of Amy's knee against hers increased. "I took her place and pretended to be her."

Silence spread through the parlor, interrupted only by the shuffling of Amy's boots.

"What's your real name, then?" Frankie finally asked.

She tried to look Frankie in the eyes when she answered, "Hendrika Aaldenberg."

"Well, then." Frankie exchanged another glance with Tess before she stood and extended her hand. "Consider yourself hired, Hendrika Aaldenberg."

Rika blinked and stared at the hand without taking it. "Just like that?"

Frankie shrugged. "Tess and I both had to lie and pretend a thousand times to make it this far." She spread her arms wide to indicate the hotel. "I won't judge you for doing the same. Just promise to be as honest as you can from now on."

"I promise."

When Frankie offered her hand a second time, it took a nudge from Amy before Rika belatedly gripped it. By the time she took Tess's hand, her insides had stopped shaking. "Thank you. I swear you won't regret it."

"Oh, I know I won't." Frankie grinned. "Because now, you get to polish all the silverware."

HAMILTON HORSE RANCH
BAKER PRAIRIE, OREGON
JUNE 27, 1868

*M*AMA AND PAPA WERE WAITING on the veranda when Amy stopped her horse in the ranch yard. Part of her wanted to run over and tell them that Rika had stayed—had stayed because of her—while the other part wanted to climb back on Ruby and gallop off because she didn't know how to explain what was going on between her and Rika.

Then she remembered. She didn't have to explain. Her parents weren't so different from her. They would understand.

When she stepped onto the veranda, Papa took off her hat so she could make eye contact. "No Hendrika? So the stagecoach was already gone?"

"Oh, Amy, I'm so sorry." Mama rushed over and hugged her.

"No, it's... The stagecoach was gone by the time I made it to Baker Prairie, but I went after it and stopped it."

Mama let go of her, her face paling. "You stopped a stagecoach? Amy! You could have been shot!"

Amy decided not to mention that Jacob Garfield had indeed shot at her. Her parents would hear about it soon enough, but for now, it wasn't important. "I'm fine, Mama. See?" She pointed at her body. "No bullet holes."

"What about Hendrika?" Papa asked. "Did she leave anyway? She didn't...?"

Amy gazed around to make sure that neither Nattie nor any of the ranch hands were within earshot. Her heart pounded in excitement. "Rika stayed. She says she..." Amy studied the weathered boards of the veranda and then peeked up at her parents. "She likes me too."

Papa gave her a hearty slap on the back. "Well, what's not to like? You're our daughter after all." Then her smile gentled in a way that it only did around her family. "I'm so happy for you. I had a feeling she was smitten with you too, but I wasn't sure she was ready to face those feelings. But where is she?"

Mama craned her neck as if looking for Rika.

"She couldn't come back here. Not with Phin..." Amy gestured to Phin's cabin. "Frankie and Tess hired her to help with their new hotel."

"Oh, that's a marvelous idea," Mama said, smiling.

"Yeah," Papa murmured. She wasn't smiling. "I just hope the townsfolk will leave her alone. You know how people are. Now that she's refused to marry Phin, there'll be talk."

Fierce protectiveness engulfed Amy like a tidal wave. She curled her hands into fists. "If anyone dares to say one word to Rika, I'll—"

"Amy." Papa laid a hand on one of her fists. "People will say what they want to say. You can't stop them any more than you could stop a herd of spooked horses."

"But I won't stand by while they pick on Rika. I just... I can't."

Papa let go of her fist, put both hands on her shoulders, and looked into her eyes. "I know. But learn to pick your battles wisely. You have to learn not to listen to what people say. Listen to your heart instead."

Amy dropped her fists and sighed. "I'll try." The whinny of a horse made her look up. Phin's horse was still in the corral. For the first time, she thought about how the townsfolk's gossip would affect Phin. "How is Phin doing?"

Mama and Papa exchanged a quick glance. "I haven't seen him since Hendrika left," Mama said.

As much as Amy wanted to, she couldn't avoid talking to Phin. He was her friend after all, and she had to make sure he was all right. She just didn't know how to look him in the eyes. "I'll go talk to him," she said but didn't move from the veranda.

"Whatever you do, don't tell him why Hendrika refused to marry him," Mama said, the expression on her face serious. "No man reacts well to being rejected for another. And if that other person is a woman..." She shook her head. "I would like to think that Phin would grow to accept it, but I just don't know."

Amy sighed again. Her life would never be easy. But then she remembered how Rika had embraced her when they had said good-bye in the hotel's parlor. She could still feel those warm arms around her and the tickle of hair against her cheek, could still smell Rika's unmistakable scent that she wanted to breathe in forever...

Mama cleared her throat.

Shaking herself out of her daydream, Amy squared her shoulders. *It's worth it.* After one fortifying glance back at her parents, she trudged across the ranch yard. In front of the cabin's door, she paused and tried to rein in her racing heart. She timidly knocked on the door. When no answer came, she knocked again, this time more loudly.

The cabin's door creaked open. Phin stood in the doorway. He looked none the worse for wear.

But that couldn't be true, could it? Amy knew that if Rika had rejected her, she would be devastated. Phin was probably hiding his true feelings, because that's what men did. "I thought I'd see how you are doing with...all that happened today. So, how are you?"

Phin rolled his eyes. "Would everyone please stop askin' me that? Like I just told Miss Nattie, I'm fine." He pointed over his shoulder.

Amy peeked past him into the cabin.

Nattie sat at the table, trailing her fingers over the burned edges on one side.

"Oh." Amy looked from her sister to Phin. "Didn't you tell me just a few months ago that it's not proper for a young, unmarried lady to visit a bachelor without a chaperone?"

Nattie flushed, and even Phin's cheeks reddened beneath his stubble. "That's what I told Miss Nattie, but it seems she's just as stubborn as her older sister."

"I just wanted to make sure you're all right," Nattie said from the table.

"I'm fine. It just wasn't meant to be, and that's that. Maybe it's better that way. I'll start my ranch soon, and havin' womenfolk around would just be a distraction."

"Thanks a lot," Amy and Nattie said at the same time.

He blushed again and scratched his neck. "You know what I mean."

I do. Even now, Amy couldn't think of anything but Rika. What was she doing right now? And how long until she could ride to town and visit her? She would try to sit next to her in church on Sunday, even if it meant putting on a dress. She shuffled her feet. "All right, then. If you're sure you're all right, I'll go get some work done." She glanced at her sister. "You coming?"

Nattie clutched the table. "In a second."

Shrugging, Amy turned and headed for the stable. *Best keep busy, or I'll go mad waiting for Sunday to arrive.*

BAKER PRAIRIE, OREGON
JULY 4, 1868

E XCITEMENT FILLED THE AIR IN Baker Prairie. People milled down the decorated street. Flags hung from roofs and windows, and garlands were strung across the street, displaying the nation's red, white, and blue colors.

While Nattie took in the festivities with wide eyes, Amy had no eyes for anything going on around her. All she could think about was Rika. How would they behave around each other when they saw each other again? What would they say? After not seeing Rika all week, her excitement and her anxiety had built.

Old Jack threw his head up as a firecracker went off just a few yards away, startling Amy from her thoughts.

"Whoa!" Luke stopped the wagon next to the Garfields' dry-goods store. Farther down the street, a procession formed, so there was no getting through to the hotel. "You'll have to walk the rest of the way."

Amy nodded and climbed down. From beside the wagon, she looked up at her family.

Everyone had put on their Sunday best. Mama was as beautiful as ever in a green dress that set off the color of her eyes, and Papa looked the perfect elegant gentleman in gray doeskin trousers, a frock coat, and a cravat, tipping her top hat at the ladies walking down the boardwalk.

In moments like this, Amy still found it hard to believe that her father was a woman. After one last wave, she weaved through the forming crowd toward the hotel.

The new hotel was even more heavily decorated than the surrounding buildings. Large signs announced that the hotel was open for business now and offered rooms at a reduced rate during the Fourth of July celebrations.

Amy's shoulders slumped. Now that there was a lot of work to do at the hotel, would Rika even have time to enjoy the festivities with her?

Well, go in and find out. As she entered the lobby, she reached up to take off her hat, then remembered that she was wearing a small ladies' hat. Nervously, she rubbed her damp palms along the sides of her dress.

In the small lobby, she came face to face with Rika.

They stared at each other.

Amy took in Rika's purple silk taffeta dress, which curved nicely along her hips and wasn't cut quite so high at the neck as the other dresses she usually saw around town. A red, white, and blue cockade was pinned to her chest, drawing Amy's gaze to her breasts.

Rika smoothed her hands over the ruffles on her shoulders.

Stop staring and say something! But what? Amy licked her lips. "Uh, your dress is beautiful." *And so are you.* She didn't dare say it, though, not sure if it was proper.

"It's one of Tess's." Rika tugged at the neckline. "You don't think it's too daring?"

Amy's gaze darted down before she quickly forced it back up. "No. The neckline is just fine."

Rika took in every inch of her. "I'm not used to seeing you in a dress."

Amy patted her dress and the petticoats beneath. Did that mean Rika liked the way she looked in a dress? Or did she prefer to see her in pants? Maybe she should have worn something else.

"You look beautiful too," Rika finally said.

Amy shuffled her feet. "Oh. Thank you."

Silence spread between them.

"Hendrika?" Tess called from upstairs. "Is it a new guest?"

"It's Amy," Rika called back.

"Why don't you take her to the parlor?"

"Oh. Of course. I'm sorry. I must have forgotten my manners. It's just..." Rika tugged on her dress again and then gestured from Amy to herself. "This is all so..."

Amy blanched. She hadn't changed her mind, had she?

"It's just all so new," Rika said. "I barely know how to behave around you."

Amy nodded, glad that Rika had the courage to say what she was only thinking. At least they were both feeling the same.

Tess came down the stairs. "Hello, Amy. Why don't you use our parlor for a visit?"

Amy untied her hat with its red, white, and blue ribbon streamers, just so she would have something to do with her hands. Should she have brought flowers or a little present as a sign of her affection? She wished there were a protocol for courting another woman. "Uh, actually, I wanted to see if you could spare Rika for an hour or two. I would love to show her the celebration."

Rika's eyes lit up. She sent Tess a hopeful glance.

Tess smiled. "Of course. You two run along and enjoy yourselves."

"Are you sure?" Rika looked back and forth between them. "We have a lot of guests coming in later and—"

"Go. Frankie and I will manage on our own." Tess pushed her toward the door.

Rika stumbled a bit, and Amy caught her. Holding on to both of Rika's arms, she looked into her eyes from just inches away.

Rika stared back before she cleared her throat and pulled away. "I have to get my shawl." She pointed over her shoulder.

Grinning, Tess watched as Amy waited in the doorway and shuffled her feet.

Then, finally, they were out on the street, where Amy could breathe more freely. She kept one eye on the busy street and one eye on Rika while they wandered toward the wooden platform that had been erected in front of the saloon. The president of the bank was delivering a passionate speech. They stopped for a moment to listen as he read the Declaration of Independence before they continued down the street.

Next to them, young couples strolled arm in arm.

Amy bit her lip. She didn't dare take Rika's arm like that.

Surrounded by the noise of gun salutes, firecrackers, and a brass band playing, they made their way down the street. Children shouted as they hopped toward the finish line in a sack race.

"I did that too when I was a little girl," Amy said.

Rika smiled as if imagining her at that age. "I bet you won."

Amy felt her cheeks heat. "I did."

Chuckling, Rika linked her arm through Amy's as they continued to weave around the other spectators.

A tingle ran through Amy's arm and down the rest of her body. She strode with measured steps, feeling a bit awkward but at the same time also proud of being the one who got to stroll with Rika on her arm.

Next to the church, picnic tables had been set up beneath a group of oaks.

"Oh." Amy stopped and looked at the people sitting at the picnic tables. "I should have thought of bringing a picnic."

Rika squeezed her arm. "It doesn't matter. Spending time together is—"

"Good day, Ms. Bruggeman," someone said next to them.

Amy turned.

Gary Snyder stood in front of them, a glass of lemonade in his hands. He nodded at her. "Hello, Amy."

Under normal circumstances, Amy would have been happy to see Gary and talk horses with him, but now he was wasting her valuable time with Rika. She barely held herself back from asking what he wanted.

Apparently, he didn't want anything from her. He turned toward Rika. "I'm Gary Snyder. We met at the dance a few months ago, but we haven't been formally introduced. Can I offer you a glass of lemonade?"

"No, thank you. I'm not thirsty."

"Oh." Gary stared down at the glass in his hands. "Well, then. Maybe another time." He hurried away.

Before Amy could breathe a sigh of relief, Alex Tolridge, the doctor's son, stepped down from the boardwalk and headed in their direction.

Amy tried to walk around him, wanting to be alone with Rika, but Alex approached them and doffed his hat. "Miss Hamilton, Miss Bruggeman."

"Aaldenberg," Rika said. At his startled glance, she added, "Bruggeman is my maiden name. I decided to go back to using my late husband's name."

Alex worried his hat between his hands. "Well, then, Miss Aaldenberg. I was wondering if you would do me the honor of accompanying me to the dance tonight."

Amy's nostrils flared. She bunched her hands into fists but had to watch as Alex directed a hopeful grin at Rika. A bitter taste coated her tongue, and she wanted to spit. *Is this how it's going to be? Will I have to watch while every bachelor in town tries to court her?*

"I appreciate the kind offer, Mister…"

"Tolridge."

Rika gave a nod. "Mr. Tolridge. As I said, I appreciate the offer, but I'm terribly sorry. I'm sure you realize I came west to marry Mr. Sharpe."

"But you didn't," he said.

"Because I realized that after losing my late husband, a veteran of the war, I couldn't bear to remarry." Rika held his gaze, the picture of sincerity.

Because she is sincere. She can't bear to remarry, but not because she's still in love with her dead husband. She's in love with me. At the thought, Amy's fists uncurled and the tension in her shoulders dissipated. *At least I hope she is.*

"I understand." Alex settled the rumpled hat back on his head.

When he gave a small bow and walked away, Rika called after him, "Oh, Mr. Tolridge?"

He turned around.

"Would you please let your bachelor friends know? It would spare them and me a lot of embarrassment if they didn't approach me with marital intentions."

"Of course." Alex hurried away and disappeared in the crowd, saving the remains of his dignity.

Rika looped her arm through Amy's again.

"You're incredible," Amy said. Instead of condemning her to suffer in silence, Rika had solved the problem once and for all.

"No, I'm not." Rika shook her head. "It's just that I finally learned not to settle for what I can have, but to strive for what I want."

Amy held her breath for a moment. She leaned close on the crowded street and whispered, "And that's me?"

Rika nodded and smiled.

Happiness flowed through Amy like golden sunlight. She felt as if she were floating as they continued their stroll around town.

It wasn't long before another man crossed their way.

Amy was ready to punch every bachelor who came within a five-yard radius of Rika, but then she realized that it was Phin. With a big lump in her throat, she let go of Rika's arm.

Phin and Rika stared at each other for a moment, then Phin snatched off his hat and kneaded it between his hands. "Hello, Hendrika."

"Hello, Phin. How are you doing?"

He stuck his finger under his collar as if it were too tight. "Oh, I'm fine. Today was my last day workin' for the Hamiltons, but I guess Amy told you that."

Amy hadn't. She had been too tongue-tied when she had seen Rika in her new dress.

"And how are you?" Phin asked.

"I'm fine too."

They stood awkwardly while people veered around them, throwing curious glances their way.

"Um, if you'd excuse me. The game is about to start." He pointed toward the field where a few of the town's gentlemen were preparing to play baseball. Before either of them could say another word, he hurried away.

Rika took Amy's arm again. Her hands were trembling, and she held on more tightly than necessary. "Lord, that was awkward. Well, at least he's still talking to me."

Amy sighed. "His pride took quite the beating when you refused to marry him. Guess it'll take some time." At least she hoped that was all it would take. She set them off in another direction, away from the baseball field and Phin.

Before they reached the end of the street, they were stopped by two more bachelors who apparently hadn't met Alex yet and hadn't been informed not to approach Rika. One of them offered to explain the rules of baseball to her while the other asked if she would watch the fireworks display with him in the evening.

After Rika had said no to both offers, she sighed. "Maybe we should have taken Tess up on her offer to use their parlor for a visit."

Their gazes met.

"Do you want us to go back?" Amy pointed in the direction of the hotel.

With reddened cheeks, Rika nodded. "As nice as the festivities are, I would rather talk to you than to every bachelor in town."

Amy set them off toward the hotel as fast as her dress and her Sunday shoes allowed.

BAKER PRAIRIE, OREGON
JULY 5, 1868

*R*ika's Sunday-polished boots squeaked over the church floor as she fidgeted. She wanted to slip past Reverend Rhodes and out of the church, hoping to escape before he could ask about her canceled wedding plans.

But the pastor stood in front of the church portal and exchanged pleasantries with Tess and Frankie, and Rika knew she couldn't leave before it was her turn to say good-bye to him.

"You should come by one morning," Tess said. "We're planning on offering breakfast at the hotel too, and my cousin is a wonderful cook."

When Rika had hired on as a maid in the hotel, she had assumed that Tess would rule the kitchen, while Frankie would take care of their guests' horses. Instead, she found that Frankie and Tess shared tasks equally.

Tess patted Frankie's hand and smiled at her, not hiding her affection.

Rika straightened her shoulders too. *Frankie and Tess hold their heads up high, even though they had to listen to the reverend going on and on about every sin in the Good Book.* They thanked the pastor for his sermon as if he hadn't just promised them eternal hell. *It's almost as if they know better and are just humoring him.*

She watched them say good-bye to the pastor and wander away, arm in arm.

They're at peace with this. With themselves and each other. She wished the same for herself and Amy.

Finally, it was her turn to say good-bye. She shook the pastor's hand, mumbled a few pleasantries, and then tried to slip past him.

But the reverend blocked the doorway. "I see Mr. Sharpe missed church today, which is very unfortunate because what I had to say in my sermon seems to fit him pretty well."

Rika squirmed. "I'm sure he's very busy preparing to set up his own ranch."

The reverend's gaze seemed to drill into her. "I won't have such behavior in my congregation. Marriage is not to be taken lightly. It's not something to toy with."

"Which is why we decided not to get married after all," Rika said, struggling to hold his gaze. "I assure you Mr. Sharpe was never anything but a gentleman toward me."

Reverend Rhodes stared at her for a moment longer. He pursed his lips in disapproval but finally stepped aside and allowed her to pass.

Rika hurried down the church steps, closely followed by Amy and the rest of the Hamilton family.

Tess and Frankie joined them. "Come over to the hotel and pick up a basket before you leave," Tess said. "We prepared too much food for the Fourth of July celebrations, and now we have a lot of leftovers."

"If you have any apple pie, I won't say no to that," Luke said. "You know I always had a bit of a sweet tooth."

"What about you young folks?" Frankie nodded at Amy, Nattie, and Rika. "Hendrika worked hard this week, and I bet the rest of you did too. Since you didn't get to have a picnic yesterday, maybe you could go on a picnic today?"

"Oh, could we?" Rika clapped her hands. "I've never gone on a picnic." Back in Boston, Sundays had been spent mending clothes, writing letters, and fighting over the magazines in Mrs. Gillespie's parlor.

Nattie shook her head. "I promised Phin one last reading lesson before he leaves, so I'd rather go home."

Rika struggled not to let her excitement show. She glanced at Amy, waiting for her answer. Maybe just the two of them could go. She longed for a moment alone with Amy.

The same longing burned in Amy's eyes. "Sure," Amy said. "If you want to have a picnic, we'll have one. I know the perfect place."

With the basket of food in one hand, Amy wandered along the river. They passed a few nice spots, but Amy kept going and Rika followed. Soon, the river meandered through the forest.

"You want to have a picnic in the forest?" Rika asked.

"Just wait and see. I promise it'll be perfect."

They wandered through the forest, padding over a carpet of pine needles and ducking beneath low-hanging branches.

"There." Amy pointed.

Rika stopped to take it all in.

The river twisted south, flowing in a wide arch. In that bend of the river, the trees parted, and they stepped onto a meadow dotted with wildflowers. A willow growing along the bank dipped its branches into the water. Colorful ducks bobbed up and down, paddling against the gentle current.

"Oh, Amy. It's beautiful." The Hamiltons had taken her to almost every part of their land, but she'd never seen the hidden meadow before.

"Papa brought me and Nattie here after Measles, our first mare, died. It's a special place."

Their gazes met and held.

Rika touched Amy's forearm and let her hand linger. "Thank you for sharing it with me."

Amy smiled and lifted her hand as if wanting to touch Rika's cheek but then pulled back and said, "You're very welcome." She turned away and spread a blanket over a flat part of the meadow. After sniffing, she wrinkled her nose. "Sorry. It's a saddle blanket and might be a bit smelly. I should have remembered to bring a clean one."

"It's all right. You don't need to impress me. Just spending time together is enough."

The worried expression on Amy's face faded. She plopped onto the blanket and immediately took off the hated sunbonnet and unlaced her Sunday boots. "Come on." She tugged Rika down next to her. "Let's get comfortable."

Rika took off her boots. When Amy rolled down her socks, Rika caught a glimpse of her bare calves. How soft and pale her skin looked, especially against her tan hands. Wetting her dry lips with her tongue, Rika imagined touching that smooth skin.

Amy nudged Rika's foot with her big toe, then let their feet linger against each other. "Hungry?"

"Starved." Reluctantly, Rika forced her gaze away from Amy's legs.

Heavenly smells wafted up when Amy opened the basket. They sampled pieces of ham, cheese, roasted chicken, and fresh bread with apple butter.

"Mmm." Amy moaned. "Either it's the fresh air or Frankie is a really good cook."

Rika hummed her agreement. "Did they pack anything for dessert? We bought fresh fruit for the hotel, and I think there were leftovers of that too."

"Yeah, I think…" Amy lifted the cloth from the basket. "Oh."

"What?" Rika leaned forward and put a hand on Amy's shoulder to peek into the basket.

Next to the last piece of bread, a box of ripe strawberries waited to be eaten.

An image of Frankie hand-feeding berries to Tess flashed through her mind. All of a sudden, she became overly aware of her hand resting on Amy's shoulder. Heat ricocheted between them.

Amy pulled back her hand from the basket as if the strawberries were poisonous.

Rika let go of Amy's shoulder and stared at her hands in her lap. The peaceful atmosphere was gone, and she hated the sudden awkwardness that had sprung up. She shook her head at herself. "You know, they're just strawberries, but we're both acting as if they are forbidden fruit from the Garden of Eden."

"W-what?" Amy stared at her with wide green eyes.

Rika sighed. "I watched Frankie and Tess at church earlier. When the pastor talked about unwed folks carrying on with each other and other sins, they didn't duck their heads in shame. I don't believe they think of themselves as sinners—at least not for liking each other the way they do. One day, I want to be able to think like that too."

"I want that too," Amy said, her voice barely more than a whisper. "I'm trying, really. It's just hard to get used to the thought that it's all right to feel like this. And when I see how easy it seems to be for you, I feel guilty about feeling guilty." Her lips formed a trembling grin that didn't reach her eyes.

Rika settled cross-legged on the blanket. "Easy?" She shook her head. "It's not easy for me either, but I've seen sin and crime and cruelty in my life, and I know that this," she touched her chest, then Amy's, "is not it. I watched one of my half brothers being stillborn because my father was too drunk to fetch the midwife. I've seen greedy overseers beat mill girls half to death and children starve because no one cared."

Amy reached over and gripped Rika's hand with both of hers.

The gentle touch sent tingles up Rika's arm, distracting her from thoughts of the past for a moment. "My whole life has been a struggle to survive, and I never thought it could be different, that there could be more to life," she said. "Now I feel like I'm living, not just existing, for the very first time, and I have a hard time believing that what I feel is a bad thing. Compared to all the cruelty I've seen, how can this," she nodded down at their joined hands, "be a sin?"

"Mama and Papa say the same thing, but I let myself believe for so long that it's wrong and that I need to hide that part of myself, so it's hard to change that kind of thinking."

Now it was Rika's turn to squeeze Amy's hands. "It's all right. Maybe it's easier for me because I never really thought about two women together before. I didn't let the thought that it's wrong fester in my head and in my heart like you did."

"Then where do we go from here?"

"Hm." Rika peered at the basket, then grinned up at Amy through half-lowered lids. "We could start by having dessert." She lifted one of the dark red berries from the basket and held it out to Amy.

Amy's gaze darted back and forth between the strawberry and Rika. Then she leaned forward and ate the strawberry out of Rika's hand, careful not to touch her fingers with her lips in the process.

Rika licked remnants of berry juice from her fingers.

Amy's chewing stopped as she watched, her eyes darkening with a hunger that had nothing to do with food. She cleared her throat and reached into the basket. "Here. You try one."

Rika moved closer and ate the strawberry out of Amy's hand. The sweet, ripe taste burst on her tongue. Before she stopped chewing, she picked up the next berry.

They fed each other berry after berry. With each one, their lips became more daring and their fingers lingered longer.

"This is the last one," Amy finally said.

"Share with me?"

When Amy nodded, Rika took the strawberry from her hand with careful teeth. She straightened and waited with the strawberry clamped between her lips.

Amy hesitated but then slid closer. Her knees pressed against Rika's. Heat shot through Rika as a warm hand came to rest against her hip, just before Amy leaned forward and bit off a piece of the strawberry.

All thoughts of strawberries vanished as their lips brushed—once, then, after they had both swallowed their piece of strawberry, again.

They separated and stared at each other.

Rika wanted to feel those soft lips against hers again, but Amy shuddered, pulled away, and rolled onto her back, breathing heavily.

Rika settled down next to her and pressed her hand to her chest. "My heart is beating awfully fast."

Amy rolled around and leaned over her with a concerned expression. "Are you afraid?"

Smiling, Rika shook her head. "Just a bit overwhelmed."

"So it was all right that I...that we...?"

Rika nodded. "It was wonderful. Kissing never felt this nice." She slid her hand into Amy's and closed her eyes with a contented sigh. Her thoughts drifted.

"Before you met me, did you ever think you might have feelings for women?" Amy's low voice interrupted her daydreams.

Rika turned her head and opened one eye. "Before I met you, I never had feelings for anyone. Not that kind of feelings. How did you know?" While Rika hadn't grown up around love of any kind, Amy had seemed aware that two women could love each other, even before meeting Tess and Frankie.

"A few years ago, I used to spend a lot of time with Hannah. One afternoon, we went riding. When our horses got tired, we rested in a meadow, just like we're doing now."

A strange feeling bristled along Rika's skin and made her clutch Amy's hand. She rubbed her finger over the calluses. Had Amy held Hannah's hand too? Had they lain together, resting against each other like this? Her throat tightened. Blood rushed through her ears, and she heard Amy's voice as if from under water.

"Rika?"

A squeeze to her hand made her blink. She shook her head to clear it.

"Hey." Amy caressed her wrist in a gesture so tender that it made her shiver. "You all right?"

"I don't like the thought of you with Hannah."

Amy's fingers froze against her wrist.

"Oh." Rika pressed her fingers to her traitorous mouth. She hadn't meant to say that out loud.

Tilting her head, Amy stared down at her. Then, slowly, a grin formed on her lips. She pulled Rika's hand away from her mouth and pressed a kiss to her palm. "You've got nothing to worry about, you know?"

"You don't have feelings for Hannah anymore?"

"No." A kiss to the inside of her wrist made Rika's arm tingle up to her shoulder. "I've never felt for Hannah or anyone else the way I feel for you," Amy whispered against her skin.

The roaring in Rika's ears finally receded. She relaxed back onto the blanket.

After a while, with their shoulders resting against each other, Amy continued. "When we were out riding together, Hannah used to go on and on about Josh and how she felt about him, how her heartbeat picked up when she heard his step, how her hands got damp and her stomach fluttered when he was close." Amy swallowed. She glanced at Rika, then away. "And it dawned on me that she could have been describing my feelings for her."

Rika tightened her hold on Amy's hand. *Don't be childish. That was years ago, and Hannah is happily married now.* She forced herself to focus on Amy. "You understood what you were feeling even back then?"

"Not at first. I told myself it was what every girl felt for her best friend."

"What changed?"

"A few years ago, two widows in town were living together," Amy said, gazing into the sky as if it showed her the past. "Some of the boys and girls made fun of them, calling them strange for preferring to keep company with each other rather than accept a new husband. But I never paid much attention. To me, it felt perfectly..." She hesitated but then said, "... natural for them to want to spend time with each other, not with a man."

"Just like you wanted to spend time with Hannah." Rika pressed a hand to her stomach until Amy reached over and took that hand too. "Those two widows...were they just friends?"

Amy's grip tightened. "No. One day, someone found them in bed together, having...you know. Sharing the bed like a man and a woman would."

Rika stared at their entwined hands, then up into Amy's eyes. "That's when you knew what your feelings meant?"

Biting her lip, Amy nodded. "I knew I was the same, but I didn't want to be. Not when it could cost me everything. People drove them out of town." She shivered. "No one did anything to defend them. No one, not even my parents. So I knew I needed to bury my feelings deep inside and never act on them."

Rika rubbed her hands along Amy's arms. "Did you ask your parents why they didn't help?"

"Oh, no." Amy shook her head, eyes wide. "At least not back then. I never talked to anyone about it. I was afraid someone would think I was too interested in such relationships. Now I know that Mama and Papa only learned about what the townsfolk did to the widows days after it happened. But back then, I thought they agreed with what the people in town said." Amy lowered her gaze. "I thought if they ever found out, it would change how they felt about me."

"Amy." A squeeze to her hands got Amy to look up. "Nothing could change your parents' love for you." She swallowed down a complicated mix of sadness, envy, and happiness.

Amy pulled one of her hands out of Rika's grasp and ran her fingers through her hair. She rolled around and stared down at Rika. "I know they love me. But how could it not change how they felt about me when it changed how I felt about myself?"

Do I feel different about myself too? Rika closed her eyes and listened, trying to reach deep inside, but all she felt was Amy's warm, almost desperate grip on her hand and the way their fingers fit against each other. She opened her eyes and smiled. "Maybe it did change how they feel about you. But change isn't always bad, is it?"

Amy's grip on her hand loosened, and she returned Rika's smile. "You're right. It's not." She sank back onto the blanket and exhaled.

Rika cuddled closer until she felt Amy's warmth. Her eyes drifted shut.

A light breeze brushed over her bare feet, and she wiggled her toes, enjoying the feeling. The wind carried the scent of wildflowers and moss. The sun shone down on them, and Amy's hand holding hers warmed up her skin even more. Birdsong and the river's soft gurgling almost lulled her to sleep.

She forced open heavy lids. When she turned her head, Amy met her gaze and smiled.

A feeling Rika had never known filled her. *This is peace.* She breathed in the scent of wildflowers and Amy. *Or maybe,* she thought, *maybe it's love.*

BAKER PRAIRIE, OREGON
JULY 25, 1868

RIKA DIPPED THE BRUSH INTO the bucket of soapy water and scrubbed the floorboards with both hands, putting all her weight into it.

"Easy, easy." Tess paused in the doorway and laughed. "We need those boards, you know?"

"Sorry." With some effort, she slowed her frantic scrubbing.

"Are you, by any chance, in a hurry?" Tess asked.

"No, it's just... No."

But Tess's knowing grin told her that her employer already knew why she was so eager to finish her work for the day. "Amy promised she would come over and take you out riding, didn't she?"

Rika took one hand off the brush and rubbed her cheek. It felt hot. "I'm behaving like a smitten young girl, not like a twenty-three-year-old widowed woman, aren't I?" When she thought of Amy, she felt like a smitten young girl. Butterflies swarmed in her belly whenever she daydreamed about holding Amy's hand during a stroll over their meadow.

Smiling, Tess walked over and took the brush from Rika's hands. "You're acting like a woman in love, and there's nothing wrong with that."

In love. Yes. Rika had admitted to herself that she felt much more than infatuation for Amy, and here, in the safe haven of the hotel, she had come to believe that there was nothing wrong with that. When Amy came to visit, Tess and Frankie welcomed her with open arms. They provided them with a place to meet in the hotel or gave Rika the afternoon off so she could ride out to the meadow and spend time with Amy.

The stairs creaked, and then Frankie poked her head into the room. "There's a suitor here to call on you."

Rika ground her teeth together. She had thought that Baker Prairie's bachelors would finally leave her alone. "Send him away."

"I'm sorry, Amy," Frankie called down the stairs. "Rika doesn't want to—"

"Amy?" Warmth rushed through Rika's belly. She jumped to her feet, hurried past Tess, and nudged Frankie aside. "Amy, wait, I'm coming!" After taking a single step down the stairs, she remembered that she was supposed to scrub the floor and turned back.

"Go," Tess said. "I'll finish up here."

"Thank you." Taking the stairs two at a time, Rika hurried down to the parlor and smoothed her hands over her wrinkled skirt. When she saw Amy fidgeting next to the front door, she slid to a stop and drank her in—the wind-blown hair, the glowing green eyes, and the slender hand worrying her hat.

"You're here already," Rika said, suddenly tongue-tied.

"Yes. Oh, here. These are for you." Amy brought her other hand out from behind her back and presented a beautiful bouquet of wildflowers. "I picked them on our meadow."

Their fingers touched when Rika took the flowers, and she let the touch linger for a moment, enjoying the tingles that shot through her body. Then she lifted the flowers to her nose. As she inhaled their sweet scent, she remembered how Amy had told her about Mr. Garfield picking flowers for his wife. *Now I, too, have someone who cares for me enough to waste an hour of daylight to pick flowers for me.* She couldn't believe her good fortune. With a lump in her throat, she said, "They're beautiful. Thank you."

After a quick glance left and right, she pulled Amy into the kitchen, leaned forward, and kissed her on the lips.

When Amy dropped her hat and wrapped both arms around her, Rika pressed closer until the scent of leather, horse, and Amy swept over her. Drowning in Amy, intoxicated, she teased the corner of Amy's mouth with her tongue.

Their tongues slid against each other. Amy moaned and nearly bit down in surprise.

Rika drew back and whispered a kiss against Amy's lips. "Careful." She brushed a few red locks from Amy's face and cleared her dry throat. "Did you bring Cin?"

"Yes," Amy said, her voice so husky that Rika wanted to kiss her again. "He's waiting for you right outside."

"Then let's go." Rika took her hand and pulled her out of the kitchen and to the door. Maybe they could ride out to their meadow, and she could pick some flowers for Amy, just to show her that she cared for her enough to waste an hour of daylight too.

SHARPE HORSE RANCH
BAKER PRAIRIE, OREGON
AUGUST 8, 1868

A T THE TOP OF A hill, Amy pulled Old Jack and the wagon to a stop. "There it is."

Rika looked down to where Phin had established his ranch. The cabin he had built was crude and small, but it would protect him from the wind and rain until he could replace it with a better one later.

The clanking of steel against wood drifted up the hill. Phin stood in the middle of his ranch yard, splitting a log. He had taken off his shirt, and his muscles bulged as he drove the wedge into the log.

Her friend Jo would have swooned over this display of masculinity, but Rika realized that it left her unimpressed. Instead, she tugged on Amy's gloves, prompting her to take them off. The feel of Amy's skin against hers was addictive.

Amy entwined their fingers and brushed her thumb over the back of Rika's hand, sending tingles up and down her spine. "Do you feel guilty for not marrying him?" she asked, her voice low.

"I feel bad about deceiving him—all of you—for so long. But I don't regret calling off the wedding."

A relieved smile darted across Amy's face. Just as she lifted Rika's hands to kiss them, Phin looked up from his log.

Rika wrenched her hands from Amy's soft grasp.

"Rika? What...?"

"Phin is watching," Rika whispered.

Amy blushed a bright red and busied her hands with the reins.

Below them, Phin set down the wedge and the ax. He shrugged into his shirt and picked up his hat before striding across the ranch yard toward them. "Amy, Hendrika." He tipped his hat and hastily buttoned his shirt.

"Hello, Phin," Amy said. "How's it going with the ranch?"

"Oh, good, good. I'm splittin' logs for a corral."

"Do you need help with that?" Amy asked.

"No, thanks. I can manage."

Silence spread between them, interrupted only by the soft sounds of Amy fiddling with the reins and Phin shuffling his feet.

Oh, Lord, this is awkward. If Rika wanted to stay, she needed to clear the air between them once and for all. "Can you give us a minute?" she asked Amy.

Amy hesitated.

"Please?" While Rika appreciated her protectiveness, it was better if Amy wasn't involved. She didn't want to destroy the friendship between Amy and Phin, and she certainly didn't want Phin to start suspecting the real reason she'd refused to marry him. Someday, they might need to figure out a way to tell him, but not now, when it was still so new.

"All right. I'll go say hello to Lancelot." Amy pointed at Phin's horse that stood grazing next to the cabin. She slid from the wagon and, after one last glance at Rika, walked away.

Phin shoved his hands into his pant pockets. "So you're stayin' for good?"

Rika nodded.

"Must have changed your mind at the very last second. Charlie said he saw you climb into the stagecoach."

"Yes." It was hard, but she forced herself to look him in the eyes. "I know it must be awkward for you. I'm sure people are talking."

He snorted. "Oh, yeah. They're comin' up with all sorts of hare-brained reasons for why we didn't wed—and why you stayed after all."

A lump formed in her throat. Did he suspect that she was staying because of Amy? She swallowed.

"Most think it's 'cause you hated life on the ranch," he said.

"No. I really liked living there."

"You just don't like me." He sounded almost calm, but Rika knew if nothing else, his pride had to be hurt.

Sighing, she climbed from the wagon seat and approached him. "I like you just fine, Phin." She touched his arm and then retreated. "But I don't love you. I'm sorry it took me so long to figure out I don't want to keep living my life making compromises. You deserve better than that too."

He rubbed the back of his neck and tilted his head, studying her for long moments. Then his shoulders settled into a more relaxed stance. "In the end, you probably did me a favor. My heart wasn't really in it either." A hesitant smile replaced his frowning expression.

The tightness in her throat eased, and she breathed in deeply.

Hesitant footsteps approached.

Rika looked up and waved Amy over.

Amy put on her gloves. "If you're ready, we should head back. I promised Frankie and Tess I'd have you back by six." She walked toward Rika to help her up on the wagon, but before she could do it, Phin stepped forward and lifted her up. Amy climbed up after her and looked down at him. "Don't be a stranger, all right? If you need help with anything, please let us know. Papa and I can ride over and help you out for a few hours."

Phin nodded.

Amy nodded back and then clicked at Old Jack.

As soon as they were out of sight, Rika slid closer on the wagon bench.

Amy pulled off one glove with her teeth and reached for her hand. "Is everything all right?"

"Everything's fine. I don't think he's too heartbroken about not marrying me."

Amy shook her head. "Strange. If I was in his shoes, I'd be devastated."

Rika had to smile at her puzzled expression. "He doesn't love me."

After stopping the wagon, Amy turned toward her on the wagon bench. Her gaze darted up and made eye contact, then veered away. "But I do," she whispered.

Rika threw her arms around Amy, causing her to drop the reins. "Oh, Amy. I love you too." She tightened her embrace. She had never thought she would find—or even seek—love, but now that she had, she never wanted to let her go.

They stayed that way, safe in each other's arms, until the stomping of Old Jack's hooves reminded them that it was time to head back.

BAKER PRAIRIE, OREGON
SEPTEMBER 5, 1868

*A*MY WOKE BEFORE SUNRISE. SHE lay in bed, not yet fully awake, until she remembered that it was Saturday. A big grin spread over her face. She would get to see Rika today. They would ride out to their meadow as they did every Saturday, pick flowers, share some bread and cheese—and maybe a few kisses—while lying on a blanket. The thought of feeling Rika's lips against hers set her blood on fire.

She scrambled out of bed. The sooner she got her chores done, the sooner she'd get to see Rika. On her way to the washstand, she looked out the window and froze.

Yesterday, the sun had been shining, ideal weather for a ride out to the meadow, but today, rain was coming down in buckets. Large puddles had formed in the ranch yard. Even the horses in the corral had sought out the shelter of the nearby oaks.

Amy's shoulders slumped. They wouldn't ride to their meadow after all. Finally, she straightened. She could still visit Rika at the hotel and spend an hour or two with her in Tess and Frankie's parlor. While it wouldn't be as nice as being alone with her on the meadow, it was better than not seeing her at all.

She struggled out of her nightgown and hurried through her ablutions.

Rain was still lashing down when Amy climbed out of the saddle and tied Ruby to the hitching rail in front of the hotel.

When she opened the door, Rika looked up from a ledger. Her eyes widened, and a smile blossomed on her face. She hurried around the front desk. "Amy! I didn't think you'd come today, with the rain and all. Oh, Lord, you're soaked. Come in."

447

At the entrance to the lobby, Amy knocked her boots together and stomped to get rid of the mud, but it was no use, so she finally took them off.

Instead of leading her to the parlor, Rika walked toward the stairs. When she pulled up her dress to climb the steps, Amy caught a glimpse of her legs. "I'll give you one of my dresses," Rika said, "then we can visit in the parlor while your clothes dry."

Amy hadn't seen Rika's room yet. Without speaking about it, they had behaved like a courting couple and stayed down in the parlor, where Tess or Frankie could chaperone. She hesitated in the doorway, taking in the narrow bed, the washstand, and the small table against one wall, until Rika ushered her in.

Water dripped from her hat as she took it off. She set down the boots she carried and struggled out of her jacket. Even beneath the canvas, her shirt was soaked and clung to her chest.

"Get out of those wet things," Rika said from her position bent over a trunk. When she straightened, she held a pale yellow dress in her hands.

Amy started to unbutton her shirt, very aware of Rika's presence. As she slid out of the shirt's sleeves, Rika's heated gaze sent goose bumps down her arms.

"You're cold." Rika let go of the dress and rushed over with a towel. She rubbed it over Amy's drenched locks, gently dried her face, and then trailed the towel over her arms and shoulders.

Waves of hot and cold raced across Amy's skin as she enjoyed the tender ministrations.

When Rika slid the towel across her collarbones, she paused and looked up.

Their gazes met.

Rika's eyes were so dark that they looked nearly midnight black. She was so close that her breath caressed Amy's face. She stared at the pink fullness of Rika's bottom lip and the elegant arc of her upper lip. Then her eyes fluttered shut as Rika's mouth met hers, connecting their bodies in a flash of heat. Her legs weakened, and she gripped Rika's hips. Through the thin fabric of her chemise, she felt Rika's bosom against hers.

After stumbling and nearly crashing into the table, they sank onto the bed.

Blood roared through Amy's ears as their kiss deepened. When she felt Rika's warm tongue sliding along hers, she thought she might faint.

Then Rika pulled back with a gasp. Her cheeks flushed, she stared at Amy, who stared back and lifted a hand to her thoroughly kissed lips.

Her whole body tingled, and despite her damp pants, she was no longer cold.

Groaning, Rika pulled away and sat on the edge of the bed. "I think..." She stopped and cleared her throat. "I think I'd better go and ask Tess if we can use the parlor to visit." After combing a handful of Amy's damp locks away from her face, she got up.

Amy sank back onto the bed, still touching her lips, and watched her go. If this was what she had to look forward to, she didn't mind the coming winter with all its rain.

HAMILTON HORSE RANCH
BAKER PRAIRIE, OREGON
SEPTEMBER 13, 1868

"ARE YOU SURE IT'S ALL right?" Rika asked when Amy pulled the wagon to a stop in front of the ranch's veranda.

"Why wouldn't it be? You've had supper with us many times before."

"Yes, but back then, I was Phin's betrothed, not your..." Rika trailed off, not sure what to call herself. Was there a word for what she and Amy were to each other?

"My sweetheart," Amy whispered, her cheeks stained a bright pink.

Smiling, Rika repeated the word to herself.

Amy reached over and squeezed her hand. "Don't worry about my parents. It'll be all right." Her voice trembled, though.

Steps thumped across the veranda, and Amy quickly let go of Rika's hand.

Phin stood on the veranda, putting on his hat. Had he seen them touch each other? But his smile was friendly when he greeted them.

"Hello, Phin. Are you gonna have supper with us?" Amy asked.

"No, I was just here to ask for some advice about my breedin' program."

"What did Papa say?"

He shook his head. "I didn't talk about it with your father. I asked Miss Nattie for advice."

"Nattie?"

"She kept notes on every foal born on the ranch for the last five years," he said, sounding defensive. "She knows which parents produce the best colors."

Amy tilted her head and then nodded. "I guess she does." She helped Rika down from the wagon. "You go on ahead. I'm gonna take care of Old Jack and then be right in."

Rika swallowed, for some reason uncomfortable with being left alone with Amy's family.

"You all right?" Phin asked when he passed her on the veranda steps. "You're white as a sheet."

"I'm fine," Rika said and navigated the steps on shaky legs. Now that Nora and Luke knew that she wasn't just Amy's friend, it felt as if she were about to have supper with her future in-laws. The thought startled her. *Oh, Lord.*

When she entered the house, Nattie was just setting the table. Luke and Nora were nowhere to be seen. "Papa is still in the stable, and Mama has an apple pie in the oven," Nattie said after greeting her.

"I'll go see if your mother needs any help," Rika said.

But when she wanted to slip past, Nattie held on to her elbow. "Did Amy tell you that I'll be leaving for New York next month?"

"She did. She's proud of you for aiming to become the first woman veterinary surgeon."

Nattie beamed. "She is?"

"Of course."

Nattie seemed to think about it for a moment before she nodded. She rearranged the cutlery on the table, even though it was already perfectly aligned. "Did you see Phin before he left?"

"Yes." Rika grinned. "Seems like he's spending more time at the ranch than when he lived here."

A blush shot up Nattie's neck. "Well, the same could be said about you. You spend a lot of time riding with Amy."

Now it was Rika's turn to blush. She clutched the edge of the table. Was Nattie suspecting anything?

Hard to tell. Nattie wasn't even looking at her. She stared at the forks and knives on the table. "I know you and Phin called off the wedding, but are you sure that...?"

Rika tilted her head. "What?"

Nattie slid one of the forks an inch to the left. "Would you mind terribly if Phin and I wrote each other while I'm away?" She peered over at Rika.

"He asked you to write him?" Rika had long suspected that Phin was smitten with Nattie, but he was too proud to court her before he had established a ranch of his own.

"No." Nattie blushed again. "I asked him."

Rika held back a grin. So Nattie was a typical Hamilton woman after all and had decided to ignore convention and do the asking. "What did he say?"

"He said he would write me." Nattie clutched her hands to her chest. "So do you mind?"

Rika crossed the room and squeezed Nattie's hand. "Why would I mind? I was the one who called off the wedding."

"Still," Nattie said. "I wanted to make sure."

"I don't mind at all."

When the rest of the Hamiltons and the ranch hands entered, Rika and Nattie shared a conspiratorial grin. Rika would protect Nattie's secret, hoping that, when push came to shove, Nattie would do the same for her.

Luke placed the tin cups back on their shelf and lingered against the wall, watching Hendrika dry another plate. She rubbed the back of her neck, a bit self-conscious about doing female chores in front of Hendrika.

But Hendrika smiled whenever she handed Luke a dried plate, apparently not thinking anything of it.

At the copper sink, Amy washed the dishes and glanced sidelong at Hendrika. "Is your shoulder all right to dry?"

"Stop worrying." Hendrika bumped her with one elbow. "It's been weeks since the shoulder gave me any trouble."

Luke bit back a smile. *Seems Amy is a mother hen too.*

A little later, Amy washed the last plate. When she handed it to Hendrika, their fingers touched and lingered. Then, as if becoming aware that Luke was watching, Amy pulled away and turned back toward the sink.

Luke threw a glance over her shoulder, making sure Nattie had left to check on the horses. "It's all right to show affection in this house, you know?"

As if demonstrating, Nora entered and wrapped her arm around Luke's hip.

"You have to be careful around other people," Luke said, "but you don't need to keep your feelings a secret from your own family."

"And you should tell your sister," Nora said.

Blushing, Amy busied herself drying her hands. "I will. But not yet. Speaking of secrets..." She looked up and gnawed on her lip. "Rika knows."

Luke tilted her head. "Knows what?"

"About you."

Dread rushed through Luke, but she forced back her instinctive reaction. Gratefully, she felt Nora lean against her. "You told her?"

"I told her a bit, and she guessed the rest."

Guessed? Luke's muscles tightened. Had she become so careless that people were able to guess now?

"Please don't be angry with Amy," Hendrika said. "She didn't intend to give away your secret, but when you first told them, she was upset and needed someone to talk to."

"I'm not angry," Luke said, more for Amy's benefit than Hendrika's. "I'm just..." She felt exposed, as if her skin had been stripped away, leaving her defenseless, but she wasn't ready to admit it and make herself even more vulnerable.

"I want you to know that I would never, ever give away your secret." Hendrika pressed one hand to her chest and earnestly stared at Luke. "I respect you so much for telling Amy." Her glance slid over to Nora. "Both of you."

Nora slipped her hand beneath Luke's vest and drew soothing circles across her back. "We told Amy so that she would have someone to talk to, someone who understands how she feels," Nora said. "Now I want to extend the same offer to you, Hendrika. If you ever need someone to talk to or have any questions, please don't hesitate to come to us."

Luke's chest expanded with love. *Here I am, acting like a scared rabbit, while Nora willingly opens up to Hendrika. Between the two of us, she's always been the brave one.* She leaned forward and pressed a kiss to Nora's cheek.

"Thank you." Hendrika smiled—a close-mouthed smile that only reluctantly spread across her face. "Actually, I do have a question, if you don't mind." She glanced at Amy, then back to Nora. "How did you decide to spend your life," she lowered her voice, "with a woman?"

"When I married Amy's father—" Nora stopped and pressed a hand to her mouth. "Lord, I keep saying that, don't I?

Some days, I forget that you girls know now." She sent Amy an apologetic glance, then smiled and rubbed Luke's back. "Some days, I even forget that Luke and I...that Amy is not physically a product of our love."

"Maybe I am," Amy said. "Having you and Papa in my life made me what I am today."

Luke sucked in a breath. Was she to blame for Amy looking for love with women, not men?

But Amy smiled, not looking accusing at all. "I learned early on to recognize love when I see it."

Do you see it when you look at Hendrika? The glances and little touches they kept trading made Luke think so.

"I only learned what love means when I met Luke," Nora said. "But my situation is different than yours. As far as people are concerned, I'm not sharing my life with a woman. I'm sharing it with Lucas Hamilton, my husband."

Amy and Hendrika exchanged glances. If they wanted to share their lives, they had to find another way. Amy sighed. "Summer is over. We won't be able to meet on our meadow for much longer."

Hendrika reached over and squeezed her hand. "We can always visit in the hotel's parlor."

"Yeah," Amy said, sounding frustrated.

Luke could sympathize. If she had gotten to see Nora only for an hour or two every week, it wouldn't have been enough either. She thought hard. Was there a way to help her daughter?

"Hendrika can visit you here too," Nora said. She looked into Hendrika's eyes. "You'll always be welcome in our home."

An idea crossed Luke's mind. "Nattie will leave soon to study back East."

"Yes," Hendrika said, "people in town are already talking about that."

"I can just imagine what they say about that strange Mr. Hamilton who lets his daughter go east unchaperoned." Luke snorted. "And even worse, he lets the girl study veterinary surgery, as if it wasn't enough to have one daughter riding around in pants."

When Hendrika looked stunned and then hid a smile behind her hand, Luke knew that was exactly what the townsfolk were saying. Not that she cared. "So, with Nattie gone, Nora back to teaching in the fall, and Amy and me out on the range all the time, the ranch needs a woman to look after it."

A squeeze from Nora let her know that she understood where Luke was going. "Yes. We might have to hire someone."

A broad smile spread over Amy's face. "You mean...?"

"It makes sense," Luke said. "We already know Hendrika and know she's a hard worker. Of course, to take proper care of her duties as a housekeeper, Hendrika would have to live on the ranch. Would you want to do that, Hendrika?"

"I—" Hendrika took Amy's hand and squeezed. "Yes, yes, of course! I'd love to live here."

Luke nodded. "Then it's settled."

Amy rushed forward and engulfed both Luke and Nora in an enthusiastic embrace. "Thank you, Mama and Papa."

Luke pressed a kiss to the reddish locks. Over Amy's head, she smiled at Hendrika. "You're welcome."

BAKER PRAIRIE, OREGON
SEPTEMBER 19, 1868

*A*MY WANDERED ACROSS THE MEADOW, gaze on the ground. She trailed her hand through the grass, parting it, and plucked a yellow buttercup. After discarding two that weren't pretty enough, she added a pink wildflower.

A few feet away, Ruby and Cinnamon lifted their heads and eyed Amy's bunch of flowers.

"Oh, no. You two go on eating your grass. These are for Rika." She lifted the flowers to her nose and inhaled their sweet scent. Her eyes fluttered shut as she imagined Rika's delighted, gap-toothed grin when she gave her the flowers. The rain had stopped her from riding out to the meadow the past three weeks, so it had been a while since she had last brought Rika flowers.

A horse snorted behind her.

Amy whirled around.

Papa slid out of the saddle and wiped her forehead with her bandanna.

Weeks ago, Amy had tried to think of her as "Luke," but it wasn't working. Nothing had really changed. Papa still worked hard at the ranch, still loved Mama, and still helped out the neighbors. She behaved the same and looked the same as ever. Man or woman, this was the only father Amy had ever known, and her brain—or maybe her heart—refused to call Luke anything but "Papa."

"Hello, Amy. I thought that was you. What are you doing here?"

"Um...nothing." Amy hid the flowers behind her back. "I'm on my way into town to take Rika riding."

"Amy." The lines around Papa's eyes deepened when she smiled. "You don't have to hide this from me. Don't be embarrassed. I think it's sweet."

Slowly, Amy brought her hand out from behind her back. She fiddled with the stems and tugged on a tiny leaf. Not hiding her feelings for Rika was still new.

"In fact," Papa said, "I'll pick some for your mother." She dropped Dancer's reins, ground-tying the well-trained gelding, and shoved back her hat.

Side by side, they wandered across the meadow and pointed out clumps of especially beautiful flowers to each other.

"Is this strange for you?" Amy asked when they stopped at the edge of the meadow to add some wild roses.

"What?" Papa asked. "Picking flowers?"

"Yes. No. I mean..." A flower fluttered to the ground as Amy gestured, and she bent to pick it up.

"You mean is it strange for me to know that we're both picking flowers for a woman?"

Amy nodded, glad that Papa said it for her.

Two more roses completed Papa's bouquet. She paused and let her gaze sweep over the meadow. "No. I think it will be harder for me once Nattie comes home with a suitor. I can relate to you loving a woman."

Sometimes, it was still hard for Amy to remember that her father was like her—a woman who loved another woman. At the same time, it made things easier for her. If she ever got up enough courage, she could ask her parents for advice. She nodded thoughtfully and used her knife to cut all the stems to the same length.

Papa's gaze rested on her.

Amy fidgeted, almost cutting herself.

"Something on your mind?" Papa asked.

Something? More like a million things. A dozen different thoughts, questions, and emotions spun through her mind.

Papa took the knife away from her. "What is it? You know you can talk to me about anything."

Amy looked down at her grass-stained fingertips. "If you hadn't been able to marry Mama, would you still...?"

"What?"

Heat climbed up her chest, and she knew her cheeks were glowing. "Would you still want to...to live with her and kiss her like a husband would?"

"Of course I would." Papa rubbed the ring on her hand. "A few words spoken in front of a judge or a priest don't change how I feel about Nora." Her eyes narrowed. "But this isn't really about your mother and me, is it? What are you asking?"

"Rika has been married once, but I can't offer her that."

"You can offer her love."

"Yes, and that's what has me so..." Other words formed in Amy's head, but she couldn't say them.

Papa laid down her bunch of flowers and gripped Amy's hand with both of hers. "Amy, your mother and I took a big risk by telling you the truth about us. We did that because we wanted you to have someone you could talk to about your feelings. So please, whatever it is, don't think you have to go through this alone."

Remnants of hurt about not being told sooner still lingered within Amy, but it paled in comparison to her gratitude. She lifted her gaze and looked into Papa's silver-gray eyes. "Is it right to want to kiss Rika and to...to touch her if we're not married and will never be?"

"Come here." Papa sank into the grass and nodded at Amy to sit down next to her.

Her cheeks still burning, Amy sat. At least this way, she wouldn't have to look Papa in the eyes.

"When I married your mother, I promised to love, honor, and cherish her for the rest of our lives," Papa said. "If you can promise Rika the same, if it's not just a passing infatuation, then I think you should consider yourself married—with all the rights and obligations that come with it."

It sounded so simple. Maybe it was. But what if she had no earthly idea how to go about fulfilling certain rights and obligations? Amy pinched the bridge of her nose.

"What is it?" Papa asked.

Amy combed her fingers through the grass and stared at the ground. "The girls in town... I heard them talk about the marriage bed."

"Oh." Papa swept off her hat and fanned her face with it. Was she blushing? Finally, she put down her hat and gave Amy a sidelong glance. "So, what did they say?"

Amy hesitated. A young woman wasn't supposed to talk to her father about such intimate matters. But Papa was not like any other father. "They said women are supposed to lift their nightgown, lie back, and wait until their husbands are finished with...their business. But Rika and I..." She swallowed against the lump in her throat. "What do you do when there is no husband?"

Papa plucked a blade of grass and studied it as if the answer were written on the green stalk.

Lord, how embarrassing. I shouldn't have asked. Amy pulled her knees up and leaned her forehead against them, hiding her flushed face.

When she opened her mouth to apologize for her inappropriate question, Papa finally spoke. "Well, if two people love each other, I would hope that the marriage bed holds more for them than just lying back and waiting until it's over, no matter if they are husband and wife or two women."

Amy wanted to ask how, but embarrassment kept her jaw locked. She ripped out handfuls of grass. Loving Rika wasn't the problem. She just didn't know what to do with all those feelings of love and passion that were bottled up inside of her. "B-but what if I don't know what to do?" she blurted before she could stop herself. "What if I get it all wrong?"

"If you touch her with love, you can't go wrong, Amy. Think of her pleasure first and foremost, not just your own."

Amy lifted her head off her knees and met Papa's gaze. Keeping eye contact was hard, but she didn't want to miss a word Papa said.

"If you have ever pleasured yourself, you know what feels good to you."

Heat seared through Amy. She ducked her head to hide her flushed cheeks.

Tapping Amy's knee, Papa got her to look up. "Rika might like to be touched the same way. Ask her what feels good to her, and let her know what feels good to you," Papa said. "Listen to what her body says. Just keep talking, and I promise you'll be fine."

Not sure what to say, Amy just nodded.

"If you think of it as a marriage, you have a lot of time together, not just one night. Even if the first time isn't perfect, Rika won't love you any less. You have the rest of your lives to get to know each other's bodies, so don't put so much pressure on yourself, all right?"

"All right." Amy took a freeing breath. Her embarrassment waned, and she squared her shoulders, proud to be having this conversation between adults with her father. "Thank you, Papa."

Papa squeezed her shoulder. "You're welcome." She stood and brushed a few stalks of grass from her pants. Her flowers in one hand, she rested the other on Amy's shoulder. "Come on. Let's go and bring our sweethearts these flowers before they wilt away."

HAMILTON HORSE RANCH
BAKER PRAIRIE, OREGON
SEPTEMBER 26, 1868

"*T*HIS IS HEARTBREAKING," RIKA SAID, raising her voice over the whinnying of the weanlings. She clutched the corral rail, then turned to Amy.

Amy smiled, once again touched by her compassion. The urge to stroke Rika's cheek made her fingers itch, but she curled them into fists. With the ranch hands riding around or sitting on the corral rails, they weren't free to touch each other. "The foals will be fine. They're old enough to be separated from their mothers." She slung one arm around Rika's shoulders, careful to make it appear like the casual gesture of a friend, and pulled her closer, comforting her with her warmth. "See how big Lucky Star is getting?"

They turned and watched the black filly galloping around the corral in search of her mother.

"Your father won't sell her, will he?" Rika asked.

"Oh, no." Amy wanted to lean closer and inhale the scent of sun-warmed grass on Rika's skin, but she held herself back. "Not when Lucky has been such a good-luck charm for me."

Someone cleared his throat behind them.

Amy let go of Rika and turned. "Hello, Phin."

"Hi, Amy. Great roundup." He looked from her to Rika. "Hello, Hendrika." His tone was friendly, as if Rika were just an acquaintance and hadn't once been his betrothed.

It still amazed Amy that he wasn't pining away.

"Hello, Phin," Rika said. "How nice of you to come over and help with the roundup. How is it going with your ranch?"

"Just fine." White teeth flashed in his tanned face when he gave them an easy grin. "If Luke and the neighbors come over to help, I should be able to finish the barn before winter."

"I can help too if you want," Amy said.

"Sure." He turned to Rika. "I hear you're hirin' on as a housekeeper for the ranch?"

Amy stiffened. Would he see it as a betrayal, now that Rika had refused to marry him?

"Yes," Rika said with a casualness that Amy knew was forced. "Someone needs to run the household now that Nattie will be leaving for New York, and we all know Amy would rather spend her time out on the range than in the kitchen."

Phin nodded. "Listen, Amy, do you want to keep Nugget's foal, or will your father auction him off?"

Amy grinned, glad that he didn't question Rika's moving to the ranch. "You've got your eye on him, don't you?"

"Yeah. He'll make a fine stallion one day."

"I'm sure Papa could be talked into selling him," Amy said. "Go on over and talk to him."

They watched him walk away.

"Do you think he suspects?" Amy looked down to where she was digging a hole in the ground with the tip of her boot.

"I'm not sure." Rika tugged at Amy's chaps until she stopped digging. "Do you think it would be better to wait for a while longer before I move to the ranch?"

Part of Amy, the part that had hidden her feelings for years, was scared. She wanted to be cautious and say yes. But what she wanted even more was to have Rika with her, to talk to her at breakfast every morning and kiss her goodnight every night. She wanted more than just a few stolen hours. "No," she said. "I want you here, with me."

"Just two more weeks until Nattie leaves," Rika said. It sounded like a promise—and like an eternity.

Darkness was falling when the neighbors, who had come over to help with the roundup, directed their horses homeward and the ranch hands retreated to the bunkhouse.

Amy reached for her hat. "I'm gonna show Rika the cabin real quick and then take her home," she said before anyone else could offer to escort Rika. She wanted to cherish every moment with her.

"It's getting late," Mama said from the kitchen sink. "Why don't you stay in the cabin tonight, Hendrika, and ride to town with us tomorrow?"

Rika looked at Amy. The same longing Amy felt glittered in her eyes. Still, she hesitated. "I'd love to, but won't Tess and Frankie worry?"

"They know you're with us, safe and sound," Luke said as she stacked the dried plates back in the cupboard. "If you're back before they serve breakfast to the guests, they won't worry."

Amy sent her parents grateful glances. She grabbed Rika's hand and pulled. "Come on." This was her chance to spend more time with Rika.

"I'll need to borrow one of your nightshirts," Rika said.

The door to the main house fell closed behind them.

"No," Amy said. "You don't."

Rika's fingers flexed. "Amy Hamilton!" She tried to sound indignant but couldn't stop a giggle.

"What? No, no. That's not what I meant." With her free hand, Amy rubbed her flushed face. "Although..."

They stared at each other, and Amy's breath caught. The thought of seeing Rika naked, of touching her skin... She didn't want to wait two more weeks to promise herself to the woman she loved.

Under the cover of darkness, Rika trailed her fingers up and down Amy's arm, sending shivers along her skin.

Amy stopped in front of the cabin. "Close your eyes," she whispered.

"Why?"

"Just trust me."

"I do." Rika squeezed her hand. "They're closed."

Reluctantly, Amy slipped her hand free, opened the door, and lit a kerosene lamp. She wrapped one arm around Rika and led her inside. "Open your eyes now."

Rika's eyes opened and then widened as she took in the cabin.

Amy had worked hard all week to get the cabin ready for Rika. Gone were the saddle blankets and the harness pieces, and Papa had helped her to finally install the wood floor. Instead of bridles and rope halters, colorful drawings covered the walls. A bunch of wildflowers on the table sent a sweet scent across the room. In the bedroom, new straw filled the mattress, and a soft quilt covered the bed.

"You…you did all this? For me?"

"Yes." Amy stared into her eyes, trying to figure out what Rika was thinking. Had she overwhelmed her? "I wanted you to have a home, not just a place to stay. Do you like it?"

After twirling and again taking in the cabin, Rika nodded. "I don't know what to say." Her eyes were damp, and her finger shook as she pointed to the horse figurines. "These are yours, aren't they?"

Amy nodded. "I thought they could keep you company when I can't be here. If I live here with you, the ranch hands will start to wonder, but they won't think much of it when I stay over sometimes." She threw a tentative glance at Rika. "If it's what you want too."

Rika rushed over and threw her arms around Amy. "Of course I do. This is a dream come true. You and your family… you are so wonderful." Her voice was choked as if she was close to tears.

Amy pulled her closer. "I want them to be your family too…if you want." *Should I…?* She gave herself a mental kick. *Do it. Now.* Her stomach felt queasy, and a ball of hope and fear was lodged in her throat, but she forced herself to move. With fear-damp hands, she reached into a trunk and pulled out a small leather pouch she'd hidden there earlier in the week.

"Another gift?" Rika asked when Amy handed her the pouch. She glanced up, regret in her eyes. "But I don't have anything for you."

Amy reached for Rika's hand and stroked it with her thumbs. She pressed a kiss to the inside of Rika's wrist, then pulled her closer until their lips touched. Her eyes fluttered shut, and she sighed into the kiss.

Both were breathless when they separated.

"You are my gift," Amy whispered.

When Rika pulled open the drawstring, Amy sank onto the trunk, her legs too unsteady to hold her up any longer.

Rika shook the contents of the pouch into her palm.

In the light of the kerosene lamp, a gold ring glinted.

"Amy?" Rika knelt next to Amy as if her legs had given out too. "What does this mean? How did you get this?"

"Don't worry. Papa got it for me on his last trip to Portland."

"But you can't afford it."

Amy frowned. Didn't Rika want the ring? "Papa and I worked with two of the goldsmith's horses every day for the last month to trade for the ring."

"So that's why you were always late picking me up?"

Since her mouth was too dry to answer, Amy just nodded. Her gaze flitted back and forth between Rika's face and her palm, which still cradled the ring. She had prepared a romantic speech and learned it by heart, but now that the moment was there, she couldn't remember a word of it. "I know you came west to marry and to start a family. I can't give you that, but if you'll have me, I can promise to love, honor, and cherish you for as long as I live. I know it's not much, but—"

Rika's lips against hers stopped her rambling. When the kiss ended, Rika touched Amy's cheek and looked into her eyes. "It's everything. When I came here, I didn't know what I was looking for. Not really. I thought I was searching for a means to survive and for a secure future. What I found is so much better."

"What did you find?" Amy asked and held her breath.

"A home," Rika whispered. "Love."

"Does that mean...?"

The dazzling gap-toothed grin Amy loved so much appeared as Rika slid the ring onto her finger. "Yes. I promise to love, honor, and cherish you forever too."

Amy slid from the trunk and pulled her into an embrace.

"I'll save up to buy you a ring too," Rika said between kisses. "We'll need to wear them on a chain, though, or people will start talking."

Not even the thought of having to hide their love could destroy Amy's happiness now. Reverently, she pressed her lips to Rika's ear, her neck, her cheekbones, then kissed eyelids that fluttered shut beneath her touch.

Rika caressed her back and whispered into her ear, "Do you want to make this our wedding night?"

Shivers raced down Amy's body. Excitement and nerves made her heart pound. Her vocal cords refused to work, so she answered with a nod.

Rika took her hand and pulled her into the bedroom, where she sat and unlaced her boots.

While Amy kicked off her own boots, she stole glances at pale, smooth calves as Rika rolled down her stockings. She watched as the apron came off next, followed by the skirt and petticoats.

As if feeling her gaze, Rika turned her head.

Amy smiled and looked away. She lifted trembling fingers and opened the first button of her shirt, remembering how Rika had helped her undress many months ago. Beneath half-lowered lids, she watched as Rika unbuttoned her bodice.

The bodice and shirt slid onto the floor together, followed by Amy's pants.

"Want to help me with the corset?" Rika pointed over her shoulder.

Amy nodded and stepped closer as if in a trance, pulled in by an irresistible force.

The skin on the nape of Rika's neck glowed a bright pink. Amy trailed her fingertip across it and watched in fascination as goose bumps rose beneath her touch. "You got a little sunburned today," she said and blinked when she barely recognized the sound of her own voice. "We need to put a vinegar poultice on it."

"Later," Rika said, her voice equally hoarse.

Amy kissed the nape of her neck, inhaling the lavender soap Rika had used to wash up before supper. She fiddled with the laces in the back of the corset, her fingers refusing to work properly. Finally, after a few breathless moments, she managed to pull it free.

They stood face to face, both in just their underwear.

"C-can I?" Amy asked, her hand an inch from Rika's hair. At her nod, she pulled out the pins, letting the mahogany tresses fall free. She combed her fingers through the softness, then trailed her fingertips along Rika's collarbone, across her shoulder, and down her arm.

When she hesitated, unsure what to do to express her love, Rika entwined their fingers and leaned forward to kiss her nose, her cheeks, and down her chest until the edges of the undershirt stopped her. She mumbled something after each kiss, her breath tickling Amy's skin and making her whole body vibrate.

"What are you doing?" Amy whispered.

"Counting your freckles."

A nervous giggle broke free when Amy remembered that her freckles trailed down her chest all the way to the top of her bosom. Would she kiss her there too?

"Amy Hamilton, are you giggling?"

"No."

"Oh, yes, you are." Rika giggled too. "And I like it. I like seeing you happy."

Amy laid her palms against Rika's cheeks and looked into smoldering brown eyes. "You make me happy. I never thought I would have this. Have someone like you in my life." She guided their faces together and kissed her again.

Wrapped in each other's arms, they sank onto the bed, Rika on top.

Her breasts, covered by just a thin chemise, rubbed against Amy's.

With a gasp, Amy pressed closer, closing her eyes briefly when she felt Rika's fingers in her hair.

"Amy," Rika murmured. Passion made her brown eyes appear midnight black. Her hands slid down, trailing heat even through the undershirt as she kissed Amy's throat. Their legs entwined, and her thigh pressed against the heat between Amy's legs.

"Oh, Lord, Rika." An unknown pleasure tightened Amy's stomach. At night, alone in her room, she had tried to imagine what lying with Rika might be like, but her fantasies hadn't prepared her for these sensations. Biting her lip to keep from crying out, she slid her hands up and down Rika's back. She felt the warmth of the skin beneath the chemise, and suddenly, she couldn't stand having that barrier between them. She ached to touch Rika. "Would you mind...?" She bunched up the hem of the chemise and paused.

Instead of answering, Rika sat up, straddled her lap, and slid the chemise over her head. Then she crossed her arms in front of her chest.

"Please, don't hide yourself from me."

Slowly, Rika dropped her arms.

Amy stared at her, drinking in every curve, every inch of the pale skin. "You're beautiful," she whispered, as if talking more loudly would break the spell.

"You don't need to say that," Rika said. "I know I'm rather plain and nothing special."

With one finger, Amy directed her chin up so they were looking in each other's eyes. "You're special to me."

Rika's chest heaved. Her eyelashes trembled against flushed cheeks. "You're special to me too." She slid her fingers beneath the edge of Amy's undershirt and lifted up the fabric. When the undershirt fluttered to the floor, she threw her arms around Amy and pulled her close.

Their breasts pressed against each other.

Every inch of Amy's body came alive. Almost dizzy with pleasure, she clutched the small of Rika's back, pulling her even closer, and felt warm hands on her bare sides.

They stretched out on the bed.

"I can feel your heart beating," Amy whispered against her ear.

"It's racing."

Amy's heart was pounding too. She wanted to touch Rika everywhere, bring her every possible pleasure, but she had no idea where to begin. "Do you know what to do?"

"I have a few ideas." Smiling, Rika kissed her collarbone, then pressed her lips to the tiny measles scars on her upper chest.

With every kiss, the urge to touch Rika increased until Amy rolled them around and leaned over, supporting herself on one arm. Her lips were drawn to a smooth shoulder, while she explored the gentle curve of her stomach with one hand. She admired the pale skin that appeared like rich cream beneath her fingers. "You're so soft," she whispered against Rika's collarbone. "I'm sorry my hands are so rough. I hope my calluses don't—"

Rika captured her wrists and pressed kisses against her palms. "I like your calluses. They make me tingle all over."

"Yeah?" Amy trailed one fingertip from Rika's navel to her breastbone, admiring the rise of her breasts and the nipples that were darker than her own. She hesitated, then carefully circled the left breast. She wanted to watch Rika's face, searching for any sign that she was doing the wrong thing, but her gaze was drawn down, following the circles her finger drew, closer and closer to the hardened nipple.

Rika moaned and arched into the touch.

Emboldened by that reaction, Amy cupped her breast. She swooned at the warm weight. "Is this all right?"

"Wonderful." As if to prove it, Rika slid her hand between them and caressed one of Amy's breasts.

Amy's eyes fluttered shut. She moaned as flashes of sensation flared through her body. Hungry for Rika's touch, she wanted to press so close that she disappeared inside of her. The feeling grew and grew until she felt as if she'd explode. She groaned helplessly and whispered, "I never imagined it could be like this."

When she buried her face against Rika's neck, Rika turned her head and kissed her ear. "That's not all there is to making love." She slid a hand down Amy's body.

A thrill raced through Amy. She held her breath as Rika caressed the sensitive skin of her lower belly, sending a flash of heat to that spot between her legs.

Rika pulled at the drawstring of her drawers. "Is this all right? I want to feel you."

No longer able to speak, Amy nodded. Her body trembled, in a hurry for something, but not sure what it was that she craved.

They struggled out of their drawers, the last barrier between them now gone. Amy sucked in a breath when they came together in an intimate embrace.

Rika's thigh pressed between her legs, skin against skin.

She panted against the damp skin of Rika's neck. A feeling of pressure and heat swirled through her belly. "Oh, yes. Lord, this is..." She gritted her teeth against the spreading sensations, trying not to get swept away by the maelstrom of feelings. Instead, she focused on making Rika feel this good too. She leaned down and pressed kisses to her breast, reveling in the pleasant fullness.

The nipple hardened beneath her touch.

Curious, Amy wrapped her lips around it and tasted it with her tongue.

"Oh. Amy." Hips arching, Rika weaved her fingers through her hair and pulled her even closer.

Amy felt her own body echo the movement as the pressure in her belly began to spread.

Rika stroked down her sensitive side, making goose bumps trail down her body. She fanned her fingers over Amy's hip and explored its curve until her fingertips rested at the juncture of her thighs.

Amy gasped for breath. Liquid heat swirled through her belly. "Rika, I..."

"Don't be scared. I'll stop if you don't like this." Rika trailed her fingers lower.

Overwhelmed with feelings and sensations, Amy covered the exploring hand with her own. She moaned when she felt the dampness between her thighs.

"Do you want me to...?"

Trembling, Amy guided her lower. She surged against Rika, wanting her closer, wanting to share this breathtaking experience with her. It took some maneuvering, but she managed to slide her hand between Rika's thighs.

The damp warmth and breathless moans washed over her senses, mingling with the sensations rushing through her.

They groaned and moved against each other in a faster rhythm.

Rika's skin glowed with a sheen of perspiration, making every touch feel like silk.

Amy searched her lips with her own, but then Rika began to move her fingers faster and she gasped for breath, trying to keep up and control her body's reaction.

Impossible.

Her hips surged to meet Rika's rhythmic stroking that became faster and faster.

Spellbound by the silky wetness beneath her fingertips, the quick rise and fall of Rika's chest, and the parted cherry-red lips, Amy pressed closer. Her heart thumped against her ribs, keeping pace with the pounding that was starting in her core.

Rika's breathless moans rained over her like kisses.

"Oh. Oh, yes." Her stomach tightened.

Rika clutched her back. Her thighs locked around Amy's hand, and she fell back against the pillow with a cry.

Tiny tremors started deep within Amy. Pleasure rushed through her. She cried out as it peaked and she fell into the darkness of Rika's eyes. For a while, she couldn't move. Her universe was reduced to the pulsing in her body and the feeling of damp skin against hers. Nothing else existed. Then, with weak limbs, she cuddled against Rika's side. Their breathing calmed, and she closed her eyes. "Wow," she whispered and kissed her cheek. "I could stay like this forever."

Rika laughed and cuddled closer. "I think your family would—" She paused and lifted her head.

"What—?" Amy asked, but Rika shushed her.

Someone was knocking on the cabin door.

Amy held her breath. She sent Rika a panicked look and pressed one finger to her lips. "Sssh. Maybe whoever it is will go away if we keep quiet," she whispered.

But instead, the knocking on the door continued. "Hendrika? Amy?" Nattie called. "Are you in there? I thought I'd bring over a nightshirt and a hairbrush for Hendrika."

Oh, no. A spasm of fear shot through Amy's belly when she remembered they hadn't locked the cabin door. She struggled into her undershirt and tossed Rika's chemise at her. "Hurry." She shoved one foot, then the other through her pant legs and hastily slipped on her shirt while Rika fought to get on her corset.

On wobbly legs, they got dressed. By the time they rushed to the front door, Amy was gasping for breath. She paused and forced herself to inhale slowly. "Ready?"

Rika smoothed her hands over her skirt and nodded. Her face, which had been flushed with passion just minutes ago, had gone pale.

When Amy opened the door, Nattie stood in front of them.

"Come in," Amy said for lack of other things to say or do.

Nattie slipped past her and held out a nightshirt and a hairbrush. "What was taking so long? It took you forever to—" She regarded them through narrowed eyes. "What happened to the two of you?"

Heart pounding, Amy glanced down at herself. She'd missed a button, and she wore neither boots nor socks. With growing trepidation, she turned toward Rika, who was equally barefoot. The laces of her corset weren't tightened properly, and now her bodice bunched in a few places.

"What's going on?" Nattie pointed the hairbrush at Amy, then at Rika. "Your hair looks as if you'd just climbed out of bed."

"Nattie..." Amy held out her hands, palms forward. "It's not what—" She stopped herself. Did she really want to live her life ducking her head in shame for loving a woman as wonderful as Rika? Did she want to lie and deny her love even to her own sister?

No. She'd never again run or hide when something scared her. She reached for Rika's hand and entwined their fingers. Slowly, she lifted her head to meet Nattie's gaze. "All right," she said, trying to keep her voice from trembling. "It's exactly what it looks like."

Nattie swallowed audibly and stared at them. "You mean you...the two of you...?"

They exchanged a quick glance and then nodded.

Pale, Nattie turned an accusing gaze at Rika. "Is this," she gestured at them, "why you didn't marry Phin?"

"I didn't marry Phin because I don't love him."

"He's a good man."

Rika tilted her head. "I know. And I thought that would be enough. But then I met your family, and I realized that I want more. I want love."

The lamp in Nattie's hand trembled, throwing flickering shadows across the cabin. "And you love my sister?"

Rika turned to Amy, a smile easing the tension on her face. She reached out and smoothed the crooked shirt collar. "Yes," she said as their gazes locked. "I love her."

Warmth spread through Amy. "And I love Rika." When she looked back at Nattie, her sister was still frowning. She swallowed. "I know this is a lot to take in. But please understand, this is who I am and who I love."

"It feels like the whole world has tilted, and nothing is right anymore," Nattie said, her voice trembling. "Finding out about Papa...and Mama was hard enough, but now you too?" She shook her head. "How can it be that in a family full of women, I'm the only one who's in love with a man? I don't understand it. And I don't understand why everyone in the family kept secrets from me."

Amy clung to the comforting grip of Rika's hand. "I'm sorry. I know it must be terribly confusing. I didn't mean to hurt you, Nattie."

Nattie's gaze softened. "I know."

"Do you think that after a while, you'll be able to forgive me for not telling you sooner and get used to the thought of... us?" Amy pointed at Rika and herself.

The new floorboards creaked as Nattie shifted her weight. "I'll have a lot of time to think once I'm in New York."

Amy's heart sank. Would Nattie even want to come back now?

Nattie crossed the cabin in a few quick steps and pulled Amy into an embrace. "You're my sister, and nothing will ever change that. I want you to be happy. If that's with Hendrika..." She let go and shrugged. "I'll make my peace with it."

Tears burned in Amy's eyes. "Thank you."

Nattie smiled at them and handed Rika the nightgown and the hairbrush. "Goodnight. And sorry for...interrupting." She blushed and hurried away.

The cabin door fell closed behind her.

Amy sank into Rika's arms. "Oh, Lord. That was... Rika, I'm so sorry. This wasn't how I wanted our first...our wedding night to end. We'll have to be more careful in the future. If that had been one of the ranch hands instead of Nattie..." The thought made her tremble.

"It's all right." Rika combed her fingers through Amy's hair, putting it back into some semblance of order. "At least we don't have to lie to your sister anymore."

"Yeah." Amy squeezed her eyes shut and pressed her face against a comforting shoulder. Then something occurred to her, and she lifted her head. "Wait a minute. Did Nattie just say she's in love?"

Rika smiled. "She did."

Her little sister was all grown up and in love. But with whom? She eyed Rika, who calmly looked back. "Did you know about this?"

Rika crossed to the door and locked it. She reached for Amy's hand. "Come to bed, and I'll tell you everything I know about it."

Amy didn't have to be told twice.

EPILOGUE

BAKER PRAIRIE, OREGON
APRIL 27, 1871

"Run!" Rika gripped Amy's arm and dragged her across Baker Prairie's dusty main street.

"I can't!" Amy gasped. "Not in these shoes."

"Stop complaining and run."

Amy stumbled. "Damn petticoats!"

Under the pretense of helping her, Rika gripped Amy's hand and encountered smooth silk gloves instead of the familiar calluses. "The organ has already started, and your father will be a nervous wreck if we're late."

"You'd think it was Papa's wedding, not Nattie's."

They slid to a stop in front of the church portal. Rika smoothed a hand over the blue satin of Amy's dress. "You look beautiful."

Amy stopped grumbling. "So do you."

Their gazes touched and held.

Rika finally wrenched herself away. "Come on. Let's go in."

When they slipped into the church and hurried down the aisle, whispers rose in the pews.

"Poor girl," Rika heard one woman say. "Having to watch him marry someone else..."

"She seems fine since the Hamiltons took her in," another woman said.

Rika sighed. After almost three years, she'd thought people had finally stopped talking about her, Phin, and the Hamiltons.

"Don't mind them," Amy whispered and pulled her into the first pew.

Nora leaned over, her red hair glowing against the dark green of her dress. "Where have you been?"

474

"Oh, she had one of her horse ideas." Rika lovingly nudged Amy's knee.

"Horses? Now?"

Amy pointed over her shoulder to the pew behind them, where Frankie sat in an elaborate lace dress. "Frankie gave permission to have Mouse and a carriage waiting for Nattie and Phin in front of the church." Her pride was so endearing that Rika wanted to lean over and kiss her, but she settled for a quick press of their knees.

Nora squeezed Amy's hand. "A gray horse pulling the carriage—what a good omen for their marriage."

Organ music started up again, and the portal opened to the first notes of the wedding march.

People in the pews turned and craned their necks.

Rika caught a glimpse of Nattie, who floated down the aisle in her pale yellow organdy dress. A veil covered her face, but her hands clutched Luke's forearm and gave away her nervousness.

Luke strode with measured steps that made Rika wonder how often she had practiced the walk down the aisle. When it came to her daughters, Luke left nothing to chance.

They reached the front of the church. Luke raised Nattie's veil, kissed her cheek, and transferred her hand onto Phin's arm. One long glance and a formal nod to Phin and she slipped into the pew next to Nora. Her hands shook when she smoothed them over her gray doeskin pants and the knee-length claret frock coat. She tugged at her cravat until Nora grabbed her hand and held it between her own.

After three years, Rika no longer found it strange to know that Amy's handsome father was a woman.

"You know what day it is today?" Nora leaned close to Luke and whispered, just loud enough for Rika to hear.

"The day we start waiting for grandchildren?"

Nora coughed and then laughed. "Oh, I can't wait to see Grandpa Luke bounce half a dozen grandchildren on his knees. But that's not what I meant. Twenty years ago today was the day we first met."

"Yeah, I thought about that too when I had that conversation with Phin earlier. Twenty years..." Luke looked deeply into Nora's eyes. "It's been quite the journey."

"And it's not over."

"No," Luke said, "it's not." Ignoring the frowning people in the pews behind them, she kissed her wife.

Rika looked away. She couldn't kiss her love so openly, but when they held on to the hymnbook together, she brushed her index finger against Amy's.

Amy leaned over. Her breath caressed Rika's ear as she whispered, "At least my parents had the good sense to fall in love during the journey to Oregon, but it took Phin and Nattie three years to marry. Three years!"

"Nattie wanted what your parents have—a true partnership. She couldn't have that before she found her place in life. But now that she's a veterinary surgeon and Phin has built his ranch..."

Amy scratched her head. "Why on God's green earth is love so complicated?"

A soft smile parted Rika's lips. "Maybe so we'll appreciate it more once we find it."

Under the cover of the hymnbook, Amy caressed Rika's hand. "And I do."

ABOUT JAE

Jae grew up amidst the vineyards of southern Germany. She spent her childhood with her nose buried in a book, earning her the nickname "professor." The writing bug bit her at the age of eleven. For the last eight years, she has been writing mostly in English.

She used to work as a psychologist but gave up her day job in December 2013 to become a full-time writer and a part-time editor. When she's not writing, she likes to spend her time reading, indulging her ice cream and office supply addiction, and watching way too many crime shows.

Connect with Jae online

Jae loves hearing from readers!
E-mail her at jae_s1978@yahoo.de
Visit her website: jae-fiction.com
Visit her blog: jae-fiction.com/blog
Like her on Facebook: facebook.com/JaeAuthor
Follow her on Twitter @jaefiction

EXCERPT FROM CONFLICT OF INTEREST

BY JAE

"*I*'M GOING TO THROW UP," Dawn Kinsley said, rubbing her nervous stomach.

"No, you won't." Her friend and colleague Ally just grinned. "Come on, you're a therapist. You're used to talking to people."

"Not to one hundred cops who would rather be elsewhere and who won't give me the time of day." Dawn knew what the police officers sitting on the other side of the curtain were thinking. Most of them would view her lecture as a waste of time.

Ally rolled her eyes. "A psychologist with glossophobia. I wonder what the APA would say about that."

"I'm sure the American Psychological Association would be much more concerned about a psychologist with your lack of compassion," Dawn answered, now with a grin of her own. Usually, she didn't have a problem with public speaking. She had held her own in front of gum-chewing high school kids, earnest college students, and renowned psychologists twice her age, but cops were a special audience for her. It was almost as if she was expecting to see her father sitting in one of the rows and was trying to impress him. *Oh, come on, Doc, this is not the time to start analyzing yourself.*

"Touché," Ally said.

Both of them had to chuckle, and Dawn felt herself relax.

"There are a few techniques that can help in these situations, you know?" Ally said.

"Let me guess—picturing everyone in the audience naked?" Dawn grinned at her friend. "And how would that help with my nervousness?"

Ally shrugged. "Well, maybe it won't." She peeked out from behind the curtain, letting her appreciative gaze wander over the men in the first few rows. "But it might be nice nonetheless."

"Maybe for you, but how would it be nice for me to picture a room full of naked men? Hello?" Dawn gave a little wave. "Did you miss the office memo informing everyone about my sexual orientation?"

"Office memo? Is that what they nowadays call kissing your girlfriend in the office's parking lot?"

"What?" Dawn sputtered. "I never did that!"

Ally rubbed her forehead and pretended to think about it. "No? Must have been Charlie, then." She pushed the curtain aside to glance at the audience again. "There are also a few female officers down there. You could look at them."

"All two of them?" Dawn joked but stepped closer to follow Ally's gaze. There were more than two female cops in the audience—but not many more.

"Pick one," Ally said.

Dawn nudged her with an elbow. "I'm here to give a lecture, not to pick up women, Ally."

Ally ignored her protests. "Pick one and concentrate on her during your lecture. Ignore the rest of the crowd. It'll help with the nervousness. So?" She pointed down to the seated police officers.

Well, it can't hurt. Dawn craned her neck and peeked past the taller Ally. Her gaze wandered from woman to woman, never stopping for long until... "Her!" she said, pointing decisively.

In the very last row, between a tall African American man in his forties and a younger man whose posture screamed "rookie," a female plainclothes detective was just taking her seat. She had short, jet-black hair, and a leather jacket covered what Dawn could see of her tall, athletic frame.

"Ooh!" Ally whistled quietly. "Nice choice! Didn't know you liked them a little on the butch side, though. Maggie isn't nearly—"

"Compared to Maggie, even you look butch," Dawn said.

"Dr. Kinsley?"

Dawn looked away from the detective and turned around. "Yes?"

One of the seminar organizers stepped up to them. "Here are your handouts." He handed her a stack of paper. "Are you ready to begin?"

Dawn clutched the handouts and swallowed. "Yes."

"Good luck," Ally said. Behind the seminar organizer's back, she mouthed, "Remember to picture her naked."

How's that supposed to calm my racing heart? Dawn she stepped out from behind the curtain and made her way over to the microphone with a confidence she didn't really feel.

Aiden slumped into a seat between her partner and Ruben Cartwright. The chair next to Ruben was suspiciously empty. "Where's your partner? Terminal back pain again?" If she had to be at this stupid seminar, so did everyone else, even hypochondriacs like Jeff Okada.

Ruben looked up from the paper airplane that had once been his seminar brochure. He shoved a strand of brown hair out of his boyishly handsome face and glanced from Aiden to her partner. "Uh, what?"

Ray leaned over to him with a grin. "There's one thing you have to know about your new partner, rookie. His back acts up every time a continuing ed seminar comes along."

"It acts up whenever I have to sit in one of these seats designed for first graders," Jeff Okada said as he walked up to them. Gingerly, he eased himself down next to his rookie partner.

Aiden sighed and glanced at her watch. She had a stack of unfinished reports on her desk, and their thirty open cases didn't get any closer to being solved while she sat here. The seminar also stopped her from spending her lunch hour in the courtroom's gallery, watching her favorite Deputy District Attorney at work. Maybe she would have even worked up the courage to ask Kade to lunch today.

Sighing again, she wrestled herself into a standing position and pointed to the back of the conference room. "I'm going for coffee."

"If you want to live long enough to enjoy your hard-earned pension, I'd advise against that, my friend." Okada raised his index finger in warning. "In more than twenty-five years on the job, I've never been to a law enforcement seminar with even halfway decent coffee."

Ray smirked. "In twenty-five years on the job, you've never been to a law enforcement seminar, period."

Over the top of his sunglasses, Okada directed a withering glance at Ray before he turned back to Aiden. "The lack of drinkable coffee is obviously a nationwide conspiracy from law enforcement brass to make sure nothing distracts their officers from the lectures. For the same reason, you'll never encounter doughnuts or attractive female lecturers at a law enforcement seminar."

"Or comfortable chairs," Ray said.

Okada threw up his hands. "Now you're starting to get it."

Aiden sank back into her chair. Giving up on her caffeine fix, she pulled the now crushed seminar program out from under her. The wrinkled paper announced the title of the first lecture: Special Needs and Issues of Male and GLBT Survivors of Rape and Sexual Abuse. The speaker was some PhD named D. Kinsley.

"Great," Aiden murmured. They hadn't even hired a cop or someone who knew the reality of handling sex crimes to give the lecture. Instead, some antiquated Freudian in a stiff suit would bore them to tears with his academic theories.

A young woman carrying a stack of handouts stepped out from behind a curtain and crossed the podium—probably the Freudian's assistant or the poor soul who had the questionable honor of introducing the speaker. The woman tapped the microphone to test its volume and nodded. "Good morning, ladies and gentlemen. I'm Dawn Kinsley, your lecturer for the first part of the seminar."

Aiden's head jerked up. That was D. Kinsley?

Nothing reminded Aiden of the academic Freudian she had imagined except the glasses on the freckled nose. Instead of a suit and tie, slacks and a tight, sleeveless blouse covered a body that was petite, yet not frail, and slender, but not model-thin. The strawberry blond hair wasn't pulled back into an old-fashioned bun, but cascaded in curls down to softly curved hips.

Seems she's the PhD, not the assistant. That's what I get for stereotyping. Of course, looking at her instead of an old man is not exactly a punishment. However boring the lecture might be, at least she would have something captivating to look at.

The lecture began, and to her surprise, Aiden found herself looking away from the pretty speaker and down to her notepad to jot down interesting details about dealing with male rape victims. The lecture turned out to be informative, practice-oriented, and witty. She even caught Okada bending his aching back to take notes. The psychologist spoke with passion and sensitivity, never even glancing down at her notes.

Instead, Aiden felt as if the psychologist was looking right at her, focusing on her as if there were no one else in the room. *Oh, come on. Stop dreaming. There are a few other people in the room, you know?* Aiden listened with rapt attention to the rest of the lecture.

Forty-five minutes passed almost too soon.

"I knew I should have tried the coffee," Ruben mumbled when they began to file out of the room with the last of the seminar participants. "If there's an attractive female lecturer, there's a chance the rest of your seminar conspiracy theory is bull, too."

Okada stretched and shook his head. "I wouldn't bet your meager paycheck on it, partner. Some government employee obviously failed to check the lecturer's picture, but there's no way they would overlook a bill for Blue Hawaiian beans at forty dollars per pound."

Someone chuckled behind them.

Aiden turned and looked down into the twinkling gray-green eyes of Dawn Kinsley, their lecturer. The faint laugh lines at their corners indicated that the psychologist was closer to thirty than to twenty as Aiden had first assumed.

"Sorry," Aiden said, pointing at Okada and Ruben. "They're not used to being out and about. We normally keep them chained to their desks."

Dawn Kinsley didn't seem offended. Her full lips curved into an easy smile that dimpled her cheeks and crinkled the skin at the bridge of her slightly upturned nose, which made the freckles dusting the fair skin seem to dance. "Don't worry, Detective, I've been called worse things than attractive."

Aiden tilted her head. "How do you know I'm a detective?"

"Oh, I don't know, could it be the fact that we're at a law enforcement conference?" Okada said.

Dawn smiled at him, but she spoke to Aiden. "The way you stand, walk, and talk pretty much screams 'cop' in capital letters. And the way you dress suggests you're a detective. Sex crimes unit?"

Aiden nodded. "Aiden Carlisle." She extended her hand.

"Dawn Kinsley, but I guess you already knew that." The psychologist nodded down at her name tag. Her handshake was as genuine and warm as her smile.

"Hey, Aiden." Ray, already halfway out the door, waved her over. "We're gonna make a run for the nearest coffee shop before the next lecture starts. You up for it?"

Forty-five minutes ago, Aiden would have jumped at the chance to leave the seminar room, but now she found herself hesitating. "Um, sure." She glanced at Dawn. "Would you like to come with us?"

"I don't drink coffee." The psychologist laughed at the look on Aiden's face. "Don't look so shocked, Detective. I'm a tea drinker, and I'd love to accompany four of Portland's finest, but regrettably, I've got an appointment."

"Maybe next time, then," Aiden said, knowing they would likely never see each other again. Not as eager to get a caffeine fix as before, she said good-bye and followed her colleagues out of the conference room.

Conflict of Interest will be published in
spring 2014 by Ylva Publishing

OTHER BOOKS FROM
YLVA PUBLISHING

http://www.ylva-publishing.com

BACKWARDS TO OREGON
(revised and expanded edition)
Jae

ISBN: 978-3-95533-026-2 (paperback)
Length: 521 pages

"Luke" Hamilton has always been sure that she'd never marry. She accepted that she would spend her life alone when she chose to live her life disguised as a man.

After working in a brothel for three years, Nora Macauley has lost all illusions about love. She no longer hopes for a man who will sweep her off her feet and take her away to begin a new, respectable life.

But now they find themselves married and on the way to Oregon in a covered wagon, with two thousand miles ahead of them.

BEYOND THE TRAIL
Jae

ISBN: 978-3-95533-083-5 (paperback)
Length: 136 pages

Six short stories that give us glimpses into the lives of Luke, Nora, and the other characters from *Backwards to Oregon*.

The Blue Hour: When her mother dies, twelve-year-old Lucinda Hamilton decides to start a new life—as a boy.

Grasping at Straws: No one knows that Tess Swenson, madam of a brothel, also owns a livery stable and a number of other businesses. On one of her secret inspections, she makes a surprising discovery.

A Rooster's Job: The Hamiltons hoped to build a home in the idyllic Willamette Valley with mild winters, but now they're snowed in and their rooster isn't doing such a great job either.

The Art of Pretending: Tess finds out that someone is stealing her money. She suspects Frankie, a woman who reminds her of Luke. But nothing is as it seems.

The Christmas Oak: Luke sets out to bring home a Christmas tree—but she finds something else.

Swept Away: The greatest flood in the history of Oregon sweeps away houses, barns, and animals in the Willamette Valley. At the same time, fourteen-year-old Amy is swept away by her feelings for her best friend.

TRUE NATURE
Jae

ISBN: 978-3-95533-034-7 (paperback)
Length: 480 pages

When wolf-shifter Kelsey Yates discovers that fourteen-year-old shape-shifter Danny Harding is living with a human adoptive mother, she is sent on a secret mission to protect the pup and get him away from the human.

Successful CEO Rue Harding has no idea that the private teacher she hires for her deaf son isn't really there to teach him history and algebra—or that Danny and Kelsey are not what they seem to be.

But when Danny runs away from home and gets lost in New York City, Kelsey and Rue have to work together to find him before his first transformation sets in and reveals the shape-shifter's secret existence to the world.

KICKER'S JOURNEY
(revised edition)
Lois Cloarec Hart

ISBN: 978-3-95533-060-6 (paperback)
Length: 472 pages

In 1899, two women from very different backgrounds are about to embark on a journey together—one that will take them from the Old World to the New, from the 19th century into the 20th, and from the comfort and familiarity of England to the rigours of Western Canada, where challenges await at every turn.

The journey begins simply for Kicker Stuart when she leaves her home village to take employment as hostler and farrier at Grindleshire Academy for Young Ladies. But when Kicker falls in love with a teacher, Madelyn Bristow, it radically alters the course of her tranquil life.

Together, the lovers flee the brutality of Madelyn's father and the prejudices of upper crust England in search of freedom to live, and love, as they choose. A journey as much of the heart and soul as of the body, it will find the lovers struggling against the expectations of gender, the oppression of class, and even, at times, each other.

What they find at the end of their journey is not a new Eden, but a land of hope and opportunity that offers them the chance to live out their most cherished dream—a life together.

CHARITY

(revised edition)
Paulette Callen

ISBN: 978-3-95533-075-0 (paperback)
Length: 334 pages

The friendship between Lena Kaiser, a sodbuster's daughter, and Gustie Roemer, an educated Easterner, is unlikely in any other circumstance but post-frontier Charity, South Dakota. Gustie is considered an outsider, and Lena is too proud to share her problems (which include a hard-drinking husband) with anyone else.

On the nearby Sioux reservation, Gustie also finds love and family with two Dakotah women: Dorcas Many Roads, an old medicine woman, and her adopted granddaughter, Jordis, who bears the scars of the white man's education.

When Lena's husband is arrested for murdering his father and the secrets of Gustie's past follow her to Charity, Lena, Gustie, and Jordis stand together. As buried horrors are unearthed and present tragedies unfold, they discover the strength and beauty of love and friendship that blossom like wild flowers in the tough prairie soil.

FERVENT CHARITY
Paulette Callen

ISBN: 978-3-95533-079-8 (paperback)
Length: 337 pages

Fervent Charity continues the story of the friendship of five women who have nothing in common but the ground they walk on and the vicissitudes of post-frontier prairie life.

Lena, a young mother living on the edge of heartbreak. Her sister-in-law, Mary, more beautiful than loved. Alvinia, midwife to the county and mother of ten. Gustie and Jordis, trying to make a home together but finding their place on either the reservation or in Charity precarious.

The women come together in the face of natural hardships—childbirth, disastrous weather, and disease—and the unnatural malevolence of people who mean them harm. In the end, they find themselves bound by a secret none of them could have predicted.

COMING FROM
YLVA PUBLISHING
IN SPRING 2014

http://www.ylva-publishing.com

LESSONS IN LOVE AND LIFE
Jae

Amy Hamilton finally has everything she ever wanted when Rika, the woman she loves, moves to the ranch. But years of having to hide her feelings leave her insecure, and her fears get the better of her. Convinced that Rika is growing bored with ranch life, Amy comes up with a daring plan. With her "father" as inspiration, Amy decides to dress up as a man so she can take Rika to Salem for a night of dancing.

Nothing goes as planned, and Amy learns some valuable lessons in love and life.

CONFLICT OF INTEREST
(revised edition)
Jae .

Workaholic Detective Aiden Carlisle isn't looking for love—and certainly not at the law enforcement seminar she reluctantly agreed to attend. But the first lecturer is not at all what she expected.

Psychologist Dawn Kinsley has just found her place in life. After a failed relationship with a police officer, she has sworn never to get involved with another cop again, but she feels a connection to Aiden from the very first moment.

Can Aiden keep from crossing the line when a brutal crime threatens to keep them apart before they've even gotten together?

HEARTS AND FLOWERS BORDER
(revised edition)
L.T. Smith

A visitor from her past jolts Laura Stewart into memories—some funny, some heart-wrenching. Thirteen years ago, Laura buried those memories so deeply she never believed they would resurface. Still, the pain of first love mars Laura's present life and might even destroy her chance of happiness with the beautiful, yet seemingly unobtainable Emma Jenkins.

Can Laura let go of the past, or will she make the same mistakes all over again?

Hearts and Flowers Border is a simple tale of the uncertainty of youth and the first flush of love—love that may have a chance after all.

COMING HOME
(revised edition)
Lois Cloarec Hart

A triangle with a twist, *Coming Home* is the story of three good people caught up in an impossible situation.

Rob, a charismatic ex-fighter pilot severely disabled with MS, has been steadfastly cared for by his wife, Jan, for many years. Quite by accident one day, Terry, a young writer/postal carrier, enters their life and turns it upside down.

Injecting joy and turbulence into their quiet existence, Terry draws Rob and Jan into her lively circle of family and friends until the growing attachment between the two women begins to strain the bonds of love and loyalty, to Rob and each other.

Hidden Truths
© by Jae

ISBN: 978-3-95533-119-1

Also available as e-book.

Published by Ylva Publishing, legal entity of Ylva Verlag, e.Kfr.

Ylva Verlag, e.Kfr.
Owner: Astrid Ohletz
Am Kirschgarten 2
65830 Kriftel
Germany

http://www.ylva-publishing.com

First edition: April 2011 (L-Book ePublisher)
Revised second edition: January 2014 (Ylva Publishing)

Credits
Edited by Judy Underwood and Fletcher DeLancey
Cover Design by Streetlight Graphics

ource UK Ltd.
es UK
2140416

K00001B/21/P